LIFE'S DETOURS

By

Percy Avram

A novel based on the life, experience and adventure of a farm lad - born in Western Canada, who through hard work and dedication achieved International recognition as a consultant on Credit Unions and Cooperatives.

"Life must be lived in the future, but it is best understood and enjoyed from it's past."
- Author unknown.

Published By
MARVA ENTERPRISES
P.O. Box 7615
Mesa, Arizona. 85216-7615

LIFE'S DETOURS

Copyright © 1996
Percy Avram
All Rights Reserved

Library of Congress Catalog Card Number 96-94253

ISBN: 0-9651737-0-4

Reproduction or utilization in any form is not permitted without the written consent of the Publisher.

If the book is coverless it may have been reported to the publisher as "unsold or destroyed" and neither the publisher or the author has received any payment for it. The sale of a coverless book may be unauthorized.

Printed in the United States of America
by Print USA
(602) 807-8030

LIFE'S DETOURS

ACKNOWLEDGMENT

The author acknowledges with pride and thanks the contribution made by - Craig D. Weber, his grandson, for the design of the cover to this book.

Special thanks are also extended to Ney Lopez, John Clontz, Dan Boghean, Ed Kessinger and other friends who read the manuscripts and offered valuable suggestions.

Also to Vicky and Andy Avram, to Emma Avram and to all the members of the immediate family who read and were helpful in numerous ways for the completion of this novel.

DEDICATION

The book is dedicated to all the readers whose thoughts and feelings might be touched in one form or another. If it adds delight and a more meaningful dimension to their lives, then I shall remain forever grateful. - The Author.

LIFE'S DETOURS

INDEX TO CHAPTERS

Chapter	Page
Introductory	(i to iv)
1. - Arrival of Joseph	1
2. - Life On The Acker Farm	14
3. - Early Recollections	29
4. - Childhood Encounters	47
5. - The Depression Year	63
6. - In Search Of Employment	80
7. - Focus On Employment	96
8. - Marriage And Farming	112
9. - The Military Episode	129
10. - Becoming A Manager	147
11. - Moving On And Up	168
12. - A Challenge To Innovation	184
13. - Too Proud To Be Humble	201
14. - Going International	218
15. - Implementing A Pilot Project	235
16. - A Shift In The Tide Of Events	252
17. - New Horizons	270
Annex "A"	280

"Draw from others the lesson that may profit yourself." Terence (Publius Terentius Afer).

LIFE'S DETOURS
AUTHOR'S NOTES

Except for the institutions, places, and people whose names are household words or of historical mention, the remaining names are fictitious, and any resemblance to real names is coincidental. The theme of the novel and the related anecdotes are derived from the experience and life of the author. The tales are embellished in some areas and suppressed in others, which results in a work of fiction.

One cannot write a book or the details of how to construct a building or the events that take place on a cruise, without acquiring a frame of mind and becoming conscious of the feelings of the people one meets and whose shoulders he touches in these scenarios. These feelings were in some instances expressed in an illusory or imaginative sense. To write about the main character's personal problems and achievements, brought the author to a state of awareness that nothing is personal in the sense that it is uniquely one's own. It is an experience shared with others, since problems, pleasures, hurts, and emotions are not exclusive feelings of the author alone. In writing this novel the author portrays a mere individual, who was caught up in what to him appears as a most exciting era in human history. An era of spectacularly productive and sometimes fearful possibilities, and whose life was touched and framed by the actions of others.

But, what a privilege it is to have walked the face of this earth; to have enjoyed sunshine and rain, and nature in all it's splendor, and to have been one of God's creations amongst the wondrous works of his hand in the society of human beings.

The author acquired a philosophy early in life from both his parents and grandparents, which simply stated - "that one should attempt to leave this world a better place than what one found." In writing the novel, this kind of motivation caused the author to create a high degree of self-reflection. In the author's personal road of life, distractions along the way diluted this philosophy and some detours left him harboring certain misgivings. For such misgivings and errors, he seeks the pardon of his family, his fellowmen, and above all from his Maker, with whom he hopes and prays to spend eternity.

LIFE'S DETOURS

What others are saying . . . .

"This is the story of the gradual development of a farm born and bred lad - who faced life and its tribulations as it came. Through a depression, employment and marriage, followed by a war, and then enmeshed in the business sector of cooperatives and credit unions - in their growth and expansion of an International scale...it is an interesting narrative of a part of life, that one seldom reads about or becomes exposed to"....John J. Clontz (Railroad Engineer).

"An interesting saga about a young man who chose to achieve his own self-development by assisting his fellowmen in the development of cooperatives and credit unions. In the process, he was instrumental in helping thousands of common, ordinary people around the world to improve their lot, by teaching them the basics of management skills, as well as the fundamentals of basic economics. Being a specialist myself in this field, I see more truth than fiction in this story. I believe it should make interesting and informative reading material, specially for cooperative and credit union members, as well as for people working in the development of self-help organizations around the world....Ney H. Lopez (International Consultant).

"The author's knowledge of events and of people associated with community development, and with such institutions as cooperatives and credit unions, resulted in the writing of a novel that contains some graphic episodes. It is both educational and fun to read".....Dan D. Boghean (Retired District Manager-Prudential Insurance Co.)

"A story of the struggles and joys of a boy of the 20th Century, who as a young adult endured the hardships of the Great Depression and the difficulties of World War II; of how he became a husband and father, and through faith and hard work and a little luck became part of corporate America and succeeded.....Vicky Avram (Corporation Executive)

"Life's Detours", is a good work of fiction from the hand and mind of an author and craftsman, who encountered in real life many of the situation narrated. It is a positive story and cause for good reading.....Ed Kessinger. (Retired Building Contractor)

LIFE'S DETOURS

Chapter 1

THE ARRIVAL OF JOSEPH

It was a glorius spring day in the month of May on the Acker farm. The sun was warm, bright and inviting to all of nature's creatures. There was a feeling and an atmosphere that gave a person a desire to appreciate life - to share, to live and enjoy it. Grandma Viola Acker was busy planting her garden. She harbored a satisfying sensation about the beauty of this day and of the security that farm life was giving her. She thought of the distance she had travelled from her simple beginnings in a village in Transylvania, Romania - which at that time was under Austrian rule, to their farm and home in Canada.

Viola Acker was small of stature, just a mite over 5 feet, and at 57 years of age was still in good physical condition. She looked after the gardening, milking of the cows, raising, feeding and caring for the flocks of chickens, turkeys, geese and ducks. She would be assisted by the men in the off-season when field work was not being done. Pausing for a moment to straighten up and give her back a break. She placed both hands on the handle of the hoe and used it for a prop. She gazed into the horizon over-looking the barnyard and enjoyed the scenery, and the heatwaves rising from the distant pasture where their herd of thirty or more head of cattle was grazing.

Lowering her gaze she observed with gratitude three newly born calves and an equal number of colts, frisking and romping around while their mothers were busy grazing.

LIFE'S DETOURS

"Thank you dear Lord, for adding this new bounty to our possessions. It will be possible for my husband and son to ship another carload of animals to the meat packing plant this fall," she thought to herself.

Catching a noisy sound which seemed to be getting closer, she turned to her left to see her son Richard approaching. He was driving a team of four horses pulling this farm implement known as a seeder, and also commonly referred to as a "drill." Richard was planting wheat into the newly cultivated soil. The puffing of the horses coupled to the beat of their steps, the clanging of the harness and the squeaky noise made by the drill were common noises to Grandma Acker. She paused long enough to see Richard reach the end of the field, step down from the platform of the drill and disengage it from seeding. At the same time he pulled heavily on the reins turning the horses back in the direction from which they came. He would continue doing this and going back and forth across the field in this manner until the field was fully planted. He gave his horses a short break, during which period he stepped to the front of the horses. He checked the fit on their neck collars to ensure that the animals were as comfortable as possible in their draft work.

He returned to his riding platform and re-engaged the drill into the seeding position. He glanced towards his mother in the garden and caught her waving at him. In his mind he interpreted that gesture as a mother's love and concern for him and for all that was going on.

"Giddyup, come-on let's go," Richard cried to the horses and they took off with the same familar noise. He glanced at the grain flutes carrying the seed into the ground to see that they were all functioning.

Besides being a farmer Richard was also a cantor on Sundays in the Romanian Orthodox Church. Everything was going along smoothly. He occupied himself with chanting hymns and chants he had put to memory while keeping his eye on the work. With the reins tightly in hand, he ensured that Maude the lead mare to his right, was following the previously marked path made by the drill wheel and to keep the seed rows as straight as possible.

At a near distance in the same field, driving a six-horse team was the family's hired hand. His six horse team was pulling a fourteen foot wide "disk harrow". This farm implement is used to cultivate and kill early spring weeds, as well as for mulching the soil for an ideal seedbed. The hired hand's name was William Cudnik, a rugged seventeen year old lad who was the son of a neighboring family. He was on his second year of employment with the Acker family. They referred to him as "Willie." They liked him for his jovial and witty behaviour. He was also an industrious and organized type of person and above all kind to animals. His wages amounted to $365 per year, or one dollar per day.

LIFE'S DETOURS

The verbal agreement was that these wages would be paid in quarterly installments, and that he would not be expected to work on Sundays.

Willie on the other hand liked working for the Ackers, because he was treated with dignity and made to feel as a member of the family. He had been given his own room and sat down at the same table with the family to have his meals. He took his Saturday night bath in the same galvanized tin tub used by the family. He had the privilege of using a pony to ride on Sundays enabling him to visit his parents and friends.

Still, there was another reason. He admired secretly and cared for the pretty fourteen year old girl that was also living with the Ackers. The girl was Pearl Molda. She was a granddaughter of the elderly Ackers. Her family consisted of her parents, three other sisters and two brothers. She was the second oldest member of the family and came to live with her grandparents because there was not enough to do at home. There was no formal agreement with regards to any wages - it was a labor of love. Pearl would help her grandparents with house work or other yard chores. In return they would see that she attended school to complete her public school education and furnish her with clothing and other basic necessities.

"We treat and love her like we did her mother, who was our child," - Grandma Acker would say.

Rising up early and putting up with all the hard physical work of having to feed, groom and harness the horses was never a problem on Willie's mind. He sat on the disc-harrow's seat and methodically steered his six-horse team all day. He made sure that every inch of ground was tilled and that the soil was properly turned over by the implement. Turning over the soil in early spring brought the flocks of sea-gulls to get their ration of earthworms. They floated gently in the air close behind Willie's disker. Each bird having her eye on the freshy turned black moist ground. Every now and then a bird would swoop down and pick up a freshly uprooted worm.

Willie had to keep somewhat ahead of Richard who was drilling in the seed. They would pass by each other with their implements and teams of horses several times each day, until this segment of the farm work was terminated. Often they would nod their head or wave at each other as they passed by. They wore dust goggles, but each one could see the white teeth and the bright smile of the other person in their dusty and grimy faces.

There was no "boss-employee" status in this relationship. It was a relationship of mutual respect and under-standing of each one's role. However, every spare moment of Willie's time not given to his work at hand, would be filled with thoughts about Pearl with whom he was becoming more and more infatuated.

"I must be careful, not to let on that I care for Pearl or that I have a crush on her," he would say to himself.

He did not want the family members to become suspicious of his thoughts and behaviour. Nevertheless, he would help her with the pails of slop when being carried to feed the hogs, or with other more heavier work that the farmyard demanded from time to time and that Pearl would undertake.

In such situations, Willie would talk with Pearl and try to impress her with his charm. She in turn would respond with squinting eyes, a few words, and light hearted smiles. In fact, whenever Willie went to Pearl's assistance, the Ackers were impressed with his attitude and his willingness to be of help. He did not take up any more time than was necessary to complete the chore.

At the last community dance held in the local school house, the Ackers went as a family and took both Willie and Pearl along. It was the custom for young people and especially the girls when going to community dances and other social functions to be chaperoned by their parents. Willie danced a couple of dances with Pearl. He did not monopolize her evening for fear such behaviour on his part would lead to suspicion of his affection for her. Such situations coupled to the good treatment offered by the Ackers, made his time and work on the farm seem easy and enjoyable.

On this day, Grandma Acker was still in her garden. She had gone back to making a series of rows in which she would plant vegetable seeds. She was in the process of planting two long rows of lettuce, which were to be followed by another two parallel rows of radishes. She looked up again and saw her husband, Grandpa Edward Acker, who had a team of horses drawing a four-wheeled wagon with a low box on it. The box was loaded with fence posts, barb-wire and other fence mending materials and tools. Repairing fences was work required to be done each spring. During the crop season the livestock would be confined to the fenced pasture land and the crops would be protected from livestock damage.

Grandpa Acker was a physically heavy set man. He carried his six foot frame quite well for his sixty-seven years of age. He did not like to work with teams of horses cultivating the land. He preferred to do building and fence repairs, painting, hauling grain to the nearest delivery point and other much needed farm work, at which he was good and to his liking. He had immigrated to Canada twenty years earlier from his native province of Transylvania in Romania. He brought with him Viola his wife, together with seven children, four girls and three boys. Their ages ranged from the eldest who was twenty to Richard the

LIFE'S DETOURS

youngest who was only three years of age.

When Grandpa Acker was two years of age his father died from wounds received in the revolutionary uprising of 1848. At that time the Romanians of Transylvania attempted to liberate themselves from the Austro-Hungarian rule. He was orphaned and raised by a great aunt. His mother remarried but her second husband did not want him as a member of his family. He grew up lacking formal education and was illiterate. In his village, he lived with his family on a four acre plot of land. They planted a garden, kept a small number of sheep, goats, pigs, a cow or two, and a few chickens.

He was also a cooper by trade, and would add to the product of their plot of land additonal income from the making and selling of his wares, They endured hardship in Romania, and more hardship as pioneers when they came and settled on their homestead in Canada. He felt deeply grateful for the consequences of his action to immigrate to Canada.

"I would have never been able to become the owner of six hundred and forty acres of land, forty head of cattle, twenty head of horses, a complete line of farm machinery, a new Model-T Ford automobile in the garage, a yard full of poultry and a bank account - if I would have remained in Romania," he mused as he paused for a moment from his work.

He wiped the sweat off his brow and took a drink of water from the gallon jug he carried along in his wagon. He knew the income prospects for the year were good. The price of wheat after the First World War had reached five dollars per bushel, and other farm commodities were enjoying good prices.

He looked toward his son Richard and the hired hand, moving their horse drawn implements across the field, busy planting the new crop. He was in a pensive mood. He knew that Eugenia, his daughter-in-law was pregnant and about to give birth to a child any day. He was hoping it would be a boy.

"It would please me so much to have a grandson from my youngest son - I would insist that he be named Joseph like my father, whom I don't remember. This farm that Viola and I worked so hard to develop, would not only be left to my son, but there would be someone to take over after him and my namesake would go on long after I'm dead," he thought to himself.

For Grandpa Acker progeny was important. He treated it like a religious commandment. He considered it a law of nature. Every living thing had to have a father, a mother and a home. He felt invigorated and thankful that he was alive and healthy. He whispered a little prayer as he turned to go on with repairing the fence, feeling that this world was not such a bad place after all.

Spring on the farm is a busy time of the year. It is a time when the farm family makes ready to greet and look after all the new life that is born or hatched. Everyone was busy this mid-morning on the Acker farm. Grandma Acker from her vantage point in the garden, could see the children on the school grounds. Pearl their granddaughter was completing her last year of study. The children were running and moving about in their bright colored sweaters and jackets in what appeared to be a game of tag. It was the morning recess period. Grandma Acker did not have a wrist watch, she knew the recess period was observed between ten thirty and ten forty-five in the morning.

"I have a few more minutes to work here in the garden, before I go into the house to render a helping hand in the preparation of the noon day meal," she said to herself.

She continued to plant more seeds in the ground and cover them lightly with top soil.

Suddenly Eugenia appeared in the kitchen doorway which happened to be facing the garden. In a voice loud enough to be heard by Grandma Acker, she cried out;- "Mama, come quickly to the house, I'm in need of your help."

Grandma Acker dropped her hoe and quickly hurried to the house. Eugenia went back in and waited. She was in pain. Eugenia was only fourteen years of age when she married Richard who was nineteen. She was now sixteen and about to give birth to her first child. She too, had come from a large family consisting of four boys and three girls. Her mother and father became embroiled in arguments during the latter years of their marriage. Her father who had also come from Romania decided to return. Her mother did not want to go back. She preferred to remain with her children in Canada.

On a cold winter's night their barn burned completely destroying the animals that were housed in it. Her father carried insurance on all of his buidlings and their contents. It was rumored that her father might have set fire to the barn himself to collect the insurance. Most everyone suspected him of arson but there was no proof.

The story was that he forgot the kerosene lantern in the barn suspended on a wire railing. By some accidental coincidence, one of the horses became untied from his manger and roamed loose through the barn. This horse could have knocked the lantern from its suspension and set the building ablaze. This conclusion was arrived at because one of the horses was found dead the next day in an area other than his own stall.

The loss of the animals and the condition in which she saw them the next morning, coupled to her misunderstandings and disagreements

LIFE'S DETOURS

with her husband, caused Eugenia's mother to become very depressed. Eugenia's father had made up his mind and after the harvest season of that year he departed for Romania. It was rumored that he took along thirty-five thousand dollars, which was a great deal of money at that time. Nobody received any letters or word from him after his departure. In the meantime, Eugenia's mother became more depressed and despondent. She wound up in the Provincial Psychiatric Hospital for treatment. She passed away during her hospital internment and was laid to rest in the local church cemetery.

This was the family and situational background of Eugenia and one of the principal causes for her early marriage. She felt fortunate to have married Richard and to become integrated into the Acker family. It gave her security and status, since the Acker family was quite prominent in the community. After her own mother had died, she looked to her mother-in-law as being her new mother - and as such called her "Mamma".

Eugenia and Grandma Acker had developed a very good rapport and there was wholesome empathy between them. They had agreed that Eugenia would do the housecleaning, cooking, bread-making, laundry and sewing. Grandma Acker would look after the garden and all of the outside yard chores, which were considered to be the domain of the farm housewife.

Grandma Acker reached the house, opened the door and quickly walked in. She found Eugenia lying down on a divan type of sofa near the entrance. It was normally used by Grandpa Acker for his short after-lunch nap. Eugenia was in pain and groaning from time to time.

"Mamma"- she uttered when she saw her mother-in-law, "I believe the time has come to give birth to my child. The pain is unbearable at times - I'm going to need some help"

Grandma Acker had given birth during her lifetime to nine children, seven of which were living. However, at this moment she did not feel qualified to act as a mid-wife in Eugenia's case. She looked at the clock on the kitchen wall. There was still one hour left before the men would be in from work and for their noon lunch.

"My dear," she said looking at Eugenia. "I'm going to walk over to where Richard is planting the crop and tell him to drop his work. To come quickly and bring a mid-wife to assist you - I will then return and be with you until the mid-wife arrives," and with that she closed the door behind her and was off on a brisk walk to where Richard was working. Eugenia was left alone on the divan. She decided to move into her bedroom and lie down on the bed.

"This might also relieve some of my pain," she thought to herself.

Eugenia had completed her grade seven at a rural public school.

Judging by the standards of the community in which she was living, this was considered good for women at that time. She could read, write and understand English better than her husband. She was good at spelling and in reality did the business correspondence for the family.

Dr. William Dammon, the only doctor serving the residents of this rural area had his practice situated about 20 miles distant. The rural telephone system was not yet installed - it came into being two years later. Eugenia had received a pre-natal examination from the doctor and he felt that she was in good physical condition, and that her birth-giving experience would be a natural event. He gave her a pamphlet on the subject of "parturition" which explained the stages of birth-giving, the breaking of the water, the labor pains associated with the encounter and the after birth sensation.

By this time, Grandma Acker had returned accompanied by Richard. He had left his team in the field with instructions to Willie, to disengage the horses from further work and take the noon break a half hour earlier than usual.

Richard looked at his wife, who was in pain.

"I believe I'll start the car and drive over to Rachel Tedesco's place, (a distance of seven miles) her skill as a mid-wife is well known in the community - I'll be back with her as soon as possible," he said and disappeared.

Eugenia's labor pains were now coming more frequently at intervals of 25 to 30 minutes and the pains would last from 30 to 40 seconds on each interval. Grandma Acker stood by, but enagaged herself in finishing the preparation of the noon day meal. The meal consisted of beef stew, mashed potatoes, fresh creamed cottage cheese, dill pickles, butter and freshly baked bread which Eugenia had earlier taken out of the oven.

Grandpa Acker suspected something out of the ordinary was happening. He quit his fence repairing temporarily and unhitched his team of horses. He had already watered and fed them their noon day ration of ground oats and sweet smelling hay. He was still present at the barn when Willie pulled in from the field with the other two teams. He gave Willie a hand in watering and feeding these horses as well. Then they walked to the house together with Grandpa Acker remarking;- "I believe we will have an addition in the family before this day is over - I saw Richard take the car and drive away, after a mid-wife, I suppose."

Willie heard the remark, nodded in agreement, but said nothing.

They both stopped outside the house where a pail of water, a dipper, a bar of home made soap and a wash basin were located on a wash-bench. A clean towel was hanging from a nail driven into one of the house's corner facia boards. Both men washed their faces and hands

LIFE'S DETOURS

and dried them, then walked into the kitchen.

The large kitchen table was home made. Grandma Acker had the table set and the food ready to be served. The conversation during the meal was brief and spoken quietly. The meal was quickly consumed and Willie departed for the barn with orders to continue his aspect of the field work. Grandpa Acker laid down on his favorite divan for a rest. He was unable to take his nap, because although the door to Eugenia's bedroom was closed he could hear her periodic groans. Eugenia tried to subdue them as much as possible, knowing that it was time for Grandpa's nap.

Grandma Acker went into the bedroom, came back out and took a glass of water back in at Eugenia's request. After a few moments she returned from the bedroom and looked at Grandpa Acker.

"Our daughter is going to have a difficult time, she's so young and its her first child. Her labor-pains are getting progressively more intense . I hope Dick finds Mrs. Tedesco at home and gets here in a hurry," she said.

Grandpa Acker had a somber look on his face. He arose from the divan and took a quick glance out the window towards the direction from which the car would be coming. He saw nothing. He turned to his wife, as he took his pocket watch out from his vest pocket and looked at it.

"He should be here shortly if nothing has happened to the car. We must put our trust in the Lord, He also has a hand in this," he commented.

The car was a 1918 Yankee Model-T Ford touring. Grandpa Acker had paid five hundred dollars for it. It was only used to go to town once per week, to church on Sunday or to visit relatives or neighbors. The car had never been driven through mud or other inclement weather conditions. That kind of weather or bad roads was for the horse and the buggy. It was housed in a garage built as a lean-to on one of the larger grain storage bins. Each fall when the snow and cold weather came, the car would be jacked up, placed on wooden blocks and stored until the next spring.

This particular Ford Model did not have a door on the driver's side and was magneto driven. It had to be cranked to start the motor. When they travelled Richard would ask his passengers to get seated in the car and be ready. He would go to the front of the vehicle, pull on the choke and crank the motor to start. At times it would balk and not start immediately, but generally a twist or two of the crank would start it putt-putting. Richard being a young man, would then hurry, climb on the running board and step over the fixed door of the car on the driver's side. Quickly he would adjust the spark and gas levers for smooth idling of the motor and accommodate his position in the seat behind the wheel.

To get the car moving he would press his right foot on the low-gear band pedal. After the car was in motion, he released with his left hand the drive lever on the left side and the gears would engage for road travel. Since this was a touring model, Richard preferred to keep the canvass top on the car folded back.

"It gives the car less wind resistance with the canvass top down," he would say.

There were times when he would operate the vehicle with the top in place. When going to church on Sundays which was five miles away, Grandpa and Grandma Acker decked in their Sunday best occupied the rear seat. Richard and Eugenia also well groomed and dressed would occupy the front seat.

The roads at that time were just "plain-dirt" roads. In many instances, they were the trails originally created by the horse drawn wagon and buggy vehicles. This explained why the automobile was a vehicle of pleasure and it reflected a measure of affluency. There was doubt in the minds of the owners about the auto's reliability. This was the concern harbored by Grandpa Acker for Richard's delay in bringing the mid-wife. The phrase was often said and heard that - "I left home with my automobile and returned with my horses." In other words, the automobile was towed home with the horses.

Another glance by Grandpa Acker out the window caught a glimpse of the car. Richard was coming down the road towards the house. Mrs. Tedesco was with him. There seemed to be a sigh of relief when the car pulled in front of the house. Rachel Tedesco quickly lowered herself from the vehicle, picked up a print satchel and immediately walked into the house.

She was familiar with the layout of the house, having been in it before on social visits as a friend of the family. She greeted the elderly Ackers with a smile. Grandma Acker pointed toward the bedroom door.

There was no need for further details. Mrs. Tedesco walked into the bedroom and literally took over. Everyone including Richard, who had also entered the house, felt that the situation was under control and that the best local help available had been attained for Eugenia.

Grandma Acker also went into the bedroom and soon came out with orders from Mrs. Tedesco. She had to warm up and have ready a large pot of water. She had to fetch an old oilcloth which Eugenia had tucked away on a cellar beam for this special need. She brought a cardboard box containing a quantity of clean rags that had been cut from bleached flour sacks and safeguarded for this event. A large basin, a bar of soap, a towel and a bottle of rubbing alcohol completed the

LIFE'S DETOURS 11

order. Viola Acker quickly and quietly attended to all of this.

Eugenia's labor pains were more and more frequent and intensive. The bedroom door was now ajar and Eugenia's groaning could be heard by both Grandpa Acker and Richard. They waited patiently as the minutes and hours seemed to drag. There was a feeling of sympathy for Eugenia's travail.

"Her water is now broken," Mrs. Tedesco was heard to say. This meant that the birth process was as nature intended it to be, but still under duress for Eugenia. There were moments of silence. Both Grandpa Acker and Richard were occassionally looking into each other's faces.

"God's power is so marvelous and wonderful - I can well remember the day when your mother gave you birth. You came into this world - the mid-wife slapped you on the back and you gave out the first cry. Son, life is the miracle of miracles, there are times when we don't appreciate the gift of life, and we fail to show in proper measure our gratitude to Him who gave it to us," Grandpa Acker said.

There was a another longer but dying groan heard from Eugenia. It marked her final contraction. It was quickly followed and overtaken by Mrs. Tedesco's shrill voice.

"It's a boy!, it's a boy!" she cried. Immediately the cry of the new born baby was heard. There was reason for all those present including Eugenia to be elated with the good news. Grandpa Acker looked to his son.

"We shall name him Joseph, so that he can carry your grandfather's and his great grandfather's name?" he said joyously.

Richard nodded approval. The name had been mentioned before during the pregnancy in family talk. Everyone knew that if the child was a boy, his name would be Joseph. Richard went into the bedroom to congratulate his wife, Mrs. Tedesco had just given the baby a sponge wash and handed him to Richard to hold. He held the baby tenderly in his arms, and gazed at him in wonder and then looked at Eugenia. "All we know, is that this child is a little bit of you and me. We've created a brand new soul unlike anyone else in this world. That's the miracle of life. We shall watch with joy his growing up," Richard said looking into the baby's face.

Eugenia spent a few days in bed recovering from the ordeal. It was customary for a woman that gave birth to rest for a few days, before returning to her daily work routine. Eugenia's work routine now had the added feature of taking care of her new born child. She was a young mother. She was infatuated with the creation she had brought into the world.She nurtured and caressed the baby as she breast fed him. She also noted that the left side of the baby's head was slightly out of the normal rounded proportion as compared to the right side of the head. She was concerned about his looks. She felt this abnormality could be camouflaged later on after his hair grew, by allowing the hair on that side of the head to grow a bit longer than on his normal side.

"I wonder, what I did wrong to have this happen to my child," she said to herself.

On her first visit to the doctor, she showed her baby to him and asked him about the abnormality of the baby's head.

"What happened"- Dr Gammon said, "is that during your pregnancy, you must have slept for long periods of time on your left side, with the result that this affected the baby's normal development of his head."

Eugenia looked back upon her pregnancy period and nodded in the affirmative, because she knew that during her pregnancy she slept on her left side facing Richard most of the time. The doctor said this was normal for a young couple, both being unaware of what this might do to the fetus.

Dr. Gammon advised Eugenia to apply gently frequent massaging with a slight pressure of the hand to the abnormal side of the head. This should be done when breast feeding and on other occassions as frequently as possible. The baby's bones are very soft and pliable during his first year of life. The abnormality should correct itself. Eugenia faithfully followed this advice and within six months a correction was obtained.

There followed the usual visits from aunts and uncles with gifts for the new born. Grandpa Acker brought home lumber on his next trip to town, and set about constructing a rocking cradle for his new grandson. A few days later Eugenia took down the family Bible from a shelf bracketed to the wall, just above the night table in their bedroom, and wrote in it with pen and ink - "Joseph Acker - born on Saturday, May 17th, 1919 at 5:30 p.m."

She made no mention of that six hour period of labor pains she suffered in order to bring this new life into the world.

The baptismal rite followed about ten days later as is customary with christians of the Orthodox faith. For the baptism the baby was held by his uncle Daniel Acker who became the Godfather of the child. A litany of baptismal prayers were recited by the priest, while the Godfather recited the CREED. The baby was dunked in lukewarm water three times with the priest saying with each dunking,

"I baptize you in the name of the Father, the Son and the Holy Spirit, Amen".

He then annointed his forehead and officially called him "Joseph"- his given christian name.

LIFE'S DETOURS

By this time Joseph was crying. However he was soon bundled in a flannelette wrap, handed to Eugenia to hold and nurse and his crying subsided.

In his brief homily the priest admonished the family to love, guide and counsel the child in the Christian doctrine and faith, so that as he grew into manhood his faith would stand him in good stead during periods of stress and tribulation.

"Just as the world is not perfect for us - it will not be perfect for him - teach him that there is to be purpose in life. That he is not to waste time, for time is what life is all about. That he is to be a good steward over his resources and to engage the talent with which he may be endowed, to the glory of God and in service to his fellow men," concluded the priest.

Everyone present chimed to say - "Amen".

Following the christening ceremony which took place about two weeks after the birth, the uncles, aunts, cousins, neighbors and friends gathered for the baptismal party. This Sunday afternoon the Acker farmhouse was full. Willie elected to remain and celebrate the occassion with the family and to render a helping hand as required. Pearl too, was neatly dressed in a cotton print dress, with a white apron, enjoying the festive occassion as she moved about obeying the orders of Grandma Acker in serving the guests.

It was a boisterous gathering with the smell of good food made up of chicken noodle soup, roast goose, slices of home-cured and smoked ham, scalloped potatoes, cabbage rolls, home-made bread, cinnamon buns, home-baked apple pies and many other goodies. There was much well-wishing for the new born and glasses filled with "home-brewed" whiskey were tingling. All the guests present extended their arms across the table to touch glasses and offer their toasts and cheers.

By late afternoon, the guests had gone to their respective homes. The Acker family was left to wash dishes, clean up, and to do the evening chores. The work consisted of milking cows, feeding hogs, and gathering the eggs laid during the day. Finally, with the chores and cleaning completed, the family sat on the screened porch in the cool and quiet of the evening and in an informal way appraised and commented on the day's activity.

Everyone felt an atmosphere of accomplishment and gratefulness. Darkness began to fall. Rather than light a kerosene lamp and continue their conversation, they opted to retire for the night. They said "good night" to each other and each one quietly left for their respective sleeping quarters. Richard and Eugenia were the last to leave. Eugenia was tired but content.

LIFE'S DETOURS

Chapter 2

LIFE ON THE ACKER FARM

The work on the Acker farm continued with rythmic tempo season after season and year after year. Every member of the household was kept busy in one form or another. Planting the crops in the spring, cultivation and weed control during the summer, harvesting and preparing for winter in the fall.

Maintenance of the buildings and fences, haying and the storage of fodder for wintering the livestock were other major activities. To these must be added the daily chores of milking cows, and feeding the hogs and poultry. Care of the animals called for year-round attention.

Practically all of this work called for manual labor. Changes in work styles or methods were slow. The Ackers were mechanizing and purchasing more and better machinery from the local dealers as they became available. This enabled them to cope with a larger volume of work in a shorter time frame. However, manual labor to operate the newly acquired implements and to care for the increase in the livestock numbers was still required.

An activity such as cutting of the grass in the sloughs and other low field areas for hay was done by a grass mower operated by one man and drawn by two horses. In the hot July sun the cut grass would dehydrate itself quickly. It would then be raked into windrows and bunched into larger piles known as "mounds". The rake was drawn by two horses, operated by one man who sat on a seat and by foot manipulated its dumping mechanism, causing it to unload at the operator's will.

The cutting, mowing and bunching of the hay was work that Richard Acker would do. When the time came to stack and store the hay, additonal manpower or hired hands would be sought. The volume of forage required to feed upwards of sixty head over a five month winter period was substantial. It took two men to a hay-rack to load the

LIFE'S DETOURS

hay mounds by hand using pitchforks. A "hay-rack" was a home-built carrier fitted on four wagon wheels and constructed specifically for hauling hay, straw and other light weight bulky materials. Each hay-rack would hold from one to one and one-half tons of hay and would be drawn by two horses.

The hay would be transported from the fields and by hand pitched into the loft of the barn until the loft would be full. The loft capacity would be about six tons. The rest of the hay crop would be stacked outside in a fenced area and stored until used.

"It takes from one to one and-one half tons of hay to winter one animal. For wintering sixty animals we need from ninety to one hundred tons of fodder," Richard stated when asked to determine how much feed was required for one winter season.

The haying season generally lasted from two to three weeks depending on the weather, and it took place during July, one of the hottest months of the year.

Spring, summer and fall seasons were busy periods, but time was always found for pleasure and relaxation. The community in which the Ackers lived was made up of some five hundred families the majority of which came to Canada from Romania and created this settlement. Their religion, language, customs and traditions, brought with them from Romania formed a part of their communal living.

Through voluntary cash contributions and donations of labor, the community had constructed two orthodox churches. They had organized a Cultural and Beneficial Society to provide themselves with basic insurance coverage for death benefits and funeral costs. Through taxes and under Provincial Government supervision several school houses were constructed. Everyone was convinced of the need to educate the children and the first school called Capitolia School, was built in the year 1907 across the road from the first church.

This was the school Eugenia attended. Richard also attended classes one winter season primarily to learn to read and write English. He had been taught to read and write Romanian as he grew up by his oldest brother during the long winter evenings. He enjoyed reading and by the age of twelve had read the Romanian Bible cover to cover. Richard was interested in mathematics and had mastered the kind of basic calculations and equations required to operate a farm. He knew the formulas for calculating the volume of wheat in a bin and the volume of water in a cylindrical well.

Richard's spelling was bad. He wrote the English words in Romanian. For example, he would write the word good-bye as "gudbai", the word night as "nait" and the word business as "biznes". He was secretary of the school board for a few years and only he could read the minutes he kept of the meetings. It took both Richard and Eugenia to write a business letter and it was generally an evening project. Richard would dictate the letter or impart the general idea and Eugenia would structure the letter in better English, correct spelling and then hand-write the letter. Her penmanship was good.

Life on the Acker farm first and foremost involved work. The principal other activity consisted of church attendance on Sunday. Here they would take time after the worship service to meet neighbors, friends and other people and to greet each other. No work was performed on the farm on a Sunday except for that which was absolutely necessary in order to give comfort to animals, otherwise the day was sacred. Other days in which farm work would cease consisted of special church holidays such as the birthday of St.John the Baptist (June 24) St.Peter & Paul's Day (July 12) and the Dormition of St.Mary (August 15th). The church attended by the Ackers bore the name of St.Peter and Paul Romanian Orthodox Church. Each year special liturgical services and prayers would be held on July 12th, the name day of these two apostles and patron saints.

Following the worship services the ladies would unfold white linen or cotton tablecloths on the green grass and spread a picnic feast in the church yard. Everyone would enjoy the various food delicacies, the outdoor atmosphere and the communal fellowship. During short periods prior to these church holidays the Ackers would observe lent and ate no animal products. Grandpa and Grandma Acker observed lent on Wednesdays and Fridays through-out the year.

However, the culture of their newly adopted country was impacting on the community and on the Ackers. There had to be some diversion from work.

"All work and no play makes George a dull boy," was a saying Grandpa Acker had heard in his new homeland and -"a young colt that fails to frolic and frisk doesn't make a good horse," was another saying he had brought along from Romania. He knew there had to be diversity.

May 24th was a holiday. It was known as Victoria Day in honor of Queen Victoria of Britain under whose reign the British Empire expanded and consolidated itself. The children had a school holiday and the day generally was observed by going into the nearest town as a family, to meet with other community folks, to a dance in the evening, or simply to visit with friends or neighbors. The Ackers observed Victoria Day because they were grateful that Canada accepted them as immigrants. This enabled them to acquire land, establish a home and find freedom.

They found Canada's laws and rules accommodating and they respected them. Later Victoria Day was changed and became Memorial

LIFE'S DETOURS

Day in honor of those who had lost their lives in the First World War. The Ackers did not have any men related to them lose their lives in that war. Richard, who would have qualified age-wise for military service was involved in food production and did not volunteer. Food was considered an essential to winning the war. They knew of neighboring young men who had volunteered to fight in that war. Two lost their lives and a few were wounded.

All work ceased on the Acker farm on July 1st. which is Canada Day and is the country's birthday. The family would motor into town and attend the annual Picnic and Sports Day. The younger men who had terminated public school had formed teams in each school district for playing baseball. On sports days they would compete with each other to determine which was the better and more superior team. Baseball, a game not heard of in Romania had taken a foothold and captivated the minds of the new generation in the community. This day also saw the civic leaders and the Member of Parliament for their area present at the affair. The folks in attendance would be entertained through a round of speeches and accolades on the progress being made in the development of their community. A degree of pride could be felt.

Other social events in general consisted of weddings, box-social dances in the local school houses and baseball games on Sunday afternoons. Wedding parties in many instances were a pleasure to attend. However at some family weddings, the wedding hosts were too liberal in serving their home-made whiskey commonly called "home-brew", and an otherwise decent party would turn into a drunken brawl.

Fist fights, personal injuries and property damages occurred as a consequence of drunkenness. At times these would wind up in court trials, and wife and child abuse. Young Richard Acker was frequently involved in fist fights or verbal diatribe during such drunken brawls. An act which the elderly Ackers and Eugenia his wife deplored, were ashamed of and found difficult to condone.

The next day or two after such a brawl Richard would be extending apologies for his misbehaviour, both to members of the family as well as to others he may have hurt.

"Any mind that is capable of real sorrow is also capable of good behavior," his wife Eugenia would say to him - "you must steer yourself away from too much alcohol."

"Drunkeness turns a man out of himself and makes room for a beast to enter," Grandpa Acker would admonishingly say to his son.

When sober Richard was industrious, thoughtful, diligent, kind, humorous and easy to get along with. His major weakness was alcohol which he could not control, and his excessive drinking took place primarily at social events. He was not the only one. The continued rise in affluence induced excessive drinking amongst more of the men. This became the largest immoral plague to permeate the community.

With the advent of the automobile a trip to Regina the capital city of the Province during the Agricultural Fair and Exhibition Week, was an event eagerly planned for well in advance and attended. The Acker family would take time off and make this once a year trip to the capital city. They would pack farm products in their Model-T Ford to take along to their city cousins with whom they would visit and stay. Products such as a crate containing 12 dozen eggs, a gallon jar of cream, cottage cheese and a pound or two of butter would be the principal items taken.

The visit to this provincial fair would put the Ackers in touch with the latest developments in farming techniques, and expose them to the new implements that were being invented and placed each year on the market. In their 1922 trip to this event Grandpa Acker and Richard purchased a threshing machine at the Fair for $2,100.00. It was shipped by rail to Truax, their nearest freight delivery point. The threshing outfit had to have partial assembly on the farm. Bill Johnson, the school teacher's husband being a mechanic, assisted in the assembly and operation of the threshing outfit during the first threshing season. He trained Richard on its operation.

The main event of the fall season was the cutting, stooking and threshing of the field crops. Several kinds of grain crops were grown and harvested. Wheat and flax were produced for the market while oats and barley were produced primarily to feed the animals and the poultry.

The implement used to cut the field crops was called a "binder," This implement would cut the crop and elevate it through a series of canvasses to a packing compartment. The packed straw would create pressure on a trigger mechanism that would bind and tie the straw into a "sheaf". The sheaf would be kicked on a set of carrier grates. When the grates became loaded with six or seven sheaves, the person seated on the binder would release the carrier using a foot pedal and dump the sheaves as bundles in neat rows.

These rows would be picked up later and manually be made to stand upright in "stooks". The people doing this kind of work were called "stookers". Sometimes the Ackers did the stooking as a family project. Richard and Eugenia would leave baby Joseph with Pearl to baby-sit. They would be joined by Grandpa and Grandma Acker all of whom would rise very early in the morning and go stooking. They would stook until the heavy dew or early frost would disappear, and then continue with crop cutting again. In three to four hours they could stook most if not all of the previous day's cut. Stooking as a family

LIFE'S DETOURS

project was done for one of two reasons. Firstly, stookers for hire were not always available and secondly it was often an economy measure.

In other words, the money saved by doing the work themselves was used for other family needs.

During this time Willie the hired hand would be cleaning the barn, spreading the animal manure on the fields, feeding, grooming and harnessing the eight horses required to pull the two binders. In addition he would grease and repair the binders in readiness for cutting.

When the crop was heavy outside help would be sought, in which case Richard would motor into town and look for harvest laborers. These men would come from eastern Canada on "harvest excursions" to assist the farmers in taking off their bountiful crops. The "harvest-excursions" were introduced by the Canadian government as a war-measure in the last two years of the War. It was a measure designed to help the agricultural industry in Western Canada with their manpower shortage. Food production was an essential input for the Allies to win the war. Many of the farm men and laborers left to serve in the war and left agriculture with a labor shortage. The government requested industries in Eastern Canada to program their employee vacations, and release the factory workers to come west and provide the harvest labor.

Factory workers and others took advantage of the Government paid-for train transportation. The five dollars per day wages paid by the farmers coupled to free board and lodging made the excursion economically attractive as well. In a bountiful crop year these same harvest-excursionists would be hired earlier and they would also do stooking. Threshing the crops would follow.

It would take a crew of ten to twelve men to adequately supply the needed manpower to operate a threshing outfit. A full crew would be made up of the excursionists and other laborers. The neighboring farmers who wanted to have their crops threshed would join forces to make a full crew.

Threshing was done by a machine called a "separator" that had a toothed cylinder into which the bundles or sheaves were fed. A tractor equipped with a pulley would transmit power with a drive belt, to another pulley of smaller size fixed on one end of the toothed separator cylinder. The ratio of the tractor pulley to the separator pulley was about 1 to 3.5 in size. This ratio caused the separator's cylinder to turn at the manufacturer's recommended rate of speed. The way the cylnder teeth were off-set in relation to each other, and the high speed the cylinder travelled was the method by which the machine would separate the crop kernels from the grain spikes and straw.

The grain would be carried by chain driven conveyor cups and elevated to a weighing mechanism. This mechanism was pre-set to automatically dump the grain in half-bushel measures into a wagon box to be hauled when full to storage bins. After passing over a series of kicker sieves the straw and chaff was forced by a blower-fan through a cylindrical tube, and stacked in a pile in the form of a pyramid some twenty feet away and preserved. When the snow covered ground and cold weather demanded that the animals be housed and cared for in their stables, the straw would be used for feed and animal bedding.

The end of the harvest season was marked by empty fields and full grain bins. Cattle would be turned loose and free to roam at large. The harvest period would last from two to six weeks depending on weather conditions. Upon completion the excursionists would leave and the Acker family would turn their attention to other work that had to be performed before the snow fell and the winter weather set in.

Some of the harvested grain would be delivered to the nearest marketing point, a distance of fourteen miles and sold to pay for harvest expenses. The largest volume of grain would be delivered and marketed during the slack winter months commencing immediately after the New Year. The grain would be hauled by horses in sleigh or wagon-loads depending on the season. The buying agency was a cooperative known as the Saskatchewan Wheat Pool. This organization had buying points at nearly every railway station throughout the province. The Ackers were members and shareholders in this cooperative and patronized its services.

Most of the province's farmers were shareholders of this cooperative marketing organization. It would handle and market the farmer-member's grain at cost. The grain was handled through a building known as an "elevator" and the "elevator agent" was its operator. The elevator was equipped with a mechanism that would elevate the grain into storage bins. A full bin containing a specific kind and grade of grain would be emptied into railroad cars. The full freight cars would be consigned to the larger port terminals situated on the Great Lakes for export to other countries.

This organized effort enabled the elevator agent to purchase and handle large quantities of grain produced by the district farmers. The Ackers supported the Wheat Pool because they felt it gave them a square deal. Later in life and after Grandpa Acker's demise one of Richard's sons became an elevator agent and grain buyer for the cooperative.

Autumn was the season of the year to haul home the winter needs and supplies. Richard would hitch a team of horses to a wagon and take into town a wagon-load of wheat. He would return with a wagon load of coal which would be emptied down a coal chute into a space reserved for coal-storage in the house's cellar. Coal was the fuel used

LIFE'S DETOURS

for cooking and for keeping the Acker house warm. It took from seven to eight tons of coal to last for one winter season. A cord of firewood would be stacked outside in a sheltered place. This activity took about ten days of Richard's time. It would take him a full day to make a trip into town to deliver a load of grain and return with the coal or the wood and unload the wagon ready again for the next day.

Grandpa Acker would hitch "Tom" and "Sandy",his favorite team of horse to a wagon load of wheat (about 65 bushels) and take it to the flour mill. The mill was located in a town called Assinaboia about 40 miles distant. This trip lasted generally three to four days. Upon arrival he would find other farmers waiting in line. He would have to wait his turn to get his wheat milled into flour. The town had a livery barn to house the horses and several stores from which food items could be purchased. Grandpa Acker took along his own lunch and blankets from home. Along with other farmers who were also waiting in line they slept in the loft of the livery barn. The only hotel in town did not have enough rooms to satisfy the demand at all times.

The flour mill was privately owned and Michael Luby the owner and operator charged 50 cents per bushel for milling. The farmer took all the flour together with such by-products as bran, shorts and grits back home. Grandpa Acker's cost was $32.50 and he returned home with 24 bags of flour, 8 bags of bran, 4 bags of shorts and 2 bags of grits, each bag weighing 100 pounds.

This yearly supply of mill products was placed in a store-room abutted on the north to the farm house. The farm had no electricity or refrigeration. Having the store-room located on the north side placed it in the shade of the main structure and kept it cool during the summer. The store-room would receive a thorough cleaning and disenfecting before receiving a new batch of mill products. This eliminated the possibility of vermin or insect infestation.

"Our bread consumption in this household averages two bags per month. Bread and butter is a staple item served at every meal. Our family plus the hired hands, vistors and guests can consume a lot of bread. Eugenia finds herself kneading dough and baking bread twice a week," Grandma Acker would say.

The two dogs on the Acker farm -"Sport" and "Kaiser" were the consumers of the bran product. Eugenia would bring fresh cow's milk to a boil on the kitchen stove and pour it to scald the dog's ration of bran. After cooling the two dogs would feed on it in gulps. The Ackers were fond of their dogs. The bran coupled to other scraps remaining from the dining table gave them nice, shiny and silky looking coats of hair. The farm-stead would have not been complete without the two dogs. They were sensitive to anything strange that appeared in the yard and mindful of their duty to guard the farm home and yard when the Ackers were away. To chase or round up the animals they were trained to be "heelers" and skilled at biting at the heels of animals. There was no animal too stubborn to resist being chased and manouvered in the direction the dogs were instructed to have them taken.

The grits was used as a breakfast cereal by the Ackers. The bran shorts were used as a feed supplement for the young calves. Three or four days after birth the calves would be weaned from their mothers and pail-fed on skim milk. A cup full of bran shorts would be added to the skim milk and mixed well before feeding. The bran shorts would be a substitute in the calves food for the cream that Grandma Acker extracted from the whole milk with the cream separator. The calves would thrive on this meal to which they became accustomed. It would be the only feed the calves would receive until they could eat hay and drink water or go out to pasture.

The cream was churned into butter every Saturday morning. A special press was used that would form the butter into rectangular blocks weighing one pound each. Grandma Acker would wrap these butter blocks in waxed paper and place them in a bucket. The bucket would be lowered with a rope and pulley into a yard well to keep cool. Every Monday saw Grandpa Acker place in the rear of his buggy, a crate with twelve dozen eggs and a wooden box containing ten pounds of butter and leave for town.

These products would be exchanged at the General Store and Mr J. L. Kelly the store owner, would provide other food products of equal value in return. Food products that the farm itself could not produce, such as salt, sugar, baking powder, yeast, cornmeal, coffee and others.

All of this animal caring and food preparation was burdensome work. However, Grandma Acker's philosophy was that - "men made houses - but women made homes, and each had a role to play." While her work and chores in the yard and with animals may have appeared tedious, she enjoyed and occupied herself with it from early morning until the late evening hours.

Late fall was the season for digging the potatoes and other root crops from the garden and storing them in the cellar. There was the onion crop to collect. Grandma Acker would weave the onions and their dried tails into braids. These braids would be suspended from ceiling hooks in the house cellar. The cabbage heads were cut and separated from the plant. Some of the heads had their cores removed and the hollow cores packed with salt. They would be laid in a wooden barrel, covered with water and allowed to ferment. The product was known as sauer-kraut. Other heads of cabbage were shredded with a hand operated shredder, and again placed in a wooden container and made into shredded sauer-kraut.

The dried bean and pea pods would be collected, placed in a bag and using a flail Grandma Acker would beat the bag to remove the kernels from the pods. The dried pods were waste. The bean and pea kernels would then be bagged and stored in the store-room for use as table food until the next garden crop came along in the ensuing year.

During the summer periods wild but edible mushrooms would appear after a rain. The mushrooms would be collected and strung up to dry and be stored. Milk would be processed for making cheese and two or three five gallon earthen-ware crocks of cheese would be stored in the cellar.

"We make our own spaghetti from the flour, then add our own home-made cheese and tomato sauce to prepare spaghetti and cheese dinners," Eugenia would say.

The Ackers seemed to know exactly when to undertake each task, how to store each food item and this made them extremely resourceful people.

During the late October weather the Ackers would attend to those needs that had to be done during this period, and before the real sub-zero temperatures set in. One such task included the castration of all male animals that were not to be kept for siring. A local farmer/rancher skilled in this respect, was employed to perform this task for a nominal charge. Later after the emasculating instruments became available, the Ackers purchased their own and the task became a "do-it-yourself" project. Simultaneously with castration, the docking of lamb's tails and dehorning of the young livestock was also done. The dehorning eliminated the possibility of the bovine animals goring one another or a human during their winter confinement to their stable.

Food preparation and storage prior to the advent of rural electricity and refrigeration, was not only a chore, but an art. The Ackers would fatten and have ready for butchering a couple of hogs with an estimated weight of between 300 to 350 lbs each. A neighboring bachelor by the name of Val Stenets was considered good at killing and dressing hogs. He would be invited to assist in this task. November days are short, therefore this task would begin at daybreak. Some preliminary work would be done the day before, such as knife sharpening, and the cleaning of the utensils used in the process.

The killing process was merciless. The hogs to be killed would be enticed to their feeding trough with a bit of food, Val would take a hammer and strike the hog squarely between the eyes with a heavy blow. This immediately stunned the animal which would drop from its legs to a stiffened lifeless position. This gave Val enough time to grab his stabbing knife, lift the animal's front left leg and plunge the knife into the animal's heart. The hog would never recover from its stunned position and simply bled to death. Later the hammer was replaced by a .22 rifle, but stabbing in order to bleed the animal properly for later dressing was still used. The dead carcass would be singed by the flames from a fire made with hay and held by Val on a three tine-fork close to the carcass. Once the hair was singed, the carcass would be covered with burlap sackcloth and boiling hot water poured over the sackcloth. Time would be allowed for the dead animal's skin to moisten, so that it could be scraped clean. The scraping was done by Val and Richard using razor sharp knives.

Both carcasses would receive the same treatment. Cutting the carcasses into pieces ensued. The separation of the different cuts of the animal was an art. The rear shoulders became roasts when stored frozen. When pickle-cured and smoked for dry storage they became hams. The bacon slabs from the animal's belly were pickled, then smoked and became cured bacon. Fat was separated from the ribs and other meaty parts. The hog fat would be separated into two classifications and ground for rendering into lard. The lard derived from the fat off the hog's back would be stored in earthen-ware crocks and used for cooking. The remaining fat rendered from other parts of the hog's body, including that gathered from the internal parts was used for making home-made soap.

The cracklings were stored to be used for food and the neck and spinal bones were used for soup bones. The intestines were skilfully turned inside out, scraped washed and then used as sausage casings. Meat not used for hams or bacon was de-boned and ground to be put into sausage. The stomach of the animal would be turned inside out, scraped clean, washed thoroughly and stuffed with a ground mixture consisting of the ears, the heart, the lungs, the tongue and rice with spices added to taste. It would then be boiled for the required amount of time, placed in cool storage and served as "head-cheese". The pork hocks and the pig's feet were initially stored frozen over the winter months, and generally used up before the warm weather arrived the following spring.

"When we kill a hog, the only thing we throw away is the squeal and the intestinal waste. Everything else can be eaten if properly cured and prepared," Grandma Acker would say.

Before departing for his home at days end, the Ackers would cut and wrap a portion of fresh pork including a bit of liver, and give it to Val Stenets in recognition of his butchering service. Since he did not raise any pigs himself the portions he obtained from custom butchering were always welcomed.

After the pickling process, the hams, sausages, and bacon slabs would be strung up near the ceiling in an empty grain storage bin, properly sealed to contain smoke. It was used as a smoke-house. The products would be allowed to dry in their hanging position for a few days. A fire would be made from hickory chips, in an old but serviceable batchelor type stove. The fire would be smothered and required close supervision in order to create and release as much smoke as possible inside this smoke-house.

The exposure of the meat to this density of hickory smoke over a one or two day period, tinted the meats with an appealing brownish color and impregnated them with a hickory flavored smoke taste. With the smoking process complete, the different products were wrapped in wax paper and buried in a binful of wheat to be used as and when required. During the hot weather of the summer months the wheat pile in the bin acted as a coolant and assisted in preserving the meats, although rancidity would set in towards the end of summer.

Early December was poultry killing time. Grandma Acker would raise turkeys, geese, and ducks specifically for the market. The Ackers themselves would keep breeding stock, plus a few birds for their own table use. The surplus was marketed. Killing and plucking the feathers from 90 to 100 turkeys, 15 to 20 geese and as many as 100 ducks, was another family project much deplored, but necessary. The birds were killed and dressed in the barn in near freezing temperatures. They would be transported and sold to a buyer who would be in town for an appointed day or two, or perhaps to some travelling buyer who would scour the countryside at this particular time of the year purchasing these products.

The purchases were made by the weight and grade of the dressed birds. Birds that were fattened for some time prior to killing, were properly dressed and made cosmetically appealing to the eye, graded better and yielded a better price per pound. Therefore, careful plucking of the feathers to avoid tearing the skin, and careful handling of the carcasses were vitally important factors in obtaining the best market price.

Although the men helped in the preparation of the birds for the market. the cash income from this activity belonged to Viola and Eugenia and was untouchable to the men. It was their pin money to spend as they pleased.

The turkey feathers were generally buried in a hole dug for this purpose and considered as waste. The feathers from the geese and ducks were saved at killing time in bags. During the long winter evenings, Viola and Eugenia, would strip the feathers and make feather-down filled quilts and pillows. Some of these products were made for their use, and some to be presented as gifts to couples getting married. Especially to couples that were related or well known to them.

By the time Christmas arrived the heaviest portion of the farm work was over. The families in the community including the Ackers, would focus on the up-coming Christmas and New Year holidays. They looked forward to the times they could spend together as a family and with their relatives and friends.

Winter with its deep snow and cold weather demanded that the farm family be constantly at work. Not with the same haste or long hours as the spring, summer and fall months, but still with some degree of urgency.

Firstly, the grain had to be transported and marketed. To transport the three thousand bushels of grain produced on the Acker farm to market with two teams of horse-drawn sleighs, each carrying about sixty bushels of grain, or about 120 bushels per daily trip would require 25 trips or 25 days. This would take most of the months of January and February, because there were days when hauling grain would be impossible. On extremely cold days the horses would not be subjected to heavy pulling. Snow blizzards would occur which would drift over and block the sleigh trails making them temporarily impassable for the sledding of heavy loads.

The month of March with the ground still being snow covered, found the Ackers preparing again for the spring work. It meant that Richard and Grandpa Acker would be repairing the machinery and equipment. Grandpa Acker would work in a heated tool shed doing harness repairs. He would stitch, mend and soak the harness in a container holding neatsfoot oil. He had crafted a wooden vise to hold the different harness parts. In repairing he would pierce the leather parts with an awl, and run the needles one from each side through the pierced hole. He would draw a heavily waxed thread through and pull it tight with his hands, then tie a knot in the thread at the end of a fixed piece of repair work. To watch Grandpa Acker do this work was a delight, because he seemed to enjoy it as he hummed some tune he had learned as a child in his native Romania.

Richard together with Willie were in a granary, cleaning grain for seed to be used in the spring planting. Seed cleaning was done by a hand operated apparatus called a "fanning mill", which was man-powered by Willie. The Ackers would require about 250 to 300 bushels of seed-wheat. This would be planted at about one and one-eigth bushels per acre of land. The fanning-mill was capable of cleaning about ten bushels per hour, thus making the seed cleaning a task of about one week duration depending on the number of hours dedicated to the task each day.

The grain contaminated with weed seeds, chaff and straw would be picked up by Richard from a wagon-box, placed by hand with a scoop measure into the bin at the top of the fanning mill. Through an adjustable slotted opening it would be fed down according to the capacity of the mill. As the grain travelled on its downward course, shaking all the while through a series of sieves the foreign objects would be removed. The sound, clean grain kernels to be used for seed would amass at the foot of the mill. The seed grain would be shovelled by hand into another partitioned section of the bin and stored until planting time.

Between hauling grain, caring for the livestock, repairing equipment and doing chores, time still remained to drive over to a neighbor's house and enjoy an evening playing cards. Or perhaps the neighbors would come over.

There were no official invitations sent out - it was understood that when someone came for a visit, they were welcome and food would be served.

The popular card games played were cribbage, rummy, Norwegian whist, and a Romanian card game known as "Seven is wild". The women were not much for card games. Their visiting time was spent in talking about their families, their work, new ideas or cooking concepts they had learned. Most of the time on social visits they carried their knitting or crocheting projects along. and worked at it while visiting. The evenings consisted of making pop corn, reviewing community gossip and talking over farm problems. They would usually wind up about mid-night with coffee and lunch, following which the guests went home.

March was also the month when the horses that would be employed in field work began receiving special attention. In the first instance more grain or ground oats would be added to their daily rations. Using a special mechanism for opening and holding a horse's mouth open, each horse would be examined to ensure that their teeth were uniform in height and in good condition. Uneven or sharp edged teeth would be ground level with a special tooth rasp. At the same time a capsule containing medication for killing stomach worms in animals was administered. This was done with a capsule gun inserted deep enough into the horse's mouth and throat, to cause it to automatically swallow the capsule when released by the gun.

The horses would have the hair clipped from their legs and the underside of their bodies, using hand operated horse hair clippers. A practise used to make it easier to comb and brush the horses for their daily grooming. Horses that bolted or misbehaved during the clipping process, would have their upper lip tightened with a "twitch", which for some unknown reason caused them to behave. Each horse was also treated to a sponge bath with water that contained chemicals for killing animal lice. These were measures taken to maintain the animals in good health and physical fitness.

The fun portion of the early spring farm work involved the breaking-in and training of young horses. Horses were generally halter-broken while they were suckling colts. As such they were accustomed to being led, handled and touched by human beings. Training a horse to accept a rider consisted of placing a saddle on its back, and securing it tightly to its body. The horse would then be turned loose, at which point he would buck and kick attempting to rid itself of the saddle. When the horse accepted defeat and became accustomed to the burden of the saddle, the next step would be to have a rider mount and train the horse to respond to the bridle and pull of the reins.

At about four years of age, the horses would be harness-broken and trained to pull weight. The breaking in and training would be done in early spring, before the snow would melt and disappear. This was important because experience dictated that the sleigh was a good vehicle from which to handle an untrained animal. The process involved pairing of an untrained horse, referred to as a "bronco", with an older trained horse. The two would be harnessed and hitched to a sleigh and then merely proceeding to drive them. At first the untrained horse would resist and even get balky; but eventually the trained horse would pull the bronco along with the sleigh, and bit by bit the young horse would adapt himself to the situation. After a season of working and pulling his portion of the load of a farm implement, in consonance with the other horses in the team, his training would be both adequate and complete.

All of this activity and more would be repeated season after season on the Acker farm. Time was also found when needed to lend a helping hand to a neighbor in distress. To pull a travelling salesman's car when stuck in a mud hole in the road,as a good deed and making no charge. Other gestures of goodwill and neighborliness were extended in hundreds of ways, always with the thought in mind that it was the right thing to do. Hoping that some day, not knowing in what way, the favor might be returned.

LIFE'S DETOURS

Chapter 3

EARLY RECOLLECTIONS

The child Joseph grew up in the spirit and the vigor of the Acker farm. Being the first born of the youngest son of Grandpa and Grandma Acker, he received a lot of attention. He was considered to be the progeny by which the ancestral name would be passed on. Grandpa Acker would utter with no holds barred, that this was "my boy". He went to his work-shop and fashioned a walker to get him started early in walking. Joseph began walking at ten months of age. Later, he also built him a wooden rocking horse with real horse hair for the mane and tail. This had to be combed occassionally, comparable to what the adults were doing to horses in real life. There were times when Grandpa Acker would braid the horses tail and tie a ribbon in his mane. During the process he would describe for Joseph's sake, that the horse was being prepared to go to town where other people would see him. To teach his grandson orderliness when the rocking horse was not in use, it had to be placed in its stable which was a special corner in the kitchen reserved for this purpose.

Recollections about his relations and life situations with his grandpa and the family became grooved in Joseph's memory at a very early age. In fact, Joseph became more attached to his grandpa than to Richard his father. In large part, this was because his father was occupied with the farm work which took him to the fields, while Grandpa Acker worked around the buildings and yard. This gave Joseph the opportunity to be near and see more of him. As time went by and Joseph became articulate the relationship grew even closer.

By the time Joseph's brother Ray was born, two years and two months later, Joseph would be spending most of his time with his grand parents. This was not difficult to understand since they all lived together in the same house. Joseph would run to the barn when his dad came in from the field with the horses. His dad would greet him, pick him up in his arms, give him a hug or a lift and ask him what was happening. It was an exchange of pleasantries in a loving father to son relationship, but Joseph's real bonding took place with his mother and grandfather.

Grandpa Acker was a cooper by trade in Romania. He had acquired a complete set of tools to enable him to do a coopers work in Canada. He did not do it for a living but rather as a labor of love. He repaired the farm's wooden barrels, kegs, troughs, and tubs. He went so far as to make new ones when time permitted or the need arose. It was usually the kind of work a person does on a rainy day when he can keep himself occupied in a sheltered area. Joseph's brother Ray, also trotted about the yard mounted on a broomstick as a horse, but Joseph who was now going on his sixth year would join grandpa in his shop and work. Grandpa made sure that Joseph had access to some tools and bits of wood, so that his mind and hands would be kept busy as well.

They would carry on a conversation. Grandpa would relate stories about his life experiences, which in turn would arouse Joseph's curiosity and prompt him to ask questions.

"Grandpa what did you do in Romania?" Joseph asked.

It was the kind of a question grandpa liked to hear, because it made him feel that his favorite grandson was actually taking an interest in his life and in his past.

"Joey, my work in the old country was much harder than here. There were so many more things I had to do. I was a cooper and did the same kind of work I'm doing here today, But, I couldn't go to a lumber yard and select the kind of wood I needed. There were no lumber yards. First, I would go to the Forest Ranger. He was an employee of the Austrian Government, because at that time the portion of Transylvania in which we lived, was under Austrian rule and domination. I would request permission from him to cut down some trees. He would issue me a permit and mark three or four trees for me to cut. Then I would go to the forest which was nearby, cut the marked trees and drag them to my mountainside home with my horse," Grandpa said.

"Did you hate the Forest Ranger - for not letting you cut more trees?" Joseph asked.

"In a way yes, I did not really hate him as a person, because he was only doing his job. But as a people all of us who lived in my village in Transylvania disliked the Austrian-Hungarian regime and foreign rule," Grandpa replied.

"Would three or four trees give you enough wood to work with?" Joseph asked again.

"No son," Grandpa replied. "There were times when I would get up in the dead of the night. At times during a rainstorm when it was

LIFE'S DETOURS

thundering and lightning, take my horse and sneak into the forest, cut down one or two trees and bring them home."

"Grandpa, isn't that stealing?" chimed Joseph.

"Yes it is - and that is one of the reasons I left Romania. You see son, any country that forces an honest man to steal, in order to make a living is not a good country, I had your grandma and seven children to feed and clothe. I had very little land, a small number of sheep and goats, two cows and a single horse. I had to depend on making wooden pails, tubs, kegs and barrels in order to make a living and care for my family. You know, when you have a family you love them like I love you. That is why I found it necessary at times to go into the forest without a permit, cut some trees and give myself wood for my work," Grandpa said.

This was a statement Joseph had heard his grandpa tell many times before to others during their conversation.

"How did you make lumber from the trees?" Joseph asked.

"It was hard manual work. I would first trim the branches, then square the tree log by hewing it roughly with a sharp axe on all four sides. Next I'd place it on a couple of tall saw horses. I'd work together with my neighbor at sawing logs. We would use a hand operated ripsaw. One person on each end coordinating our "push and pull" motions, we would saw the log into boards. These boards then became the lumber or wood that I would use to make the staves for the barrels, tubs, and kegs or for repairs to the existing ones," Grandpa replied, while using his hands to assist him in making the explanation.

Joseph sat down on a little wooden block, he listened and watched his grandpa using a drawknife, shape a piece of wood into a semi-round shape to be fitted as a repair piece to the bottom of a barrel. He was trying to square in his young mind how his grandfather could have been stealing. He had heard him say on numerous occassions that a person is not supposed to steal.

"Thou shalt not steal, is one of the Ten Commandments," his grandfather was heard to say. His father would reinforce the commandment by adding that- "anything you take from anyone, without that person's permission is stealing."

"What did you do with the products you made?" Joseph asked, full of curiosity.

"I had a covered wagon and a horse and after crafting enough products to fill my wagon, I would add some rough lumber and my tools to the load, bid my family farewell and depart in search of a market to sell my wares. We would seek to travel in pairs as much as possible. In my case I had a neighbor who was also a cooper and a close friend, so we would pair up and depart from our village together.

Our best market would be in the Province of Banat, a part of Romania with abundant vineyards and the people were engaged in the production of wines. Upon arrival we would go to the village markets and sell our products privately to customers. But, more important it was at these village markets that we would make our contacts and appointments with the wine producers, to go to their private wine cellars and repair their existing wine casks, or craft new ones."

Joseph's dad who had been standing in the doorway of the toolshed and listening to grandpa's tale also found it interesting. His childhood memories from Romania were partially forgotten, because he was brought to Canada when he was four years of age, a little younger than Joseph was at this moment.

"How much were you paid to repair those wine casks?" Richard asked his dad. Joseph listened intently.

"The price of my labor and materials would be arrived at after some negotiation and bartering. The amount would be decided based on the number of items to be repaired and the amount of material and time required to do the job. I'm unable to say now, just how much I would earn per hour or per day, because that was not the way us coopers worked. It was piecework and we would quote a price for a certain volume of work. When the price was agreed upon, work would commence and payment would be received at termination. Then I'd go to the market and with some of the money earned, I would purchase a few hundred kilograms of corn and wheat and bring it back home. We could not raise corn and wheat in the mountain area, only potatoes and garden vegetables. We had to buy the grain required for making bread, and for the cornmeal cooked and known as `mamaliga', which formed part of our daily diet," grandpa replied.

"What do you think, Joey?" his dad said. "Grandpa had a hard time and hard work making a living in Romania, don't you think?" Joey responded in silence by taking in a long, deep breath.

"My main reason for coming here," Richard said, "is to call you in for lunch. So drop your work and let's go eat."

The dinner table was set. The men had washed their hands and everyone sat around the table.

"Joseph now knows the Lord's Prayer, so we shall ask him to say it," his grandpa said.

Joseph always sat at the table on a higher chair and to the right of his grandfather. He repeated the Lord's Prayer loud and clear without any prompting. Everyone, including Willie looked at Joseph while his grandpa gave him a pat on the head and praised him. The food served at this meal being a cool rainy day, consisted of plenty of home-made bread and butter, a huge bowl situated in the center of the table from

LIFE'S DETOURS

which a ladle handle was protruding. The bowl contained boiled pork hocks and sauer-kraut. It was a favorite family dish and one of grandpa's real favorites. He ate each spoonful of cabbage and each bite of pork hock with gusto and with a smack of his lips after every mouthful. Grandpa's zest for this dish also made the food taste very good for Joseph, because he liked to be a copy cat and to be considered manly like his grandpa.

One April day Eugenia had dressed Joseph in a one piece red wool suit that buttoned up in front. It was equipped with a hood that could be pulled parka style over the head. When Joseph was dressed with this red colored suit, only his ruddy face would be exposed to the weather. He was allowed to go outdoors, to play around the yard and amuse himself. At first Joseph chose to play with Sport, his favorite dog, but later drifted away from the house and into the barnyard. An old rooster caught sight of him in his all red suit and decided he didn't want this creature around the barnyard. The rooster attacked him viciously by jumping at him, pecking and scratching. Fortunately his face was not scratched or hurt.

Joseph ran for safety into the barn and crawled into a space under a manger. He began crying and shouting -"Grandpa! Grandpa!" - the rooster stood by and kept an eye on him and he did not dare come out from his place of safety. He cried again, in fact he cried several times - "Grandpa! Grandpa!"- Joseph knew that his grandpa was somewhere in the yard and was hoping he would hear him. Grandpa did hear him and came to determine what the problem was. He found Joseph under the manger, crying.

"What's the matter, Joey?" grandpa asked.

"The rooster, the rooster - see him," Joseph replied sobbing and sighing. "He fights with me and scratches me, and he's bad."

"Come on out from there," his grandfather said. Joseph came out and taking his grandfather's hand, they both walked away from the barn and to the house. The incident was reported to the whole family. His mother Eugenia praised him for deciding to take shelter under the manger and to cry for help, as she wiped his dried tears with a wet cloth. But, to put an end to this episode, Grandpa Acker ordered that the rooster be killed and served for dinner the next day, which by coincidence happened to be a Sunday. The conversation piece at this meal centered around this mean bird and what it had done. Joseph felt content and vindicated. The rooster had paid a price for it's misbehaviour. Grandpa's judgement was to be respected.

The old house on the Acker farm was getting more and more crowded each year. It was built in 1908 and it's rooms were small. Initially the house had two bedrooms. Another two bedrooms were added later. However, the year now was 1923 and Richard and Eugenia, by this time had two boys and a girl. Joseph, Ray and Virginia. Then there were the grandparents, Willie the hired hand and Pearl the niece. All of which pointed towards a need for increased accommodation. A decision was reached to build a new house on the farm, and construction began in early May with the completion date programmed for late October. The main carpenter for the project was Nick Haraniuk and the assistant was Nick Vesea. Three of the neigbors came over for a day to help with the mixing and pouring of the cement. The old house was torn down and the salvaged lumber was used in the building of the new house. The same site was chosen but the cellar required enlarging. Joseph could recall how his father removed dirt and enlarged the old cellar. With a team of horses pulling a metal scraper, he would remove about a quarter of a cubic yard of dirt on one pull. The cellar measured fourteen by twenty-eight by six feet deep. The four corners of the cellar excavation had to be squared off by hand with a pick and shovel. It was hard physical work.

Once the cellar was dug, the foundation forms were laid and cement was poured. After two days of allowing the cement to cure, construction began.

Richard and Willie continued on with the farming operations, while Grandpa Acker became the supply man. With Tom and Sandy his favorite team of horses, he would haul gravel, make trips into town and bring back lumber, nails, cement, plaster, shingles, doors, windows, and whatever hardware and other items were required. When grandpa was not coming or going into town, he would put on his carpenter's apron and assist the two carpenters in their work.

During the construction period Joseph recalls taking the carpenter's hatchet from their tool box and chipping away at bricks with it. Nick Vesea while shingling on the roof of the house caught him in the act.

"Joseph, drop the hatchet, don't chop bricks with it - run! or I'll jump off this roof on top of you," Vesea cried.

Joseph scrambled away as fast as his two little legs could carry him to a granary. This granary had been converted and used as a kitchen while the house was being constructed. In fact, a number of the empty granaries were being used for sleeping quarters, and for storing the household furniture and clothing during the building period.

Sundays as usual was a day of rest on the Acker farm. One Sunday afternoon the family decided to take a ride to see the operations taking place in the construction of a new railway line. This new railway line would enable the formation of a town and shipping point, at a distance of only seven miles from the farm. The three children went

LIFE'S DETOURS

along. Joseph took his usual place in the front seat on his grandfather's knee while his father drove the car. This placed Joseph in the midst of the more serious conversation. In reality it exposed him to adult thinking. He could also visualize and appraise the interaction between his father, his grandfather and the rest of the family.

At a site known as Ormiston, about 20 miles to the south-west of the Acker farm a large deposit of sodium sulphate had been discovered. There was a demand for this mineral in the manufacturing of paper. The development could not take place without a railroad to transport the commodity from the mine to where it could be used. Through negotiation the mining company together with other vested interests convinced the Canadian Pacific Railway (CPR) to build a rail line to serve this industry. This was to be a spur-line, taking off from the main east-west railway line that connected the city of Weyburn and Swift Current in the province. The spur-line would take off at a junction known as Amulet and continue in a north-westerly direction, allowing the formation of such towns and grain delivery points along the way as, Bures, Edgeworth, Dahinda, Kayville, Wheatstone, Ormiston and terminating at Crane Valley.

The Horse Shoe Lake Mining Company launched mining operations at Ormiston, very soon after the railway line was completed. A good number of the local farmers or their sons obtained employment in this industry. Kayville then became the shopping center, the mail, freight and delivery point for the Ackers. It was seven miles to Kayville, while Truax the previous town the Ackers patronized was fourteen miles away. The closer proximity of the new town was a time saving feature. Time which they could put to productive use elsewhere on the farm.

There were no paved roads at the time. Richard would steer the Model-T Ford along the existing wagon and car trails until they arrived at the construction site. The site was a large encampment consisting of many men, machinery and animals. There were no caterpillar type tractors to be seen anywhere around. A large steam driven engine was used to draw a huge plow with several furrows. The ground plowed by this unit would be hauled by teams of four mules hitched to metal scrapers, and there were at least ten of these teams and scrapers. The dirt would be piled in the low areas in order to elevate the ground to where it would be level for laying down the steel rails. The ground would be soaked with water sprayed from a water tank drawn by two mules. The packing and levelling by a grader implement drawn by a team of twelve mules hitched in tandems of four mules to each tandem.

The rails, the wooden ties, the sand ballast and the other supplies required for the levelling, grading and dressing of the rail bed, would be brought in by the train. As the railway bed construction advanced, the wooden ties would be dug in and the rails laid on top and spiked to these wooden ties.

In other words, the rail line would simply follow the rail bed and the encampment as it advanced.

The men slept in tents and had a dining place in another large tent. The kitchen and the kitchen crew were actually occupying a caboose or cook-car on wheels, which would be moved by a team of mules from one encampment site to another as the work progressed.

There were a lot of black men working driving the mule teams and working on this project. It was the first time Joseph had seen a black man.

"Why are those men black?" Joseph asked.

Grandpa Acker said - "Well, that's the way God created them."

However, Richard decided that a better explanation was forthcoming and since he had read something about slavery and the black people in the United States, he offered his interpretation to Joseph and the rest of the passengers in the car.

"Those black people come from Africa. Their ancestors were brought to the United States by wealthy landowners as slaves, but Abraham Lincoln freed them from slavery. They are now free to work like anybody else, they are supposed to be good workers - slow but steady - I understand. It wouldn't surprise me one bit to discover that the contractor might have brought them in from the States to work here on this project," Richard said.

At that time, border crossing between Canada and the United States had few restrictions. Richard who could talk good English approached one of the project's foreman at the site and spent a few moments talking to him.

"Are the black people working with you Canadians?" Richard asked.

"Oh, I don't know. We don't ask questions. They are good workers and that's all we worry about," the foreman replied.

"Where do you obtain all the feed necessary for the mules and horses and the food and drinking water for all the men working on this project?" Richard asked the foreman.

"We get all the drinking water for the men by train and we store it in tanks. We buy some of the food locally from the farmers and bring the rest in by train. The drinking water for the animals is hauled by tank and mules and is obtained from nearby sloughs or farmer's wells. Sometimes we have to pay for it, other times a good farmer merely says "help yourself." The feed on the other hand must be purchased. We have a crew that goes out amongst the farmers and scours for hay and

LIFE'S DETOURS

oats to feed the mules and the horses. All the feed is paid for with cash but we insist that it be delivered to our campsite," the foreman said.

The Ackers marvelled at the contractor's encampment and it's layout. They returned from the trip in time to get the evening chores done. They were tired, but wiser in terms of having a better understanding of the planning, the organization and work that must go into a project of this magnitude. They had never seen or even visualized in their mind's eye anything undertaken in construction that came anywhere near this dimension.

"When I arrived in Regina from Romania, the first job my oldest son Jacob (who had since passed away) and I obtained, was on the transcontinental line of the this same railway company. The Canadian Pacific Railway or the CPR. We worked on the rail line that ran across the southern belt of Canada and connected Regina and Calgary. We did maintenance ten hours each day, six days per week, for one dollar and seventy-five cents per day. Of course, I only worked until I saved enough money to buy a team of oxen, a wagon, a plow, a cow, ten chickens, a rooster, and two little pigs and we moved with grandma to the homestead. Do you remember that Richard?" Grandpa Acker said.

"And we lived in that sod shanty for two winters and one summer. We also built a sod shelter for the animals. It had a straw roof. The animals were kept nice and warm during the winter months, but in summer the straw roof would allow the rain to penetrate and the inside would be muddy and slushy. We had to move the pigs to an open pen outdoors. The cow and the calf were all right in the pasture. Those first few years on the homestead were very difficult times," Grandma Acker remarked.

The move into the new house was a relief for Eugenia and Grandma Acker. The men working on construction had gone which meant there was less cooking to do and especially less laundry which had to be done by hand. During the summer Eugenia would place her wash stand and tubs in the shade of a building. She would scrub away by hand on the scrub board for three to four hours to get all the clothes washed. Heavier denim, wool and cotton clothing such as men's pants, jackets, sweaters were usually washed separately in a tub, using plenty of home-made lye soap and a plunger. The clothes were hung on an outside clothesline and allowed to dry in the sun.

Pressing was done by lighting a fire in the kitchen stove and placing two or three sad irons on the stove to get hot. Using a special handle, Eugenia would take one of these irons at a time and press the clothes. When one iron got cold, she would return it to the stove and pick up another. This practice would continue until ironing was finished.

During the winter months this work was done by Eugenia in her kitchen. The clothes were often hung to dry over night on a retractable make-shift clothes line, stretched from hooks placed in one corner to another in the kitchen. It was impossible to dry them outside. The clothes would freeze due to the cold frosty weather.

"Are you not tired after a full days work of this kind?" Grandma Ackers would ask Eugenia when they sat down in the evening for a short chat or merely for assessing the work that had been done and looking at what tomorrow brings.

"Oh, I'm somewhat tired. The knuckles on my right hand are sore from all that scrubbing on the scrub-board. Some of the boy's clothes were very dirty and that last batch of soap we made contains quite a bit of lye. Its hard on my hands. Anyway, it sure helped to get the soiled clothes clean. The washes aren't always this big. To-day's wash with all the bed sheets and blankets was a big one," Eugenia replied.

Joseph was present. He did not say anything, but thought to himself that truly his mother had worked hard all day. Grandma Acker hadn't washed clothes for a long time. She had growing daughters, four of them, who spelled her from this chore. After her youngest daughter married she had granddaughters come and help her, until Eugenia married Richard and came into the family. Nothing much was thought of the whole affair, after all it was routine work and the kind of work that women did. It would be on occassions such as this, that Eugenia would think about her own mother, how hard she worked and did the laundry by hand for her father, four brothers and three sisters.

"Children never think about the hard work and sacrifices their parents make, until they have children of their own and come face to face with the realities of life," Eugenia thought.

She didn't mind the work. She loved her husband and her three children and she had great respect and cared for the elderly Ackers. The labor it took to make for a happy and provident home was no hardship.

During their year in the new house, the Ackers found themselves with a full time boarder. He was a Romanian Orthodox monk, who had been brought by the parishes from Romania to officiate and be their priest. The community had two churches but no parish house for the priest to live in. The parishioners decided to build a parish house near one of the churches known as the St. Mary Orthodox Church. The monk's arrival took place at the on-set of winter and the work was postponed until the following spring. During this waiting period which lasted about eight months, the priest known as Father Teofil Marin remained as a boarder with the Ackers.

Joseph was now six years old and the priest had brought with him books from Romania. One book was a primary reader used as a

LIFE'S DETOURS

beginner's book when children started school in Romania. Father Marin, encouraged by Joseph's father and grandfather made a point of holding school with Joseph for two hours each day except Sunday. By the time Father Marin moved away from the Ackers and into his own parish house, Joseph could read and write Romanian.

He could not speak or read English. His parents were not concerned. They knew he would learn to speak English as soon as he started school. Once Joseph was able to read and write, his father decided to teach him simple arithmetic. This involved the basics, consisting of addition, subtraction, multiplication and division. Joseph was studious and quick to catch on. He put the multiplication table to memory up to the figure twelve. By the time he was seven years of age and began attending the rural public school, he knew the basics of arithmetic and was able to do long division using three digits. All of his mathematical skill to this point was expressed in the Romanian language.

Grandfather Acker would take great pride in Joseph and in his ability to read and write and work with figures at such a young age.

"Joseph, I received a letter today from Romania and I'd like to have you read it for me," grandpa would say, when he would bring home the mail. Grandpa was illiterate. He could have asked Richard or Eugenia to read the letter for him, but Joseph read the letter and that made him feel important. Additionally, Grandpa Acker had subscribed to a weekly newspaper from Alba Iulia, which was the capital city of the Judicial District of Alba in Romania. His village was located in this Judicial District. The newspaper would arrive anywhere from four to six weeks after being published. It was still news for Grandpa and Grandma Acker, because they knew the region, places, family names, and therefore of interest to them. Richard would read the newspaper, but Grandpa Acker would ask Joseph to also read it for him. This familiarized Joseph with the names of people, of regions and of events in Romania and sparked more conversation between him and his grandfather.

By this time Grandpa Acker was economically quite well to do as a farmer in Canada. On one occassion Dan Balan and his wife, who were close friends of the Ackers paid them a social visit.

"Edward, my wife and I are going to Romania for a visit - how would you and Viola like to come along? We can travel together and it would be fun. What do you think?" Balan said.

Grandpa Acker gave a smile and thought for a while.

"Tell me more about it, when are you leaving?"

"We plan to leave right after harvest, about the beginning of October and return early in the New Year. It takes about 12 days to get there. We will be three days and three nights on the train from here to Montreal. From there we will board a ship and sail for about six or seven days across the Atlantic Ocean to Hamburg, Germany. From Hamburg by train across Europe to Bucharest, and to our village near the city of Ploesti," continued Balan.

Joseph looked at his grandpa and was wondering why he wasn't getting excited and jumping at the opportunity to return back to the country and the place where he played as a child and where he grew up.

"Boy, if I was in grandpa's boots, I'd sure go," he thought to himself.

"You were a sergeant in the police force in Romania. You are younger and you can also speak English, French and some Hungarian. Your two sons here in Canada are old enough to take care of the farm in your absence and you have brothers and a sister there. Your wife has relatives in Romania. It is very fitting for you to go. In my case I have no relatives to visit. My wife Viola has three sisters and a brother left behind there. We talked about making a return trip but Viola is not enthusiastic about it and I am not anxious to go either. Romania doesn't mean so much to us anymore. I became a Canadian citizen through naturalization shortly after I obtained title to my first and second homesteads. My children and grandchildren are all here in Canada and this is where my roots are. I have no desire to go back to Romania, not even for a visit. I hope you have a good trip, a good ocean voyage and after you return, I would be delighted to talk to you and to find out about the changes that took place in the 25 years since I left there," Grandpa Acker concluded.

The Balans departed for their home and later journeyed to Romania.

"I could afford to make the trip but I truly have no desire to go back. I could easily sell the farms and everything else we own and return to Romania. With this money I could buy plenty of property over there. But my children are here now farming on their own; my grandchildren have gone to school in this country, they speak the English language and would never think of going to Romania. Canada is their country and Canada is a good country - it has been good to us," and with those thoughts Grandpa Acker brushed Romania out of his mind.

"Joseph, I have your dad's permission to take you along with me into town to-morrow. I will be taking in a load of grain and return with some lumber - would you care to come along?" his grandpa asked him.

"Sure,"- Joseph replied. "I'd be very happy to go."

"Then listen, get to bed early, because the town is 14 miles away and with a wagon load of wheat it takes about three and one half hours

LIFE'S DETOURS

to get there. Then by the time we unload the grain and load the lumber, and stop for at least one hour to feed the horses and for us to eat, time flies by pretty fast. We want to return before sunset. We will leave about seven o'clock in the morning," his grandpa said.

Joseph was off to bed early. The next morning, a bright August day, found Grandpa Acker and his grandson Joseph, seated on the wagon seat mounted on a wagon load of wheat. Grandpa would incite Tom and Sandy the two horses, to adopt a brisker walking pace. There were a few valleys and other slightly inclined areas, in which the horses could be made to trot, because the wagon and it's load would practically force them into a trotting pace. The driving time into town and back, gave grandpa and Joseph plenty of time to talk about many things.

"Grandpa, what is God like - do you think he sees us?" asked Joseph.

"Joey, I believe in God - I know he exists. God is an awesome power and I don't know exactly how to describe him to you. You see, I have never read the Bible because I can't read - but you can read, and you should begin to read it as soon and as early in life as you can. As you know, I go to church regularly and I listen to the preacher's sermons. I memorized my prayers when I was your age and I say them every morning and every evening. I pray to God. I pray and ask him for good health and good crops. I pray for you and for our whole family and for good neighbors. I also thank God for the many, many good things, he has given me," grandpa said.

Joseph knew there was truth in what his grandfather said. He had seen him light a candle on many occassions, then kneel and face a small icon of Christ suspended on a nail on the east wall of his bedroom, repeat his prayers and cross himself in the traditional Orthodox fashion. His prayers were lengthy and said with a tone of supplication.

"You see Joey, everything we behold with our eyes in this world had to have a Creator. The sun, the moon, the stars and this earth we live on didn't just happen. There had to be a master mind, a super power to make these objects and to place them in their proper place and order. We human beings are just a part of everything that God created - we are above all the other animals, because we have the power of speech and our minds and ability to think are made in God's image. God also sent his son Jesus Christ to be our Saviour, so we must abide in Him, cultivate a close intimate relationship with Him and make Him our nearest and dearest friend," grandpa said.

Grandpa was no theologian. He had picked up his faith and belief in God from his great aunt in Romania, who had raised him. It was a deep subject. It was one that was difficult for grandpa to explain and even more difficult for Joseph to comprehend but it energized his imagination. It was a moment of decision for Joseph and in his child's mind he made a secret commitment that he too would be a believer like his grandfather.

By this time, they were fast approaching town and the talk turned to other subjects. There was much to be observed along a fourteen mile drive and much to talk about. The first place they pulled to upon arrival was the grain elevator. Grandpa was greeted by the agent who quickly weighed the loaded wagon of wheat. He then opened the end-gate of the wagon box and allowed the grain to flow into a pit. With the aid of a mechanical device the agent turned a wheel by hand, which in turn lifted the front end of the wagon to an angle of about 45 degrees causing all the grain to flow out of the box. The wagon was lowered again to it's horizontal position, and the agent weighed the empty wagon and wrote out a slip which he gave to grandpa.

"Mr. Acker, to-day you brought sixty-two bushels and twenty-seven pounds of wheat. I have taken the twenty seven pounds as a dockage allowance for the foreign objects that the screening showed was in your grain, and I have made your grain ticket for sixty-two even bushels. Your wheat graded number One Northern and the Winnipeg street price according to yesterday's telegram is one dollar and ninety-two cents per bushel. Your check is written for one hundred and nine dollars and four cents," the elevator agent said looking to grandpa.

Grandpa Acker spoke only enough broken English to be able to greet people and to do his business.

"Thank you and good day," Grandpa said, and they drove out of the grain elevator and to the livery barn. The two horses were unhitched and led to a water trough, where they drank their fill of water. Then into the barn where a ration of oats and a manger full of hay was waiting for them.

Grandpa and Joseph walked to the main street in town and to the restaurant, which was operated by a couple of Chinese men called Jim and Tom. No one was quite sure of what their last names were. They sat down in one of the table booths. Tom, a short fat chinaman came to the table and took the order. Grandpa ordered - soup, one order of pork chops for himself, a half order for Joseph and raisin pie. Coffee to drink for himself and orange pop for Joseph. It was Joseph's first meal in a restaurant and the best meal he had ever tasted. They finished eating, grandpa paid the bill and walked out and towards the bank.

They met Mr. Lusted, the bank manager, who was walking towards them on the same wooden plank sidewalk.

"Good afternoon Mr. Acker," the banker said as he tipped his hat

LIFE'S DETOURS

slightly in a gesture of respect to grandpa - "how can the bank help you to-day?" he asked.

"I'm only in need of changing my grain check into cash to-day," grandpa replied, and after a few more pleasantries they parted.

Inside the bank the teller greeted Grandpa Acker. He asked him to sign and endorse his grain ticket, counted the correct amount of cash, which grandpa took, expressed his thanks and gently placed the money in his wallet as they turned and walked out of the bank.

"Joey, I'm in need of a shave and a haircut, let's go in the barbershop and you wait for me, while the barber gets my beard and hair trimmed," grandpa said, as they walked into the barber shop.

The barber knew Grandpa Acker and knew he couldn't talk much English, therefore after the greeting and grandpa ordering a "shave and haircut" there was silence. Grandpa laid his head back on the head-rest in the barber's chair, closed his eyes and the barber went about the business of grooming grandpa's hair and beard. Joseph sat on a chair and he was sure he heard grandpa snore once or twice, but he kept watching the dexterity with which the barber handled the razor, the comb, the scissors and the hand clippers.

Joseph's own hair and that of his brother Ray would be short-cropped by their dad at least once a month, on some Saturday night at home using the horse clippers. Joseph's mother would turn the crank on the manually operated horse clippers, while his dad handled the clippers that sort of rattled, as he manipulated them around their ears and up along the sides of their head.

"Grandpa's hair cut would be much nicer than the one his dad gave him and when he grew up, he too would get his haircut by a barber," Joseph thought to himself.

Grandpa's grooming over and paid for, they went to the general store owned by Louis Lozinsky. Mr. Lozinsky was a Jewish merchant, who also came to Canada from Romania and could speak the language. Grandpa liked doing business with him because they could communicate and understand each other. Joseph understood what they were talking about. Grandpa handed a list written by Eugenia to Mr. Lozinsky, who went about wrapping the items in brown paper and packing them in a suitable cardboard box.

Grandpa paid for the goods, said "Good-day" to Mr. Lozinsky in Romanian. He picked up the box of supplies and together they walked back to the livery barn. The horses were watered again and hitched back to the empty wagon. They drove to the lumber yard, where Grandpa selected the lumber he required, paid for it and off again homeward bound. As they passed by the restaurant Grandpa Acker stopped the horses. He tied them momentarily to a heavy post located at the corner of the street, specifically for that purpose. He walked into the cafe and returned with a cone of ice cream, which he gave to Joseph.

"What a fantastic day and what a good man grandpa is" Joseph thought to himself, as he said "thank you" and began licking on the delicious ice cream cone.

It was early afternoon and they were homeward bound. The return trip took less time because the load was lighter, and the horses were made to trot periodically. The conversation between grandpa and Joseph continued, with Joseph again asking a leading question.

"Grandpa, why did the banker lift his hat slightly, when he greeted you on the street?"

"Joey, that is a mark of respect. The banker respected me for two reasons. First, I'm a much older man than he is and it is customary and right for younger people to respect their elders. Older people have more knowledge and experience about life, because they have lived many more years and have encountered many more situations. Much of this experience and knowledge they can pass on to the younger people, and many mistakes can be eliminated this way. There is an old saying - `that there is no need to invent the wheel over and over again.' One must only learn how to use the wheel already invented."

Intelligently raised young people are aware of the knowledge and skills of the older people, they will listen. learn, analyze, sift and apply suck knowledge and experience in their own lives to the degree that it can be applied. Secondly, the banker knows that I am one of his clients and he also respects that. He wants me to be his friend and to continue doing business with him, and I want to continue doing business with him and to be his friend. In Romania, people carried their money in a money-belt. If the quantity was more than it would be safe to carry in your moneybelt, than a person would hide it or bury it in a secret place in the ground. Since I came to Canada, I learned to use the bank for my savings because the bank pays me interest. The bank also lends it to other farmers who can use it for productive purposes. A person can make good use of the bank if he borrows wisely, is honest and develops a good reputation of repaying his loans on time," grandpa replied.

"Grandpa, do you have much money in the bank?" Joseph asked.

"Grandson, yes I have some money saved in the bank. It is money that your grandmother and I are saving for our older age when we can no longer work. Also for a rainy day. In other words, for some unforeseen incident or catastrophy that could emerge. Every person should set aside some of his earnings into savings. Joey, you will soon be starting school and you should study hard and get a good education, because nobody can ever take your knowledge away from you. A

LIFE'S DETOURS

person can lose his property or have his money stolen, but your education and knowledge is yours to keep and you can impart or share it with others to the degree you wish. You must remember that irrespective of how well educated you are, if you cannot manage your money or your income in reality you are a fool. A fool with money is considered wiser, than an educated person with no money. If a person earns one dollar per day and spends one dollar and one cent, he will always be in debt and obligated to others - but, if he earns one dollar per day and spends ninety-nine cents or less, some day he will become his own boss and master of his destiny," his grandpa said.

All of which sounded like a sermon and a warning and rang a little bell in Joseph's mind.

The sun in the west was slowly lowering itself to the horizon, when grandpa and Joseph pulled into the farmyard. Willie greeted them and took over the horses to look after them, while Richard came and lifted the box with supplies and carried it into the house. Grandpa and Joseph also followed. The lumber was left for unloading the next day.

"How was your trip?" Eugenia asked Joseph. "What did you bring me?" his brother Ray asked.

Grandpa had a bag of candy in the box which he shared with everyone in the house. In fact, neither grandpa or Joseph's father Richard ever went into town, to return empty handed without some sweet items or fruits for the family.

All of the trip's experience was recounted and shared with the family in detail over the supper meal. It had made a great impression on Joseph as he related what he saw and heard. Of course, Joseph was unable to articulate in detail the conversation and the lessons he had learned from his grandpa, but he thought about them. It made him feel good and kind of grown up. He said "good-night" to everyone and went upstairs to his bedroom. There was no need for his mother to remind him to say his prayers. He had learned that lesson from his grandpa. The ride to town with grandpa was a journey forever imprinted in his mind. He was tired and soon was sound asleep.

This was the year that the Acker family broke up. Richard felt he wasn't getting a fair shake from the joint operations of the farm with his father. Joseph had heard them arguing. He didn't like what he heard and the way his father talked to his grandfather. Grandpa Acker talked it over with Viola and they decided to turn the farm over to Richard. They bought a house in the city of Regina and moved. They reasoned that at their age they would be more comfortable and secure living in the city. They would be closer to church, to medical attention and other facilities. They reached an agreement whereby Richard would get three quarters (480 acres) of land which included all the buildings, and grandpa would retain one quarter (160) acres for himself. Everything else, like machinery, livestock, grain stored, would be shared half and half except for the household furnishings which Richard and Eugenia would keep.

A farm auction sale was held at which all of grandpa's goods were sold. It was in the fall and the livestock belonging to Richard could be seen in the pasture. But having reduced the numbers of both horses and cows by half so abruptly as a result of the sale, made the farmyard and pasture look bare.

A week after the sale, Mr. George Jonescu a local merchant and trucker appeared in the yard very early one morning in late October. He came with his Model-T Ford truck to load Grandpa and Grandma Acker's belongings and bedroom furniture, and deliver them to their new home in the city.

After the loading was completed at which Richard gave a helping hand, Grandpa and Grandma Acker kissed and hugged all of the children. Then they embraced and kissed Eugenia who was holding the youngest member of the family in her arms. His name was Charles and he was only five months old. Finally they turned to Richard, they embraced, shook hands and said farewell.

They said "good-bye" several times. Then just before getting into the cab of the truck, Grandma Acker looked towards the east, she crossed herself religiously and said "God help and save us all." She sat in the middle of the seat in the truck cab with Mr. Jonescu at the wheel, and Grandpa Acker to her right. The Model-T Ford truck began to move, as the grandparents gave one more look to the ones they still loved, and to a labor that took a good portion of their lives. Waving their hands they disappeared down the road.

Richard, Eugenia and the children stopped for a moment and gazed after the moving vehicle. They heaved a sigh. The separation was real, a vacuum was felt. Back in the house they re-arranged the furniture and took over the empty bedroom. Joseph knew and felt that he would miss his grand-parents and especially Grandpa Acker. But, he said nothing.

LIFE'S DETOURS

Chapter 4

CHILDHOOD ENCOUNTERS

The year was 1926 and classes at the rural school which Joseph would be attending began on the first day of March. Joseph's father drove him to school with horses and sleigh. Many parents drove their children to school on opening day because there were books to carry, and the snow was knee deep making it difficult for the smaller children to walk. Richard arrived early, introduced himself to Mrs. Louisa Bills the teacher, and asked her where Joseph would be seated.

"Can he speak English?" the teacher asked.

"We've been trying to teach him just a bit of English in preparation for this day, but we haven't been very successful. During the last few years when my parents were living with us, we spoke only Romanian. We had to - they couldn't speak English," Richard replied.

"I have taught Joseph and he can do basic arithmetic. He can read and write Romanian, which should enable him to learn to speak English very rapidly," his father added.

The teacher commended Richard for having taken the time to teach Joseph the basics, and pointed to a desk in the first row, second from the front facing the blackboard.

"He can occupy that desk," the teacher said.

Joseph's father assisted him to place his two scribblers and a pencil box in his desk. Then he took Joseph's hand and showed him the cloakrooms, where he would leave his lunch pail and the extra winter clothes not required in class. He walked with Joseph to the outdoor toilets and in Romanian instructed him saying - "When you find that nature tells you to use the toilet, raise your hand and ask permission to leave the room. You will say -

"Please Mrs. Bills may I leave the room?" - "Can you remember that?" - "Please Mrs.Bills may I leave the room?"

Joseph nodded to indicate he understood, but deep inside he felt insecure about this situation.

Richard knew that Joseph would feel strange, so he took Joseph to Sarah Acker, who was a thirteen year old, grade seven cousin and the daughter of Daniel Acker. Daniel Acker was Joseph's uncle and also his godfather. Joseph knew her and he immediately felt much better.

"If you need some help, go to Sarah and tell her your problem and she will talk to your teacher and help you," his father said. Sarah assured him that she would be pleased to help.

By this time the school bell rang, and the children from the previous year's classes stood at attention besides their desks. Joseph looked around and copied what he saw the others doing.

The teacher asked all the children to bow their heads and repeat the "Lord's Prayer" after her. Then they sang "O Canada" the National Anthem. The teacher asked the children to be seated. She gave them a short lecture on study habits, punctuality in attendance, neatness in their work, good behavior and what the new school year held in store for them.

Then she asked each child to get up and introduce himself or herself. Those children that were prior year students acted accordingly - but a number of new students just like Joseph, could not speak Engish, and were unable to comply with her request. Joseph's father stepped in and gave his son's name and age. Other older brothers, sisters or parents present did likewise for their beginners. Following this activity, the parents departed.

Joseph attended school regularly. He found it very difficult at the beginning due to his language deficiency. But he was making new friends and learning something new every day. His attendance was always punctual and the attendance chart on the wall was full of red stars for each day of class. Later his brother Ray and sister Virginia joined him as students. Richard and Eugenia as parents gave the teacher their support and made sure that their children were taking their school work seriously.

There were days in class when the teacher would write a simple arithmetic problem on the blackboard, and ask the beginner's class to work it out.

"How many of you are finished?" the teacher would ask. Joseph would always be the first to finish and raise his hand.

"Joseph, would you go up to the blackboard and show the rest of the class how you arrived at the answer," she would command.

Joseph would look to Sarah first for an interpretation of the teacher's command, and once informed, without any hesitation walked up to the blackboard, wrote the problem figures and explained his results in Romanian. His explanation and his answers were correct, but

LIFE'S DETOURS

the exercise was always followed with a good laugh by the teacher and all the students, because he explained his results using the Romanian language, and the teacher would have to explain Joseph's work in English to the remainder of the class.

The headstart Joseph received from his father stood him in good stead. As soon as he was able to understand, speak and read English, he was way ahead of the others in his class. He made good progress in school and at the end of his first year, he skipped over grade two and was promoted to grade three. He spent one year in grade three and skipped over grade four to grade five. At the age of thirteen Joseph wrote his grade eight examinations, which would have completed his public school education in six years. However, Joseph failed his grade eight test the first time and was forced to repeat the grade for a second term. The failure was due to Joseph's own fault, because throughout the year he became lackadaisical in his study habits. At exam time he discovered he did not have all the answers. He repeated his grade eight studies and re-wrote his tests the following year passing the grade with honors.

Joseph being the eldest in the family was called upon by his parents to assist more and more with the farm chores. School hours were from nine o'clock in the morning to four in the afternoon, five days a week. There was a 15 minute break period in the mornings, one hour for noon lunch and another 15 minute break period in the afternoon. Walking to and from from school took about 20 minutes each way. During the summer months plenty of daylight remained to assist with the farm and yard work, both before leaving for school in the morning and after returning in the afternoon.

On most days his mother, a hard working and resourceful woman, had lunch ready for Joseph and his brother and sister when they arrived from school. At least once per week there would be freshly baked home-made bread with butter, cinnamon rolls, and home-made apple and rhubarb jam or honey. Another favorite of the family consisted of bread dough, rolled fairly thin and cut into square or rectangular pieces. These would be deep-fried and served while hot with a bit of honey. Sometimes these same pieces of bread dough would have a mixture of cottage cheese and egg folded in, and again deep fried for a delicious snack. These were called "cheese- blitzes." There was always plenty of fresh whole milk, either hot or cold to drink, and this kind of a snack would hit the spot on any school day of the year. This mid-afternoon lunch was a "quick-deal" intended to supply energy, and invigorate them long enough to see them through the chores and other work. The main meal of the day was supper which was served at a later hour in the evening.

The work consisted of bringing the cows home from the pasture and milking them. This was a chore that had to be done both morning and night. As soon as Joseph was ten years of age he was obligated to milk cows along with his mother. From six to ten cows were milked daily, depending on the season of the year. Ever since Grandma Viola had gone to the city, the separation of the cream from the milk, the churning of the butter, and its packing and storage was done by Eugenia with the help of her children. Each child was assigned the kind of work that was within his capability to perform. There were the hogs and the poultry to feed and water. When these chores were all done, the homework assignment from school was often completed by the light of a kerosene lamp.

The work most despised by Joseph was helping his mother do the gardening. It seemed to consist of never ending weeding, hoeing and hilling the plants.

"Mom, why must you plant such a big garden?" Joseph would ask.

"Dear, we are a big family and the winters are long. We must have vegetables put away to see us through until next year when a new garden comes along," She would reply.

Joseph would look at the 20 rows of potatoes with each row 200 yards in length that required hoeing or hilling.

"When will we ever finish this work?" Joseph would murmur grudgingly to his mother as he surveyed the potato patch.

"Don't look at the length of the rows, but rather ask yourself - how long does it take me to do one row. Then multiply that time by 20 rows. If it takes you one hour to do one row, then twenty rows would amount to twenty hours. With two of us working, we can reduce it to ten hours. Once we get it done, the garden will look good and the potatoes will grow and produce. We'll also have the satisfaction of knowing that our food supply for the winter months will be adequate and we can be grateful. You must learn to work by objectives. The objective in this case is to get this particular phase of our work done. There is no task that should be worked at begrudgingly. In the first place, the need for the task should be determined, and if the need is there, then the action to fill that need should be applied," his mother said.

Joseph exchanged ideas regularly with his mother and would confide in her with many of his personal problems.

"Mom, I had a fight with Victor Robles at school to-day. He came up to me and called me names, and said that I was acting too smart for my breeches. I am better than he is in school - but he is bigger and stronger than me, so I fought back the best I could. I grabbed him by

LIFE'S DETOURS

the hair and pulled him to the ground - then I kept him there until the bell rang. The other boys were watching and my friends clapped their hands and kept with me, while his friends kept with him. But, they did not interfere in our fight," Joseph told his mother.

"Joseph my dear boy, it is not good to fight with the boys at school because they are our neighbor's boys, and we don't want to become enemies with our neighbors over the quarrels of our children at school. Now, I believe you did the right thing in defending yourself, but remember he will bear a grudge against you and will constantly look for the opportunity to get even. So that, even if you came out a winner in this fight, you may come out a loser and hurt on another occasion. Remember that bashing others, either physically or by word of mouth in order to make yourself look good will have just the opposite effect. Here's what I think you should do. Tomorrow, take an extra apple to school. Then invite Victor to one side and quietly tell him you are sorry about the fight you both had yesterday. Ask him to forgive you. Offer him the apple and ask him not to call you names anymore, because you really want him to be a friend of yours. To be good to people is a challenge and without goodness we cannot please God or accomplish our purpose in life. Goodness is the secret of really succeeding in life. On the other hand for your own sake do not slacken on your learning or on your studies. Try to be helpful to him and others if you can. Don't take the attitude that you must reduce yourself to the lowest common denominator, just to have Victor or anyone else have you as a friend. Remember this Joseph, that you must at all times learn to be yourself and do your own thing. Excellence stands out, it will be noticed and it will make a difference in your life," his mother admonished.

It was difficult for Joseph to understand and to consider this kind of passive behavior, but he had noticed this trait in his mother when she would face tension and stress in dealing with his father, who was by far a rougher and more complex person and outright mean at times. She would remain calm. He respected his mother's admonition. Joseph's mother looked forward to the day when he would be a grown man, and would defend and protect her from his father's abuse. They empathized with one another.

One rainy afternoon the telephone rang. Three long and two short rings meant the call was for the Ackers, It was a rural telephone line and everyone knew by the number and length of the rings, who the call was destined for. Quite often, the neighbors would lift their receivers gently and listen in on the conversations taking place. The Ackers did not follow the practice of listening in and on following the gossip line. They cautioned their children not to develop this habit. The call was from Mrs. Ebert, who extended an invitation for Mr. & Mrs. Acker to

LIFE'S DETOURS

go over to their house, and spend an evening with them and a group of friends visiting from the city.

Richard and Eugenia finished the chores early, and Joseph was left in charge to baby-sit his younger brothers and sisters and to make sure they behaved and went to bed on time. The Acker family had grown in number by this time to five boys and two girls. In addition to Ray (9) and Virginia (7). there was Charles (5), Libby (4), Louis (2) and Allen a baby in arms. The parents took Allen along with them while the remainder were left at home.

"Joseph, do not play with matches and do not run around outside and track mud in the house. Be good children and we'll take you into town Saturday evening for ice cream. All of you be sure to mind Joseph," their mother Eugenia cautioned as she pulled the door shut behind her.

The evening at the Eberts was a pleasant one. It so happened that Fenley Merrell, one of the visitors from the city was an astrologer, capable of preparing horoscopes. He had brought with him his required paraphernalia, and most of the evening was spent in preparing and reading the horoscopes of those present. There was much bantering, small talk and laughter.

After most of the excitement had worn off, Eugenia broke into the conversation.

"How much would you charge for a detailed horoscope for our oldest son?" she asked Mr. Merrell.

"My charge for a complete horoscope is $2.00, and I'll put it down in handwriting for the individual," he replied.

Eugenia glanced at her husband Richard, who signalled with a slight nod of the head that she should proceed to engage him. But, she was also an astute person.

"Mr. Merrell, we really have no money at this time. (It was 1930, and the first year of the Great Depression, following the economic crash of 1929). But, if you are willing to drive by our farm on your way back to the city, we can pay you the equivalent of $2.00 with some farm products, such as cream, butter or eggs. Would that be all right?"

"That will be just fine," Mr Merrell countered. "Tell me where and when was your son born?"

"He was born on a Saturday at 5:30 p.m. on May 17th, 1919," she replied.

"He was born at home, situated on the North-East quarter of Section 14, Township 10, Range 24, West of the 2nd Meridian," Richard added.

A couple of days later, Mr. Merrell and his company drove by the Acker farm in their automobile on his return to the city. He picked up

LIFE'S DETOURS

the dairy products which Eugenia had already prepared in good measure, and he in turn handed her an envelope containing the hand-written horoscope for Joseph.

"How have you found the horoscope reading for Joseph?" Eugenia asked Mr. Merrell.

"Mrs. Acker, your son is under the zodiacal sign of Taurus. It is a good sign. According to the reading, your son should attend school and prepare himself, because he will become a leader of men, he will be someone great - I cannot predict with absolute certainty what he will be, but the prediction is good. He could be a high ranking military person or an ambassador or hold a high position in government," Mr. Merrell replied and with that he cranked the motor, got into his automobile, waved farewell and took off.

Curiosity took hold of Eugenia, she went into the kitchen, sat down on a chair and rested her elbows on the kitchen table. First she read Joseph's horoscope over to herself. Then she called Joseph into the kitchen, and she related all that had taken place during their visit to the Eberts.

"I have your horoscope here before me in Mr. Merrell's handwriting, and I would like to read it to you, would you care to hear it?" she asked.

"Sure," Joseph said.

At that moment, his father appeared in the kitchen door, He was dressed in his work denim overalls, a sun bleached red workshirt and the old dusty, greasy, black felt hat, which he wore most every day when working. He wanted a drink of water before going to the north forty to finish plowing. He heard his wife ask Joseph if he wanted to hear his horoscope, so he took a dipperful of water in his hand and sat on a chair for a moment to listen to the reading.

Eugenia read about the fact that he was born under the zodiacal sign of Taurus, and all about the lunar positions and how it highlighted his physical attraction. How other planets affected his opportunities negatively, or enhanced them in a positive manner. Eugenia read hurriedly, until she arrived at that portion that dealt with the probability of him becoming a leader of men. At this point, she read more slowly as if to underscore the significance of this statement.

"Joey, you have a wondeful horoscope, the future looks good for you, but you must study and acquire at least a high school education, then you will be on your way to doing great things," his mother said.

His father joined in the conversation and re-inforced what his mother had told him.

"And Joseph if you do well in school, your brothers and sisters will emulate your capability, and they too will become good students. It is important that you commence exemplifying your leadership from now on every day. You can do it if you put your mind to it," his father added.

His team of six horses were waiting in front of the house. Emotionally he had been moved when he thought about the future of his children. Inspite of his drinking problem, he wanted the best for his children. He took a few more minutes to share some of his own thoughts with his son.

"Joseph, your life will become a wonderful and interesting journey. We hope that your situation in life will be better than ours. Lives are made of chapters which eventually are written into a book. After the book is written and printed it cannot be revised. Every worthwhile accomplishment big or little, has its stages of drudgery and triumph. A beginning, a struggle and a victory. There is strength in knowledge. Try to fill the chapters in your book of life with courage, faith and good deeds. Your mother and I will try to equip you with courage and faith to confront life's difficulties as well as its pleasures and successes, but the deeds will depend on you. Apply yourself in earnest to everything you do. You will be a winner. We love you." With that his dad departed to attend to his work.

For that moment, Joseph took his parent's advice quite seriously and he tried to visualize in his mind's eye what he would be like as a general or an ambassador or some other government official. During the remainder of his childhood and adolescent period, in times of stress or dissatisfaction with the way things were going for him, this thought of greatness and of becoming a leader of men crossed his mind many times.

There were times when Joseph could not square his father's actions with his counselling and teaching. He could remember vividly the time his mother was to give birth to his brother Louis. The year was 1928, It was on the last day of the month of March. There was still snow on the ground. His father hitched a team of horses to the sleigh, put on a light load of thirty bushels of wheat and drove into town, to deliver and sell the grain. He was to bring back a ton of coal and a written list of food supplies that Eugenia had provided. Evening came and he had not returned. Eugenia did the chores with Joseph's help and returned to the house. She was not feeling well. She sat down and wrote a quick note, placed it in an envelope and handed it to Joseph.

"Joey, go to the barn quickly, bridle Queen and ride over to the Peakes and hand this letter to Mrs. Peake. Then come back as quickly as you can and before it gets dark."

As Joseph took off on horseback, a distance of one mile across the fields, a large bright, silvery moon was rising over the Eastern

LIFE'S DETOURS

horizon. He arrived at the Peakes and handed the envelope to Mrs.Peake.

She read it quickly and said to Joseph - "Thank you,- go back quickly and tell your mother I will be over to her house right away."

With that Joseph returned back home. He stabled Queen. She was the kind of a horse that children could ride safely.

A half-hour later, Mrs. Peake driven by her son with a team of horses arrived. Her son departed for home very quickly, but Mrs. Peake remained. Joseph thought something strange was going on. Why should Mrs. Peake come and stay at the house as an overnite visitor. But being only nine years old, he accepted it as his mother's invitation to Mrs.Peake to remain, considering that she was ill and more so in view of the fact that his father was not yet home. Mrs.Peake and Eugenia retired to the bedroom for a while. Then Mrs.Peake returned to the kitchen. She looked at the children.

"Your mother is not feeling very well and that is why I'm here. She told me to tell all of you to go upstairs to your respective bedrooms and retire for the night," and with that all the children went to bed.

The next morning, when the children woke up and came down stairs, their father was in the kitchen preparing breakfast for them. Joseph noticed him looking groggy, ashen and haggard. He hadn't shaved. He had stopped in town the day before, took to drinking with some of his buddies, forgot all about his family and did not get home until four o'clock that morning. In his absence and before mid-night, Eugenia had given birth to her baby.

Mrs.Peake, an elderly and matronly looking farm woman, had a husband, and two grown up children of her own. She brought the newborn baby into the kitchen and showed him to the rest of the children. Shortly thereafter she had some very unkind words to say to Richard, about his comportment as a father and responsibility to his family. Joseph heard Mrs. Peake's censuring words and comments to his dad. She was a person to be respected and Richard sat with a glum look on his face and accepted all she had to say without a single murmur.

"Boy when I grow up, I don't want to be like my dad, that's unfair to my mother," Joseph thought to himself.

Apart from his drinking, Richard did pay fatherly attention to his family. He was a strict disciplinarian and often expected too much adult behavior from his children. He would not stand for any back-talk. Any new suggestion or idea by any member of the family had to be diplomatically introduced and brought to his attention. Joseph recalls one incident that occurred during his public school days. He came home from school on a rainy day and found his dad in the house.

"Well, tell me what new thing have you learned today?" his father asked.

"Mr. Gorchan, our teacher explained to the class the phenomenon of thunder and lightning and how it was caused," Joseph replied.

"Well how is it caused?" his father asked looking him square in the eyes.

"According to Mr. Gorchan the moist atmosphere in cloudy weather is loaded with electricity, and lightning is a discharge of electricity from a negative portion of a cloud to a positive portion. This discharge could also be down to earth, resulting in a light and electrical flash. Thunder is the sound which follows the lightning flash and is caused by the sudden and violent expansion of the air during the electrical discharge making a loud rumbling noise," Joseph replied.

His father listened to the explanation but felt it was somehow artificial. As a matter of fact, Joseph's father was never really convinced that the earth was round, and at times this made him look ignorant in the eyes of his children.

"Joey, I think you should tell Mr. Gorchan, that God created thunder and lightning when he created the earth," his father said.

There was no room for further argument. The very next day, Joseph wanted to test the teacher's reaction to what his father had said.

"My Dad said that thunder and lightning was created by God, and that man doesn't really understand how it functions. Is that true?" Joseph asked his teacher.

"Joseph, I never said that God did not create thunder and lightning. I too believe He did. I only explained how God created it to function. You see, God created a wheat plant for example, but man has been able to plant and raise wheat, to analyze it's chemical composition, to determine what material it is made of and to adapt it for human use. In fact, in some cases through genetic engineering, a new variety has been created by man. For example, the "Red Fife" variety which your dad planted previously grew tall, lodged and had a four-row grain spike. The new variety developed called "Marquis" has a six row spike, the plant grows a shorter stem, it is better yielding, and produces flour of better quality. So you see, through scientific research and study man has been able to unlock some of the secrets of nature created by God and to understand them," the teacher explained.

This argument enabled Joseph to explain the teacher's answer and position with relation to thunder and lightning situation to his dad. Joseph wasn't sure he had convinced his dad, but at least he had convinced himself. He was certain in his own mind that man was created to learn how to utilize the natural elements placed at his disposal by God, and to control them in accordance with his needs.

Richard loved and cared for his family and when he was not

LIFE'S DETOURS

under the influence of alcohol, devoted time and encouraged their participation in extra curricular activities. During the public school years, he encouraged his children to take an active part in drama, singing, reading and memorizing poetry. Eugenia too, supported those kinds of activities that provided for child development without incurring huge outlays of money. He hauled lumber and built stages and platforms for the school concerts, and rendered Mr. Gorchan and other teachers a helping hand in this respect. Some of the best Christmas concerts in the region, were staged by the teacher and pupils at the school where the Ackers were students. Joseph played a leading role in drama, debates, spelling contests, and the annual year end Christmas concert. His brothers and sisters did equally as well.

The latter part of the 1920's was a period when drastic changes were taking place in agriculture. The immigrant farmers that had settled in the community, were now gradually leaving behind some of the more traditional farming practices to which they had accommodated themselves, and were adopting newer and better methods of farming. Animal power on the farms was being replaced with tractor power. Joseph recalls his father selling 12 of his work horses and purchasing a 15-30 McCormick-Deering tractor and a new "Durant" automobile in 1928. Following the purchase of the tractor, most of the field work was done by the tractor pulling the implements, and the new car replaced the old Model-T Ford. The old car was classified as junk and put to rest in a hidden corner of the farmyard. Each farmer maintained from four to six horses for other than field work, such as grain hauling, haying, and for transportation purposes during the winter months when the ground was snow covered.

In the beginning they were unable to rely totally on mechanization. Oddly enough one of the debates at school in which Joseph participated debated the subject of "Tractor power vs horse power on the farm". Joseph was a good debater and he would have liked to be on the affirmative side of the debate. However, the teacher assigned Joseph the task of defending the status quo. Together with another fellow student they defended the horsepower situation and on the basis of the student vote, won the debate.

Joseph remembered vividly the economic crash of 1929. The Ackers felt the impact of this crisis for several reasons. In the first instance, the dry spring and summer season created an unprecedented drought resulting in a poor crop and garden. Secondly, the price of the farm products also declined, thus minimizing the family income. Harvest terminated early and the yield was only sufficient to provide feed to winter the livestock, and seed for planting next spring's crop. For the first time Eugenia's garden did not produce. The family did not harvest any potatoes which was a staple food item. The situation was bleak. Richard went to the western part of the province near the city of Swift Current, where rains had been plentiful and the crops were good. There he worked as a harvest hand for 28 days at five dollars per day. On his return, together with Eugenia, they drove by wagon and horses into town and purchased 12 bags of flour, one bag of beans, one bag of rice, 2 bags of cornmeal. These bags weighed one hundred pounds each. They purchased no clothing, except one pair of two buckle overshoes for each of the school age children. Everyone had to make do with last year's clothes.

As soon as the freezing temperatures set in they butchered a hog and a young steer. They ordered by mail two hundred pounds of fresh frozen fish, which came in by train from Lake Winnipegosis in Manitoba. The farm still supplied milk, cream, butter and eggs. In reality the family faced winter with a good supply of food, and were comfortable until the next year when the new crops were harvested.

However, there were other problems. Richard had purchased the automobile in 1928 with a down payment and a further payment to be made in 1929. Likewise, the tractor had not been paid in full and a final payment came due later that year. Richard was able to sell two head of cattle and satisfied the tractor payment. He could not meet the automobile payment, so he arranged to have the dealer repossess the vehicle. This was a stigma for the family. The neighbors would learn of the situation and that would be a clear indication that the family had no reserves. The land taxes remained unpaid and a note at the Mortgage Company had to be renewed.

One evening Joseph overheard a conversation between his parents in which his mother sounded rather perplexed.

"You were unwilling to increase our herd of milk cows with the loan from the mortgage company, so that we could ship more cream. Cream would bring us in weekly checks, with which we could run the household, buy food and clothes for the children and have cash on hand. The pasture land you plowed under with that money, could have been used to pasture a larger herd, and we would not need to rely so heavily on the grain harvest which can be a failure when rainfall is inadequate. Additionally, we could have had more cattle to sell which would have provided us with more income, and we could have met our financial obligations and had some reserves to see us through this period," she said to him.

Joseph did not hear his dad respond argumentatively. He merely heard him say - "hindsight is always better than foresight."

In his own mind, Joseph sided with his mother and felt she was right. He seemed to think that she was a better planner and manager of

LIFE'S DETOURS

resources than his dad.

"When I grow up, I'll seek to copy and apply my mother's managerial skills. She is a good planner and is result-oriented," he would intuitively say to himself.

As a young boy, Joseph was also involved in his share of childhood pranks and mischief. On one occassion, he went over to the Frentzs, a neighboring family who had a boy of the same age to visit and play games with him. During the visit he noticed a small pair of pliers, only 4 inches in length placed on one of the window sills. He looked at them with envy and while no one was looking, took them, put them in his pocket and came home with them. A few days later his Dad noticed him playing with these pliers.

"Joseph, where did you get those pliers from?" his father demanded to know.

Joseph, did not know exactly what to say, but he knew that any punishment that might be meted out, would be lighter if he told the truth. He hated to admit that he stole them so he offered a half-truth as an explanation.

"I played with them last Sunday afternoon at our neighbor's place, and I forgot them in my pocket and I came home with them," Joseph replied.

His father suspected theft. He quickly ordered him to walk back to Mr. Frentz and to hand the pliers to him, apologizing for having taken them. This placed Joseph in an embarassing situation, but he knew that disobedience to this order from his dad would bring physical punishment. He followed the order.

He walked slowly the one quarter of a mile to the neighbor's house and with a red face, he shamefully approached Mr. Frentz - "Mr. Frentz, I am returning a pair of pliers, that I took from your house last Sunday. I know I shouldn't have done this and I'm very sorry. Please forgive me."

Mr. Frentz immediately understood the dilemna that Joseph had found himself in. He asked Joseph and his son Sammy to sit for a moment beside him on a bench in the shade of the house. He related a story to them about an experience, similar in nature that he had committed as a small boy in Romania and how his father ordered him to go and admit wrong doing and to ask for forgiveness.

"Joseph you have done the right thing. All of us will make a mistake from time to time, no one is perfect. The point is, when an error is committed, that we own up to it and ask for forgiveness," Mr. Frentz said.

He rose from the bench, apologized again and said good-bye. He walked rapidly towards home. Somehow he felt relieved. A weight had been removed from his shoulders and he had a spring in his step. He was glad his father ordered him to admit his wrong doing and he vowed never to repeat such an act again.

On another occasion curiosity got the best of Joseph. It was during harvest time, and the threshing crew hired by his father was made up of men who had come from other parts of the country in search of harvest employment. The Ackers provided sleeping quarters for these laborers in a caboose. It was a building on wheels, which made it portable for moving from one farm to another as required. The caboose was rustically finished on the inside with bunk beds and provided accommodation for eight to ten men to sleep. There was a table at each end fastened to the walls. Joseph was cautioned not to go into the caboose, since this was the private domain of the workers. But he could not contain himself and one day snuck in to see what the inside was like. There were unmade bunk beds with the grey woollen blankets strewn whichever way across them and some ruffled up pillows. There were clothes hanging from several nails driven into the walls above the bunk beds.

On one of the tables he noticed a bar of chewing tobacco, from which someone had cut off a portion. Joseph picked it up in his hand and looked at it. It had the smell of tobacco but the appearance of chocolate. The jacknife laid handy on the table. He thought to himself that if he cut himself a small bit, the workman to whom it belonged would never notice it. So he took the knife, sliced himself a fairly thick sliver of this bar, put it in his mouth and vacated the caboose.

At first it tasted sweet. He chewed on it as he saw the workmen doing while walking to the house. He sat on the front steps and took several good swallows of the juice and then began to feel sick. He felt like he was about to faint and began vomiting. The original sweet taste had gone. In his mouth he now had the awful taste of tobacco, mixed with taste of the vomit. His mother happened to notice him vomiting and quickly came to see what had happened.

"I'm sick, and I don't know why," he said to his mother.

His mother, not knowing what he had been up to, took the genuine view that perhaps the child had eaten something disagreeable and his stomach was reacting to it.

"You better come in and lay down on the sofa, while I prepare a medicinal drink for you," she said.

The medicinal drink consisted of drinking a tablespoon of an Anti-Pain oil in a half glass of warm water. This was quickly followed with a level teaspoon of sugar to sweeten the after taste. She gave this to Joey, who sipped it down and allowed the sugar to slowly dissolve in his mouth. Already he was beginning to feel better, but the pale color

LIFE'S DETOURS

on his face remained. His mother touched his forehead with her hand.

"You have no fever, so just rest for awhile and you'll get over it soon," and with that she went about her housework, for it was harvest time.

In a few minutes Joseph was up and around again. But, his chewing tobacco sickness remained a secret he shared with no one until he reached manhood.

After his move to the city, Grandpa Acker would come back to the farm every spring for a couple of weeks to lend a helping hand with the farm work. He would do the same at harvest time for a similar period or longer. However, the intimacy and the familiarity that once existed between Joseph and his grandfather had lost some of its magic. This was due to the fact that Joseph grew older, and over a five year period had spent only periodic visits with him. Now he had to attend to chores and other responsibilities, and there wasn't sufficient time left for the two of them to re-create the bond that once existed.

The last good visit Joseph had with his grandparents, was in the winter of 1927/28 when he travelled by train to Regina with his father to visit them. His grandfather took Joseph and his father to the movies. They were silent movies, with written captions explaining the scenes as the dramas unfolded. Joseph could read them faster than his father. Grandpa simply viewed the movie and formed his own opinions and fantasies about what was happening. After the movie was over they compared notes, and Joseph was able to explain in more detail the movie story and piece it together in coherent fashion for his father and grandfather.

"Joseph, you're a clever boy. If you study hard and continue going to school, someday you'll write a book. If I could read and write, I'd write a book about my life experiences. I hope you will do it. God bless you my boy," his grandfather said.

However, as expected back on the farm in the absence of his grandfather, Joseph was now continually learning more from his parents and his school teachers. His father took time to assist Joseph in training their dog Sport to pull the toboggan, and to give the kids a ride around the farmyard. Joseph would go as far as the neighbors and back if there was a need to run an errand. Sometimes if Sport spotted a rabbit, he would take off after the rabbit with the toboggan behind him, dumping off Joseph in the snow and forcing him to walk back home.

Their father allowed time for the children to enjoy other winter sports, such as ice skating, down-hill sledding or tobagganing, but doing chores, attending to homework and reading a good book had top priority. The situation was wholesome and Joseph grew up enjoying his childhood. But if anyone was to ask him, whom he felt was his best friend and teacher, he would still place his mother at the top of the list.

LIFE'S DETOURS 63

Chapter 5

THE DEPRESSION YEARS

The aftermath of the economic crash of 1929 in the United States, soon spilled over the 49th parallel into Canada causing a similar impact. The depression was ushered in by the spectacular crash of the Montreal and Toronto stock markets in the late fall of the same year. The economic impact of this crash was felt world-wide, but certain features were peculiar to Canada.

As an exporting nation, it felt an immediate decline in foreign trade, with the high tariffs of France, Germany and Italy as well as the Hawley-Smoot tariff of the U.S. damaging Canadian agriculture. This caused a decline in railway traffic and income. Coal and wood pulp, two other export items also suffered reduced volume of export sales and coupled with sagging farm prices affected government revenues. Unemployment became general, and as many as 100,000 farmers were receiving some form of government aid. The Acker farm fell in this category.

Farms were not electrified and battery operated radios were just emerging on the market, The cost prohibited many farm families from purchasing a radio. The news on world and national events, on markets and other items of interest to farm families came from weekly newspapers. These came through the mail by train and were always a week to ten days late. In fact, on many occasions the main reason for going to town on a train-day, was to pick up the mail of which the newspapers were the most important items. The Ackers were receiving the "Western Producer" - a weekly newspaper owned and published by the Saskatchewan Wheat Pool, the farmer-owned grain and livestock marketing cooperative. This newspaper highlighted events of national importance, and a fairly detailed coverage of provincial and local news.

It was a newspaper that the Ackers patronized and read with dogmatic fervor because it defended the farmer's plight, and the role that consumer and marketing cooperatives could and did play in regulating the markets. The farmers organized cooperatives in order to correct abuses created by the unscrupulous marketing practices of the petroleum, grain and livestock companies at that time.

One such glaring abuse was the purchase of grade No.1 wheat for a No. 2 grade, with a possible difference of five to ten cents a bushel in price. Joseph remembers his dad telling of his experience, in which he took a horse-drawn wagon load of sixty bushels of wheat to a privately-owned elevator company. A distance of fourteen miles. He drove the load into the grain elevator and the Agent or Buyer looked at his wheat sample, and remarked:-

"Mr. Acker, the grain you have here today is No.1 wheat, but I'm sorry, I have no space in my elevator for No. 1 grain. The only bins in which I can place your grain are holding No. 2 and No.3 grades. If you wish to dispose of this load I'll have to buy it for a No.2."

"What could I do?" Mr.Acker thought. "Take my load of wheat back to the farm?"

He was forced to sell his grain at the grade and price offered. In addition to this maneuvre, there were such other practices as short changing the farmer on scale weight, or deducting a heavier percentage of "dockage" for weeds and other foreign matter content from the grain delivered. Such practices aggravated the farmers and compelled them to band together and organize farmer-owned cooperatives for fair and better treatment.

The other weekly newspaper that came into the Acker home was called "The Family Herald and Weekly Star." This was an independently owned newspaper published in Montreal. It focussed on national events and rural Canada's agricultural problems. Both newspapers reported political events at all levels of government including the international scene. Joseph became an avid reader of the newspaper, and became well informed on marketing scenarios, political developments and local current events. His father played an active role in the local farm organizations, being a member of the local Wheat Pool Committee and the local Farm Supply Cooperative. From an early age, he took Joseph along with him to many meetings of these organizations.

The plight of the farming industry, as well as the injustices that pervaded the economic and social fabric of society of that day, became ingrained in Joseph's mind as an injustice that required mending. He felt he had a role to play in this scenario. Many a winter evening, neighbors would come to the Acker home to discuss politics, and Joseph's father encouraged him to participate wisely in those exchanges of ideas and information. Joseph would refer to news items and

LIFE'S DETOURS

clippings from the newspapers to buttress his arguments. He would translate information from English to Romanian, since most of the neighbors could not understand English well, much less read it. All of them spoke Romanian. Joseph sensed that he was making an impact on the neighbors and although he was young, they treated him with respect. This in essence contributed immensely towards building his self-esteem and developing a personal socio-political philosophy.

News had arrived by telegram from the city, that Grandpa Acker had passed away. This was in September 1930. The harvest had been poor due to a spring drouth, and high winds which caused soil drifting, Nevertheless, Joseph's father felt he had to attend the funeral. He looked to Eugenia and asked;- "Mom, do you want to go to the funeral with me?"

"No, I know we can't both go, because we simply cannot leave the children and the farm alone for two or three days. I believe you and Joseph should go and I'll stay at home, do the chores and see that the children attend school," she replied.

There were neighbors close by that would have gladly taken care of the chores and arranged for the chidren to go to school. Eugenia knew that her son Joseph wanted to be at his grandpa's funeral, so she wisely chose to dissent, and allow him to take her place. In additon, she knew that money was too scarce for all three of them to go.

A half mile away Dan Acker, Richard's brother was also preparing to go, driving his own car and taking along his son George who was the same age as Joseph. Both Richard and Joseph would ride with them in a 1926 Chevrolet sedan. Not a very reliable vehicle, but one that took them to the funeral and back, a distance of seventy-five miles each way. It was a three hour journey one way over a dirt road. The arrangement was that Richard would pay for the fuel the car used and the meals, while his brother Dan furnished the car. Richard had two uncashed cream checks totalling eleven dollars, which he cashed and filled the gas tank on the car for two dollars. He gave one dollar to Joseph and kept the rest for meals and for the return trip.

They arrived at Grandpa Acker's home in the late afternoon, just as the funeral home delivered the emblamed body to the house. The elderly Ackers lived in a modest two room house, one of which served as the kitchen and dining area. The other served as a sitting room during the day and a bedroom at night. The coffin was rolled into the bedroom-sitting area, with the result that there was only sufficient room to walk around it and view the remains. The coffin was one of Grandpa Acker's do-it-yourself projects. He built it a few years before, and had suspended it indoors from the roof of his outside shed. It was out of the way until the time for its use arrived. A funeral wake was observed for two late afternoons and evenings. Many of Edward Acker's relatives and friends came to view the remains, and to pay their last respects to Grandma Viola Acker and members of the family. Joseph viewed the remains several times during this period. He stood by the half-opened, black cloth covered, home-made casket and gazed at Grandpa Acker's face, with his closed eyes. There was silence, silence with sorrow, yet in the midst of this sorrowful silence, there was a conversation going on in Joseph's mind.

In retrospect a thought emerged about the time they walked hand in hand through the grain fields, and Grandpa Acker knelt in the wheat field and thanked God for the bountiful crop.

"This is my grandfather, my best friend and counsellor, and he will talk and pray no more. I hope God has a special place prepared for his soul in heaven - he was a good man," Joseph thought to himself.

The next day, they took Grandpa Acker's remains to the church. A litany of liturgical and burial prayers were said. Everyone in attendance filed past the coffin one more time. Joseph saw the tears in the eyes of Grandma Acker, his father, his uncle and cousin, and he could not contain himself. He too cried. He felt his own deep sorrow. He cried even as the last person in church filed past the coffin, because he felt a void in his being and because he would see his grandfather no more except in his mind's memory.

The undertaker closed the lid on the coffin and signalled to the pallbearers to gently remove and walk the coffin to the hearse. The drive to the city cemetery was a short one, and the dark, open grave was waiting to devour his remains. The coffin was placed on a mechanism which unhurriedly lowered it gently to its last resting place. The final act that took place, and which Joseph clearly recalled was the Orthodox priest taking a sharp pointed spade in his right hand, and nicked the grave at the head, at its foot, and on the right and left side, in the form of a cross, and uttering with priestly authority a petitional directive containing words along the following lines:-

"In the name of the Father, the Son and the Holy Spirit, Edward thou servant of God, we commend your soul unto Him, and we commit your body to the ground from whence it came, ashes to ashes and dust to dust, in sure and certain hope of the Resurrection unto eternal life, through our Lord Jesus Christ."

Everyone murmured quietly - "Amen."

Joseph felt those words were very appropiate and deserving as a final and culminating reward for his grandfather, and for the closing chapter on a life of almost eighty years. A life in which, had it not been for his grandparents as progenitors, he most certainly would have not been born and enjoying the life he had.

LIFE'S DETOURS

Back on the farm there was still harvesting to be done after the return from grandpa's funeral. Because of the light crop harvested, threshing was estimated to last for only one day. Richard did not operate his own threshing outfit, but chose to have a district farmer come with his outfit and crew and thresh his crop. The harvest crew this particular year was made up of the local neighbors or their sons. Richard was a part of that crew as a teamster hauling bundles or grain as the situation warranted. The threshing outfit pulled into the Acker farm in the evening. The next morning very early, the purring of the McCormick-Deering tractor, the humming of the grain thresher and the timely half-bushel dumps of grain into the wagon box were as regular and steady as clockwork. The steady stream of straw coming out of the straw blower and being piled unto a newly formed straw pile gave any farmer a feeling of contentment. The threshing crew was small in number, and those that were unable to go to their homes in the evening, bedded themselves down with blankets in the barn's hayloft. That is where the crew had slept upon the night of their arrival. The outfit shut down for noon lunch, which generally took one and one-half hours. This allowed sufficient time for the crew to feed their horses, and also come into the farmer's home for a satisfying noon-day meal.

The Acker family had developed a reputation as being good hosts, even on occasions other than harvesting. Eugenia Acker was renowned for being a good cook. This particular day she served a noon-day meal consisting of chicken noodle soup with crackers, roast leg of lamb, scalloped potatoes, creamed cucumber salad, with a baked apple cobbler and fresh whipped cream for dessert.

The noon-day meal and break period being over, work in the harvest field resumed. Richard was conversing with Edward Vall, the owner of the threshing outfit, when one of the teamsters began hollering at the tip of his voice,-

"FIRE" - "FIRE" - "FIRE" - and he was pointing towards the Acker farmyard.

Sure enough, the Acker barn was on fire and the fire had burnt a hole through the barn's roof. An idle team of horses hitched to a wagon and standing by, were quickly recruited and several workmen and Richard climbed into the wagon and hurriedly headed for the burning barn.

Richard remembered leaving a young colt tied to the manger in his stall, as well as four little pigs that were being weaned in another stall. They arrived in time to save the animals, all of the harness and other barn equipment.

Joseph noticed the sad look on his father's face as he sustained his loss, with his hands fixed on his hips. Together with the other men they simply watched the building burn to the ground.

Most of the crew members smoked. It was determined that the fire was caused by the careless throwing of a cigarette butt, that had not been properly extinguished. The fire originated in the stairwell space which was used for climbing into the loft. There was much speculation about which person might have been the culprit responsible for the deed, but no one was specifically identified as being solely to blame.

There was no need to repeat the words of caution - "People should never smoke in the barn, there is too much combustible material to begin with, then there is always the concern for animal life, and lastly the monetary loss itself." An expensive lesson was learned by everyone.

The incident not only dampened spirits for the day, but prolonged the threshing, carrying it over to the next morning for a few hours. Richard did not continue working on the threshing crew for the balance of the season and the neighbors understood his dilemna. He had to construct a make-shift outdoor manger, at which the cows could be tied during their milking period. He also required a place to feed those horses that would be used for chores and for the building of a different barn.

The building was insured, however the mortgage company had first claim to the insurance proceeds. Richard agreed to let the mortgage company retain the insurance proceeds as a payment on his loan and delinquent interest. This reduced his mortgage amount from three thousand to two thousand dollars, and brought him to a current status with the mortgage company. There was another barn on one of the farms that Grandpa Acker had purchased earlier on for Richard. It was decided that since it wasn't being put to use at that location, they would move that building and with a few added repairs, replace the building that burned.

The building was moved with the help of a few neighbors and two tractors pulling it on skids made from four cut down telephone poles. The rural telephone system was no longer in operation. The farmers were unable to pay their phone bills, and there was no money available for repairing the system. Finally, the telephone company was dismantled. Each farmer became the owner of the telephone poles and wire that was on his property, and this is how Richard became owner of the poles used for skidding his barn. The building was pulled to its new site and was placed on a foundation of stones, with earth packed tightly around it. The required repairs to the barn door, the loft door, and the windows were made, and before winter set in, the Ackers were again in a position to provide shelter and housing for their animals.

For eight years the economic climate and living conditions,

LIFE'S DETOURS

caused the popular conversation to become depression influenced and oriented. Joseph often wondered about the kind of a future that lay ahead for him. Little or no money in circulation. The situation looked hopeless and at times he felt that life for him was a continuous damp, drizzly cold November month with very little sun. He was reminded of an excerpt from Locksley Hall, one of Tennyson's poems he had read,-

"For I dipt into the future, far as the human eye could see. Saw the vision of the world and all the wonder that would be." Then in his mind Joseph added another line -"But, little do I see for me."

He continued going to school day after day, week after week and year after year.

He graduated from public school, and now had to go on to high school. The nearest high school was located fourteen miles away, An attempt to enroll as a student at this school was not impossible, but highly impractical because of the distance and lack of funds to enable boarding away from home.

"Joseph, you must continue to study, and try to complete your grade nine and ten by correspondence. The Government Department of Education is offering these courses by mail and your father and I decided to ask you to consider seriously studying in this manner for the next two years. Perhaps by then our financial situation and conditions will improve, to enable us to assist you financially to attend a town or city high school and complete grade eleven and twelve - what do you think?" his mother said.

Joseph at age fourteen could not refuse the suggestion, As he looked into his mother's eyes he could see how apologetically and lovingly she had offered the proposal.

"I will certainly try and do it," Joseph replied.

They filled in the enrolment application, included the fifteen dollar tuition fee and on the next trip to town, mailed the envelope to the Department of Education.

As it was, conditions did not improve, in fact they had deteriorated. The year 1932 brought about a very good harvest of quality wheat, after two bad years of drought, high winds and dust storms. The dust storms were so bad at times, that any cars running on the roads had to have their headlights on, and the kerosene lamp would be lit to provide reading light within the home at mid-day. Dust banks formed around buildings and other stationary objects, similar to snow banks in the winter time. Poor Eugenia would be wiping dust from the window sills of the home, and shaking and airing bed blankets and clothing outside on a clear day. The livestock would come to the barnyard from a dried out pasture with mud around their eyes and nostrils, and famished for something to eat.

LIFE'S DETOURS

The Ackers had to sell most of their livestock, and retained only a basic herd of four cows and four horses. There was simply no feed, and the Municipal Government assisted with financial grants from the Provincial and Federal Governments, brought in fodder for the livestock from other parts of the country. It was rationed and given as relief aid to enable the farmers to feed and retain their basic livestock herds. The Ackers also retained a few head of sheep for both wool and table meat, and wintered them on Russian Thistle, a weed that grew during the drought periods.

The weed was mowed while tender and before the thistle weed grew needles. After drying it was stacked in the same manner as hay and fed sprinkled with a solution of stock molasses diluted with water. It then became palatable to the animal's taste. They were fed no grain. The protein and fibre content was adequate to sustain the animals throughout the winter months.

The economic conditions were such that by 1933 nearly every family in the municipality was receiving "relief-aid" in some form or another, and openly talked about it.

They were not the kind of people that felt good about receiving relief-aid. They were hard working and had not lost hope. They merely found themselves trapped into a situation that lowered them to a level beneath their dignity, and still somehow had to learn to stand tall.

Living in a rural community, people get to know what everyone is doing. There's no way to keep it a secret and is one reason why there is less abuse, theft or moral degradation than in a large city. The old saying - "that it takes a whole village to raise a child," was very applicable and held much truth for the Ackers and their neighbors. Farm families as a rule were close families.

Joseph's younger sister Libby, became ill in 1931. She was five years old. Her parents did everything within their power to attend to her illness. She suffered with leukemia, and there was no known medical cure. Dr. Dammon the family physician located 20 miles away, prescribed certain blood building medications which had to be taken with either orange or tomato juice. Oftentimes, the family sacrificed other needs in order to buy the right kind of juice for Libby. There was no improvement. Finally, Richard drove Eugenia and Libby to the nearest train depot, and sent them to the city to see a specialist in child infirmities. The doctor placed her in hospital and two days later on December 6th, 1932 she died. Her mother brought her home in a casket. It was a sad and shocking event for the entire family.

This incident brought the family even closer together. Stark reality revealed that even a young person was subject to death and to be called home by his Maker.

LIFE'S DETOURS

"How could this be? It is so cruel and untimely. Only a few days ago we played with her. She would have been ready to start school in the spring. Everyone loved her including visitors. She would be asked to put on her mother's higher heeled shoes and pretend she was a school teacher. She would dramatize her ideas and thoughts, which always brought appreciative comments from those around her. Everyone loved her and now the space in our lives that she once filled remains barren," Joseph thought to himself.

Her brothers and older sister Virginia witnessed with sorrow her small face and her body dressed in one of her best Sunday white dresses lying in a white brocade covered coffin. The parents felt a degree of guilt, blaming themselves because they did not understand the nature of her illness.

"She was about four and half years old, and I allowed her to go outside to play on a day of an intermittent rain drizzle. She came in somewhat wet and must have caught a cold. She never regained her health or strength after that. The other children were with her too. Nothing happened to them, but all children are not alike, you know." Eugenia was heard to explain to those in attendance at the funeral.

The entire family, followed by a few sleigh loads of caring neighbors and their children, went bundled up in horse drawn sleighs to the church where funeral prayers were said. She was laid to rest in the church cemetery. Everyone stopped for coffee and sandwiches after the burial.

The ride home was slow. It was a gloomy cloudy day and being December, it was also a short day. No one in the sleigh said very much. Every member of the Acker family felt an emptyness and harbored the feeling that they should not have left Libby behind and alone. Everyone felt that Libby's death gave their lives new meaning and purpose.

"Motherhood isn't just a sexual relation, and a series of contractions, its part of a woman's nature, its a state of mind. From the moment I knew there was another life inside of me, I felt a responsibility to protect and defend that human being. It was a part of me. I tried to protect everyone of my children, and I love them all, and I shall miss Libby," Eugenia was thinking quietly as the sleigh slid along in the crisp snow.

Finally, she fled from those thoughts and broke the silence by shedding a few more tears and saying:-

"This day we have celebrated Libby's wedding and funeral. She was dressed in white as a bride in her coffin. There will be nothing more we can do for her. At her age, surely her soul will be with the angels. May God rest her soul in peace, eternally."

Richard, the father made no comment. He called on the horses for a trot and silence prevailed until they arrived home.

Richard hauled three hundred and twenty bushels of wheat and sold it at thirty-two cents a bushel to pay for Libby's funeral expenses. It was an unforseen set-back for the family. The prices on all farm products had reached an all time low. Eggs sold for as little as four cents a dozen. A five gallon can of cream would net three dollars and fifty cents. The children had to wear the "hand-me-down" clothing from their older brothers and sisters. Joseph wore shirts to school his mother made from empty flour bags, that had been washed and dyed a dark color. He recalled on another occasion, his dad took a sleigh load of thirty bushels of wheat to the grain elevator, and after weighing and dumping the wheat, he loaded the sleigh again with one and one-half tons of anthracite coal. To his dismay, his father discovered that he received ten dollars and sixty cents for his wheat, and had to fork an additional sixty cents from his pocket to pay for the coal.

The years of 1933 and 1934 were noted for heavy grasshopper infestation and drought. The municipality supplied the farmers with insect poison and the poison was spread according to instructions. The army worm infestation was a bit easier to control, because the farmer would plow a furrow or two around his field, and lay the poison in the furrow. When the army of worms came crawling to enter the field, they would first feast on the poisoned food laid in the furrows and become poisoned and reduced in numbers.

However, the grass-hoppers came by flight and one year they were so numerous in their flight migration, which appeared to be from the State of Montana that at times the sun was obscured by the cloud of these flying insects. Insect poisoning was applied by many farmers including the Ackers, but the results were far from satisfactory and from totally saving the crops.

Joseph continued his correspondence studies, but also helped his father on the farm. The severe drought had lowered the water table under ground and many of the form wells went dry. The Acker's wells were affected and they were forced to haul water with horses and a water tank of ten barrel capacity from a neighbor's spring about three miles distant. It was a thrice weekly routine, and indicative of the volume of water that was being consumed, even under the circumstance of careful management and rationing. The drawing and hauling of the water happened to be Joseph's responsibility.

For a long period there was no rain, snowfall was light and the drought persisted. Joseph recalls how his father, and a few other community elders organized a "Prayer For Rain" day. A huge crowd of farm families came to the prayer meeting held at the church. Joseph also attended and he too, knelt and asked God with a deep and

LIFE'S DETOURS

soliciting personal supplication to make and grant rain. The prayer meeting concluded with the entire crowd joining in a procession, in which they circled the church's ten acre property, chanting hymns and prayers and asking God to have mercy, to order rain, and to bless them, their land and their animals. Strange as it may seem on that very day, and before the Ackers returned to their farm home by horse and buggy, a heavy downpour of rain caught them on the way, and for a good hour the rain came down in bucketfuls. Everyone was soaking wet and yet happy.

"Thank God, He does answer prayers," Joseph's father said.

For Joseph it was a day never to be forgotten. The colossal two hour down-pour filled one of the sloughs on the Acker farm that had been dry for some five years, to a near record level. The dry and cracked earth absorbed the water very rapidly, and within six weeks after the downpour the Ackers planted oats in it, to be harvested for green feed. Enough green feed was produced to furnish the fodder needs of the livestock for that coming winter.

Hard times continued. The Conservative party had formed the Goverment in Canada, and Richard Bedford Bennett, a renowned Calgary lawyer became Prime Minister. Farmers who had scrapped their Model-T Fords including the Ackers, now brought them out of the scrap heap, removed the body from the main frame and with a little bit of ingenuity, converted the chassis into a rubber-tired wagon. The wheels were equipped with new tires and the chassis was adapted to be pulled by horses. This made an easier pulling vehicle for the horses and of more comfort for the farmer. In many instances the conversion was a "do-it-yourself" project, made by the farmer himself. The vehicle became popularly known as the "Bennett Buggy," and was the chief vehicle of transport for the Ackers and for many other farmers.

The Conservative party had made an effort to rectify some of the economic ills that prevailed, but the weight of the world-wide depression was so great, that Canada in isolation could not remedy all of its problems. The end result culminated in the people blaming the Conservative party for being unable to cope with the problems and to remedy the situation.

During the 1935 elections, the Liberals were swept back into power with William Lyon McKenzie King as Prime Minister. The party acted immediately to alleviate the economic pressures that the people were feeling, by taking such measures as:
  a) Signing a treaty with the U.S. to reduce tariffs on manufactured goods, in return for preferred treatment on farm products, fish, lumber, wood pulp, nickel and asbestos.
  b) Securing new export trade outlets.

c) Signing a trade agreement with Japan.
d) Initiating a series of public works, the largest of which was the construction of the St. Lawrence Seaway, in cooperation with the U.S.
e) Creating the Bank of Canada to regulate the Banks and the money supply.
f) Creating the Canadian Wheat Board to stablize grain prices, and explore International markets.
g) Creating the Canadian Broadcasting Corporation to regulate the growing communications industry.
h) Creating a number of Royal Commissions to hold hearings, to study, and to recommend ways and means for improving the economic and social conditions of the people.

Due to the depression, and the ineffectivess of the old line political parties, new parties sprung up, particularly in Western Canada. The Social Credit Party which was based on a theory developed by C.H. Douglas' "Credit-Power and Democracy," formed the government in the Province of Alberta in 1935. At the same time it sent 17 Western Members to the Federal Parliament in Ottawa. The broader based Cooperative Commonwealth Federation (CCF) party, which advocated a program of socialized economic order, was founded about the same time by J.S. Woodsworth, at a party convention held in Winnipeg.

The antithesis of the development of the CCF party was that the farmers who are the most rugged of individuals, and the greatest believers in private ownership and individual freedom, embraced the socialist theory. The Province of Saskatchewan, with a predominantly rural population and an agriculturally based economy, kept a socialist government in power for 20 years under the leadership of T.C.(Tommy) Douglas.

Joseph supported the CCF theory and political party and even though he was too young to vote, he attended meetings with his father and was able to influence many farmers to support and vote for the party.

Joseph recalls the increase in the price of gold announced by the United States Government during the depression from $20.00 to $35.00 an ounce. Young as he was, he would muster his energy and wisdom and at political meetings request the floor and ask the speaker:-

"How is it that the United States could raise the price of gold, but could not raise the price of wheat. Who eats gold and why is gold more important than food, clothing or education?"

He was only sixteen years of age, and many of the local farmers were admiring his penetrating questions and valiant behavior. They were the kind of questions they would have asked, but didn't dare for

LIFE'S DETOURS

fear of being ridiculed or because their English wasn't very good.

In fact, many neighbors would bring their corres-pondence on business matters to the Acker farm, and Joseph would draft replies and attend to their personal needs in hand-written letters on scribbler paper. The cost of a postage stamp was three cents. Each farmer would bring his own envelopes. Joseph made no charge for the service, but quite often a farmer would give him a tip of twenty-five cents.

Unemployment became widespread and Joseph knew of many young farm men who went in search of employment across the length and breadth of Canada. They travelled by riding on the top of the railway freight cars. "Riding the Rails" or "Riding the Rods" were common expressions, and begging for a meal, became "bumming for meals," and was not an uncommon occurrence. By 1935 unemployment conditions had climaxed to the point where a huge number of unemployed laborers had organized a "March on Ottawa" - however, acting on orders from the Federal Government, the Royal Canadian Mounted Police intervened, and broke up the organization in the City of Regina. Some loss of life took place and the leaders of the movement branded as being Communists, were tried in court and some were imprisoned for short periods.

By the mid-thirties, most farm families had acquired a battery-operated radio and were therefore quite current on the news and current event happenings. In the evenings, after the chores were done, the whole family, and at times including some of the neighbors would crowd around the radio. Some sat on chairs, while others would sit on the floor and listen to the popular radio programs of that day.

"I enjoy Fibber McGee and Molly," Richard would say - while someone else would chime in and say -"What about Amos and Andy?" Then there was discussion on subjects such as the boxing match between Joe Louis and Max Schmelling - the kidnapping of the Lindbergh Baby - the capture of Trapper Johnson, and the Dionne Quintuplets.

Ray would interrupt by uttering "What about Hockey Night in Canada with Foster Hewitt, or the World Series in baseball games?"

Besides radio and newspapers, in the long winter evenings, Joseph would engage in a game of "checkers" with his dad or younger brothers, or another game imported from Romania called "the mill." During Joseph's early years, his father would win at the games of both checkers or the mill, but as the years progressed and Joseph entered his mid-teens, he would handily beat his father. Quite often Joseph would allow himself to be beaten so that his dad would not became disenchanted with the game and quit.

There were times, when the neighbors would drop in and spend an evening playing cards, or vice versa, the Ackers would visit the neighbors with the same objective in mind.

Crop conditions in 1935 were unfavorable due to a disease known as "stem-rust," which caused both the quality of the wheat and the yield to be very low, and in some cases uneconomic to harvest. Many farmers set fire to whole fields of their wheat crops. In 1936 the Ackers obtained seed and planted forty acres of a new rust resistant variety of wheat known as "Thatcher." When harvested the sample looked very nice, but again the yield was low due to drought conditions. A sufficient quantity of the Thatcher variety was harvested to furnish the seed requirement for the ensuing year and a bit for sale as seed to the neighbors. The remainder of the wheat crop yielded even less. Prices had improved somewhat but with low crop yields - nothing more could be said, other than "times are hard."

The depression conditions continued and after having seen his father's barn burn down, and the lack of money with which to provide an added degree of comfort to life, Joseph wondered if farming would be the thing he wanted to pursue and if not, what if anything could be different for him in life. He reminded himself of the horoscope his mother read for him a few years back.

"Would I be a leader of men?"- "What would I have to do?"- "How much would I need to study?"- "Where would I need to go?"

Joseph's lessons began arriving weekly by mail. The Department of Education sponsored a one hour radio program each Saturday morning from nine to ten o'clock, in which questions or problems submitted by correspondence students would be discussed and answered. This caused the Ackers to purchase a PHILCO battery-operated, table model radio, which together with two batteries cost about $33.00. One battery would be in use, while the other was in town being re-charged. Additionally, Mr Gorchan, the public school teacher had agreed to allow Joseph to study at school, and he further agreed to assist Joseph with problems and to coach him in his studies.

He was the only student in the community taking his classes by correspondence and it worked extremely well. Joseph joined in the extra curricular activities and the teacher welcomed his participation especially in the Christmas concerts. It was at the concert held in December 1935, that Joseph caught a glimpse for the first time of what to him appeared to be an extremely pretty girl, and who would later play an important part in his life because she became his wife. She came with her parents as spectators to the concert. She was a student at a neighboring school. Joseph would have liked to give her some kind of a gift. He wanted to make an impression on her. He might have done something to obtain a gift had he known, but he didn't expect her to be

LIFE'S DETOURS

a spectator at a concert in which he played a couple of leading roles. Fortunately for him he was the oldest student in the school and the teacher appointed him in charge of packaging bags of candy and nuts for all the school students, as well as for the younger children at home and not yet students.

A bag with candy and nuts for each child was supplied by the School Board out of the school's meager budget, and was the only gift many children received during those depression concerts.

In the distribution of the presents to the students, after the concert was finished, Mr.Gorchan, the teacher called the names of the students and asked them if there were any brothers and sisters at home, and how many. Then he would order Joseph to hand out the number of packages called for, to some member of the family. When the distribution was completed, by coincidence and not by design there was one package left over. Joseph asked Mr. Gorchan if he could have it and he nodded in the affirmative. With that package in hand, Joseph ducked out from behind the curtains, watched for an opportune moment and with a smile handed the package to Suzanne, the pretty girl saying: "Merry Christmas To You and a Happy New Year."

Through correspondence Joseph completed his grade ten studies in June 1936. He was now ready to go to the city for his grade eleven and twelve. By this time, the Department of Education had approved a policy whereby the first senior year of high school or grade eleven could also be taken by correspondence.

"Joseph, the situation is such, that we cannot afford to send you to the city for completion of your high school education. Take your grade eleven by correspondence also, and surely a break will come along somewhere. These crop failures cannot last forever. We used to harvest good crops, and they should come back again. Conditions will improve, so that we can offer you support next year," his father said.

Joseph understood, shrugged his shoulders and agreed. Along with everyone else, he had accustomed himself to the "next year" hypothesis. He continued to study his correspondence material, but found it more and more difficult. There were theories in geometry, problems in algebra, and grammatical structure in the French and Latin languages he was studying that he was unable to fathom. Mr. Gorchan, the teacher who had been very helpful and to whom he had become accustomed, took a more senior position at another school, and his replacement was unwilling to render similar problem-solving assistance.

There was no way to compel the new teacher to allot time to Joseph, after all he was hired to teach public school and not high school.

LIFE'S DETOURS

"I don't believe he is adequately prepared to teach the high school curriculum," Joseph thought to himself.

Later, based on the teacher's own admission this was the actual case. Joseph did his best, but by Christmas of 1936 he was convinced, he couldn't make it and dropped any further study.

Joseph's brother Ray earlier in the year had seen an ad in the newspaper of a farmer nearby who was known to the Ackers, who wanted to lease two hundred head of sheep to anyone interested in pasturing and looking after them on a share basis. The sharing consisted of the lessor and the lessee, sharing equally in the lamb and wool crop, with the basic flock remaining intact and belonging to the lessor.

Ray reasoned with his father saying, "Let's lease this flock of sheep. We have pasture and between me and my brother Joseph and my younger brother Charles we can herd the flock. This will bring in added income from the sale of the male lambs and the wool. If we keep the herd over a two-year period, we might have enough female lambs to start our own basic herd and return the original herd to its owner."

The suggestion was endorsed by their father. A lease contract was signed and two hundred sheep were brought walking on foot to the Acker farm. Sheep are easy animals to winter. Their housing must provide wind shelter, but doesn't have to be elaborate since their wool fleece gives them protection from the cold. The Ackers erected a pole and straw barn, which had three sides closed in to shelter them from the prevailing north-west winds, and the one side facing the east was left open. This method of loose-housing proved satisfactory and Ray's idea soon became significant and made an impressive impact on the family income. There were two crops coming in from this herd of sheep. The wool crop in the spring and the lamb crop in the fall.

Joseph had trained himself to shear sheep. He had read in the farm newspaper that an Australian shepherd could shear an animal in five minutes.

"If an Australian can do it, I can do it too," Joseph said.

In practice he discovered that holding the animal with one hand, then bending over and manually operating the shears so as not to cut the animal's skin, at the same time have the wool came down in a fold likened to an inverted blanket, was no easy task for a seventeen year old. He had developed relatively good speed, and with one animal following another on the clipping floor, he could clip an animal with hand operated shears in ten to twelve minutes. His brother Ray was equally as good. Between the two of them they could shear about seventy to eighty animals in one day, and over a three day period the entire flock would be sheared.

LIFE'S DETOURS

After shearing they would be passed through the dipping trench to be chemically treated for ticks as they swam through. This task together with careful vigil at lambing time during the month of April proved to be the most arduous effort with regards to caring for the herd. The shepherding was done on horseback and the dogs Kaiser and Sport had been trained to assist with rounding up the flock without hurting the animals.

The Acker farm began to make progress. The last year in which the farm was affected by drought was 1937, following which the price of the farm commodities began improving and the yields realized from both the crops and the animals were better. This enabled the Ackers to purchase a better used car, a new tractor and some new implements.

Even Eugenia was able to make demands for some new things in the home, For many years, the mattresses on the family beds were home made. They were made from heavy cotton cloth, sewn by Eugenia on a sewing machine operated by foot treadle. Basically, it was simply a large bag, stuffed with fresh hay and placed over the bed spring. Joseph and his brothers would help in changing the hay contents three to four times a year. For the first week after a fresh stuffing and change, one could smell the fragrance of the fresh hay and sleep quite nicely before the hay became matted down and hard.

"I want new mattresses for all the beds," Eugenia demanded,- "and we must replace, blankets, pillow cases, towels, window curtains, new linoleum on the kitchen floor, and the house painted throughout. We must also buy clothes for the boys, and furnish a bit of a wardrobe for Virginia who is now a teenager and who also works very hard."

That was typical of Joseph's mother. Everyone else had to be taken care of first and she would come in last.

Chapter 6

IN SEARCH OF EMPLOYMENT

To make the winter months go by, a group of neighbors with growing children, which also included Richard's brother Dan Acker and his family, decided to hold weekly social evenings at one or another of their homes. After completion of the farm chores in the evenings, these families would drive by horses and sleigh to one of the neighbor's homes. The men would play cards and on occasion alcoholic beverages would be served. The ladies talked about their children, new recipes, community gossip, and at the same time kept busy with their handiwork of embroidering, crocheting or knitting. Work they took along with them.

The younger set visiting in another room, would talk about the happenings of a past or an upcoming dance or social event, while they were engaged in a card game of their own. At other times they would lower the flame on the kerosene lamp and listen to an Alfred Hitchcock type of ghost or mystery story. A serial drama that was popular on the radio at that time. It was an opportunity for both the parents and young set to communicate and socialize. The evenings generally wound up before mid-night with a pot-luck lunch, with the hosting family providing the coffee.

There were evenings when the parent's conversations focused on the the future, and primarily on what was in store for the rising generation of which their children formed a part. Every family had one or two children, who were now in their late teens or early twenties. The depression lasting as long as it did destroyed some of the plans that parents had set as goals for assisting their children to take their rightful place in society.

On one occasion Richard Acker led the group discussion by saying,- "The depression hurt us badly. Eugenia and I knew that we couldn't purchase land in order to put each one of our boys on his own farm. Our aim was to give them an education, enabling them to move into society and find appropiate jobs. That didn't pan out because the farm income was low, and we got strapped financially to the point where we couldn't send them to school beyond what was locally available."

This opened the discussion, and other families expressed similar concerns. Joseph Frentz spoke up saying;- "We have four boys altogether. The eldest who is 22 is now in Timmins, Ontario, and is working as a miner in one of the gold mines. He writes and says - he's making $5.25 for an eight hour shift and he's doing very well. In fact, he has invited our second son to join him. He is sure that there is work for him also at the same mine. You know our boys were raised under conditions of scarcity and hard work, and apparently this kind of upbringing has done them a world of good. My son says the mining companies like to recruit the young men from Western Canada because they are good workers, careful and make good miners."

"My oldest son is 21, and he left for the west coast of Canada. He is now in Vancouver and found work in a garage. He was always handy with tools on the farm and he repaired our tractor and farm implements. At times he did repair work for the neighbors. He said he found his job soon after he arrived there and is earning $1.10 an hour. My son did not want to go to school beyond his grade eight, but he is handy with tools and understands mechanical work, so he's happy and we're happy," Jacob Pater, another neighbor said by way of contributing to the conversation.

"You know, we had no money to give him, and I believe all he had was about $20.00 in his pocket when he left home. He rode the freight train from here to Vancouver. He wrote and told us how a good freight yard-man allowed him and another young fellow to get into an empty box car and ride from Calgary to Vancouver inside the car. He said that riding the freight train through the mountain tunnels was impossible due to the smoke and steam emission from the train's engine. Riding that portion of the trip inside the freight car was a life saver. He's even indicated, that he was coming back home to select a bride from here to take back with him. He said he wants a farm girl to be his wife. I suppose that is his mother's behavioral influence on him. He says Vancouver is a large city, and if so, any girl he takes from here ain't gonna milk no cows there. But that's his business," Pater added smilingly.

Marilyn Chase, the wife of Donald Chase broke into the conversation saying;-

"Our oldest boy Charles, rode the freight train to Windsor, Ontario and spent six months working on the tobacco farms and other odd jobs. Then he was able to get employment with the Chrysler Corporation and is now working full time in this car manufacturing plant. Earns about $10.00 per day, and that's lot of money. Can you imagine what we could do here with that kind of daily income? I wrote and told him to mind his money and send it to us and we would buy him a farm somewhere nearby. But, he says that farming is not for him. It's too risky. He bought himself a car on monthly payments and he wants to save enough to make a down payment on a house and then to seek a girl for a life long partner. He wants his sister to join him and he thinks she could also get work at Chrysler, but if that fails, there are other jobs available for her. It would cost her nothing, because he would pay for her room and board until she found work. You know, our kids will make it all right because they were brought up to respect others, to be industrious and to give an honest day's work for an honest day's pay. They may not have a good education, but they can read and write and use common sense and that's important in today's world. I always told my kids that - quality and honesty never go out of style and never to burn the bridge behind you. That's what my parents taught me, so I just pass it on."

These discussions and findings with the neighbors gave Richard and Eugenia Acker ideas and a kind of an uplift too. Joseph their oldest son was now nineteen years going on twenty. They were just coming out of the depression, things were a bit better - but money was still a very scarce commodity. There were four more boys at home, with an age spread of about two years between each of them. Richard Acker was barely 40 years of age himself and considering the size of the farm, as the boys grew there would be enough help to do the farming for some years to come.

Although they hated to think of the idea of having their children leave home to seek employment in other parts of the country, they also realized that this was inevitable and that sooner or later they would be facing a situation of this sort.

It took place on an evening in early March. It was after the evening meal. There was a howling wind and snow blizzard outside. Inside the house, the coal heater was keeping the place warm, the livestock in the barn had their mangers filled with hay and were bedded down for the night. There was an air of contentment in the Acker home as the light flickered from the burning coal fire. The family sat around, some crouched on the floor with their back against the wall and some on chairs with their elbows on the table. Richard and Eugenia sat on an older and much maligned sofa. The topic of conversation centered on the future and what provision should be made for members of the family.

LIFE'S DETOURS

"Joseph, what plans have you made for yourself, and how do you see the situation?" his father asked him.

His brothers looked anxiously at Joseph to see what his reply would be and Eugenia his mother paused for a moment from her knitting, as if to be sure she did not want to miss a word of what was going to be said.

"I have been giving it some thought. Most of my friends and guys my age or older have left or are leaving for other parts of Canada and the United States in search of employment. There is nothing much left here for me to do and I would also like to go and try my luck, but I have no money to speak of. I made a little money from my trap line on weasel skins, and from the jack rabbit pelts I sold but it is not nearly enough. I could ride the freight train like some of my friends have done, but I feel I must wait and save a few more dollars, for some clothes and a few meals,"

Joseph said in a serious and thoughtful mood.

"It's tough and we don't want you riding the freight train. It's too dangerous," his dad said.

"However, we can sell one or two of the hogs we have ready for market and raise a bit of cash for you, but where would you go and what would you do?" his father asked.

"My intention is to go down east to Windsor, Ontario. My cousin Nicholas Acker moved there about six years ago. He left the farm and headed for Windsor. At first he had it tough, only part-time work and most of that on the tobacco or dairy farms. Now he is working in the Chrysler Automobile Factory and is doing quite well. I wrote him a letter and asked him what the prospects were like for me to get a job, if I were to go there. I also asked him if I could stay with them while I seek work. He replied, that I could stay with them and that I could obtain employment right away, if I wasn't fussy about the kind of a job I would get," Joseph informed the family.

"When did you write him? I never saw you writing him a letter and there was no letter in our mail from him as far as I know," his mother said.

There were times, when Joseph's relations with his dad were strained because his father was temperamental on the one hand and a perfectionist on the other. It was somewhat difficult to engage in conversation with him, except on very rare occasions. In many ways he was a very good father, except for his drinking which aggravated Eugenia as well as Joseph and the rest of the family. For this reason, Joseph wrote the letter without telling his parents about it, and he told his cousin to send him the reply in care of their batchelor neighbor who lived close by. Nicholas his cousin, was aware that Joseph's father was inclined on heavy drinking at times and when this occurred he would abuse his family, so he complied.

"I wrote Nicholas secretly because I was afraid of dad's attitude, and I asked him to send the reply to Valerian our batchelor neighbor, which he did. That's how we communicated," Joseph said.

Joseph's dad felt hurt to learn that his child had to hide information from him, but he did not lose his temper. Rather he took a positive posture, picked up on the conversation again, and said:-

"Son, I make my mistakes and I grieve for them, but I'm also interested in your welfare. If you are planning to go, we don't want you to run away. We want you to leave and always feel that this home will always be your home. If you go and things don't pan out like you anticipate, then by all means come back - and we will find something here. Something that we can either do together or you can do by yourself. When were you planning to go?" he asked.

"I would like to leave as soon as possible," Joseph replied. "As you know, I do not have enough money - I was going to borrow a few dollars from Valerian our batchelor neighbor, but I haven't asked him yet, so my time for leaving is dependent on money. The truth is that I was going to leave home about April 1st and go down on the flats near Regina. I was going to seek employment with a farmer for a month or two until I could raise enough money to pay my way and then leave for Windsor," Joseph replied.

It was at this point that it dawned on Joseph's dad that his son was not a little boy anymore, but that he was a grown up man - ready to accept responsibility and to paddle his own canoe.

"He does not need me anymore," his father thought quietly.

Because of his drinking and his temper Joseph harbored a respect out of a love/hate relationship with his father. In the hate relationship, he would not dare to talk openly to his father and discuss his problems. In the love relationship he would go all out to please his father. It was not a wholesome relationship in Joseph's opinion.

Joseph celebrated his eighteenth birthday in May. On the following July 1st there was an all day picnic and a dance in the evening in their hometown. His cousin George, who was of the same age was going, but Joseph would not dare ask his father to allow him to go. Oddly enough, on that July 1st date, which is Canada's Birthday, his dad came to him and said:-

"Joseph, would you like to go today to the picnic and dance in town?"

Joseph couldn't hardly believe his ears. He worked hard on the farm, he would rise early in the morning without being called by his parents and begin the day's chores without being told.

LIFE'S DETOURS

"I guess dad appreciates my work after all," he mused in his mind.

"Sure, I would really love to go," Joseph replied.

"You can have this day off. Dress up, take the pony and away you go. Remember don't come home too late, we will be pitching hay tomorrow and we'll need your help. Here is a five dollar bill, take it - but don't spend it all. Joseph, I want you to have money in your billfold when you open it. That doesn't mean, that just because you have money you must spend it. Go and enjoy yourself, but be a gentleman. We would like to hear good news about your public behaviour," his father said as he set off to go about the farm work.

"A good thing has happened, I can now join my peers in social activities," Joseph said to himself.

He had more than enough money for the day. The admission to the sports area was fifty cents, and for the dance in the evening it was another fifty cents. A cup of coffee was ten cents, a sandwich fifteen cents, a piece of raisin or apple pie (which was really a quarter of a pie in size) was twenty five-cents. He could even take Suzanne to lunch if she were at the dance, but she was absent. He jumped on his saddled pony and rode into town. The pony was stabled and fed in the livery barn for another fifty cents. He returned home with two dollars and fifty cents still in his pocket. For a long time he recalled how much he enjoyed that particular day.

"Joey, we will arrange for you to leave within two weeks. I will ship the hogs to market this week and as soon as we receive the check, we will provide you with sufficient money to buy a one-way bus fare and a little pocket money. You said you had $20.00 of your own, and that should take care of your getting there," his father said.

The evening went by fast. The bedtime hour had arrived for the younger children, but no one was sleepy and no one was asked to go to bed. Eugenia, Joseph's mother began to talk:-

"Joey, we hate to see you leave home. I hate to see you leave and I will miss you. When you go and wherever you go, do not forget about us and be sure to act mature and conduct yourself with decent behavior. Think of all the good things we tried to teach you and apply them. Work hard, be honest, be truthful and sincere. Treat this going away as if it were one of your wishes being fulfilled. If someone were to grant you three wishes, what would they be and how would you go about fulfilling or administering them? Select your company - don't pick on losers. Remember, that if you tell me who you keep company with, I can tell you what kind of a person you are. Enjoy yourself, engage in humor, listen to good music, smile at people, be polite and be nice. Above all, I will not be with you to remind you to take your hat or cap off, when you enter into people's homes. It is a mark of respect that you give to people and in return they will respect you for being considerate and mannerly. I hope you will always treat the ladies with courtesy. You must remember that every girl has a mother. I hope you remember all the things I'm telling you," she concluded.

It was bedtime and everyone seemed to feel good about the event of the evening. Joseph was sharing a bed and sleeping together with his youngest brother Allen. After they settled under the cold blankets and warmed up a little, Allen was filled with feelings about Joseph's leaving. He said to him:-

"Joey, I have learned so much tonight. If you go away, will you come back to see us? I will miss you. Someday, when I grow big I will travel to see you, maybe I can get a job too."

Everyone fell asleep harboring the thought of Joseph's departure.

Richard's forecast was fulfilled, two weeks went by very rapidly and the morning had arrived for Joseph's departure. He was riding by car to Regina from where he would take the bus for Windsor. Uncle Dan Acker had arrived to pick Joseph up. He was going to the city by car and had offered Joseph a ride. Joseph was all dressed in clean travel clothes. His mother had pressed his two good shirts and the only suit he had. All his clothes had been freshly laundered the day before and everything was packed in an old suitcase. Joseph was now saying good-bye and hugging every member of the family. He left his mother to the last and as he gave her a hug and a kiss on the cheek, she said to him;-

"I roasted a chicken yesterday, and I baked fresh buns. I put them in this paper bag for you to have lunch on the bus as you travel. Good bye and God Bless You - Don't forget to write and let us know how and what you are doing. We are all anxious to hear from you. We love you."

With that Joseph got into his uncle's car and they left for the city. It was a two and one-half hour drive, and his uncle struck up a bit of conversation with him.

"Joseph, if you get down there and things go all right for you, would you be willing to help your cousin George to go down there as well? He will be staying home to help me farm this summer, but when fall comes he'll be ready to go and it would be nice if the two of you were together. You grew up together here and you could be together there too." Joseph felt a degree of importance by being asked to be of help to his closest friend and cousin.

"Sure deal, I'd be very happy to have George come to Windsor, to find employment and for us to be together," he replied.

After all, the Richard and Dan Acker farms were border to border and their homes less than a half mile apart. They played together, did Christmas carolling together and went to the same school and church.

LIFE'S DETOURS

There was only one distinct difference between Richard and Dan Acker. Dan was an easy-going person and had more patience, while Richard was quick tempered, aggressive and a perfectionist. Joseph had received more scoldings and the odd beating from his father for simply not putting things back in their place or on their hook after using them. His father would always say:-

"Things are here for everyone's use, but put them back in their place after using them so that when the next person needs an item he knows where to find it." He was right.

Uncle Dan drove Joseph right up to the bus depot, embraced him, said "good-bye" and left to attend to his business. Joseph went inside the depot and learned that the bus would depart in four hours time. He purchased his ticket, placed his suitcase in storage and decided he would take a walk and look over the city. As he walked along he passed by a cafe and noticed a sign in the window that said - "TEA CUP READER INSIDE - 50c." He paused for a minute, attempting to determine whether he should have his tea cup read or not. Since he was going on this long journey of two nights and two days, he decided to go through this experience and have his tea cup read.

He had heard that some gypsy ladies could foretell events by doing tea cup reading, but also that some folks had been mesmerized by their trickery and had their pockets emptied. He felt that he would be safe in a restaurant because it was daytime and it was a public place. But to be safe, he left two dollars in his pocket and folded the remaining twenty-eight dollars carefully and put the folded money inside his sock on his right leg. Then he walked into the restaurant, sat down at a table and lingered awhile until a waitress appeared.

"I'd like a cup of tea please, and I'd like to have the tea cup reader, read it for me," Joseph said.

"Is there anything else you'd prefer to have with your tea, or will that be all?" she asked.

"That will be all - thank you," he replied.

The waitress gave him a ticket with a number on it and advised him that his number would be called when his turn came, and when called he should take his cup with him to the cubicle where the tea cup reader sat. His cup of tea was served. Without adding any sugar or cream, he sipped on it slowly. After he finished, he gazed into the bottom of the cup to see what if anything he could see or decipher, but he saw nothing more than a cluster of wet, black tea leaves. He waited patiently looking up at the clock on the wall, which told him he still had about two and one half hours to spare.

Soon his number was called. He picked himself up quickly, grabbed his cup and headed for the tea cup reader. The reader was a gypsy lady, she had a dark complexion and was wearing a red kerchief on her head and a band of red beads around her neck. She had a dark wart on the lower left hand side of her face, but otherwise attractive. On her fingers she wore several rings with large colored stones that appeared expensive to Joseph. She asked him to sit down and greeted him with a smile. She picked up his cup and looked into the bottom of the cup very intensely, while twisting and semi-turning the cup from time to time.

"Young man," she said. "You are presently embarked on a journey. You will be travelling under a foreign flag," She looked at Joseph and asked, - "Am I correct?"

Joseph kept looking at her. "Yes, you are correct, I'll be leaving shortly for Windsor, Ontario and I will be travelling through the United States," he replied.

At the same time he thought to himself,- "She is right. How did she know? - She had never seen me before - She must possess some magic powers."

The lady peeked into the tea cup again and scrutinized it further. She looked at Joseph again and said:-

"You are going in search of employment and you will find work. It will not be the kind of work you'll like, but you appear to be a rugged individual and a survivor, and you'll work at whatever you get until something better comes along. I see friends or relatives offering you help and in close relationship and harmony with you. I cannot foresee any immediate sickness or bad luck in your future. According to your tea leaves you will do very well. Do you have any questions?"

"No, I don't - thank you very much," and with that Joseph got up and walked back to the bus depot.

He still had a short time to wait, but the bus arrived on time from Calgary and would leave on time for Winnipeg, Fargo, Minneapolis/St.Paul, Chicago, Detroit, and finally Windsor. Four o'clock in the afternoon came and the boarding call was announced. Joseph took a window seat in the center of the bus. He had checked his larger suitcase and placed the cloth bag containing the lunch his mother packed for him, in the overhead storage place. They departed on time and being his first ride on a bus, he thought it rode quite smoothly.

No other passenger sat beside him and for a long time he set alone, and in a pensive mood, simply viewing the passing landscape and events through his window. He thought about Suzanne, his girl friend and he felt content that he had been able to spend a Sunday afternoon in her company and to tell her that he loved her. He meditated on what the tea cup reader had told him. She didn't mention anything about his love relationship with Suzanne, and he didn't ask her

LIFE'S DETOURS

about it for fear her reading might have been negative. He thought about his mother and the horoscope predictions she had obtained for him. He was pondering two alternative questions in his mind.

"Am I going in search of something better, or am I escaping from something that held no real hope?"

Suzanne was still his girl friend and he admired and loved her, but he wasn't sure whether she loved him in return to the same degree. There were other young men his age paying attention and courting her as well, and some had jobs and could offer her more than he could. He would write to her. Hopefully, he would land a good job and eventually he could prove to her that he was equal to or better than some of her other suitors. He would come back with money, dressed in good clothes and propose marriage to her. He tried to think big. He remembered reading a quotation written or stated by a certain William James which said:- "The most important thing in life is to live for something greater than life."

"What else can be greater than life?" Joseph asked himself. He was tormenting his brain, trying to get a satisfying meaning out of this saying.

"If I could only locate a good job," he fancied, "I would try to help my parents too. They were hit by `hard times' and the depression and I'm sure they would have tried to do better for us children, but they just couldn't afford it. Sometimes, I think my dad could have been in a better financial position, but he was not a very good manager and too much a man of this world. He loved his bottle and good times. I'm going to do better and Suzanne is my sweetheart and I'd like to win her and have her for my life-time companion."

The depression had left with Joseph a legacy of fear, but also a desire for the acquisition of property and security.

"What else can be greater than life?" this question popped up again in Joseph's mind. "I suppose, it's putting the best effort to live this life well; to be of help to others; to live with someone you love; to have children of your own; to leave this world a better place then when you found it, and to earn your way to eternal life with your Maker, would be the sum total of that saying," he concluded.

The journey took fifty-four hours. The bus would make stops of 20 to 30 minutes, at two to three hour intervals. Joseph would remove the shoes off his feet during the driving periods, recline his seat as far as possible and catch some sleep. His hunger would be satisfied with the roast chicken and buns his mother had packed for him. He spent a few cents on soft drinks to quench his thirst. A bottle of Coca-Cola would cost five cents or ten cents if you took the bottle with you.

The arrival in Detroit was about ten o'clock in the morning, and after a thirty minute stop at the bus depot, the bus driver announced that we would proceed through the tunnel linking Detroit and Windsor. We were to prepare ourselves for the stop which would be at the Canadian Customs in Windsor, Canada. This exercise did not take as long as Joseph had anticipated. He was asked where he was born, where he was coming from, where he was going to and for what reason.

"I'm going in search of employment and work," he boldly stated.

The Immigration officials on both the American and Canadian side, merely looked at Joseph's birth certificate and signalled him to move on. They did not order him to open his older and somewhat battered suitcase. The last stop for Joseph was the Windsor bus depot. Joseph had written his cousin Nicholas advising him about his time of arrival and expected to have him meet the bus. It was noon, and Nicholas was at work in the Chrysler factory.

Waiting for him at the bus depot instead, was a step brother to Nicholas whose name was Pete Koster. Pete and Joseph were old acquaintances. They had attended the same public school back west in Saskatchewan but had not seen each other for six or seven years. Pete and Nicholas were step brothers coming from the same mother, and Pete was boarding at his brother's place. After a handshake and a few exchange of words, Peter drove Joseph from the bus depot to the Nicholas' home in his own car.

Nicholas was married to Marianne, a young girl from the West, who had been a very good friend of Joseph's mother Eugenia. They had two children, a boy and a girl, and he owned his own home. The home had three bedrooms upstairs and a semi-finished basement, which also provided some living accommodation. The home was not finished completely on the outside and Nicholas would work his week-ends on finishing the construction, landscaping and the completion of the garage.

That evening after Nicholas came home from his work shift they talked about Joseph's trip, his arrival and surprises, and they asked questions about the people and places out West that were also known to them. Nicholas and Marianne assured Joseph that he was welcome to stay with them and that it would be no problem. They had discussed Joseph's staying with them prior to his arrival and they agreed that Joseph would share the same bedroom alloted to Pete.

"You can stay with us, as long as you want to, but after you find employment, we will ask you to pay us $2.50 per week for the room and laundry and if you would like to have your meals included, that will cost you $10.00 per week. But, only after you find employment," Marianne stated.

Joseph willingly agreed because as he found out later, his cousins

LIFE'S DETOURS

were giving him a good deal. The very next day, Joseph set his sights on finding employment of some kind. The mornings were usually taken by getting up at the crack of dawn and walking to the main factory gates in search of employment. The big automakers in Windsor were Ford's of Canada and Chrysler Corporation. Then there were a goodly number of small jobber factories and foundaries, that manufactured automobile parts and accessories for the assembly plants. There were jobs to be had in the city and county governments and in the service industries.

Joseph sat and thought to himself, -"What would I like to do, - where and how should I begin?"

There was also much unemployment and many people in search of jobs.

Each morning, he would rise up early and go one morning to the Chrysler main gate and another morning to the Ford main gate. The idea was to get there early enough so that he would be near the front, if not the first in line. The hiring procedure was done by the respective Employment Officer, who came to the main gate and strictly on the basis of "eye contact," he would point out to people saying:-

"You, you, you and you," until he recruited the required number. Then he would say to them - "follow me" and to the rest of the men standing there, sometimes as many as two hundred, he would say - "Thank you, come again to-morrow, you might have better luck," and walk away.

Doing this day after day was no fun. Joseph would pick up the Employment Ad section of the newspaper, look over the advertisements and walk to one or two agencies who were looking for help to apply for work. There were times when he would get an immediate interview and other times, simply left a filled in application form with his cousin's phone number for contact. He never received any phone calls and was becoming quite impatient.

Ten days had gone by and no work. His own $22.00 was dwindling away, although he was very careful with his money. He had paid $4.75 for a new pair of walking shoes and he purchased a few other personal items. Pete Koster was working as a waiter in a Greek-owned restaurant. He was earning $22.00 per week, was the owner of a car and also had two or three suits hanging in his closet and a number of shirts. In Joseph's judgement he was doing pretty well. Another cousin, Victor Cozma, from one of Joseph's aunts who was his father's sister, was working full time in the Ford factory and his net take home pay was $45.00 per week. His cousin Nicholas was earning as much as $60.00 per week in Chrysler, but that included some overtime.

Joseph had many more cousins and friends in Windsor. They had migrated to Windsor from other parts of the West, also due to the hardship conditions caused by the depression. All of them were Canadian born, but of Romanian parentage. They sort of huddled together by having purchased their homes in close proximity, and were in a cultural and social setting somewhat similar to that enjoyed on their farms. All of them had employment of one sort or another, but the ones considered to be better off, were those employed in the automobile factories or allied industries. They had purchased homes on installment payments, driving cars, were well dressed and some even had purchased fishing boats, which was considered a luxury and a mark of affluence.

Their living standard was several levels higher than those sustained by the relatives they had left behind in Saskatchewan. Sunday afternoons during the summer months, were spent at family and friends get-to-gethers and "beer picnics" at a farm owned by a Romanian Canadian in rural Essex County. The farmer had built a band stand, a platform for dancing, a set of bleachers for watching a ball game, and a shed with a stand for dispensing soft drinks, beer, hot-dogs and hamburgers. There was a fifty cent admission charge to pay for the use of the grounds, while the food and drinks were paid for individually according to consumption. Joseph would attend these parties and picnics, which enabled him to become acquainted with more people. He would allow everyone to believe that he was happy and enjoying himself, but deep inside he was both unhappy and insecure.

In response to an ad which appeared in the newspaper, after two weeks, he was able to obtain employment as a dishwasher in a restaurant situated at the main gate to the Ford factory on Drouillard Road. He would commence working immediately. His work hours were from midnight to eight o'clock in the morning, seven days a week. His wages were one dollar per eight hour shift, plus two meals each day. His work consisted of washing dishes, scouring pots and pans, washing floors, windows and counters, cleaning the refrigerators and stoves and anything else the night chef might order him to do, such as peeling potatoes.

Joseph had been working six months and had bought himself a bicycle for getting to and from work, a new suit, and a couple of shirts, and he was current in his payments of $2.50 per week for his room and laundry to his cousin. In addition, he had saved $65.00 in cash and had given them to his cousin's wife Marianne to safekeep for him.

Then a letter came from his dad at home.

"Joseph, can you send us enough money to enable us to purchase four barrels of tractor fuel, in order to get our crop planted. I had money to take care of planting the spring crop, but your mother took ill

LIFE'S DETOURS

and she had to have a gall-bladder operation and our funds went for medical expenses for her. I simply don't know where else to turn for financial help. Please help us if you can," the letter read.

Joseph liked his dad in so many ways and loved him, but at times because of his behavior he despised him, sometimes openly and sometime secretly. However, Joseph had a profound attachment to the family and especially to his mother. He read the letter and tears welled in his eyes as he reflected on what he should do.

"I know that four barrels of tractor fuel costs forty dollars and I have sixty five dollars saved. I'm going to send dad sixty dollars to get his spring crop in and I hope that mother is okay," he said to himself.

He explained his situation to Marianne, and asked her for his money. Then he sat down and wrote his parents a letter, and enclosed a postal money order for sixty dollars and mailed the letter "registered" to be sure they receive it.

Joseph kept working as a dishwasher in the restaurant, but he knew that wasn't what he wanted to do for the rest of his life. He was saving every penny he could always with the thought in mind, that some day an opportunity may come along and he wanted to be able to take advantage of it. Theater admission to daytime movies would cost 15 cents and he had rationed himself to two movies a week. There was a daily door delivery of the newspaper, which didn't cost him anything because his cousin was a subscriber, He read the newspaper cover to cover.

Twice during the entire nine month period that Joseph stayed in Windsor, he went across the river to Detroit with Peter Koster to visit with some of Pete's relatives. On one occasion they stopped to attend a burlesque show. It was the first time in his life, that Jospeh had seen naked women and a "strip-tease" show. Both Pete and Joseph had purchased the lower priced tickets, therefore they were seated in the rear seats of the theater and did not have the best view of the stage. At intermission time when the lights went on, from his vantage point, Joseph was surprised by the number of bald heads that he saw in an audience made up entirely of men. He quickly deduced that many older adult males liked to see naked women. Joseph also thought they were attractive and lustful.

A letter came from home. It was written by his mother. She thanked him for sending them the money, talked about his dad, brothers and sister and concluded as usual with her motherly expression of love and concern for Joseph's welfare. Joseph was not happy. His work was boring, tedious, and required little or no use of his mental ability. He was learning nothing that was new or helpful.

When his friends and relatives were sleeping, he would be

working. His pay was increased after six months to one dollar and twenty-five cents for an eight hour shift and he had taken only three Sundays off in nine months. His peers were working only a forty hour week,- they were off on Saturdays and Sundays and were earning more money. He thought about his girl friend Suzanne out West. He would write to her and she would reply - but the situation was not conducive to making any firm commitments, and Joseph felt, that unless the situation would change he would lose her.

Once in a while Joseph would receive a note from his sister Virginia who would fill him in on the latest events and gossip, as well as any conversation she may have had with Suzanne. Receipt of good news and comments from home and from his sister filled Joseph's days with delight and renewed his faith and hope that better times were in the offing. Somehow things would improve.

The days dragged on, the year was 1939 and September came along with the news that Britain had declared war on Hitler's Germany. At first Joseph never gave this news much thought. There was speculation in the newspapers as to what Canada's role would be in this situation. As a former British colony would Canada officially take Britain's side and become a war declarant against Germany. It was becoming clear that Canada would mobilize it's industries and it's resources to produce both armaments and food and support Britain. There was a growing feeling in defending the cause of obtaining freedom in Europe for those countries that Hitler and his armies had overrun. The Canadian Government announced the formation of a Volunteer Military Force to fight on Britain's side. It also began the expansion of its military foundation, which included the full development of army, navy and airforce training bases. There was no talk of mobilizing manpower other than by the volunteer method. Joseph was not interested in any aspect of the war and least of all in volunteering for military service.

"What the hell has Canada done for me, and last of all Britain? Depression, hard times, no money, no jobs, no future - and now, jump at the opportunity to get hold of a gun and march off to shoot some innocent bastard, who is probably forced into the army and the war against his will. The International Cartels and big money boys are at it again. And all of this, in the name of patriotism and the defense of freedom. Freedom to go hungry, freedom to be without a good job, I'm not volunteering, because in the first place I don't believe in war and in killing, and secondly how do the christian nations square their belief in God, when one of the ten commandments specifically says, `Thou shalt not kill.' In this war, I'm going to be a conscientious objector," and with those thoughts Joseph justified his own position and plodded along in

LIFE'S DETOURS

daily life.

His cousin Victor Cozma received a telegram from Timmins, Ontario where his parents were living. The telegram was from his mother, Joseph's aunt and it was brief.

"Your father passed away last night - funeral will be on tuesday, try to come."

Victor had his own car. He phoned Joseph and asked him if he cared to go along as a companion, to attend the funeral and to visit the Cozma family. There were some members of the Cozma family that Joseph had actually never met. He asked the restaurant owner for one week vacation, which the owner refused to grant. He then requested time off for one week without pay which the owner reluctantly approved. Timmins was located about 710 miles to the north of Windsor, in the same province.

It was renowned as a mining center primarily for gold, but other metals such as nickel and copper were also being mined. Joseph had heard that the mining industry was doing more hiring and while the wages paid were not as high as in the automotive industry, the jobs once acquired were far more stable and without seasonal lay-offs. He decided to go along, see the country, meet the new relatives, and explore the possibility of obtaining better employment.

That weekend Joseph packed all his worldly belongings in his suitcase. He didn't have very much. He had informed Nicholas and Marianne Acker that he was going to attend the funeral of Victor's father and that he would return by the coming weekend. Very early on Sunday morning, Victor came by with his car, picked Joseph up and they departed. Their objective was to drive the seven hundred miles non-stop and arrive there late that evening.

Chapter 7

FOCUS ON EMPLOYMENT

At nine o'clock that Sunday morning Victor and Joseph stopped to refuel the car, and have coffee at a service station on the outskirts of Toronto. They had travelled 260 miles. Joseph was fascinated by the good roads as compared to Western Canada. He was captivated by the population density, nice farms, and the stacks pouring rich black smoke from the factories located in most towns along the way. The next stop on the trip would be North Bay a distance of 210 miles.

"That's where we're going to stop for our noon day meal," Victor said.

"It's okay by me," Joseph replied.

The car zipped right along on that portion of the trip, and the scenery had changed from the settled and developed areas, to forests, rocks, and lakes. They would drive through the odd little hamlet, where there was very little more than a general store, a post office, and a railway station. They would stop periodically to satisfy their thirst with a cold soft drink, and while doing so, Joseph asked some residents,-

"What do you do for a living here?"

"Some of us work on the railroad, some of us in lumbering, some are trappers and some work in mining," they replied, kind of in unison. Joseph could see a measure of contentment in their rugged faces.

At one fifteen that afternoon Joseph and Victor were seated at a restaurant in the city of North Bay enjoying their noon-day meal. North Bay was a mining town, but of more strategic importance was its location, since all of the railroad lines and motor highways leading to Western Canada, channelled themselves through this city at the northern tip of the Great Lakes.

Joseph and Victor still had another 240 miles to drive to make Timmins that afternoon. Victor had resided in Timmins, but a divorce

LIFE'S DETOURS

and separation from his wife caused him to move to Windsor and seek employment in the automotive factories. Joseph asked Victor many questions about work in the mines, his divorce and the conversation also reviewed early recollections that Victor had about life on their prairie farm.

It was a beautiful August afternoon and the good road coupled to the passing scenery, made the hours and the miles pass quickly. At six o'clock that evening Victor drove his car into the yard of his parent's home in Timmins.

The reception received by Victor and Joseph consisted of embraces and kisses. For Joseph it was an exhilarating moment because he was meeting for the first time members of the Cozma family, who were his cousins and whom he had never seen before.

The funeral of Myron Cozma his uncle, was held the following Tuesday in accordance with family tradition and the Orthodox rites. For a moment Joseph was reminded of his grandfather's funeral. Myron was an immigrant from Romania, an original pioneer who had homesteaded in Saskatchewan. He died after a lengthy illness and bout with asthma at the age of 73. He was a heavy smoker. There was an air of grieving and sorrow for Myron's death by the family members. However, Joseph at his age, inwardly felt that anyone having lived 73 years had to be realistic and accept death as a part of the cycle of life.

After the funeral, Joseph got to know his cousin Peter who was of the same age. His sister Leanna, who was a beautiful little damsel of fifteen and his aunt Maria who treated him as if he were one of her own children. In addition, Joseph had a cousin Dorothy who came to Timmins at the invitation of her boy friend Wayne, and soon after her arrival they married. Wayne was working as a bartender in the Kingston Hotel at the time, but later transferred to the Three Star hotel. They were living in a two-bedroom basement suite of another cousin, also known to Joseph. This quick connection to so many relatives gave him a high degree of comfort.

During the two remaining days prior to his return to Windsor, Joseph explored the possibility of obtaining employment in Timmins at wages and conditions that would be superior to what he had in Windsor. Everyone assured him that finding employment would be no problem. At that time, gold mining in the Porcupine basin was in full operation. The Timmins area was noted for having an annual output of 1,000,000 ounces of gold, which was 25% of Canada's total gold production. It was situated in a rich mining area in the Pre-Cambrian shield of Northern Ontario. This shield held the abundant auriferous quartz rock from which the gold was mined.

His cousins filled him in on wages, working conditions, and

LIFE'S DETOURS

living in general in this mining city of about 22,000 people. Everyone appeared to be well housed, well dressed, well fed, drove an automobile and unlike Windsor nobody spoke of unemployment. Wayne, his cousin by marriage said to him:-

"Joseph, we have a sizeable Romanian-Canadian community here. We have an Orthodox church and a social hall. We have a young people's group in which you would be interested, and there are some exceptionally good looking girls in the group. We have four hotel owners who are Romanians and I'm sure that if you decided to remain in Timmins, you would have no problem obtaining employment at better wages and working conditions than you are presently having in Windsor."

"Sounds good to me," Joseph thought. He had two days to think about it.

"Should I remain in Timmins and seek new employment or should I return to Windsor at those miserly wages and slug it out at the mid-night shift in that restaurant in the hope that I might land something better? I think I'll take a chance and remain. Surely, it can't be any worse."

He advised his cousin Victor, that he was not going back to Windsor, and asked him to convey this message to Nicholas and Marianne Acker, and also to Mr. Nicolapolous the Greek owner of the restaurant he had worked in.

Joseph moved in and became a boarder with Wayne and Dorothy Polymer. He shared a bedroom with his cousin George Acker, who had arrived in Timmins a short time before and was working as a miner in the Paymaster Gold Mines.

Through Wayne's influence, a week later Joseph was working in the Three Star Hotel as a waiter in the beer parlor. The starting wages were $22.00 per week, and when coupled to tips that averaged about $10.00 per week, produced a weekly income far superior to what he was earning in Windsor.

His job consisted of mopping the floors in the men's section of the beer parlors, washing tables, chairs and ash trays, cleaning the bathrooms, and serving the beer drinkers with their orders. He had to learn how to manipulate a tray containing full glasses and bottles of beer, watch for empties and walk in between the various tables and take orders. It was a job that kept a waiter continuously on his feet from nine o'clock in the morning to midnight, six days a week, and this was tiring even for a young man of twenty-one.

It was the kind of a job that placed Joseph in a position to meet miners. There were two mine superintendents and three shift bosses whom Joseph served, particularly on Saturday nights when they came

LIFE'S DETOURS

in to spend a few hours in the company of their wives. Joseph made sure he gave them special attention and service and the tips they left for the waiter were always better.

"What are the possibilities for me to get a job as a miner?" Joseph asked Jim Hobbs, the mine superintendent at the Nabob Gold mines.

"Are you interested in working in an underground tunnel, and getting those lily white hands of yours soiled?" Jim Hobbs retorted.

"I'll do anything to make more money," Joseph replied."I was born and raised on a farm and I've been exposed to hard work and dirty hands - I can work alongside and keep up with the best of them," Joseph said, as he picked up some empty glasses from Hobb's table, emptied the ash tray, and wiped the ash tray and the table clean again.

"All right, I'll tell you what! On your next day off come to the mine office, get your physical examination by our doctor, and if he says you're fit for underground work, you've got a job," Jim Hobbs said, as he helped his wife fix her fur stole, left a fifty cent tip on the table and walked out of the beer parlor.

Joseph finished cleaning the table, re-arranged the chairs, all the while sheltering a feeling of accomplishment for having talked to Mr. Hobbs.

"My working time will be reduced from 12 to 13 hours per day and a six day week, to 8 to 10 hours and a five day week. My wages would increase from $22.00 per week to about $30.00 per week and more if some overtime were involved. If the job becomes permanent I could eventually bring Suzanne here from the west - get married and settle down. It would be a victory for me to get away from serving late night drunks and these long hours," Joseph thought to himself.

He broke the news to Wayne and Dorothy the next morning at breakfast, who were pleased to learn that he was able to obtain a job to his liking. Wayne himself, was now the bar room manager and making wages of about $40 per week. This was comparable to what most miners were earning. However, Wayne did not expose himself to mine dust which caused many a miner to suffer from silicosis, and for this he was quite content with the job he had.

Joseph was not concerned about silicosis. He had already made up his mind that he would work, save his money and in a few years he would be in business. His goal was to own a corner grocery store, where he and Suzanne could work together. This was also Joseph's day off, so he hopped on the bus and went to the Nabob Mine office for his interview and physical exam. Everything went Joseph's way and the following Monday, found him in miner's work clothes.

He wore a hard hat carrying a miner's lamp on his head, a lunch bucket in his hand and on the cage with eight other men and Ben Benik his shift boss, were being lowered swiftly by elevator down the mine shaft to the one thousand foot underground level.

Here Joseph was introduced to his mining partner, who was of French Canadian descent and whose name was Charles "Chuck" Lacroix. Chuck was an experienced miner and operated the pressurized air drilling machine, while Joseph was assigned to be his helper. He took a few moments to tell Joseph that his job would consist of helping him set up the machine ready for drilling.

"You must be nimble with the chuck wrench in loosening these bolts on the drilling machine. Then you must add the required length of drill bit and tighten back the bolts in readiness for continued drilling," Lacroix said, as he pointed to the pile of drill bits and the drilling machine. He continued,- "Our job is to drill about 18 holes, each eight feet deep in the face of this tunnel drift. We will then have to fill these holes with properly fused dynamite, in readiness for blasting by the end of our eight hour shift. Comprendre?"

"If you follow what I tell you, you will learn as you go along on your job. It's not easy work. It's wet, messy, and lots of noise made by the drilling machine. In one 8 hour shift we must load on cars the broken rock from the previous night's blast, drill all the required holes, tamp them in with properly fused dynamite, light the fuses and execute the blast before the day's shift is over. In all of this work, safety is important," Chuck instructed Joseph

The days and the weeks that followed found Joseph going to work five days a week. Each shift he would put on his miner's hat and clothes, join Chuck Lacroix and descend to the same underground level. Here, they would hose down the working area with pressurized water and scale down with scale bars any loose rock to ensure a safe working place. Every day consisted of loading by hand shovel, the rock from the previous shift's blast into the empty rail cars. This exercise was called "mucking." The empty rail cars would be coveniently placed on the underground spur tracks by the night shift. The cars loaded with muck would be pushed on the rails by a "railman," with a motorized battery driven engine to the mine shaft. The loaded cars would be sequentially lifted by the elevating cage to the surface for unloading, grinding and smeltering.

Once the muck was loaded and the area cleared, the drilling machine would be positioned and the drilling of the eighteen holes to a depth of eight feet in the face of the drift would commence. Joseph observed that this operation required some skill, since the center three holes had to be drilled in the form of a pyramidic cone. The holes were in the form of a triangle on the face of the drilling area. They were pinpointed to be about 18 inches apart and had to be drilled at an angle,

LIFE'S DETOURS

so that they would meet with each other at the eight foot depth.

These were called the "blast start" holes and were critical for a successful blast. The shortest fuses were specifically inserted in these holes, in order to be the first to blast off and knock out the core or center of the pre-determined blast. The remaining holes would then follow with the bottom three holes left to the last. These last holes would lift the entire blast and spread it back into the drift, making for easier shovel loading the next day. After the holes were drilled, the fuses would be pushed into them and dynamite sticks tamped in. Chuck and Joseph would then dismantle the drilling machine and remove it from the scene. They would lay down steel plates, about 3/16" in thickness and about 2 1/2'x 4' in size, to cover an area that would take up the spread from the blast. These pre-laid steel plates made it easy to run the shovel under the blasted ore and made for quicker and easier mucking.

Finally, the fuses were lit and Chuck and Joseph hurried out of the blast area to a safety zone area. They would sit quietly waiting for the blasts to go off. Each detonation had to be counted to ensure that all the drilled holes had exploded, thus making the area safe to enter on the next day's shift.

It didn't take long for Joseph to become an old hand at mining and at his particular job as a machine man's helper. He began to enjoy life somewhat more. With the added income, he had added two more suits to his wardrobe, a top coat, shirts and underwear, leather gloves and a "homberg" hat.

Together with his cousin George, they took studio photos and proudly sent them back to their respective families in Saskatchewan. They wanted to indicate the degree of prosperity they were enjoying. Joseph was also hoping that his girl friend Suzanne would see the photo and maintain her interested in him.

They had joined a young people's club which existed at the St. Mary's Orthodox Church Hall and were beginning to tie links of friendship with other young people. The social agenda consisted of singing in the church choir, Friday night dances and other social evenings, as well as invitations to private homes.

They had invitations to those homes belonging to families of Romanian descent who had daughters ranging in age from eighteen to twenty. Joseph was intelligent, handsome and now that he had a job, was considered a good catch for any young female. He took advantage of that status and enjoyed the company of a number of the local girls, but secretly inside he yearned for Suzanne his childhood sweet-heart from out West.

What he didn't like about his new mining job was the distance he had to travel to and from work. This added two to three extra hours to his working day. The Hollinger Gold mines were within walking distance of Wayne's apartment, and Joseph knew he had a connection in that mine through Alex Connor, his cousin by marriage who was a long time employee of that mine.

"I have six months of mining experience and I wonder, if I talked to Alex if he knew of a way in which I could get hired at that mine," Joseph thought to himself.

The opportunity soon presented itself when he was invited for a Sunday evening dinner to Alex's home. Here he met his wife Anne and the three small boys that made up their family. Alex and Anne had moved to Timmins from the West as well. Joseph's parents Richard and Eugenia Acker had stood up as best-man and matron of honor for Alex and Anne when they were married in Saskatchewan, and this together with him being a first cousin with Anne made the bond between Joseph and the Connors a bit tighter.

The dinner and after dinner chat included talk about the West, it's people and places that were known to both Joseph and the Connors. Finally, the talk got around to mining, the labor unions, the mines and their working conditions. Alex had a surface job in the Hollinger Gold Mines. He worked as an engineer in their machine and blacksmithing shop. He was a shop steward and on the union executive committee and he knew many of the administrative people by name.

"What possibility is there for me to obtain a job with the Hollinger Gold Mines?" Joseph asked Alex.

"The opportunities are there," Alex replied. "I was talking to Mr. King the personnel and employment manager and he told me they were hiring men every day. What you should do if you are interested, is go to their employment office and fill in an application. You have some mining experience, which will serve you well, but I believe you should apply for a surface job like I have. It is safer than underground and you will not be susceptible to `miner's lung.' You may use my name as a reference."

"I'm very grateful Alex, for your suggestions and for your willingness to assist me in obtaining a job at Hollinger."

Joseph knew that it is one of Canada's largest gold mines, so he was delighted to have an opportunity to work for them.

"Please bring me an application form. I'll complete it, then if you will, you can take it to the employment manager's office for their consideration. I hate to lose a day's pay in order to get this done," Joseph said.

Alex agreed to Joseph's request and within a matter of two days this exercise was accomplished.

LIFE'S DETOURS

"I've had a chance to talk to Norm King, the employment manager again, and he sort of hinted that a surface job was in the cards for you," Alex stated. "You'll be hearing from them shortly."

The following week Joseph had a call for an interview at the Hollinger employment office. He took a day off from the Nabob Mines and attended to this request.

"Is Mr. Joseph Acker in the crowd?" one of the secretaries called. Joseph rose to his feet with a smile and walked up to her, as she waved him to come forward.

"Mr.Norman King, our employment manager wishes to talk to you," she said as she led Joseph into his office.

"Good morning, Mr. Acker, I'm so glad to see you, have a chair. Would you like a cup of coffee?" Mr. King asked as he had risen from his chair to shake Joseph's hand.

Joseph found himself in an elegant office and unaccustomed to being treated with such courtesy, he was somewhat confused and at a loss for words.

"Thank you very much," he replied as he sat down on the chair offered to him. "A cup of coffee would be fine, just make it black."

Mr. King eyed Joseph with a degree of curiosity and began the conversation.

"You know," he said."Way back before the depression, I was a teller in the Canadian Bank of Commerce in Truax, Saskatchewan, and I knew your grandfather, Edward Acker, your father Richard and your uncle Dan. I did business with them and they were good clients of the bank. Then the depression came, the bank closed down, I was laid off and I came to Timmins in search of employment. I started off in this mine's office as an accountant, but through the process of attrition, promotion, and some extra curricular study and dedication, I have worked my way to become this company's employment and personnel manager."

Joseph listened intensely to a man, who it seemed to him had a run of bad luck but picked himself up and made good.

"Well, Mr. King, our folks stayed with the farm, and things were not much better when I left there two years ago. My desire to finish high school remained unfulfilled, because my parents were simply unable to afford the cost. My dad writes and says that the prices of farm products have improved, but as you know, the debt load became heavier due to the unpaid and accumulated interest on the loans. As a matter of fact, I've had to assist them financially at one sowing season with the planting of the crop," Joseph said.

The conversation lasted for a good half-hour. Mr. King was also a musician and played the saxophone. He had played at many of the public school dances and was acquainted with the names of most of the families who were living in the area Joseph came from. Finally he looked at Joseph and said.

"Mr. Acker, we will give you surface employment at this mine. I know that coming from the farm you are acquainted with machinery. These machines are somewhat different, but you will soon learn to operate and maintain them. You will report to Surface Depot No.2 the day after to-morrow. Before you leave here today, you will complete all of your required documentation and receive your identification badge. Welcome on board with the Hollinger Gold mines. I hope you will like working with us," Mr. King stated as he turned Joseph over to his secretary, with instructions to facilitate the documentation and to issue the badge. They shook hands again and parted.

Joseph felt like a million after this interview. The secretary who took his employment particulars looked at him and asked.

"Does Mr. King know you personally? - he seldom treats new employees with the courtesy he extended you!

"Well, he knew my grandfather and knows my parents. He once lived and worked in the same area I come from, so we had a few things in common to talk about," Joseph responded.

Two days later, Joseph reported to Surface Depot No.2, where his foreman Ralph Kelly was waiting to offer him his work assignment together with a series of instructions. He paired Joseph with Jean Roberge, an elderly man of French Canadian lineage. Jean was extremely good at cursing and Joseph had taken French as one of the high school subjects, but had not read or heard any of words that Jean would sometimes utter. Their first day's work consisted of unloading a carload of timbers that were to be used for underground mine props. It was the kind of work that called for lots of muscle and very little brain power.

"Where are the machines, Mr. King talked about, and when will I be exposed to them," Joseph thought as he daily confronted the assigned manual labor.

It was an all day shift work, five days per week which commenced at 08:00 a.m. and terminated at 4:30 p.m. The work consisted of loading and unloading freight cars coming in with mine supplies. The sorting and arranging of the supply inventory in the various sections of the warehouse. There was grass and weeds to cut that the mechanical mowers would miss in tight corners and close to the buildings. There was the keeping of the surface rail track in good condition, and filling in orders with supplies ordered by the underground miners. There was never an idle moment except for the 30 minute lunch break.

LIFE'S DETOURS

Joseph now found himself with ample time on his hands. He would be home daily by 5:00 p.m. and his evenings were free and long. He would read the daily newspaper, write letters and listen to the radio. Television had not yet arrived on the scene. Friday nights were usually social evenings at the church hall. Saturdays were days when one would dress up and go downtown to do some shopping. Joseph would eventually wind up in one of the hotel beer parlors where a few hours would be passed in drinking beer, visiting and comparing notes with other young men, who were miners and who also came from the West.

These beer parties would get pretty boisterous, but would always break up by the evening meal time. The chatter would include talk about the kind of job each one would be doing in their respective mine areas, latest news from home, upcoming parties or dances, who was going around or courting with whom, present or future plans, mine accidents if any, the latest jokes and other small talk. It was really "camaraderie day."

It was a kind of a peer group, with each member of this group having a status level, based on the kind of work he performed at the mine and the size of his weekly pay check. Joseph was considered to be a lucky guy to have been able to obtain a surface job.

"Whose leg did you have to pull, in order to get yourself employed on the surface at Hollinger?" Joseph was asked by a member of his peer group.

"Nobody's leg guys. I just happened to be lucky," Joseph said.

Then he went on to explain the episode with regards to Mr. King, the employment manager at the mine and the fact that he knew the Acker family from his days in the West.

Victor Short, one of the young men in the group piped up and said:- "Joseph you can have the surface job. It's okay, you're always working in fresh air and no danger of silicosis, but you'll never make any money at it. I've got an underground job. I'm a machine man, and together with my partner we work on contract with the mine. In other words, we are assured of our basic wages, then if the volume of ore we mine and muck out exceeds a certain tonnage during a monthly pay period, we receive a bonus. Last month my bonus checque alone was $750.00. I don't intend to be a miner all my life. As soon as I can put together enough cash to buy me a good farm, I'm a gonner back West. Farming is the life for me."

This set Joseph to thinking. Even the surface job at the mine was not what he really wanted to do for the rest of his life, but to do anything else required money. Money which he didn't have. Northern Ontario's climate consisted of extreme heat during the months of June, July and August and extreme cold in the winter months. To cope with this climate, he had to furnish himself with spring and summer, as well as fall and winter work clothing. The miners working underground did not require seasonal work clothing. But, his real anxiety rested on his low daily wages of $4.65, and for his immediate desire to save enough to offer Suzanne a marriage proposal and to bring her to Timmins and marry him.

He had made up his mind to seek an interview with Mr. King and to request a transfer from surface to underground. The interview was arranged and granted.

"Mr. King, I've been working at this surface job for six months, and while I enjoy it - I want to be truthful with you and tell you that I'd like to earn more money and to do so, the underground appears to be the place to find it. If it would be possible, I'd like a transfer to the underground and I'd like to work particularly with someone who is a contract miner. I've heard that the mine offers such contracts and I'm prepared to work hard."

"Okay Joseph," Mr. King said. "We'll respect your request and you can start working underground beginning with your next shift. I'll take care of the documentation. There aren't too many people that were given the opportunity to work on the surface, but you were, and to go underground is your prerogative. Check with the front office to see which shift boss, mine shaft and level you're to report to. Good luck."

"Thank you, Mr. King," Joseph said. "I'm sorry if I caused you any inconvenience, but really sir, I'm planning to get married and I'm in need of earning more money. This is the reason for my request."

Mr. King paused for a moment,- "Whose the lucky girl?" he asked.

"She's a girl from down West. Her name is Suzanne Parker, you might know the family," Joseph replied.

"Parker, Parker, yes, I think I do remember the name. Good for you! Let me know when the wedding reception will be held," Mr. King said as he shook Joseph's hand and departed.

Joseph reported to Shaft No. 3 one half hour early. He changed from street clothes to miner's garb. He was given a hard hat with a miner's light again. He was cautioned about the mines safety measures, and about the consequences of hygrading (the act of stealing gold from the mine). He was then introduced to Larry Schaefer, the shift boss supervising the mining activity at the 6,000 foot level below surface at this Shaft, and together they were quickly and quietly lowered by the elevator cage to that level.

"Ever worked in a mine before?" Schaefer asked.

"Yes sir, six months in the Nabob mine, at the 1,000 foot level - machine man's helper," Joseph replied.

LIFE'S DETOURS

"You'll be a machine man's helper here also. You'll be working with one of our best mine contractors. He's been with Hollinger for more than twenty years. He's a Finlander and his name is Henry Skala, very good man. You'll be working in a "stope" above this level," Schaefer informed Joseph.

They began walking through the mine drift to where Henry would be located.

"Pardon me sir," Joseph interjected. "Tell me what is a stope? I've worked in the Nabob mine for six months, but can't recall any reference to a stope,"

"A stope is an excavation from which gold ore is removed in a series of horizontal steps between underground mine levels. In other words, if we must follow a vein containing gold in a vertical direction from this level, we do it by developing a stope. The ore is removed and the space is backfilled with sand or crushed rock that has no mineral value. You'll see pretty soon," Schaefer said.

They arrived at a spot in the drift, that had a ladder and the shift boss began to climb, ordering Joseph to follow him. They climbed a series of twelve foot ladders from one landing to another, until they finally popped their heads into the work area. They looked like gophers popping their heads out of a gopher hole. They were about 100 feet above the 6,000 foot drift level below. They saw Henry's light. He was busy hosing down the face of the stope with pressurized water.

"Good morning Hank," Schaefer said. "How does it look?"

"Good morning, Henry replied. "It looks okay, still got good quartz here, the analysis should be good."

"Hank, this is Joseph, Joseph Acker, he will be your new machine helper and partner. He looks to be a sturdy and rugged young fellow and should make a good miner. I hope you two guys will get along and make good bonuses."

"Bonus," was the word Joseph wanted to hear and at last it came out. "I must be grateful to Mr. King, I'm sure it is his influence that brought me to this miner and to this level."

Mr. Schaefer departed, after which Joseph and Henry took a few more minutes to chat and acquaint themselves with each other. Contract mining called for full use of your working time, if you wanted to receive a bonus and Henry lost no time in telling Joseph what to do. Joseph was not afraid of work. He reminded himself of his mother, the potato rows and the garden. He pitched right in and wanted to convince Henry, that he was a good machine man's helper and a good worker. Henry on the other hand was glad to see that he had a good worker and partner.

It was hard work, but Joseph enjoyed the working hours and the

LIFE'S DETOURS

increased pay. His bonus for the first month amounted to $410.00, and when added to his regular wages, began to make some sense and to pay for the extra effort. One morning, as they washed down the face of the stope they noticed a vein of pure gold about 3 feet in length and about one inch in size at its thickest end. The vein looked like a flash of bright lightning, streaking from the right upper half of the stope's face and narrowing itself to a point at the lower left of the face.

Henry looked at Joseph and said,- "You and I can share in some of this gold if you can keep a secret. What do you think?"

"I'm game," Joseph replied. He had heard how some miners had made themselves rich by hygrading gold from the mines and selling it to black market buyers.

"Then you go and keep an eye on the stairwell, while I chisel away at some of this metal. I will place it in sample bags which we have with us and hide it. Then at some future date, we will take it out of the mine. Okay? Keep your eye on the stairwell and if you see anyone coming up, come quickly and let me know," Henry commanded.

Joseph followed his instructions and kept watch at the stairwell. No one came. After an hour Henry called on Joseph to suspend the watch and return to their work.

"How will you take it out?" Joseph asked.

"It won't be easy," Henry said. "We'll have to work on Christmas Day. That's a day when very few people come to work, except for money hungry contractors like us. We will then bring it out of the mine, seat ourselves on the right side of the tram that takes us to the main shaft where we shower and dress into street clothes. As the tram passes by the mine property fence, we can throw the bags over the property fence. After we are in street clothes we'll walk around the outside of the fence at a later time and pick them up."

"Henry, you've got it all figured out," Joseph said. "About how much gold did you stash away?"

"I've got two sample bags, which I consider hold about 80 or 90 ounces of gold quartz each. You see it's not pure. It has yet to be refined, but we can get about $20.00 an ounce for it, as is. The sample is quite pure."

In addition, to the gold placed in the bags for hygrading, Henry also had an extra bag or two from which he would take a bit and add to the bags containing samples of the ore. These samples were being sent up to the laboratory each day for gold content analysis. Contractors were not only being paid for the tonnage output of ore, but also for it's gold content. In other words, the more gold content that was found in the ore mined from that particular stope, the higher would be the bonus paid.

LIFE'S DETOURS

"Yes, Henry knows his mining business," Joseph chuckled to himself. He was now the owner of about $1,500 worth of gold quartz hidden in the mine and an accomplice to the heisting of gold or "hygrading" as the act was called in mining terms.

One evening Joseph happened to be alone in the Polymer apartment. There was a knock at the door. Joseph answered and opened the door. It was the daughter of the next door neighbor. The Thornes.

"My name is Ruby Thorne, I live next door. I was talking to your cousin Dorothy and she told me that you are quite good in mathematics. I'm in my second year in high school and I'm having difficulty in resolving some algebra problems. Would you be willing to help me?" she inquired.

Joseph considered himself relatively good in algebra, geometry and straight arithmetic. But he had only completed grade ten and did not feel qualified to become a tutor on the subjects. He hesitated for a moment. He looked at her pretty face and lean body and asked her to come in.

"I'm not sure that I can really help you," he said.

He related his story to her about being unable to complete his high school education, due to the depression and lack of funds.

"Let's have a look at your problems and see if I can be of any help," Joseph commanded.

They drew two chairs side by side at the kitchen table, and together worked out the problems for that evening. They did not appear extremely difficult problems for Joseph. But, how was he to judge her capability in one session. They sat and chatted for a while and then she rose to go home, and as she was walking towards the door, she said:-

"Do you mind if I come again? You've been very helpful and I'd appreciate your help again if I should need it. Thank you very much and good evening."

Joseph nodded approval to her comments, smiled, closed the door and remained totally non-plussed. Here was a beautiful seventeen year old girl, looking to him for tutoring in her mathematic classes. Why didn't she look for someone more qualified. He shared the evening's event with his cousin Dorothy, when they returned later that evening.

"Yes, she talked to me about you and she asked me what education you had. I told her we were students at the same time and school and that you were pretty good in math. She said she was having a problem with her algebra and wanted me to ask you if you would help her. I didn't get a chance to talk to you about it yet. She beat me to it. I also think she has a crush on you," Dorothy stated.

"I'm not sure how much tutoring I can do in algebra, but I guess at some point, I'll just have to admit that I'm not qualified to help her because of my own limitations. She is a nice girl and about her crush, I'm old fashioned, I want a girl, a western girl, just like my mother," Joseph said smilingly to Dorothy.

Every workday, Joseph walked carrying his lunch bucket past the railway station on his way to the mine. The morning walk would take place about 7:30 a.m. and at this particular time, the Temiskaming and Northern Ontario Railway (The T&NO) train would pull out of the station, westbound for North Bay with connections for other Western Canada points. That whistle, as the train pulled out of the station would make Joseph homesick and yearn for his childhood sweetheart and for home.

"One of these days, I'll have enough money saved up to catch that train and go back west, get married and bring her here. All I need is $2,000 and if my bonuses come along good, I should have that amount saved by the end of August." he would say and comfort himself with that objective.

The relationship between Ruby and Joseph had developed somewhat beyond tutor and pupil. She would come once or twice a week over to the Polymer apartment and they would work together on her algebra problems. They arranged to see some movies together. Then it switched to where Joseph would go over to her parent's home. Some evenings they would walk and visit together. One evening she phoned and asked Joseph to go over to her home and assist her with her homework. Joseph agreed.

He knocked on the door, entered and found Ruby's parents had gone out for the evening, and being the only child in the family she was home alone. There was no homework to be completed, she was only looking for Joseph's company - but, the exercise books were opened on the kitchen table to make it look like they were being worked on. It was a precautionary measure in case her parents returned early.

She took Joseph's arm and led him to the living room sofa which could be seen through the kitchen door. They sat down close to each other, held hands for a while and followed with intimate kissing. patting and hugging."Joseph, I don't really need your help in doing algebra. I asked for your help as an excuse to get to know you and to allow you to get to know me better. I really care for you. My parents don't know you - but they have observed that you are a pretty clean living fellow and the folks you are staying with are really nice people. I like your cousin Dorothy and so does my mother. Do you think we could become steadies?" she asked as she looked into Joseph's eyes inquisitively.

This caught Joseph off guard. He felt that Ruby had a crush on him but he didn't think it was that serious. He reminded himself quickly of Suzanne, but then felt that she too, might be in someone else's arms at this particular moment. He pulled himself away from Ruby somewhat and was trying to think of what to say.

"I rather felt that you were quite capable of solving your algebra problems, but I wasn't quite sure of how to handle the situation. I appreciate your candidness, however, I do think we should mull it over. You are seventeen and still in school and I'm twenty-two. I have a job - but I'm not yet ready to enter into a serious relationship. You've suggested going steady and we might try this for awhile, and see how it all develops," Joseph responded.

At this point, the automobile lights from her parent's car swung into the driveway, which helped to break up the conversation and to get Joseph and Ruby quickly to the kitchen table. Ruby's parents entered and appeared delighted with the fact that Joseph was a visitor at their home. The hour was getting late and after a few exchanges of pleasantries, Joseph bid them "good-night"" and departed.

A few more weeks went by, with Joseph attending to his regular shifts of work at the mine and also spending one or two evenings every week in Ruby's company under the pretense that he was tutoring her in her homework.

Then a telegram arrived from his mother. "Come home at once if you can. Your father had a bad accident. We need you."

Joseph looked at his bank book, which showed he had a balance of slightly over $2,000.00. His month-end pay check, was more than enough to buy his ticket for returning back home. He had planned to go back West in the fall anyway, but this sort of accelerated matters. He wired back home that he would be coming at the end of the month. This gave him enough time to request a one month "leave of absence" from the mine, settle a few personal matters and pack ready for departure.

He departed on the third of October. He informed everyone that he was taking a one month leave of absence due to his father's illness and that he would return. In the few days before leaving, he had said farewell to all of his relatives and most of his friends. He instructed his cousin to send him any important mail to his parent's address in Saskatchewan. He left by taxi early in the morning for the railroad station. Sure enough Ruby was there to give him a hug and a kiss and to see him off.

"Send me a postcard after you arrive, and I promise to write you at least once before you get back," she said.

She waved from the station platform as the train blew its whistle. Joseph waved back as it chugged away and departed on time.

Chapter 8

MARRIAGE AND FARMING

Most of the passengers on the train were men dressed in uniform. The newspaper headlines, and the main topic of conversation on the train was related to the war. Hitler and his armies together with Mussolini were making advances on all fronts. Canada had declared war against Germany in September, 1939 and committed itself to assist the United Kingdom with military resources in the form of food, munitions. air force training grounds, and manpower made up of volunteers for the army, navy and airforce.

Joseph did not concern himself with the military for several reasons. First, Canada had not committed itself to furnishing manpower militarily, other than on a volunteer basis. Secondly, there was a shortage of manpower in agriculture and producing food was a vital component of the war effort. He might have to remain on the farm anyway to help out the family and would then fit this category. Lastly his personal philosophy about wars was incompatible with the majority of the country's mood. He knew that French speaking Canada was not overly anxious to jump into the war. Then the depressive economic conditions under which he grew induced him to develop a bitter attitude towards the entire system.

He felt the only justice that existed was enjoyed by the rich, and they were the ones that should be making the patriotic sacrifice to the cause. He simply did not feel patriotically motivated at this particular time to volunteer for military service. He had other plans.

Three days and two nights later he stepped off the train at the Union Depot in Regina. There was no one there to greet him. He phoned Gary Pinchuk,one of his city cousins to get the scoop on the condition of his father. He was told that his father was resting in the Grey Nuns Hospital and that while his condition was critical, it was by no means fatal. He was also invited to be a guest at their home for the

LIFE'S DETOURS

short time he would be in the city. He grabbed a taxi, dropped off his baggage at the Pinchuk's, and on this slightly windy and cool October day hurried to the hospital to visit his dad.

"Hi there dad," he said as he entered his dad's hospital room, walked quickly to the bed, took his extended right hand and shook it - then kissed him on his forehead. His dad had tears in his eyes. "How are you and what happened?"

"Look at my left hand," his dad remarked. The left arm was in a cast and resting on a pillow, from just below his arm pit to the palm of the hand. The fingers could be seen but were a dark blue color. He looked weak, tired and very unlike the person Joseph knew to be his father. His father related how the accident occurred.

"We were threshing on our farm. It was late in the evening and we wanted to finish up. I was in charge of the threshing outfit. I went to give a twist to the grease cups that feed grease to the cylinder shaft on the separator. The drive belt had a clip on it which grabbed the sleeve of my sweater and gave my arm a swift twist around the pulley of the drive shaft, with the result that I now have a damaged elbow and a broken left arm. What's worse, I've lost a lot of blood, I've had one transfusion and I need more. My blood is of the RHB Positive type, which the doctor says is not as common and easy to find. They are looking," his father remarked.

"I wonder if my blood type is the same as yours," Joseph said. "I'll have the hospital check it right now - maybe we have the type in the family."

The hospital laboratory took a sample of Joseph's blood and determined that it was of the same type as his fathers. Without hesitation the hospital intern doctor was notified, who authorized the immediate taking of one pint of blood from Joseph and transfusing it to his father. Joseph was also told that another pint might be required within a week or sooner, and would he agree to a further donation. He nodded approval.

Joseph sat by his father's bedside as his blood was going drop by drop into his father's veins and bloodstream. They continued their conversation.

"Your mother is at home on the farm with the rest of the children, except for Ray, who has joined the army. I'm glad you came back to help with the farming. Charles, your brother is at home but he is only 16 and not finished with his high school education, and the other two boys are too young. Of course, there is your sister who can help - but, the farm needs a more mature person. As you can see I'll be out of commission for a long while, therefore your presence and your effort is crucial at this time," his father said.

Joseph chose not to tell his father at this moment about his personal ambition, which was to get married and within the month return back to the mine. He had to have more time to think the situation over, now that his father seemed to think that he would remain to farm.

His father continued talking.

"Since you left home, I have also made a major decision in my own life. I have become an ordained priest in the Eastern Orthodox faith."

At this juncture Joseph kind of swallowed hard. He had heard his dad had become a priest, but he wasn't quite sure his dad would be so committed and talk about it to him so soon.

"What prompted you to arrive at this decision?" Joseph asked.

"Well, you know that I've been active in our church all my life. I may not have been the best person - but I have been a cantor; always supported the church and attended it on a regular basis. Since the war began and Romania has taken sides with Hitler, Canada suspended diplomatic and immigration relations with Romania. The Romanian Orthodox churches in this country are unable to bring any more priests from Romania as in the past. Our local priest passed on to eternity and our parish was without a priest. The parishioners have asked me to take on the priesthood, and serve their spiritual needs and I have consented. I was ordained by the Ukrainian Orthodox Bishop from Edmonton. and have been fulfilling the priesthood functions for the past year. This situation in which I find myself now is going to hurt our parish, but I hope our people will understand. You know the doctor has suggested the amputation of this arm down from the elbow, but I have not consented. I cannot visualize myself in church and in the priest's robes with only one and one half arms. I would rather die attached to this arm than part with it," his father said, as he searched Joseph's face and eyes to see if he could read an expression of approval.

He looked at his dad and felt sorry for him. He purposely suppressed any facial expressions that might reflect disapproval of his father's decision and action.

"Your arm must have been pretty badly mutilated, if the doctor felt that amputation might be necessary," Joseph said.

Richard Acker had no medical knowledge, but tried to explain his condition to his son in the best language and terms he knew how. He spoke softly.

"The elbow is crushed and the main artery carrying blood to the lower part of my hand has been badly damaged. You can see the dark color of my fingertips due to poor circulation. This artery has been stitched, repaired, in the hope that it would serve to circulate a minimum of blood, while other arteries and veins heal and develop

LIFE'S DETOURS 115

helpful capillary action. It is the doctor's hope and certainly my hope, that this healing process will evolve on that basis and the arm could be saved."

"You are presently in need of hospital and doctor care. I'm so glad to see you as well as you are," Joseph said. "Take it easy and rest and you'll be okay. I'd like to take a quick trip to the farm to see Mom and the rest of the family. This will also give me time to think over your proposal about farming. 1 can come back early next week or sooner if the doctor feels you need more blood right away. In the meantime, take care and give yourself plenty of rest, don't worry - we will see what can be done and after I consult with Mom too we will be back to see you - as soon as possible, okay?" Joseph touched his father's right hand and as he parted walking backwards toward the door, his father reminded him not to forget to come back soon.

That evening Joseph visited with his cousin's family, conversing about events that took place during his absence from the area. The next day he was able to catch a ride to the farm with their nearest farm neighbor and by noon, he had greeted his mother and his sister on the farm. His brothers were all at school. They reviewed the incident of the accident, and talked about family matters and the economics of the farm.

"Whatever made dad become a priest?" Joseph asked his mother.

"Son, I think the Lord came into our family in a real way. It has made a big difference in your father's behavior. As you know, your father was a good man in so many ways, but he was steadily consuming more and more alcohol and in reality he was an alcoholic. He was, as you know at times very abusive and hard. Difficult to get along with, but since he accepted the responsibilities of priesthood, he has become a different man. He has shied away from alcohol and is attempting to correct his character deficiencies. He is by no means perfect, but far easier to live and get along with. I'm praying that with more time he will improve even more. It's the best thing that ever happened to him and to us," his mother said.

The topic then turned to farming, to the autumn field work that had to be done and to the uncertainty about the date of a hospital release for his father. There was grain to be marketed; coal be be hauled for the winter heating of the home; more fodder to be garnered for wintering the livestock; taxes to be paid and other farm expenses and debts to be taken care of.

"We're just not equipped to satisfactorily take care of these burdens without your help," his mother said.

Joseph related his plans to his mother.

"I did not come back to remain on the farm. I took a month's leave of absence from the mine. My thoughts were to see dad and offer any possible assistance that I could during this short period. As you know Mom, I've been corresponding with Suzanne and at this time I'm going to propose to her. If she consents like her letters to me indicated that she would, I'm going to marry her and take her back with me."

"Joseph, I respect your plans, but we are now at some kind of a crossroad in which we all need your help," his mother said.

He respected his mother's advice, perhaps more than anyone else's in the world.

"I want you to listen to what I have to tell you and then make your decision, but my advice to you is crucial. As you know, the Federal Government passed the National Registration Act in 1941. All single men of ages 21 to 35 had to register. You had to register, did you not?" his mother questioned.

Joseph nodded agreement.

"This means that should this war continue you too, are liable for military service. There are some exceptions applied to that age group which exempts from military service, those who are involved in basic wartime industries of which agriculture is one. At this particular time you are needed on the farm. If you get married and return to mining, particularly gold mining, you are liable to be called for military service and the farm would be left short-handed.

However, if you get married and stay with farming, chances are much better for you to be exempted, which would be better both for you as a married man and for us because we need your help. Your brother Ray is already in the service and your other brothers are still in school. Think it over, we could arrange to have you lease some land from the neighbors. The farm implements we now have can be shared, and your land and ours could be farmed together," his mother advised.

This made a bundle of sense to Joseph. He asked about the family car.

"Yes, we are driving a 1937 Whippet," his mother said. "We bought it second hand. New cars are not available because of the war effort."

Joseph asked if he could make use of the car to go and see Suzanne, who lived on the Parker farm about 4 miles away.

"Joseph, you are now 22 years of age. I expect you to act as an adult. You may take and use the car or anything else we have on the farm, but in all situations act responsibly and in the best interests of the family and the farm," his mother replied.

Joseph wasted no time in arranging his time table to allow for a visit with Suzanne. It was on the first Sunday afternoon, after his return from the mines. They drove about the countryside talking about events

LIFE'S DETOURS

that took place during his absence and exchanging pleasantries. They parked for a long while on a lonely countryside road, to embrace, to kiss, to hold hands, to express and share their passion, as a kind of an excessive making up for that period in which they were separated from each other.

Joseph felt and knew for sure he was now in love with Suzanne and that he wanted to marry her. He told her all about his plans and the developments that took place since he returned. He talked about the plans the family had for him as a result of his father's accident. Susanne listened intently, giving him a squeeze of the hand every now and then as he told her all about his intentions.

"Above all, I came back to ask you to marry me and to take you back with me. I do not have a ring to present you with right now, but I'm going to pop the question to you this very moment. Honey, will you marry me? Joseph asked Suzanne, as he held her tightly in his arms in the front seat of the car.

It may have been the precise question that Suzanne had been waiting for, and if it was, she hesitated in replying. She chose to ask a few more questions.

"I like your idea of getting married and going back to the mine, but what if you should decide to remain and fulfill your parent's plans to assist them with farming during this crucial period, where would we live?" she asked.

"I've been thinking seriously about the situation you posed and my plan is to take over the Hreniuk farm. which our family has currently under lease. I have about $2,000.00 which I saved and brought back with me from the mine. I would repair the house, make it liveable and move there. It's only one mile from the main farmstead and I could do the farming for both myself and my parents. You see I'm still liable to be called for military service and I would hate to take you to Timmins and be forced to leave you there alone, while I go for military duty. We could live on the farm until this war situation corrects itself. Then if we don't like it - we could call it quits, sell out, and being familiar with mining go back East," Joseph said.

"That sounds reasonable," Suzanne remarked. "But I have one other concern."

"What could that be," he asked

"We have now been going around together for some time on a regular basis, but not steady-steady. I like and admire you, but there were times when I had the feeling that you were a jealous person. Am I correct in my assumption? Are you a jealous person?" she asked.

This question put Joseph in an awkward situation. He never thought of himself as being a jealous person. He was confused as to why she would venture forth such a question at this particular time. What was Suzanne's fear? What was the strategy? Was she sincere and what kind of an answer was she expecting? He did not feel that his proposal would be turned down, but just in case it was - what would his next step be? He thought of Ruby the girl he left behind in Timmins as an alternative. She was there. She would be waiting for him. He wasn't quite sure that was what he wanted.

After a few moments of silence and a pause, he made an attempt to respond.

"Honey, I love you and I care for you, before and now. I do not see myself as being jealous. I feel I'm a possesive person. In other words, I like to look after things that are mine or that belong to me. If in the past I have appeared to you to be jealous, it was because, although in fact you weren't mine, I could mentally picture you as belonging to me and therefore I cared. I have no other explanation to offer."

Suzanne, seemed to be pleased with this response. She snuggled close to him, placed her head against his chest, her arms around him, and looking up into his face, smiling she said, - "You are my sweetheart. I will marry you."

That evening Joseph had dinner at the Parker home. Suzanne's parents were courteous, and throughout the evening's conversation asked many questions about the East, about mining and living conditions. Joseph made no hint of any plans he had to marry their daughter. He thought the parents might feel it's too hasty. He felt it would be better if Suzanne broke the news to her parents herself, at a time when she felt it would be most appropiate.

As each day went by, Joseph became more and more engrossed in the farm work, and began to assume the concerns that go along with planning the work and then executing it. By the end of the third week of his leave of absence, he had determined to remain and associate himself with farming and with helping the family. He telegrammed Mr. King, stating his inability to return to the mine and that a letter of explanation would follow. At the same time he wrote a letter to his cousin Wayne explaining his decision to remain in the West and some of his reasons for doing so. He thought about Ruby but did not write to her, knowing full well that she would get the news from his cousin.

An urgent telegram was brought to the farm by the local telegraph agent.

"Your father requires additional transfusion of blood, come in at once," the message read. It was sent by Dr. Ritchie.

Joseph and his mother immediately departed by car for the city and drove directly to the hospital. They found Richard Acker in a semiconscious state and not anxious for conversation. The attending nurse stated that Dr. Ritchie had just been there and was still in the hospital and she would locate him immediately.

"Mr. Acker requires another blood transfusion," she said as she left to search for the doctor.

In a matter of minutes Dr. Ritchie appeared on the scene and quickly explained what had transpired.

"Due apparently to over-swelling of the arm, the pressure created inside the cast caused the damaged artery to rupture again which led to the loss of blood. It is this blood that has to be replenished. Joseph, you know where the lab is - I have already requested the technician to extract another pint of blood, so let's get this activity out of the way as soon as possible," the doctor concluded.

Joseph walked out of the room to the hospital laboratory.

Mrs. Acker remained talking to Dr. Ritchie.

"Mrs. Acker, we may not be able to save your husband's arm. You see, it was in a cast - and the fact that it swells, forces me to avoid placing it in cast again."

Looking at Richard, Dr. Ritchie kept on talking.

"He will not accept amputation, therefore we must try to treat it in some other way. What I will do is make a half-cast to support the under half of his total arm. This cast mould will still maintain his arm firm and allow him to rest it on a pillow. It will allow the arm to swell and for the nurses to treat the open wound. At the same time keep his arm steady to permit healing."

"Does this mean he will be bed-ridden for a long time," Mrs Acker asked.

"Precisely," Dr Ritchie added. "He will have to lie in bed until the swelling goes down and the wound will stop releasing abscesses. Then we can cast another mould to hold the arm steady and allow him to get out of bed and perhaps even go home. This can take from three weeks to one month."

"It will be near Christmas, before he can be released to come back home," Eugenia Acker remarked.

By this time, Joseph had returned from donating the blood and a nurse walked in with the pint of fresh blood. It was quickly arranged for the transfusion to occur. Dr. Ritchie asked to be excused and disappeared.

"We'll leave you now," Eugenia informed Richard. "We'll be staying at the Pinchuk's tonight and we'll drop in and see you again tomorrow. Try to rest as best as you can. We'll pray for you," she gave him a kiss on the cheek and began to leave the room.

Joseph also touched his father's right hand with his and held it a moment, then he too bade his father farewell and followed his mother out of the room.

The next day's visit at the hospital proved more positive. Richard felt better. He regained some color in his cheeks and stated that the pain in his arm had subsided. They visted for an hour or so longer. However, everyone including Richard, was aware that there was work to be done on the farm and that Joseph and his mother had to get back as soon as possible. They bid each other farewell and assured Richard they would come to see him soon.

The ride back to the farm from the city, a distance of 70 miles lasted the usual two and one half hours. Joseph and his mother talked about Richard's condition, the hospital expenses that would be incurred and the hope that his condition would allow him to come home by Christmas.

Joseph also told his mother that he had proposed to Suzanne and that she had accepted. Suzanne was to discuss the proposal with her parents and on their next meeting she would inform him about their decision.

Back on the farm he went about his work. Snow was sure to come any time and as much field work and gathering of fodder had to be done before the snow fell.

The following Sunday Joseph went to visit Suzanne again. He picked her up in the car and went for another drive in the countryside.

"I talked to my parents about our plans to get married, and they offered no objection," Suzanne said.

"Good, then to-day I suggest that just between us - we should make an engagement commitment, I will arrange for our wedding to take place as soon as possible, but in the meantime you are mine. I will love you and take care of you as long as I live," Joseph said as he stopped the car on a rural road and they hugged and kissed in what seemed to be an insatiable manner.

"I want to be your companion and I'll try to be just the kind of a wife you'd like and be proud to have," Suzanne replied.

In this amorous atmosphere they continued to talk about their plans. Joseph told her that it would be late December before he could expect his father to come home. That in setting a wedding date, his father's situation would have to be taken into consideration. They agreed to tentatively set February 1st, being a Sunday, as a target date and to begin making arrangements for the wedding with that date in mind.

Subsequent visits to the hospital made by Joseph and his mother noted steady improvement in his father's situation. His father was released from the hospital in early December, but chose to remain in

LIFE'S DETOURS

the city and close to the doctor and to further medical attention should the need arise. He remained as a guest in the Pinchuk home until a couple of days before Christmas, when he returned to his farm home.

By this time, Joseph's father had been apprised of the wedding plans and while he could offer no physical help, he nevertheless offered his concurrence and blessing. Joseph continued his plan and preparations for his marraige.

Since Joseph's father was a minister, he would conduct the marriage ceremony in the Acker home. This would be followed by a dinner and dancing for the invited guests. The Ackers had a four bedroom home. The main floor consisted of a large kitchen and dining area, a reasonably large living room and a large bedroom. The living room and the adjoining bedroom could be used to entertain the wedding guests, as well as some of the kitchen area. At any rate the quarters would be cramped for holding such an affair, but it was the way things were done at weddings held in the community at that time. This would have to suffice for this wedding as well.

January was a busy month preparing for the wedding. A short shopping trip was made to the city to enable Suzanne to select a wedding gown and other bridal necessities. Joseph was going to use the last suit he had bought while mining, which he had only worn once or twice. Additionally, they purchased an inexpensive set of wedding rings.

There was a hog to kill and dress. The menu would consist of beef stew, home-made sausages, roast chicken, mashed potatoes, cabbage rolls, pickles and relishes, apple pies, strudel, a variety of cakes and other pastries, freshly baked home made bread and a myriad of other little things that the groom's mother felt had to be served. This is not to recount what was going on at the bride's residence.

The alcoholic liquor for the wedding was the most difficult situation to contend with. Purchasing whiskey by mail order for such an occassion from a government liquor store was prohibitive due to its high cost. Therefore, Joseph in collaboration with Michael Ritter, his chosen best man for the wedding, opted to make and distill a quantity of home-brewed whiskey. This was illegal and the activity had to be executed under very hush hush conditions.

In the barn, an excavation was made large enough to accommodate two 45 gallon wooden oak barrels. About two gallons of sprouted rye kernels were placed in the bottom of these barrels, to which a quantity of sugar and yeast were added. The barrels were then filled with lukewarm water to a level of about four inches below the top. Wooden covers were placed on these barrels, on top of which an oilcloth was laid, and a couple of horse blankets to keep an adequate temperature for the fermentation process. The fermentation period would last for a period of one week. The whole excavation was covered over with sweet smelling hay from the loft, camouflaged and made inconspicuous. At the end of the one week period the excavation was re-opened. The entire fermented mash was distilled with a kit of copper made distilling equipment, borrowed from a near-by neighbor. The distilling exercise took place in the farm blacksmith shop, where the coal-fired blower forge was used to bring the mash to a boil and keep it steaming. The forge was hand powered and Joseph's brother Louis was the manpower energy behind the crank. The process began in the late afternoon and continued into the late night. A total of twelve gallons of "home-brew" was realized. The excavation was back-filled, the whiskey was stored away from the premises, the distilling kit returned and a general clean-up ensued.

For a winter's day, February 1st, started off as a reasonably nice day. Michael and Pearl Ritter, the best man and matron of honor, arrived early at the Acker residence driving an older model one ton Ford truck. Other neighbors and friends began to arrive. The orchestra which consisted of a violin, a trumpet player and a drummer had arrived the night before and had been housed at the Ackers. A convoy of five automobiles left the Acker residence on a four mile drive, partially on the road, and partially across the snow covered stubble fields to the Parker residence to pick up the bride.

The Ritter truck which was loaded with a few bags of gravel to give it added weight, was used for breaking a trail through the foot deep snow for the other cars to follow. Joseph with his car and the other three cars followed the lead truck. They arrived at the Parker farm home without any incident.

A few friends and neighbors together with members of the Parker family were on hand to greet the groom and his entourage. The custom called for the groom to drive to the home of the bride, pick her up and drive to the church for the marriage ceremony. In this case, the ceremony was to be held in the Acker home, therefore the wedding party after picking up the bride would return to the Acker residence.

The three piece band, which came along led off with typical music played at Romanian weddings and after the usual greetings and chit chat, the matron of honor took on her normal task of putting the finishing touches to the brides hair, a slight cosmetic touch to the face and fixing on the bridal veil. The customary bridal farewell to her parents, brothers and sister was executed before leaving her parent's home. She was departing as a girl and in her future returns whatever the occasion might be, she will be treated as a married daughter and visitor. She was now leaving to make her life permanent elsewhere.

LIFE'S DETOURS

Joseph looked at Suzanne, she was smiling radiantly, and appeared more beautiful than ever in her white bridal attire. He stepped outside and waited for her exit. He offered his arm and walked her to the automobile, opened the car's door and assisted her by lifting and tucking her veil to prevent both damage and soiling, while she accomodated herself in the car. He walked around the car's other side and sat beside her in the rear. Michael and Pearl Ritter drove the car on the return trip, while their truck was being driven by Suzanne's brother. The return of the wedding party took up the entire morning. Everything was ready and waiting at the Acker residence.

Joseph assisted Suzanne out of the car, lifted her in his arms and walked her over the threshold of his parent's home. They entered the main floor bedroom that had been prepared before hand as a chapel. The bedroom furniture had been removed and it was furnished with a small table covered with a white table cloth. A home made twisted bread ring (kolachi), a candle holder with three lit candles, a glass of wine, a small glass with anointing oil were placed on the right side of the table. Two crowns that would be placed on the heads of the bridal pair during the ceremony sat on the left side of the table. On the wall a permanently hung icon of the Last Supper would face the young couple as they were taking their vows.

Father Richard Acker, his left arm still in a cast, wore the simple and permissable orthodox priest's attire for performing religious ceremonies. He was dressed in a long black robe, draped with only the front piece of his priestly garb. He was ready to begin the marriage ceremony. Joseph and Suzanne were facing the table, flanked by the best man and matron of honor and a few more people that were able to squeeze their way into the room. The rest of the wedding guests stood in the main room of the house and listened to the prayers, gospels and conjugal commitments.

"This will be the first marriage ceremony, that I am conducting since I became a priest. I am grateful that God has enabled me to confer this blessing upon my son," Father Acker declared prior to beginning the prayers.

"Blessed be the Kingdom of the Father, and of the Son and of the Holy Spirit," Father Acker began.

Joseph could not remember all the prayers and details of the ceremony, but some of the highlights that made an imprint on his mind were the taking of the vows; the exchange and placing of the rings on their respective fingers; the prayers associated with the placing and removing of the head crowns; the bread and wine communion and the oil annointment at the conclusion. A concluding prayer that Father Acker repeated slowly, reading it as if there was a purposeful intention for it to be really meaningful, was the following:-

"O God, our God, who didst come to Cana of Galilee, and didst bless there the marriage feast; Bless, also, these thy servants Joseph and Suzanne, who through Thy good providence are now united together in wedlock. Bless their goings out and their comings in; replenish their life with good things; receive their crowns into Thy kingdom, preserving them spotless, blameless, and without reproach, unto ages of ages, Amen."

The marriage contract was then signed and witnessed by Michael and Pearl Ritter. It was one o'clock in the afternoon, and the bridal couple together with the best man and matron of honor moved from the room that served as a chapel and took their places behind the head dinner table. In the meantime, the chapel room was quickly furnished with tables and chairs and equipped to accommodate more wedding guests for their meal.

The weather outside had turned colder, and a blizzard was in the making. A few guests had arrived by car from the city. Other local guests arriving late travelled by horse drawn sleighs and had to have their horses stabled in the barn. The Acker barn was full to capacity. Joseph's brother Allen and Suzanne's brother Edwin, who acted as "horse parking valets" took a number of horse teams for sheltering to neighboring barns. The Acker home was jam-packed with people, but plenty of good-will prevailed.

Due to late arrivals, the dinner meal continued on into late afternoon. The home-brewed whiskey flowed freely and the reception took on a boisterous din, which was only outstripped by the three piece band with its musical interludes. After the main meal the tables were lifted, leaving only one table at one end of the room laden with finger-food for anyone wanting to munch at desired intervals. The floor was cleared for dancing and the band played, enabling 8 to 10 couples to dance at any one time. About midnight most of the guests departed, but those whose homes were more distant and travelling with horses and sleigh, kept on partying till daylight broke the next morning.

Joseph and Suzanne stayed with the party till after midnight, and after the bride's dance went upstairs to their room and retired for the evening. Father Acker had retired earlier to his room upstairs. Eugenia and Charles stayed up with the guests until they all finally left.

The next day was clean-up day. Joseph and Suzanne had taken stock of who gave what as gifts at their wedding. They realized $580.00 in cash, and numerous other gifts ranging from household and kitchen items to two milk cows, two horses, a couple of piglets, six chickens and two roosters. Everything of course was gratefully received, since these were items that a young couple starting to farm could use.

Life went back to routine following the wedding. Joseph and Suzanne were going to live with his parents, until the warmer weather would arrive enabling them to rehabilitate the vacant house on their leased farm and to move there.

The time arrived when they were in their own two room, wall papered farm cottage. Spring farm work came upon them, and Joseph took to his farm responsibilities. Together with his brother Charles, who could only work in the hours before and after school, repaired fences, planted the crops, sheared the sheep, marketed the crops and animals and literally did all the farm work.

On their own farm, Suzanne became a farmerette. She planted a garden, raised chickens, milked the two cows they had and did other yard chores. In July, Susanne announced that she was pregnant, Joseph joined in her happiness and felt manly and content. The news were imparted to their families who were delighted to hear about the event.

"What are we going to name the baby?" Joseph asked his wife.

"Let's think about it. Whether it's a boy or a girl, we ought to have a nice name to give our baby," she replied.

The year 1942 was a good crop year, and Joseph and Suzanne had realized a bountiful crop. The problem was marketing. Wheat could only be sold under a quota system. The government was forced to initiate an orderly marketing procedure due to lack of storage space; wartime usage of railway cars and boats and the curtailed demand on the export market.

The first marketing quota allowed the sale of three bushels of wheat per acre. Joseph's quota was for one hundred acres making for an initial sale of 300 bushels. He had harvested 40 bushels per acre. Rainfall had been both timely and adequate and in one crop season alone, the myth that the drought years had made Sakatchewan farms unproductive was killed when the current year's bumper production came along.

Joseph's cash resources including his mine savings had dwindled. He had found his parent's cash situation tight when he returned from the mines. He contributed his cash to overall farm and living expenses and on medical expenses for his father; then on his wedding, and on rehabilitating the cottage they were living in plus their own living and farm expenses. They had a good garden and enjoyed meals that Suzanne resourcefully prepared from the vegetables and meat that were produced on their farm.

New marketing quotas opened periodically and at three bushels per acre, it would give them about $300.00 for spending, which was sufficient cash flow to cover needed farm expenses as well as their living necessities. They drove to town, to church, or to visit their in-laws or friends with their team of horses and buggy. There was little money available, so life consisted of love, simplicity and hard work.

On the international scene the war seemed to be escalating, with Britain and its Allies holding their ground but unable to make gains and to overcome the mighty war machine Hitler had mustered. Approximately three months after Joseph's marriage, April 27, 1942 the Canadian Government held a plebiscite asking for a release from its initial commitment of mobilizing manpower only on a voluntary basis. In the referandum the nation approved the release, and two months later, single men up to age 35 were made liable and called for compulsory military service.

The Japanese had attacked the U.S. Navy Fleet at Pearl Harbor on Dec. 7th, 1941, which caused a vengeful United States to immediately declare war on Japan, and at the same time actively entered the European war theater in April of 1942. British and American forces were now working together, and the war planes coupled to the famous American built Sherman tanks, played a gigantic role in beginning to turn the tide of the war in favor of the Allies.

Nevertheless, in early 1943 the Canadian Government extended the conscription of men for military service to include married men up to age 35. Joseph was in this category. He knew he would be amenable to conscription and by June of 1943, he had received his call to report for military duty.

During this time, Suzanne had given birth to their first child. A little baby girl which they named Carolyn. Joseph having concentrated on his farming, by the time his call was received, the crops had been planted and were in their pre-heading stage. He was certainly not keen to leave the farm and his small family and report for military duty. His father's arm had healed enabling him to carry on with his priestly duties, and his brother Charles had terminated his high school. His brother Ray, who had been serving in the army received a medical discharge and had returned home. There was now sufficient manpower on his parent's farm and no need for his help any further.

Joseph appealed to the Recuitment Board for an extension of time, stating that he had a vested interest in his own farm and the need to take off his current crop. He advised the Board that after harvest he was prepared to respond for military service. The appeal was denied and Joseph reported in early July for induction into the army and for his basic training.

By the middle of August his basic training had been completed and again he appealed to the Commanding Officer of his battalion for a six week leave of absence, to allow him to harvest his crop and to move

LIFE'S DETOURS

his wife and daughter from the farm, to a more desirable and permanent place of residence. He pointed out to the Commanding Officer that he operated a leased farm, from which his wife and daughter would have to move when the lease expired.

Again the Commanding Officer turned down his request. This made Joseph extremely angry. The battalion known as the Prince Albert Volunteers was now quartered in a campsite near Courtney, B.C. on Vancouver Island. The battalion was about to embark on six weeks of advanced infantry training, following which they would be dispatched as reinforcements to the main overseas battalion in Europe.

Joseph's concern was his wife and daughter. He did not wish to leave them on the farm in a state of uncertainty. The crop could be taken off by his two brothers and marketed in timely fashion. But, his wife and daughter had to be more adequately provided for and settled somewhere during his absence, where they would enjoy a degree of comfort and security both for his sake and theirs.

At the military barracks, this one evening Joseph was assigned to clean the Commanding Officer's office. While dusting and cleaning the top of his desk, he noticed the form pad for authorizing "Leave of Absence" lying on the desk. The top page of the form pad was blank, but oddly enough, the form carried the Commanding Officer's signature. Joseph made a snap decision.

"I'll take this form, fill in my personal data and go absent without leave (AWOL). I'll go home find a place for my wife and daughter to live during my stay in the army, take off my crop and then return for duty. I know I'll be penalized, but what the hell, a few days in military detention ain't going to kill me," he thought to himself.

He finished cleaning up the Commanding Officer's office. He took the blank form, stamped it with the rubber seal that had also been carelessly left on the desk top, returned to his barracks and filled in the blanks with the required particulars. He packed all of his soldier's belongings and together with his rifle laid them on his bunk bed. Then carrying only a small bag containing a change of clothes and his shaving kit, about ten o'clock that evening he walked into the bus depot in Courtney. He purchased a bus and ferry ticket to Vancouver and departed.

At the Canadian Pacific Railway station in Vancouver, he purchased a ticket to take him to Regina. Two Military Police requested him to show his "leave pass". He quickly whipped this out of his billfold and showed it to them. They waved him on to board the train which was due to leave within the hour.

He purchased a copy of the newspaper as he passed by the newstand. One of the headlines highlighted President Roosevelt and remarks he made in a speech - "More than an end to the war, we want an end to the beginning of all wars," he stated. Inside the train he seated himself comfortably and waited for the train to depart.

A number of thoughts ran through his mind. As a child he was taught to obey orders from his superiors. He knew he was running away from duty and felt somewhat guilty. On the other hand he had to protect his family and garner the fruits of his labor and that of Suzanne's for the past year.

He recalled having read somewhere,- "that you are not to take life's experiences too seriously. Above all, you're not to let them hurt you, for in reality, they are nothing but dream experiences. Play your part in life, but never forget it is only a role. I wonder if the role I am now playing is the right one?" he was asking himself.

Then as he braced himself and sat a bit more upright in his seat on the train, another old Cree Indian saying came to his mind. "You can't let anyone else walk your distance."

In other words, whatever you feel you have to do, you alone must do.

LIFE'S DETOURS

Chapter 9

THE MILITARY EPISODE

The remainder of his train ride and return trip back to the farm went smoothly. Suzanne was not aware of his coming, although he had told her in his letters that he was applying for a "harvest leave" and was hoping to have it granted. When he arrived at his farm home, Suzanne simply assumed that his request for a harvest leave had been approved. He didn't disclose to anyone that he was actually a runaway and on the loose from the army. Later he informed Suzanne about the escapade and asked her not to breathe a word to anyone about it. She didn't.

He donned on his civilian clothes and went about the business of farming. It was mid-August and harvest was just beginning. His crop was average, not as good as the prior year's, but according to the neighbor's estimates and his own hunch, he was placing the production at about 25 bushels per acre. Joseph would be faced with one major problem. The marketing of his current year's crop, as well as the carry over from the previous year.

He submitted an application to the Canadian Wheat Board (CWB) requesting permission to market all of his crop in one fell swoop. The CWB was granting such permission to farmers who were being called for military duty, or who were voluntarily joining the armed forces and had to dispose of their crop before leaving.

Then another good thing happened to Joseph. An elderly couple living in a two-room house in the town of Kayville, had listed their property for sale at the price of one thousand dollars. This included the house, the land and a backyard shed. Kayville was the town where the Ackers did their shopping, obtained their mail and marketed their products.

"Not a pretentious piece of property, but it would be a suitable place for Suzanne and Carolyn to live in during his absence. She would be close to her parents, as well as to the Acker family and could receive help if necessary," Joseph said to himself.

Without consulting Suzanne or anyone else, he offered a deposit of $100.00 on the property with the balance to be paid within a month, or as soon as harvesting was completed and his crop was sold. He came home and broke the news to Suzanne, who also felt that this was a good move.

Financially, Suzanne would receive her military marriage allowance of $55.00 per month, plus an additonal $20.00 per month for the child Carolyn and that would provide adequate income for their living.

During the harvesting operation which lasted about three weeks, Joseph had received the permit from the CWB to sell all of his grain. The Saskatchewan Wheat Pool (SWP) and McCabe Brothers, were two buying agencies in Kayville. The two grain buyers knew Joseph, and were aware of the fact that he would be going back to the army. They considered it their patriotic duty to assist Joseph in solving his marketing problem and arranged for loading a carload of 2,000 bushels of wheat. This took care of 80% of his crop production. The price was $1.05 per bushel. Joseph gained sufficient funds to complete the payment on the town property they had acquired, and to pay the current year's farming expenses. Another 500 bushels would be marketed at a later date when storage space would become available. His brother Ray would attend to that matter.

By the end of September, he had settled Suzanne and their little baby daughter in their newly acquired home. The weather was nice and he took the time to fix and repair a few things, as well as to put in the winter's supply of coal. It was time for him to report back to the army, but decided to spend a few more days at home with his family.

In the following week, one afternoon there was a knock on the door. Joseph and Suzanne were enjoying their noon day bowl of soup and a sandwich. Carolyn was sleeping.

He rose to answer the door. When he opened it, there stood Constable Bob Walton, from the local detachment of the Royal Canadian Mounted Police (RCMP). Constable Walton knew the Acker family.

"Good afternoon, I'm sorry to disturb your noon day lunch. You are Acker Joseph, Regimental Number B129074. aren't you? the Constable asked.

Joseph nodded in the affirmative.

"I've received a notice from your battalion head quarters that you are Absent With Out Leave(AWOL). I have instructions to pick you up. Do you want me to pick you up under an arrest warrant, or would you prefer to go back on your own? It would make it easier and more honorable for you, if you went back on your own," the Constable said.

"Yes, I am AWOL from my battalion duties. Thank you for allowing me to go back on my own. I prefer to do that. However, since you are here Constable, give me half an hour to pack my belongings, and I'll catch a ride with you back to Avonlea. From there I can catch a train ride to Regina," Joseph pleaded with the mountie.

"As a matter of fact, I have police business to attend to in Regina tomorrow, and you can ride with me right into the city," the Constable said.

"Good, I can spend the night with friends in Avonlea, and tomorrow you can then drop me off at the barracks and I'll report back," Joseph said.

"Okay," he said. "I'll run over to the cafe, catch a cup of coffee and I'll be back to pick you up in half an hour."

Joseph took a quick wash and a shave. He changed into his military uniform and packed a few personal belongings in his knapsack. Time went by rapidly. He had a few moments to chat with Suzanne. The policeman returned. He went to the crib and kissed Carolyn "good-bye" as she was sleeping, he gave Suzanne a hug and a kiss with tears in his eyes, then let go of the hug, said "good-bye" to her and walked away to the policeman's car.

Constable Walton was a good policeman. As they drove back to the city. He looked to Joseph and said,- "What was your reason for going AWOL?"

Joseph explained his farming and his family's situation.

"Twice I requested a leave of absence. While other recruits were getting a "harvest leave" I was refused both times. I felt my personal problem was a pressing one, so I deliberately went AWOL to solve my problems. I'm thankful that I've been able to resolve them satisfactorily, and I was ready to go back on my own before the week's end anyway, but you beat me to it."

"Well, you'll be court martialled for sure and probably receive some detention time for this misbehavior. How long have you been absent?" Constable Walton asked.

"It'll be seven weeks next tuesday," Joseph replied.

The next day they drove up to the gate of the military compound and recruitment center in Regina. Here Joseph got out of the car, thanked Constable Walton and walked through the gate into the compound. He walked directly to the Commanding Officer's (C.O's) quarters and reported in.

There was a sergeant sitting behind one desk and a lieutenant behind another desk. The door to the C.O's office was closed. Joseph stepped up to the lieutenant's desk.

"Sir, my name is Private Acker Joseph, Regimental No. 129074. I have been AWOL since Aug.15th, and I am now reporting back for duty," he said as he saluted.

The lieutenant returned the salute, picked up a file, looked to Joseph and curtly said.

"Since you belong to this district your documents have been sent to us. We know all about your capers. For your misdemeanor you are subject to be Court Martialed, and I'm scheduling you to appear before the Commanding Officer (CO) tomorrow morning at 09:30 hours. Here's an order for you to report to the Quarter Master Sergeant, to obtain your blankets and be assigned temporarily to barracks. You won't be here very long. Be here tomorrow morning promptly at 09:15. You are now dismissed."

"Yes sir," Joseph replied.

He saluted smartly and making a sharp about turn, he walked out and to the quartermaster's office to receive his blankets. To his surprise, he found his kit bag and rifle had been shipped from Vancouver Island to Regina and all his equipment was there waiting for him. He was assigned to Barrick Unit C7 and was handed both his personal equipment and the blankets. He signed for them. He thanked the Corporal in charge and walked to Unit No.C7, where he would temporarily house himself and await the results from the next day's hearing.

At 09:30 the next morning, Joseph appeared before Col. Stan Gibson, the Commanding Officer at this military post.

"You are Private Acker,Joseph - Regimental No. B129074?" the CO asked.

"Yes Sir," Joseph replied.

"You are charged with being Absent Without Leave from the duties at your battalion since August 15th. How do you plead?" the C.O. asked as he looked Joseph straight in the eyes.

"Guilty Sir, I plead guilty," Joseph replied saluting.

"What have you got to say, if anything, in your defense," the C.O. asked.

Joseph took the opportunity to state his case, explaining his two requests for a harvest leave. He talked about his vested interest in the farm and the situation with his family. Anything less than a harvest leave would have caused him and his family hardship, a substantial financial loss and mental anguish.

The C.O. listened attentively, then closing the file folder he held before him, looked at Joseph and said:-

"You are guilty of a misdemeanor. However, in view of your

LIFE'S DETOURS

situation I will impose a light sentence on you. You are to serve 28 days in detention at the Military Detention Barracks in Dundurn, Saskatchewan. You will be taken there by the Military Police (MP) tomorrow by train."

"Thank you Sir," Joseph said as he saluted and made an about turn to leave. However, he found himself now under escort. He was being escorted by an MP who took him to his barracks to pick up his belongings, then led him to an improvised cell and locked him up overnite. He was a prisoner. His limited military freedom had been taken away from him. It was the price he would be paying for his misdemeanor.

The next day, accompanied by his MP escort they travelled a matter of three hours by train, and then with a military vehicle he was taken to the Detention Barracks. Again, he had to face the Commanding Officer at these quarters, where he was told about the detention rules and the rigid discipline that he would have to undergo.

"Failure to submit to this discipline would be punished by a restricted diet and solitary confinement," The new CO admonished him.

"On the other hand, for good behavior, we might consider shortening your sentence. You will be shown to your cubicle by your escort. You are now dismissed," the C.O. commanded.

Time in detention was taken up in the main with military drill, washing pots and pans, scrubbing of the kitchen and bathroom facilities. Additionally, general housecleaning of the barracks and yard was performed routinely every day. There were at least 50 other inmates serving detention time for various causes. A few were conscientious objectors, a couple were on a hunger strike, while a few just simply refused to bear arms. The majority were serving time for being AWOL just like Joseph.

The wearisome part about being in detention was the isolation that one was subjected to. During off-duty hours, one would be confined to his cubicle. This was a small room with a cot, furnished with a thin mattress, a blanket and a pillow. The only reading material was the Bible. There were no newspapers and no radio was allowed. The prisoner was allowed to write and send and to receive one letter per week, both of which were censored. The bottom line was that as a detainee one was constantly under a measure of surveillance.

Joseph would lie down on his cot and think. A thousand thoughts would cross his mind.

"Why am I in this situation? In my mind lies the kingly power to control every function of which I am capable, yet here I am, robbed of the physical power to respond to the dictates of my mind. Why do we need wars for anyway? Why can't mankind settle their differences through discussion and mutual agreement? Here I am a young man, married, with one child, simply seeking a break in life and I am being robbed of it. Who created the present crisis? Wasn't it Britain and France, and the United States that helped Hitler to amass his power? Didn't the countries now known as the Allies, using the profit motive, furnish Hitler with much of his military needs. They exported vital commodities to help him build his war machine. Am I unpatriotic? Do I not believe in defending my country? Who attacked us anyway?" he was saying to himself.

One morning, he was advised by the guard that he was to be paraded before the Commanding Officer. Joseph readied himself, but wondered what the purpose of the interview would be. His behavior had been good. At the appointed time he appeared before the C.O and in customary military fashion, saluted and stood at attention.

"Private Acker, I have been going over your file, and I am disposed to make a new assessment of your detention sentence, but first I want to have you take a psychological and aptitude test. You will write your aptitude test this morning, following which you will be interviewed by the post psychiatrist. As soon as I have these reports, you will be summoned here for another interview and disposition of your case. You will now carry on," the C.O. concluded.

Joseph was led by the guard to a room that looked like a small library. He was directed to sit at one of the tables and was handed the Aptitude Test sheets. He had 90 minutes in which to complete all the questions. He finished on time and handed the work to the guard, who in turn handed it to another officer for appraisal.

Joseph was then taken to another office for his psychiatric interview. He saluted the officer, who carried the rank of a captain.

"My name is Captain Jenkins, I am the post psychiatrist, and for the next little while we're going to have a chat about you personally and your situation. Please sit down and make yourself comfortable," he said.

Then he turned to the guard and said,-"Corporal you may be excused, please stand by in the waiting room, I'll call you as soon as we're finished."

The first question that Captain Jenkins posed to Joseph was,- "Private Acker, are you a draft dodger?"

"No Sir, I'm not a draft dodger, but I'm not a believer in war either," he replied.

"Are you not patriotic, don't you believe in defending your country," the Captain asked.

"Sir, in my mind patriotism is like a fever, it is blind, when compared to the philosophy under which I was raised and it is irrational. Both at church and in my parents home, I was taught the ten commandments. The 7th of which says - Thou shalt not kill, then how does this square and uphold the act of war? Furthermore, in the Bible again, God did not create only one country, he created the Universe and the Earth and all things that dwell therein. My country, to this point has brought me through an economic depression, which deprived me of furthering my education. In truth, I have nothing to defend but life itself. My life and that of my family and life for me begins each morning because God ordained it so. No power on earth can grant a person life, but powers exist, that can regulate and take away the life of even a peaceful law abiding person. I believe that one should defend his country, like he defends his home. Should he kill in the process? I'm not sure. Maybe it is better to turn the other cheek. I am not a draft dodger, I'm prepared to defend my country and bear arms if I'm forced to. But, I'm not too sure that I want to kill to fulfill these objectives," Joseph concluded.

Joseph felt at this point, that he had probably said too much in reply to a simple question. But, somehow he felt better for having said it. He got it off his chest.

"What prompted you to go AWOL?" the Captain asked.

Joseph repeated his situation once more for the captain's sake. The captain listened intently and appeared to be sympathetic to his situation, but did not orally express concurrence.

"Private Acker, you appear to be honest and sincere and to have the makings of a solid citizen. You have a chance to do well in the military also. Your intelligence is above average in relation to other men I've interviewed. Would you be prepared to participate in military action overseas at this time?" was the final comment made and question the captain asked.

"I have returned from being AWOL, with full intentions of abiding by whatever course, the army will choose and direct for me. If I must go overseas, I will do so," he replied.

With that the Captain called the MP guard back in, shook hands with Joseph, and following the routine military salutations, the guard led him back to his confinement cubicle. He was also told that at 15:00 hours that same day, the C.O. wanted to see him again.

Joseph's curiosity was more aroused than ever. What is this testing and interviewing all about. Does this mean he will be dishonorably discharged. He was well satisfied with the morning interview with Captain Jenkins and felt a degree of pride, when he was told that he had above average intelligence. Joseph felt that the volume of reading and the kind of books he read had contributed to his status.

"Maybe I have failed," he thought to himself. "But failure is nothing more than success that has taken the wrong road."

He remembered what his grandfather had told him about his experiences. "The test of a person is not whether he has failed - but whether he is content to lie there and whine, and blame others, or to get up and make a fresh start."

Thomas Edison was a great success, I wonder how many failures he had before he became a success, Joseph thought.

Joseph Billings once said,-"It ain't no disgrace to make a mistake. The disgrace comes in making the same mistake twice."

"Private Acker, let us report to the C.O's office. The time is 14:50. We have ten minutes," the guard called from the corridor.

At the appointed hour, Joseph stood anew before the Unit's C.O. He felt impatient and insecure.

"Private Acker, I have good news for you. Your aptitude test taken this morning ranks you as potential officer material, and the interview report from Captain Jenkins also came in positive. Are you willing to go overseas?" the C.O. asked.

"Yes sir, if that's where the army determines I must go. But, I do not feel that I'm adequately prepared to face physical combat, because I have not yet completed my advanced training," he replied.

"If you are willing to go overseas you will be given your completion of training there - before being assigned to physical combat," the C.O. stated.

"I'm willing to go sir," he replied.

"Based on your willingness to go overseas, you will be pardoned for your misdemeanor and your time spent in detention will go unrecorded. You will get prepared to depart for England tomorrow at 08.00 hours. Good luck to you and Godspeed. You are dismissed," the C.O. concluded.

All at once Joseph found himself to be a free person inside of a detention camp. He was no longer being escorted back to his cubicle and his cubicle door was left open. He took a little time to stroll over to the kitchen and talk to the kitchen staff. On his return to his cubicle, he bumped into the C.O. whom he saluted, and who returned the salute with a smile but made no comment.

The next morning, he was handed an envelope containing his official documents.

"You are going on a one-man draft and carrying your own documents. Do not lose them," he was warned by the staff-sergeant who delivered them to him.

He was driven to the city of Saskatoon, from where he boarded a train for Camp Debert in Nova Scotia. The ride lasted three days and

LIFE'S DETOURS

two nights.

At Camp Debert, Joseph was assigned to a company of new recruits, who like himself, had not completed their advanced training. They were in this camp for one week, and under strict orders to stand-by ready for overseas departure. The exact time and place could not be disclosed due to the secrecy that was involved in all military operations. The soldiers had been informed of the fact that they would be transported overseas by ship, and Hitler's submarines, were still very active off the Atlantic coast of North America.

"It is just as well for security and safety's sake, that such matters are kept a secret," Joseph thought.

Finally, the day of embarkation arrived. Ten thousand Canadian soldiers marched up the gang plank of the "Louis Pasteur" ship. It was a ship taken over from France before its downfall to Hitler. It was a former luxury liner, now converted to a troop transport ship. It took a couple of days to get all the men on board and settled.

The soldiers were crowded into cramped quarters. They slept on hammocks slung from the ceilings of the various decks, in which they happened to be housed. It was a sight to look at from your hammock at night, and see the hundreds of hammocks swinging back and forth as the ship swayed up and down on the Atlantic waves. The food was served military style, with each soldier using his mess tins and going to a spot on his own deck level to receive his rations.

The ship set sail early in the morning and sailed due south from the port of Halifax. This was hard for Joseph to understand. "Why weren't we sailing in a north-easterly direction if we were going to England?" he thought.

Nobody seemed to know what was going on and no one was supposed to ask questions anyway. It was a matter of wait and see.

Late in the same day, the Pasteur docked outside of the New York harbor, and the next day the Queen Elizabeth ship loaded with more than 20,000 American soldiers steamed out of port. It was accompanied by a number of gun boats, destroyers and submarine chasers. Overhead a number of planes of varying descriptions were flying. The transatlantic convoy for transporting the two troop ships was taking formation.

Joseph stood on the deck of the Pasteur, overwhelmed by all this military strength that had been mustered and displayed. He also felt a measure of safety and security and harbored a feeling of strength.

"There is no way, that Hitler can win this war. The fact of the matter is that we are just beginning to give him a dose of his own medicine. The Allies are powerful, and we are lucky the United States is on our side," Joseph thought.

During the first three days the convoy sailed in a south-easterly direction. Everyone became aware of this by the tropical warm air breezes that were blowing. After the first day, part of the naval and air convoy disappeared and only two destroyers accompanied the two troop ships, one on each side. On the third day, the convoy arrived into the company and formation of a new number of Allied gun boats, submarine chasers and destroyers. It was an "escort party" which came from an Allied Naval Base located on the Azores. At this juncture, the entire convoy swung in a northerly direction, and the two troop ships were then escorted right into the port of Liverpool in England. The troop ships were met by a welcoming military band, who opened up the band concert with great flair by playing the song, "My Bonny Lies Over The Ocean." This brought a lump in Joseph's throat. He knew that other soldiers did not feel the same way as he did. He could tell by their actions and behaviour. Some were waving to a group of good looking English gals, who were on the bank waving their handherchiefs, smiling and somehow transmitting their happiness at seeing the two troop ships docked there. England as a country was war-weary by this time. Troop reinforcements of this nature bolstered their morale.

The troops were advised that the disembarkation process would take a couple of days, since an insufficient number of trains were available to carry all the troops at once to their various destinations. Joseph's platoon was given their time of disembarkation, their train number and told that they would be going to the Canadian Army Camp at Aldershot. He had to board a midnghit train and arrived at Aldershot early the next day. He did not see much of the countryside travelling in the night. As a defense measure the country as a whole was dark. It was November 1943, and the "black-out" was still in force. The bombing of London and other British cities by Hitler's "Luftwaffe" and the V-1 and V-2 bombs continued. In camp at Aldershot, Joseph was immediately assigned to a company of soldiers for completion of their advanced training.

He took everything in its stride and decided he was going to make the best of it. He wrote at least one airgram letter each week to Suzanne, to his parents and others as time permitted. He took along his hand operated hair clippers and his iron for pressing clothes. In the evenings and on weekends he would be busy cutting hair or pressing uniforms for his buddies and others. He charged 50 cents for haircuts and 50 cents for pressing a complete uniform (tunic and trousers), 25 cents for pressing a shirt. All in all, he found a way to make good use of his spare time, stay out of mischief and earn some money in the meantime. This lasted into early 1944.

The paymaster's office grew concerned over Joseph's lack of

drawing funds from his soldier's pay and questioned him on the issue.

"I'm trying to save every penny I can," Joseph explained. "One of these days the war will be over, and I will require funds to rehabilitate myself in civilian life."

"You're a rare bird," the paymaster sergeant said, "I wish there were more guys of your kind. Too many of the boys find themselves borrowing from one pay period to another." He was satisfied with Joseph's performance and accounting.

One morning, as the company was ready to appear on the parade square, a second lieutenant accompanied by the sergeant major walked into the barracks and called for order.

"Do we have anyone here who can speak, read and write other languages, and Romanian in particular?" the Sergeant Major bellowed in a loud voice.

Joseph hesitated for a moment, but then stepped away from his bunk bed and replied.

"Yes sir, I can read, write and speak a couple of languages, of which Romanian is one. What's the scoop?" Joseph asked.

"There's a group of Romanian prisoners that have been captured fighting along with Hitler's Forces in Northern Italy. They've been brought to the prisoner's camp at Woking. We need some interpreters for interrogation and documentation. Have you done translation before?" the lieutenant asked Joseph.

"Well sir, I haven't done any translation in an official capacity, but back in Canada I did translation for Romanian people who could not speak, read or write English," Joseph replied.

"Okay, then pack up your stuff. I'll clear your transfer with the C.O. and we'll drop by here to pick you up and take you to your new post," the lieutenant said.

There were five soldiers including Joseph and the lieutenant in the jeep. The drive from Aldershot to West Acton in London took about two hours. They arrived before lunch. Joseph was escorted by the lieutenant before a staff sergeant, who explained the nature of the job he was to perform and the conditions under which he would be working.

"You will be taken on strength here at Canadian Military Headquarters (CMHQ), and will be doing translation and interrogation as called upon and necessary. You will be doing office and clerical work as assigned. You will be furnished with a written job description. There is a five day work week from 08:00 hours to 16:30 hours with a half hour lunch break. There is no work on week-ends, except on rare occassions when some special issue involving your specialty comes before us and calls for immediate attention. There are no bivouacs or barracks to house the military personnel working at CMHQ in London, therefore you will be living as a civilian. You must locate for yourself a boarding place. The army will pay you a subsistance allowance of One Pound Sterling (equivalent to $5.00) per day and provide you with a ration book. There is a medical unit attached to headquarters here and you may use it at your convenience or need. You will turn your rifle into the quartermaster's office. You won't need it. You will draw your clothing needs from the quartermaster in accordance with basic army rules. You are expected to keep well groomed and dressed; to carry on with good behavior; to be law abiding and to maintain the good image of the Canadian military personnel in this country. You will take the balance of today and all of tomorrow off and try to obtain lodging. Report for work here on Friday morning. Do you have any questions?" the staff sergeant asked.

"Yes sir, I have one question. May I leave my duffle bag here, until I locate a place to live," he asked.

"Sure, we will store it right here for you. You may now leave. You are dismissed," the sergeant ordered.

Joseph felt like he had been awakened from a dream. Little did he think, that he would land such a favorable position for himself. He walked out on the street and just stood for a moment to get his bearings and his thoughts straight. He saw a gentleman dressed in a non-military uniform standing at the bus or trolley stop. Joseph walked up to him.

"Good day sir, my name is Joseph Acker, I'm a Canadian soldier and I need some information. Can you help me?" he said to the stranger.

"Good day, how are you - what is your problem?" the gentleman replied.

"Sir, I've just been taken on strength at our military headquarters here. The Canadian military have no barracks in London. We must find lodging among the civilian population. I was wondering if you knew of a family nearby, that would be in a position to accommodate me. I have been supplied with a ration book and have a subsistance allowance to take care of the rental," Joseph informed him.

"My name is Ralph Hawthorne. I'm a bus conductor for the London Transit System. I live a couple of blocks from here at 253 Uxbridge Road. The street that runs diagonal to this. I have three sons and two daughters. My three sons are all in the British Armed Forces. One is with the Royal Air Force in India, the second is with the Royal Navy on the high seas, and the youngest is with the Royal Air Force here in Britain. My eldest daughter is married to a sailor, who is also in the service and our youngest daughter is a student. We have ample space at our house and we'd like to do something for our servicemen.

However, I must first talk to Mrs. Hawthorne about this before I make a commitment. Can you come and see us tomorrow morning? Write down our address- 253 Uxbridge Road," he said.

"Thank you sir, I'd be glad to see you in the morning." Joseph replied.

A trolley pulled up to the stop. It was the moment for a change of shift for the conductors. The two exchanged a few words, and finally Mr. Hawthorne got on the bus and in short order disappeared from sight. The off-shift conductor walked his way down the street.

The next morning Joseph showed up at the Hawthorne residence. Mr. Hawthorne introduced him to his wife, who was a matronly looking woman, wearing a near ankle length dress, and a bleached white apron on her front. They immediately made it known to Joseph that they would be happy to provide lodging for him, and showed him the room that he would occupy. It was a spacious and bright bedroom on the second floor. The two double paned glass windows were open. The glass panes were painted black. This was done to avoid having night lights shining in London and to making the city vulnerable to bombing. Every window, in every building in the city had the windows painted black or covered. The bedroom windows when open were overlooking the street. "It could be a bit noisy," Joseph thought, but he liked the location and the idea of being close to his work. He also took an immediate liking to Mr. and Mrs. Hawthorne, a couple in their mid-fifties.

"I'll take it," Joseph said. What are your house rules and your charges? he asked.

"Our charges will be 15 shillings per day or 100 shillings per week. You will follow the same house rules as our family. We do not suffer unruly guests, late hours and noise. No rowdy parties. We will serve two meals daily (breakfast and dinner) and we will do your laundry. You are free to move in at your pleasure. We will treat you as a family member in the hope that our boys will receive nice treatment from other folks, wherever that may be. You will be filling in a vacuum at our home," Mrs. Hawthorne said.

"Thank you," Joseph replied. "Here is my ration book, and payment for the two days remaining for this week. Commencing with Monday, I will pay you for each week in advance. I shall now go and fetch my personal belongings and settle in."

After concluding his move, he was given a key to his room and the front door. Conversation topics during mealtimes involved talking about the war, comparing notes in terms of the living conditions between England and Canada and about their families. Joseph would receive letters from home with the latest news, and Suzanne would send food parcels which Joseph would share with the Hawthornes. Since Joseph did not smoke, when cigarettes came, the Hawthornes would purchase them from him. Most everything was scarce and rationed.

Joseph enjoyed the work he was doing. He felt extremely grateful and fortunate. His subsistance was one pound (20 shillings) per day. He would pay the Hawthornes 15 shillings per day, and have 5 shillings daily left over for bus fares, for the odd pint of ale at the corner pub, for his weekend browsing around London and his R & R vacations and for other small personal needs. His income from cutting hair and pressing uniforms had disappeared with his transfer, but was adequately made up by the subsistance allowance.

At first translation and some interrogation took up most of his time, but this was a diminshing activity, so he found himself filing documents in the Records Section and working in the Military Postal Service. Both tasks were huge and important. Documents had to be filed promptly and soldier's files kept as current as possible. New files had to be added as new soldiers came on strength, while other files for those killed in action or wounded, had to taken out and returned to their home base or Department of National Defense. In the Postal Service section, the task was ample and called for keeping abreast and posting all the address changes for the thousands of soldiers in all branches of the service. Address changes had to be posted hurriedly, and letters and parcels redirected, for nothing demoralized a serviceman more than failure to receive news from home and from his loved ones. Joseph knew this from his own experience. The work never became humdrum, but it soon became routine.

Conditions in London at that point were still very war like. The sirens would squeal frequently at first, and less often as time went by, letting everyone know that the V-1 and later the V-2 bombs were coming. Everyone would run and scramble for the underground shelters and stay there until the all-clear signal sounded. There were times, when Joseph and the Hawthornes would grab a blanket and run in their night pyjamas to the underground shelters, and remain there till the break of day. In fact, at times it was even funny, because one never really knew whom one was sitting or lying down next to in the shelter. It was routine, and people took it in stride, while at the same time praying and hoping that the war would come to an end.

"These people are fantastic," Joseph thought to himself. "In spite of all this hardship, shortage of goods, rationing and inconvenience the war has imposed on them, they retain their loyalty to duty, their sense of humor and their good natured composure. They're incredible."

Joseph soon assumed the character and disposition of the people.

LIFE'S DETOURS

It sort of grew upon him and he shared in their happiness, as well as in their sorrow and anguish. However, he kept pretty much to himself. He would spend his off duty time reading or studying. He took a course sponsored by the army on Free Lance Writing and Newspaper Reporting.

On weekends, he would tour the city of London, both by trolley and by the underground railway or "tube" as the Londoners called it. He had arranged to visit Buckingham Palace, Hyde Park, Westminster Abbey, the Houses of Parliament. He walked down 55 Downing Street, and saw Petticoat Lane. On at least two occassions he went to the Hammersmith Dance Palais to observe the activity and some of the military night-life in London. The servicemen often referred to the Dance Palais as the "gonorrhea-racetrack." Joseph had no desire to get involved or acquire friends from the opposite sex.

On his Rest and Recuperation vacations, he had been to Manchester, Liverpool, Brighton, and Birmingham. He spent many a Sunday afternoon in Hyde Park, listening to the soap-box orators give talks on any number of subjects. He had a particular liking for a certain Dr. Frederick Lohr, who was a graduate from the University of Berlin. He was forced to flee from Germany to avoid imprisonment, because he disagreed with Hitler's "Mein Kampf" theory. Joseph learned a great deal from this person. He gave lectures on philosophy and then engaged himself in oral debate, with anyone who questioned or disagreed with his point of view. His style of debate paralleled that of Plato. He would raise questions or engage in dialogue gradually bringing the other person to agree with him or accept his premise. His lectures were weighty and significant.

Notwithstanding, news about the battle gains the Allies were making on the war front, and the involvement in his work and other activities, there were times when Joseph felt lonesome, and longed to be back home with Suzanne and his little daughter Carolyn. He had composed a poem, dedicated to her.

TO CAROLYN

My dear daughter, It seems you've just arrived
  At two, you look so well behaved-
Your style and your manner capture me,
  As I sit here alone and think of thee.
The doll carriage made of painted tin-
  And the little dolls you lay therein,
Minus an arm, or leg or hair-
  You drag them with you everywhere.
Around the house you demonstrate your powers,

I know, I can imagine, thinking here for hours.

You cannot understand as yet, the pride
 I have, to be your daddy walking by your side;
To have you look at me, and gaze so unafraid,
To feel your trust in me my little maid.
Your smile - it always makes me want to sing -
 A trick of yours, it brings you anything.
I'd like to be at home - putting you to bed,
 Straightening up the pillow for your head;
Rocking your crib, whispering a prayer
 As you nod off to sleep, in our Creator's care.

Worldly wisdom doesn't bother you - as yet,
 Most things you haven't heard, some you'll forget-
You'll learn so many things when you have grown,
 That an olive has a seed - and not a bone,
And mamma's hat a veil - and not a shade,
 And to sit still while mamma makes your braid.
But there are natural things - that somehow you know,
 I think God taught you ere he let you go.
For two years would be otherwise too short,
 For learning the ways to get to my heart.

A year and a half had gone by since Joseph's arrival in Britain. Then on the morning of May 8th, 1945, the radio and the newspapers announced that the war in Europe had ended. Hitler had committed suicide, and the German Military Forces had signed the agreement of surrender the day before. It was V-Day in Europe.

The troops were now coming to Britain from inland Europe, and preparations had to be made to transport them back to Canada. The preference was given to those soldiers who had volunteered to fight in the Pacific Region against the Japanese. The others followed in accordance with the availability of space on the troopships.

The Canadian Military Headquarters (CMHQ) would certainly be the very last Canadian unit overseas to fold up. Joseph being attached to this unit would naturally be amongst the last soldiers to be repatriated. The work that he was doing along with some others, in the Records and Postal Section, increased tremendously in volume. This was due, of course, to the increased movement of personnel from the overseas bases to their regimental bases at home, and the need for their documents, parcels and mail to follow them.

Letters from Suzanne would ask him when he would be returning. He was unable to offer a date, because no one was certain

LIFE'S DETOURS 145

when their work would diminish in volume to a point where he could be released for repatriation. For Joseph and Suzanne, the war was not quite over yet.

However, on December 22nd, 1945 he received his embarkation orders. Trains were arriving every hour at Southampton with homebound troops, mostly Americans but the Canadians were also included. About 23,000 soldiers, including Joseph, marched up the gangplank unto the Queen Elizabeth troop ship. As the ship slowly pulled out of port to set sail for New York harbor an atmosphere of joy prevailed throughout. The return voyage aboard the Queen Elizabeth was more comfortable and the sailing was smoother, than on the initial voyage to Britain. The troops were in the mid-Atlantic on Christmas Day, and they were served a "turkey-dinner," a dinner that many of them had not had for a long time. An outstanding treat and change from mutton. Radio messages were received from President Roosevelt, as well as Prime Minister McKenzie King of Canada.

One of the most unforgettable sensations that Joseph felt, was the shiver that went up his spine, when he first spotted the "Statue of Liberty" on the dim ocean horizon as they were approaching New York harbor. Joseph was not an American, but even as a Canadian and a neighbor, he revelled in its image and what it stood for.

"Maybe we do have something worth fighting for. Something that perhaps I haven't quite understood up to this point. If our countries are democracies, then democracy cannot be a spectator sport, it must be made to work. The people must roll up their sleeves, get involved in it, strive for improvement and then defend their freedom and their gains," he thought to himself.

The troop ship was about one hour out of New York harbor, when a "Welcome Home" smaller ship came to meet it.

After it had turned and realigned itself to sail on the right side, at a distance, but parallel to the Queen Elizabeth, a troupe of entertainers emerged with welcoming messages, music and song. The song "Sentimental Journey" sung by three pretty young ladies touched the hearts of most of the men on board, including Joseph's, and teary eyes were being wiped with khaki handkerchiefs.

Disembarkation lasted for two or three days. Joseph's turn came on the second day. After disembarkation, he boarded the Chesapeake and Ohio passenger rail line to Niagara Falls, then switched to the Canadian Pacific Railway line, which brought him to Regina on New Year's eve, 1945.

They had been issued with 30 day passes on board the train, making it unecessary to report to barracks upon arrival. There were families, wives and sweethearts waiting at the train station for the arrival of their loved ones. Joseph knew there would be someone waiting for him at home, not at the station.

Fortunately, he was able to catch a ride with a petroleum freighting truck that same evening, and at an unconventional hour past midnight, he knocked on the door of their home in Kayville. There was no response. He rapped on the window and called Suzanne by name, telling her it was him. A light went on, and soon Suzanne unlocked and opened the door. The meeting, the hugging and the kissing were moments of pure ecstasy.

Carolyn, who was almost three years of age, had been informed by her mother of her dad's whereabouts and had been shown pictures of him. She awoke. She was sleeping with her mother. She lifted herself up and sat on her pillow in bed.

She looked with anxiety and curiosity at the stranger that had walked in the house in the middle of the night and disturbed their peace and quiet. Joseph picked her up in his arms and kissed her, then laid her back on the bed.

Moments were spent in a bit of get acquainted chatter. Joseph was tired from the long trip. He could not control his eyelids. He prepared himself for bed, but one thought stood on his mind, as he looked at Suzanne and Carolyn, lying in bed beside him.

"It's so good to get back home and to those you love, but what do I do now and where do I go from here in civilian life? I'll face that situation later," he thought as he fell asleep.

LIFE'S DETOURS 147

Chapter 10

BECOMING A MANAGER

Kayville was located on a spur line of the Canadian Pacific Railway, that ran west from Weyburn to Cardross, about 60 miles as the crow flies north of the U.S. Border. It was one of the better small towns within a radius of 20 miles in almost any direction. It was incorporated as a hamlet in the Rural Municipality of Key West in the province of Saskatchewan. It's estimated population at this time was about 200 people. It served as the trading center for an area comprising of two and one half townships with a total of about 500 farm families. As the Second World War ended it became a thriving community and a center of economic activity. It had a community hall, four general stores, three implement agencies, three major oil companies, a lumber yard, two grain elevators, two coal and wood dealers, and a livestock shipping yard. It did not have a bank and a few other services normally found in a bigger town, such as a pharmacy, a doctor's office or a lawyer's office.

After spending 30 days at home on leave, Joseph returned to the Regina Military Depot for his discharge. He was granted an honorable discharge with the General Service and European theater badges as recognition for his service. He was given a discharge allowance of $250.00 and was told that a further grant would be available for the construction or purchase of a home.

He walked out as a civilian on the streets of Regina and met up with Johnny Huston, a friend whom he had known for some time.

"Hi there Joe, what are you doing, still wearing the army uniform? his friend said to him as they shook hands.

"Well, I'm on my way to purchasing new civilian clothes. I've just received my discharge this morning and will be returning back to civilian life," Joseph replied.

"Well, that's good to hear. I did very well for myself during the war and am now well-heeled in business," Huston explained.

"Tell me about it. I knew you didn't make the grade for the army, so then what happened?" he asked his friend.

"I was declared medically unfit, but we did pull some strings you know. I had friends on the Medical Examination Board and they helped me out a lot. Then my dad, assisted me in acquiring the Allis Chalmers Agency, you know, selling and handling heavy machinery for road construction. With that I was able to get a defense contract from the Federal Government for the construction of a portion of the Alaska Highway. It was a war-time contract on a cost-plus basis, but it still paid off well," his friend said

Then with a grin on his face, Huston added, "For every big tractor or scraper that went over the cliff, we chalked it up to expenses and made an extra 10%, because our contracts called for cost plus ten percent."

"You mean to say, that if you took me out to dinner, you could say it was for a business purpose, then claim it as an expense and add an additional 10% to that bill?" Joseph asked.

"Precisely, that's the way it works. It was a boon for the contractors. There was no way one could lose money, because the higher your cost became, within certain liberal limitations, the more one was protected by the cost-plus feature of the contract," his friend remarked.

"I'm happy for you," Joseph replied."In my case, I have to start from scratch and I don't know exactly where to scratch to begin with," Joseph added as they shook hands and parted.

He returned back to Kayville, this small community and it's milieu and began to investigate it's potential and possibilities. He found similar reports of people who did well during the war years. Some of his friends, had no more than he did at the beginning of the war, but after four years they were now considered good and well established farmers.

These situations were aggravating and rubbed Joseph the wrong way. He felt sorry for himself only to the extent of the time he lost. But then, he thought about the veterans that lost time and came back wounded, and those who made the supreme sacrifice of losing their lives. Here's these guys sporting a sense of pride and seemingly unashamed to tell one to his face, that the war was a waste of life and time.

Joseph still felt he had much to be thankful for.

He reserved his opinions in such discussions and kept continuously focused on trying to get something suitable and more lucrative that he could do. Suzanne suggested that he complete his last

LIFE'S DETOURS

two years of high school, but Joseph had no income, other than the few savings that Suzanne and he put together out of their military pay and allowances. He decided this was not the best course for him to pursue at this time.

He opened up a small office, obtained an appointment as a Notary Public and a Justice of The Peace. He began doing secretarial and para legal work. He secured appointments as an agent for several insurance companies, did income tax and bookkeeping work for others and he would cut hair on Saturdays. He had purchased an autombile for $400.00 and went selling newspaper and magazine subscriptions on a commission basis, two days per week. At first the income was adequate for a living, but there didn't appear to be any substantial future in it.

One year later, the Board of Directors of the Kayville Cooperative Association (the Co-op) found themselves searching for a qualified person to manage their business. The former manager had resigned to go into a partnership business in the same locality, and to some degree in direct competition with the Co-op business he formerly managed.

Joseph applied for this position and received the appointment. As a manager, he would receive $75.00 per month and no other benefits. He would be allowed to carry on with his established lines of business. The volume of trading the Co-op was doing at that time was just slightly over $25,000 annually and primarily in petroleum products. During the winter months when farming operations were idle, there was no business activity. The Board of Directors had visions of an expanding business and were constructing a new building on the same location. They were looking for an active and aggressive person as manager and Joseph assured them he had those qualities.

Joseph had a lot to learn and he had to learn fast. He assumed his responsibilities on April 1st, and this is the time of the year when farmers begin their field operations. All of the Co-op's business was generally done from April to the end of October. If the Co-op was to flourish and increase it's trading volume, it had to add other lines of merchandise beside petroleum products. Lines that would permit commercial activity for the association during the idle winter months. Increased trading volume would bring greater revenue to the association and subsequently a better salary for him. When the construction of the new building was completed, the facitilies enabling expansion into other lines would be there. What would be required is a plan for development, and his job was to draft this plan, which he did.

The year 1947 concluded with a slight increase in sales over the previous year and a patronage refund of 8% on each dollar of sales. This surpassed any previous record this Co-op ever had and was a feather in Joseph's hat.

At the annual meeting of the association held in March of 1948, after the usual reading of the minutes, and a brief discussion on Board policies and future plans. Mr.Bruce Sanborn, the president of the Co-op introduced Joseph in a very positive way to the fifty odd shareholders and their wives present at the meeting.

"Ladies and gentlemen, we are fortunate to have Mr. Joseph Acker as our new manager. As you can see from the financial statement for last year, this is the first time in the history of this co-op that we have received a patronage refund of eight percent. He is a young man. He is aggressive. He is a good businessman. I'm going to turn the meeting over to him. He will summarize the business operations for last year, and also reveal the plans we have made for the future expansion of the Co-op." He then requested Joseph to present his report.

At that moment Joseph felt he had to take full advantage of the situation, and to do that, he would have to leave two important thoughts well embedded into the minds of the co-op members. He would have to do that during and in the manner of presentation of his report. First, he had to instill confidence in his shareholders that he had the capability and could do the job, and secondly he had the responsibility of educating the members who were actually shareholders and owners of the business.

He had to point out the benefits that could be derived from supporting their Co-op, and the tremendous potential that they were facing. He had prepared a visual aid in the form of a flip-chart with figures, graphs and diagrams to assist him in making the presentation as understandable as possible.

"Mr. Chairman, ladies and gentleman," Joseph started out. "I'm your new manager, and I'm delighted with this opportunity to tell you about your business and how grateful I am to be it's manager. Let me begin at the beginning, by telling you that a co-operative is any group of people, who band themselves together for the purpose of obtaining their needed goods and services at cost. This is exactly what you folks have done. You have organized this co-op and last year, the patronage refund amounted to 8% on every dollar of purchases you made from your co-op. This means that the price of the goods you purchased from your co-op was reduced by 8% across the board on all items."

"Any one of you, and I see three or four of you in this crowd, that made purchases of $1,000.00 or more last year, are entitled to $80.00 or proportionately more as a patronage refund. Now, in my books this means prudent judgement and good management on your part. Consider that one has to put savings in a bank to earn 3% interest. However, at your coop you have earned 8% not on your savings, but on what you had to spend in order to carry on your farming operations. I would call that good business, and perhaps you could save more if you made more of your puchases at your co-op; but, since the co-op does not carry a full range of commodities, you are being forced to shop elsewhere for the other portion of your needs."

"In addition to petroleum products, we ought to be carrying a complete line of groceries, hardware and staple items in dry goods. Here's the way I look at it, and I've discussed it with the Board of Directors and I have their support." he said as he turned to his flip-chart and a map of the area.

"We have the potential to serve some 500 families in the two and one half townships in which Kayville is situated. At an average expenditure of $2,000 per family, we can calculate an annual sales volume of some $1,000,000. If however, our average figure is too high, let's reduce it by 50% to $1,000 per family, and that would still result in an annual sales volume of $500,000.00," he emphasized.

At this point, a number of the members of the audience, were looking at each other with smiling faces and nodding agreement with his argument.

"What this will mean for our community is strictly this," Joseph continued. "We will be in a position to effect greater savings for you. For example, an 8% dividend on sales of $500,000 - would net savings of $40,000 that would be retained right here for the benefit of you, the Co-op shareholders. If we expand our lines of goods and services, it will call for more employees, again giving employment to more people in our own community. So there are additional benefits to be garnered."

Joseph paused for a moment, and one member raised his hand seeking permission to ask a question. The chairman recognized him and gave him the floor.

"Mr. Manager, I believe your plan is great, but if the Co-op is going to monopolize and grab all the business in this town, we will force the other merchants out of business, and that's not going to be good for the community, either or is it?" the member shareholder asked.

The chairman looked to Joseph to furnish the answer.

"You are correct in your assumption sir. If the Co-op took all the business, the other merchants would cease to function. In the first instance, none of the existing merchants carry complete lines of merchandise in other than groceries. The Co-op proposes to carry a sizeable inventory in weed chemicals, fertilizer, hardware, dry goods, batteries, tires, and other farm needed supplies. Secondly, we will endeavour to be competitive with the other merchants in price and service. If they do a better job than the Co-op at serving you and their prices are right, they will survive. Remember the Co-op is not an instrument to put people out of business, it is an instrument to put people like you and me into business as shareholders. It should act as a balance wheel in our community to regulate the prices and the quality of the goods you need to buy," he replied.

At this point another member in the audience stood up and signalled his intention to ask a question. He was granted the privelege.

"Sir, I'm a member of the Co-op. I used to purchase fuel oil for my tractor from you, but have stopped doing so, because the quality of the Co-op fuel oil is not as high as that of your competitor. I'm rather convinced that my tractor performance is better with the fuel oil procured from your competitor. Can you explain that?" he queried.

At this point, the chairman looked again to Joseph to advance the response.

"Sir, I believe, firmly believe, that the refinery located in the city of Regina, which is our source of supply, and is owned cooperatively by you the farmers, draws it's crude oil out of the same pipeline that feeds the other local refineries. It refines and puts out a quality of fuel oil that is second to none. I would be willing to take a sample of your fuel oil and a sample of the Co-op fuel oil, and have you send it to an independent laboratory for testing. I'm sure the results would reflect such a minute difference in quality, either way that it should not effect performance," Joseph said.

One other farmer member in the audience, quickly rose to his feet and asked for permission to talk. Permission which was granted.

"Mr. Chairman, I'm a member of the Co-op also, and I've been buying my fuel from the Co-op. I run two tractors and a couple of stationary engines and they have excellent performance. Maybe the gentleman that spoke needs to have a tune-up on his tractor. I don't think the fuel is the problem," he said.

The discussion on the merits of the business, the products and the service carried on into the late hours of the afternoon. The final upshot of the meeting was that the general annual assembly endorsed the recommendation of the manager to proceed with the expansion of the business by introducing new lines of goods and services.

As a result of the endorsement, Joseph received more work and responsibility. He did not request an increase in wages at this time. He felt he would surrender another year of his time in order to prove that he too, was a community builder, and not in the co-op business merely for the sake of making money and a better living for himself.

From his previous year's experience, he found he was immediately faced with two new business problems and one personal problem.

Firstly, he felt that if the business was to expand. he would have

LIFE'S DETOURS

to be personally in charge and responsible for the transportation of the commodities from the central refinery and warehouses in the city to his place of business. The previous manager had been freighting the Co-op's merchandise and was still doing so under Joseph's management, but it wasn't working out.

The reason being, that the owner of the truck was doing custom trucking for his own business and others. He was not assigning the truck solely for freighting the Co-op's goods. Joseph had no control over the freighting aspect of the goods, and thus never capable of being firm in his promises to make the goods available to his members at the appropiate time. This matter was solved when the Board of Directors authorized Joseph to purchase a truck of his own and to give him the franchise for trucking all of the commodities required in the Co-op business.

Joseph went to one of his farmer friends who lent him $2,000 to purchase his first Ford 3 ton truck. He hired Andrew "Curly" Banks as the truck/driver and henceforth was in the freighting business.

The second major business problem concerned the granting of credit to the Co-op members. The basic co-op principles enabled and called for members to:
 a) Voluntarily join or withdraw as a member from the co-op.
 b) Each member had a vote, regardless of the number or value of his share capital. This provided for democratic control.
 c) Trading was to be for cash only.
 d) Payment of limited interest on capital.
 e) Equitable distribution of the surplus earnings.
 f) Continuous education of the membership.
 g) Integration of services and resources at regional or other levels of operation.

Joseph discovered that the Co-op he was managing was fulfilling all of these principles, with the exception of Item c), which emphasized cash trading.

Immaterial as to how well intentioned a farmer was to do business with cash only, at some point throughout the crop season he would be forced through circumstances of one form or another, to purchase goods and request that the goods be advanced on credit for periods of 30 to 90 days, or as the farmer would say "until after harvest."

The problem rested on the fact that the Co-op did not have the capital to be both a source of supply for the goods, and at the same time a credit institution or bank to finance the sales. The Board of Directors, were the more well-to-do farmers and community leaders and they constituted the cream of the farming community. They always paid cash for their purchases and felt everyone else was doing likewise or ought to do the same.

Joseph did not want to lose sales due to the Co-op's shortage of capital and it's inability as an institution to extend credit. This forced him to do some manipulation that worked in his favor but was risky.

In the first instance, he extended some credit out of his own funds. Funds that he borrowed personally from the bank. Secondly, he reported inventory stocks as being on hand, when in truth the inventory had been sold on credit.

The reality of the situation was that 100 credit accounts at an average of $200 for each account, meant having $20,000 of capital to provide for this accommodation.

For two years, he extended lines of credit on this basis and was extremely lucky because the accounts were paid up after harvest as promised. One account amounting to $150.00 was lost due to the death of a shareholder who was a bachelor, and whose successors did not wish to recognize the indebtedness. The amount was too small to take legal action for its recovery.

The interest paid to the bank on Joseph's personal loan for the extension of credit came out of his pocket and was an added expense. He did not like this arrangement. He submitted it as a problem for the Director's consideration. They discussed it, but took no action. He decided to do something about it.

At the annual provincial convention of the Co-operative Managers Association, held in Regina the previous year, he became knowledgable about credit unions and the role they could play in the extension of credit. Particularly, in those small communities that were not being served by a branch or office of a commercial bank.

Some managers who had credit unions in their communities reported on how they would direct the farmers to borrow for their farm operating needs from the credit union and pay with cash at the supply cooperative. It sounded so logical, and an idea that intrigued Joseph to the point, where he made a decision to give leadership and spearhead the organization of a credit union in his community.

On the other hand, Joseph's personal problem was tied to provide more adequate housing for his family. In addition to the one daughter Carolyn, who was four years old now, another daughter Tabetha was born in February 1947. Suzanne travelled by train to Regina right after New Year to stay with a friend and to be closer to medical facilities for bringing Tabetha into this world. The winter was a heavy one with much snow and with daily snow storms and blizzards, making it both ineffective and impossible for the train to plow open the rail line to come into town.

LIFE'S DETOURS

The residents and farmers were without mail for three solid weeks. The Co-op along with two other coal dealers ran out of coal and some farmers had to resort to keeping their homes warm by burning wheat or flax straw. Suzanne and baby Tabetha were ready to come home from Regina, but roads and rail lines were blocked. They were flown home in mid-February with a small Cessna plane, which landed on a stubble field on the outskirts of the town. Joseph and Carolyn walked to meet the plane and to welcome Mom and the new sister home.

Joseph had access to a grant loan amounting to $1,200 from the Army, but could only use it for the construction of a home or the purchase of a small holding. The increase in the family made the construction of a new home a priority, thus plans were made to construct a new home this same year.

In total, Joseph's area of responsibility now consisted of expanding and managing the supply co-operative, directing the trucking and freighting business, organizing the credit union and building a new home. Suzanne like a brave soldier jumped in to help her husband. She would bring the baby in the carriage into the Co-op store and mind both the store and the baby, while Joseph would be out filling orders and delivering goods to the farmers. Both their efforts were focused on serving the Co-op members without asking for additional pay.

"I wonder if this is the field of leadership, I'm supposed to find myself in?" Joseph thought, as he would remind himself occasionally about what his mother told him, and his early astrological forecast had indicated.

He knew he was socially inclined and motivated to serve others. He believed that good in this world could only come, if people agreed to work together and share that common good as equitably as possible. To him, the cooperative philosophy came next to the church and its teachings, and he often felt that cooperation was the physical and material expression of the Christian doctrine.

Organizing the credit union went very smoothly. The date of the organization meeting was announced. Posters were tacked unto a few corner telephone poles and in the post office lobby. On the appointed day in the month of March, a beautiful sunny day, with a brilliant white cover of snow on the ground, a substantial crowd of rural and town folks packed themselves into the community hall. They were eager to hear about the wonder of "people being able to organize their own bank," which would be known as the Kayville Credit Union.

The Department of Cooperative Development of the Provincial Government, sent out a representative in the person of Mr. Gary

Hamman, to explain the legality, the nature and the function of the institution. If the idea met with approval, the meeting would elect a Board of Directors, a Credit Committee and a Supervisory or Audit Committee. Mr. Hammon would spend some time with whoever would be appointed as manager to introduce and acquaint him with procedures and the bookkeeping system.

Joseph acted as chairman of the meeting, and after a few words of introduction, he called on Mr. Hamman to explain and direct the organization of the institution.

"Mr. Chairman, ladies and gentlemen," he started off. "First I want to bring you the greetings of the Department of Cooperative Development, where I work and from the Minister, the Hon. T.C. Douglas, who is also the Premier of the Province of Saskatchewan."

This introduction always struck a solid note in the community, since T.C. Douglas was leader of the Cooperative Commonwealth Federation (CCF), and it was the political party in power. A party that had united the farmers and the labor group under one banner, with a view to socializing some of the province's resources and improving the services for it's citizens. Under the Douglas leadership the party was elected to power consecutively every four years, and governed the province for a period of 20 years. Douglas himself had been a former Baptist Minister, had a dynamic personality, and an unsurpassable capability for public speaking and for explaining government policies. The Kayville community by majority supported the party. Joseph himself was actively engaged and supported the party. He rendered leadership at local and district conventions for the formulation of grass root policies, which he felt met the needs of the times.

Mr. Hamman continued explaining the functions of a credit union and to try to convince the skeptics, he advanced some illustrations that stuck with Joseph throughout his life's career.

"Ladies and gentlemen, I'm going to relate to you a story that fits your community and your situation almost like a glove. It seems, that early on here on the prairies another town existed just like yours. It had most every kind of business established. There were two or three general stores, there was a cafe, a hotel, a blacksmith shop, a lumber yard, a few petroleum agents, a barber shop and so on. The town had most businesses that people wanted or could use, but did not have a bank."

"One day, a clever individual came into town and took a look around to see if there was room for him to launch forth an enterprise of some sort. He soon discovered that the town had no bank. He quickly made up his mind to open a bank."

"He rented a small building on a corner lot. He converted the

LIFE'S DETOURS

interior to make it look like a bank, with a counter that had a teller's cage made from an old iron grill. He bought and installed a sizeable steel chest for safe-keeping the money and documents, and equipped a small office with a desk and a few chairs. He then hung up a huge nicely painted sign that read "BANK".

Hamman continued, - "The sign was grist for the mill of the skeptics. Jokes were made by them about the bank and it's sign. Who has money in our community to invest in a bank of this kind? It ought to be a brick building with bars on the window, some said. Others were saying - We'd rather do business with a bank thats further away, so the rest of the community will not learn about your business affairs, while still others simply questioned the integrity of the person who was the banker."

"No one visited the newly formed bank during the first week, but on the second week one of the merchants came in, sat for awhile and talked to the banker, and then made a deposit. During the third week, other merchants and businessmen walked in and did likewise. The fourth week got even better, more people and more deposits were coming in, and at the same time one of the local farmers came in applied for a loan and got it. Word was spreading and from that point forward the bank had developed roots and was growing steadily."

"It happened at church some three or four months later.

After the worship service a few of the neighborhood women approached the banker's wife, and in casual conversation asked her how her husband's bank was doing. "Oh, it's doing very well," the banker's wife replied. "So well in fact, that we have also placed our own money into it."

"The moral of this story is that a bank cannot operate unless the people have confidence in it. We are here today expressly for the purpose of electing honorable people from amongst yourselves to be on the Board of Directors, on the Credit Committee, and on the Supervisory Committee. We must appoint a manager for this credit union, who is honest, responsible and can be bonded. The credit union will be audited periodically by an inspector from our department, and the condition of your assets and liabilities will be reported to your Board of Directors, who in turn will report them to you at your annual meeting. The credit union is democratic in nature, and you people will be involved in its democratic structure. You have nothing to fear," Mr. Hamman concluded.

A farmer in the audience rose to ask a question, and Joseph as chairman granted him this privelege.

"Mr. Chairman, I'd like to ask the speaker, where the capital for this credit bank is going to come from. This is not a wealthy community and many of us need to borrow money. The private banks have plenty of money, but this credit bank that you talk about has no funds whatsoever, so what are we going to have - a paper bank?" he asked.

Mr. Hamman appeared anxious to respond.

"Sir, the private commercial banks have plenty of money, I agree with you. But, it is still money from the people. When you go to a private commercial bank, to ask for a loan, you will only get it if you can prove to them that you don't need it or can get by without their loan," Hammon responded jokingly.

Everyone in the audience started laughing, sort of in agreement with Hammon's statement based on some of their own personal experiences in dealing with the commercial banks.

"With regards to capital," Mr. Hammon continued. "This credit union will not have sufficient capital at the beginning to satisfy fully the credit needs of this community. So, the credit union begins by launching a capital mobilization or savings program."

Then turning to the blackboard behind his back, Mr. Hammon picked up a piece of chalk and slowly but deliberately led his audience through a "thinking process" on the matter.

"Look," he said. "Mr. Acker, your co-op manager tells me there are about 500 families in this area. Families that could be served by your co-op and credit union. Let's take 50% of these families, and assume they will become credit union members and supporters. Right? that would give us 250 families to work with.

Now if a family could be motivated and convinced that it is good for them to save an average of 50 cents per day, or a total of $3.50 per week. This is not much money, many people smoke tobacco for that amount. Then if this money is deposited in the credit union and the family receives a dividend of let's say 5% annually, and the dividend is left to accumulate and is added to the principal, this family could save $1,000.00 in five years. Savings that would be hard to accumulate in one lump sum, but savings that would come together by bits and pieces. In five years 250 families could save $250,000 and this is the kind of capital formation that families must seek to follow, both for their own family welfare, as well as for the capitalization of the credit union. Do you understand me?" Mr Hammon queried his audience.

The audience responded with applause. Two things became clear. That those present at the meeting were in favor of proceeding with the organization of the credit union, and that a potential existed if properly exploited, and with time would ensure its capitalization and it's capacity to serve the community.

The chairman then brought the attention of the meeting to the

LIFE'S DETOURS

day's agenda, which included the election of members to the Board of Directors, and the two Committees. With this item concluded, the appointment of the manager became the next item for consideration. Joseph Acker found himself appointed to the position by unanimous consent.

After the meeting, that evening he was coached by Mr. Hammon on how to make the book entries. The system was a standardized credit union accounting system, very simple in nature, but difficult for Joseph to comprehend in a two hour session.

"The system is one that accountants call double-entry. In other words, for every debit entry, there must be a corresponding credit entry. For example, when a member comes to make a deposit of say $20.00, he will receive the duplicate of the deposit slip as his receipt. For the credit union this transaction becomes a debit entry in the cash column of the journal ledger because the credit union owes this amount of cash to the member. At the same time it becomes a credit entry in the deposit column of the journal ledger. Now then, if you take this $20.00 from your cash and make a bank deposit, then a credit entry is entered in the cash column, because you took it out of cash, and a debit entry is entered in the bank column, because now the bank owes the credit union this money. At the same time, in the Individual Member's Ledger, the entry is posted as a credit entry, and when the member withdraws funds from his account, the entry made is a debit entry. The important point to remember is that every debit entry must have a corresponding credit entry. Do you understand that?" Mr. Hamman asked.

Joseph indicated that he understood some of the bookkeeping procedure, but certainly not in it's entirety.

"The important point for you to remember is to be sure to write down every transaction, and to post your entries in the ledgers as best as you know how. Then at the end of the month, put the books in your car - bring them into Regina, and we will go over your work with you. We will correct your errors and teach you new aspects that will affect the credit union operations as it grows," Mr. Hammon counselled.

The hour was now getting late, and Mr. Hamman would have to catch the next morning's train to get back to the city, but they discovered they both liked whiskey. With the front door of the Co-op store locked, they sat comfortably in Joseph's office and imbibed in several drinks of scotch whiskey, while they continued discussing the merits of the credit union and the co-operative enterprises, and the role they could play in the community. Next morning, Gary Hamman caught the train back to Regina and Joseph turned to the work at hand that was awaiting to be accomplished.

His first move was to purchase a safe, and to re-arrange the office to accommodate the credit union operations.

At the same time, he was able to locate a local carpenter who had agreed to tear down his old home, salvage as much of the lumber as possible and to construct the new one. Joseph was to provide him with additional labor for digging the basement and for pouring the cement for the basement walls and foundation. The other extra labor required would be provided by Joseph and Suzanne in the evening hours after the store closed and whatever free time was available on weekends. The total budget for the house was not to exceed $2,400.

Joseph felt confident and knew he could prove to the community, that the co-operative enterprises he was now managing could be of great economic benefit and were the right kinds of businesses to serve their member's needs. He considered the share capital invested by the members in the Kayville Co-op Association, and in the Kayville Credit Union, as an off-the-farm investment into institutions that would work, in the interest of and protect the direct investment of capital and labor they were making into the family farm itself.

Such was his conviction of the merits of this philosophy, that he put all his effort into serving the members with quality goods, competitive prices, and a service that was second to none. He would go out of his way to render good service. If a farmer came in and ordered to have 200 gallons of fuel delivered to his farm the next morning, Joseph would deliver it that same evening, even if it was midnight. This kind of service met with favorable comments from the members, and by word-of-mouth, the co-op and the credit union were developing favorable and acceptable images in the community.

The Co-op purchased the grocery inventory from one of the private merchants in town, moved it into it's new building and hired the lady-owner of the store to be the grocery clerk. It opened a meat department and hired a butcher. It expanded it's tire and tube inventory through a consignment contract with a leading tire firm. He had the Co-op take on the agency for the Canadian Co-operative Implements for the sale of farm machinery.

On a part-time basis he hired his young brother Allen, and his brother-in-law Edwin Parker, who were high school students to make petroleum and other deliveries after school hours. They would unload carloads of coal and assist Curly the truck driver to haul grain or livestock. Service was good and the sales volume steadily increased. Joseph's work-load kept steadily getting heavier.

As an indicator to the shareholders of how the business was progressing, Joseph had painted and erected a sign inside the store in the form of a thermometer. This was graduated in weekly increments forecasting the expected sales volume for the year. On a weekly basis

LIFE'S DETOURS

he would enter the actual sales of the co-op and a comparison would be made to the forecasted figures. The actual sales figures were consistently above the forecasted ones, and this item became a topic of conversation between the shareholders in the beer parlor, at the post office, on the street corner, and even after the worship services at church.

The growth of the Kayville Co-op, under Joseph's management considering the size of the community was phenomenal. Over a five year period many of the early forecasts were realized. Commodity and petroleum sales increased from $25,000 in 1947 to $252,000 at the end of 1951. Joseph's salary however had only doubled from $75.00 to $150.00 per month. Naturally, he was making additional income from his trucking enterprise, from insurance commissions, and from notarial and accounting fees. They were now living in their newly constructed home and during this five year interval another daughter was born in the family. They named her Eleanor. He was now the father to three daughters.

The hours were long and Joseph was beginning to feel it. Additionally, the early pioneers brought with them from Romania a traditional custom, which took roots as well in their new community in Canada. It was the habit or custom, to conclude a successful business transaction between two people by calling for a drink of whiskey. This drink was generally described as "one on the horses mouth." Joseph now having some 250 member clients, and feeling obligated to take a drink with each one of them at one time or another, found himself drinking alcoholic beverages in greater quantity than would be prudent. He was careful not to let it interfere with his work, but it was beginning to show in his personality traits by becoming irritable, by drinking with his buddies when he should have spent time with his family, and quite often became abusive to Suzanne and the children.

Nevertheless, life went on. The Kayville Credit Union had also grown in assets to the point where it's share capital exceeded $250,000 and exemplified a tendency towards continuing growth. The period that Joseph managed and worked for these enterprises, enabled him to gain as much knowledge and experience in business administration and human relations, as he might have received from taking a basic university course on the subject matter. He did attend a few short non-degree courses in city during the winter months which were extremely helpful to his work.

He recalls with great fervor one particular incident which took place in the credit union aspect of the operations. An incident which brilliantly illustrates what transpires daily in the financial world on a much larger scale.

LIFE'S DETOURS

It was a cool cloudy morning, with one of those misty rains in the atmosphere during the last week in June. He peered out of his office window and noticed Kristofer Wanless, wearing a raincoat and a pair of rubber boots walking slowly towards the door of his office. Kristofer was a local farmer and a member of the Co-op, but not as yet a member of the credit union. He walked into Joseph's office.

"Good morning, Joe," he said. "Nice rain we're having, very good for the crops."

"Good morning, Kris," Joseph replied. "What brings you so early in the morning and on a rainy day into town?"

"Well, I wanted to discuss a bit of personal and private business and by coming early, I felt I could do it before other folks come in to bother you," he said.

"Oh good," Joseph uttered. "How can I help you?"

"Mr. Acker, how safe is it to deposit money in this credit union you are managing?" he asked.

"Kris, the credit union is a legally chartered corporation, supervised by the Provincial Government. It is affiliated with the Saskatchewan Co-op Credit Society, which is a kind of a central bank for credit unions on a provincial scale. We have over $250.000 of local money in share capital and growing. As far as I'm concerned, take it from me - it's safe to deposit funds with us," Joseph stated.

"Well, in that case, I have some money to deposit, but I must warn you, I may require it on short notice. You see my neighbor said he intends to quit farming soon. Maybe this year, maybe next year, and I want to buy his farm. So, when he is ready to sell, I want to be ready to buy and I'll need the money," Kris explained.

"No problem, you can have your money whenever you like. All you need to do is come in and ask for it," Joseph assured him.

"Okay, then I want to deposit $20,000 today," he said as he put his hand into the pocket of his blue denim overall jacket and pulled out a roll of $100 bills, big enough to choke an ox. He counted the money while Joseph was looking on, then he handed it to him.

Joseph took the money and recounted it. He divided it into two bundles of 100 bills to each bundle. It had a musty scent and some bills appeared to be rusty. He prepared a deposit slip, an individual member account book and other required documents, opened the safe door and placed the money in it, then he turned to Kris and asked.

"Kris. where did you keep or store this money, it has a musty smell ?"

"I had it rolled and placed into a one inch iron pipe, cap screwed on both ends and buried vertically in a hidden spot in the ground," Kris replied.

LIFE'S DETOURS

They parted company and time went by. At year end the credit union declared a 5% dividend, and for the six month period Kris's money was invested it earned $500. Once a year each member received an audited statement of their account with the credit union by mail. Kris received his and in late January he walked again into the credit union office.

"Mr. Acker, I'd like to make another deposit," he said.

"I have another $15,000 to add to my account. but again I must warn you, I will need the money as soon as my neighbor decides to sell his farm. Is that okay?"

"Sure deal Kris," Joseph replied, and quickly made a deposit slip, counted the cash, put it back in the office safe, and brought Kris's personal savings book up to date.

"You can have your money any time you like on very short notice."

Two years went by, and one late Friday afternoon Kris walked into the credit union office. He advised Joseph that within the hour his neighbor would be coming in to finalize the deal on the sale of the farm, which he was now buying.

"I have $38,300 in my account. The deal is for $40,000. Can I borrow an additional $2,000 from the credit union to close the deal? I told my neighbor this would be a cash deal, that I had the money with you and that you would be doing the notarial work and the tansfer of title documents. Can I have the money and can we close the deal today?" he asked.

Joseph told him, that he did not carry that much money on hand. That the funds were deposited with the Saskatchewan Co-op Credit Society, the central credit union located in the capital city. That this was too late in the day to motor to the city and return with the funds, since the city offices would all be closed and stay closed until Monday of the following week.

"But you assured me, I could have the money at any time and I promised the neighbor, the deal would be for cash," Kris said as he appeared to be growing a bit angry.

"I'll tell you what we'll do," Joseph said. "We'll write him a check for $40,000 and we'll complete the transaction. If your neighbor refuses to accept the checque, then we'll offer him a deposit of $2,000 as earnest money. I have that much in the safe, and we'll ask him to wait until Monday, when we can drive to city and obtain the funds and close the deal then. Is that okay by you?"

"Sure, I hope he takes the check or the earnest money offer, I simply don't want to miss out on buying his land," Kris countered.

By this time, Ernest Paul, the neighbor came in. Joseph explained the situation to him. His neighbor simply said - "I'll take the check."

Joseph prepared all the documents and had the neighbor sign the documents for a Transfer of Title to Kris. In return he handed him the checque for $40,000. Kris was happy with the "done-deal" and shook hands with his neighbor, then departed.

"Mr. Acker, I would like to deposit this check here in the credit union until a later date. I will not be requiring all the money immediately, but will draw on it as I need to. Can I do this?" Mr. Paul asked.

"Sure deal, be happy to serve you. As you know, this is where Kris Wanless had his money too," Joseph replied.

The transaction was completed again in the usual and formal manner, and Mr. Paul walked away a satisfied person.

Joseph sat and pondered on the situation. Here is a huge transaction that took place without any exchange of cash funds. Even the additional $2,000 advanced to Kristofer Wanless were covered. The cash was replaced by "confidence." Confidence in a paper transaction, that merely transferred funds from one account in the credit union to another. This is what is going on all over the country, and this is the kind of a role that banks are performing. It served to strengthen Joseph's faith in the credit union and it's function in serving the community.

This led to other similar practices, that eventually brought the credit unions into the Canadian banking system. A farmer would obtain a loan from the credit union to finance his farming operations. Once the loan was approved, he would leave his money on deposit. A week or ten days later he would order a quantity of fuel, which the Co-op would deliver. The Co-op delivery man would request payment for the fuel delivered, and the farmer would simply advise him that he had money on deposit at the credit union, and could not pay the driver at that moment. The driver had instructions not to dump his order unless the fuel was paid for in cash. To remedy the situation, the farmer would take a piece of paper, and write an order addressed to Joseph, who was the manager of both the Co-op and the Credit Union. "Mr. Acker deduct sufficient funds from my account in the Credit Union to pay for this fuel delivery," The farmer would add his signature to it.

The driver would bring this grease stained piece of paper back with him. The deduction would be made from the farmer's account and the transaction was treated as cash.

Credit Unions by law, were not considered as banks, and were therefore not permitted to issue checks to their members. Situations like the above, made Joseph print credit union checks with the mimeographing machine on plain white paper, and giving a pad of 10

LIFE'S DETOURS 165

to each farmer-member of the Co-op. They became known as "negotiable orders" and were used as checks in the local community. Other credit unions were experiencing the same situation and this practise became wide-spread over the entire province. Credit unions began printing their negotiable orders on quality checking paper and were being recognized as acceptable monetary instruments. The Central Credit Society became the clearing house for the credit union negotiable orders. Eventually, the Government and the Canadian Banker's Association, recognized the credit union system as an integral part of the overall financial infrastructure, and passed legislation permitting the entry of credit unions into the total banking system.

Just as the Kayville Co-op and Credit Union were becoming meaningful community institutions, another post-war phenomenon was taking place. The small family farm was no longer an economic unit that could provide a living for the farmer and his family. This resulted in many small farmers selling their farms to their neigbors, and moving to the larger urban centers in search of employment and other benefits, such as a better education for their children. The consequence of this transition resulted in a gradual reduction of the number of families in the community, and a corresponding decrease in the volume of commercial activity. One or two of the merchants caved in and left town due to this situation, as well as the impact the Co-op had made with its substantial growth. Small towns were on the brink of disappearing from the scene and many of them did. Larger centers capable of offering a wider choice of services, coupled with better roads and the increased use of the automobile, were other factors that contributed to the disappearance of the "family farm" and along with the family farms the towns were also affected, Kayville included.

The Kayville Co-op Association was affiliated to Federated Cooperatives Limited (FCL), which was a central purchasing, distribution and wholesale organization serving its co-op affiliates. Along with the merchandise FCL provided the managers of the affiliates with technical and managerial counselling.

In early 1952, Mr. Don Zirkle, the FCL representative walked into the Kayville Co-op. By this time FCL was well aware of the unqualified success that Joseph Acker had stacked in his favor as an aggressive promoter, salesman and manager.

"Good morning Mr. Acker," he said. "My name is Don Zirkle, I'm from FCL, and I'm on a special mission here to day. It's a matter I must discuss with you personally and I'd like to have a bit of your time, whenever it's convenient for you."

The Co-op store and the office happened to be busy at that point, because it was train day and many customers were in town. The activity

LIFE'S DETOURS

soon dwindled away and Joseph called Zirkle into his office.

"My purpose for coming here today, is simply to ask you to consider moving from Kayville and taking over the position of manager at the Prince Albert Co-op Association. Allow me to continue," Zirkle said.

"Kayville is a small town. Small towns are on the decline in terms of economic activity. You have peaked right now at the maximum of your potential in this community. The Co-op sales have surpassed $250,000, a goal you've reached in five years. The Credit Union has surpassed $250,000 in assets in four years. You have demonstrated outstanding ability to stimulate and manage growth, and FCL would like to have you harness your ability at a center with greater potential. I'm speaking now about the city of Prince Albert in Northern Saskatchewan. This should be good for you and good for Prince Albert as well as FCL. Prince Albert is a city of 18,000 people. It is situated in a rich mixed farming area. The present manager is 65 years of age and retiring. The Co-op has current sales of $252,000, eleven employees, and handles petroleum products, lumber and home building supplies. There is enormous room for growth at this point. We certainly feel you are the right candidate for this opening and we'd like to have you give it serious thought. What do you think?" he concluded.

"Thank you very much for bringing me this information, and for the invitation to take advantage of this opportunity," Joseph replied, feeling jubilant about the fact that someone, somewhere had noticed the results of his performance. "What would the starting wages be?" he asked.

"The present manager is receiving $225.00 per month. We talked to their Board president and he stated that they would be willing to start a new man at $300.00 per month. Currently you are receiving $150.00 per month here. This would double your salary immediately," Zirkle replied.

Joseph knew his wages at Kayville were low, but he had income from his other sources that netted him more than $300.00 per month. However, he felt he wanted to specialize in management and to test his promotional skills on a larger scale. This appeared to be the opportunity.

"Mr. Zirkle, give me a few days to consider your proposal. I must discuss it with my wife. We are pretty well settled here, and this means uprooting my family and leaving behind a community in which I have become a leader, so to speak," Joseph said.

Joseph was delighted with the surprise that had come his way. He told the store staff, he was going out on business and would return early in the afternoon. Actually, he went straight home and broke the news to

LIFE'S DETOURS

Suzanne. They talked about it over the noon lunch hour. They looked at every aspect of the move. Their three daughters would have access to better schools. They would move into a better community served with electrical power and running water, something Kayville did not have at the time. Secretly, Suzanne felt the move would be good for Joseph.

"I have no doubt about his capability, and I'm anxious to have him break away from his drinking buddies with which he gets involved. Perhaps life in a new community would bring a change and moderate his drinking vice," she said to herself.

Suzanne bought the idea and agreed to make the move.

Joseph advised the local Directors of his decision to move away, and gave them two months to search for a replacement. The entire community felt that Joseph's departure was a great loss. At the farewell party given in their honor, Bruce Sanhorn, the president of the Kayville Co-op paid tribute to his efforts in words like the following.

"Joseph Acker, is a man that would not allow grass to grow under his feet. He is a true cooperator, and has served our community well. You know, it has been said that `there are those people who make things happen, there are those who let things happen, and then there are those, who don't know what's happening.' Joseph is a man who can make things happen. We know he will be successful in his new venture.

What is our loss is the gain of the Prince Albert Co-operative. It has also been said -`that behind every good man stands a good woman' and Suzanne is no exception to that rule. They are a great couple. We want to wish them well in their new environment."

It was in the month of August, 1952 the Ackers sold their home in Kayville, packed their household and personal belongings, loaded the family in the car and departed to their new location in Prince Albert.

Chapter 11

MOVING ON AND UP

Joseph Acker had gone the previous month to Prince Albert for a look-see trip and the job interview. After having agreed upon the terms of employment, he purchased a home for $7,500 using as a down payment $4,000 from the sale of his previous home. He felt good about the move. He had a home for his family and a job for himself, even though he harbored a certain amount of anxiety and uncertainty about the job.

"Relinquishing a position that one builds and in which one feels a degree of comfort and security, for one that has promises, but also uncertainties is not an easy change to make," he thought to himself.

He thought about his childhood and about the home-spun philosophy that entered the topic of family conversation. He would hear his grandparents or parents say that "a bird in a cage is worth two in the forest." Joseph wondered if he had bit off more than he could chew, and if he was embarked in the proper direction for his welfare and that of his family.

But since his main objective was to develop and sharpen his managerial skills, he felt this undertaking offered him that challenge. He did not express or show his fearfulness to his family and at any rate, it was now too late to make an about turn. He was committed and would have to sink or learn to swim.

The Ackers drove the 275 miles from Kayville to Prince Albert leisurely, in order to give the family an opportunity to observe, enjoy and savor the countryside. They stopped for noon lunch in Watrous and arrived at their new home early in the afternoon. Their household and personal effects were being brought with his own truck, which he later sold. Curly the driver arrived with the load within the hour.

The truck was unloaded, furniture and household goods were placed in position, with some boxes left for later unpacking. That evening meal consisted of hamburgers and soft drinks. Everyone in the family, tested the hot and cold water taps to see if it was real. Everyone was ready for the biggest treat of their lives. A shower before retiring to their bedrooms.

Settling in the family took top priority. A few innovations and additional installations around the home were necessary. Suzanne registered Carolyn and Tabetha for school and at the public library. She purchased the required books and additional clothes for their school wear.

Joseph took to his responsibilities as manager. He made the acquaintance of Mack Darnell, the president of the Prince Albert Co-op (P.A. Co-op), and the principal person to whom he would have to report, He spent time with Allan Gill the bookkeeper who was a staff member in place. He was a key person, who would be reporting to both Joseph and the Board of Directors.

He took the first six weeks to make an assessment of the business operations. He had no written report to present to the Directors at the first monthly meeting following his appointment. The Board of Directors consisted of nine persons (eight men and one woman). President Darnell requested him to offer oral observations he wished to make at this time.

"I have spent most of my time since my appointment making an analysis of the current operations. I have uncovered some loose areas that could be made tighter in order to realize more savings. However, based on economies of scale, most of any additional profits we seek had to come from making more efficient and increased use of the existing assets, and a higher productivity per man-hour of labor input. All of this points to the need for an increase in the volume of sales."

He continued."I have made a thorough analysis of which wholesalers are our suppliers, and I have examined the purchasing and pricing methods and techniques used in detail. I have conducted a similar analysis of the cost of the products purchased by our consumers, to determine the price structure and the competitiveness of the Co-op in relation to the consumer prices charged by the other businesses in the community. Adjustments were made where necessary to ensure we are in line. I will be presenting a written report with added documentation of the complete results of my analysis at the next Board meeting," Joseph concluded.

Two months later, he presented his first written report at the Directors meeting, which summarized the findings of his analysis. Furthermore, the report suggested and requested the approval of salary adjustments for two employees and an across the board increase of 5% for the remaining employees. This was important in Joseph's mind, since a systematic salary evaluation and wage comparison to other local industries of similar character had not taken place in the P.A.Co-op before. Employees had been engaged, more or less in ad hoc fashion, with a salary agreed to between the manager and the employee at the time of hiring. Additional increments were offered at the manager's pleasure. No official salary or wage structure had been established and Joseph sensed that this was an area of concern with the employees. By redressing this situation, Joseph knew he was doing the right thing and could win the favor and support of his employees.

There wasn't much Joseph could do by way of capital investment in facilities to enable him to increase volume by adding additional lines of merchandise. The Co-op simply did not have the additional funds for acquiring new property or expanding their present facilities.

The existing facilities embraced a service station occupying a strategic location on the main highway passing through the city. It dispensed gasoline to members and motorists alike. It offered a mechanical service and handled a complete line of tires, batteries and accessories. It also carried farm hardware and supplies, weed chemicals, baling twine, and some basic livestock needs. A bulk petroleum and fertilizer distribution center, coupled with a small lumber yard were located on railway property, somewhat on the outskirts of the city.

The potential for growth and development of this Co-op was evident. The riddle facing Joseph in this larger community of 25,000 people comprised of both urban and rural residents, was how to go about mobilizing the Co-op's resources, so as to capture a larger slice of this retail market.

He began by joining forces with Jack Powell, the district representative for the Saskatchewan Wheat Pool (SWP). The SWP was the province's largest grain marketing organization. Being a cooperative marketing organization, and having been in operation for more than fifty years, it had many supporters and clients in the local trading area. It also shared the same common denominator with the emerging and growing cooperative consumer sector, which was to protect and improve the welfare of its members.

Jack Powell, worked with the membership of the SWP in general and specifically with the local committees at each grain delivery point. His job was to carry on educational and informational programs with the membership. and to receive feed-back for improving the operations of the SWP. Jack was also a member of the Board of Directors of the P.A. Co-op and was therefore knowledgeable about the philosophy and objectives of both the producer and consumer segments of the cooperative movement and their development.

LIFE'S DETOURS

One way the SWP would attract farm families to school house or cottage meetings was to offer free movies, during a period when the rural areas were not yet electrified. The SWP representative was equipped with a gas-engine powered generator, which produced electrical energy to operate the projector. The movies were shown in the evenings and generally consisted of a fifteen to twenty minute news reel, followed by two regular films of about one hour duration each. A fifteen minute break would be observed between the showing of the two major films, at which time, Powell took the occassion to brief those in attendance about the latest events in terms of the grain marketing problems and always a few words about cooperatives in general.

He requested Joseph to accompany him to a number of these meetings, and he took the opportunity to introduce him to the leading and influential farm families. This gave Joseph an opportunity to determine,"what's what and who's who?" in the trading area. It gave him an appropiate time frame in which to appraise the economic potential and the attitude of the farm folks towards their cooperative. All of which led him to believe that the P.A. Co-op was over due in terms of expanding it's facilities, to serve the growing needs and demands of it's shareholders and members.

Joseph spent a considerable amount of time in planning and elaborating a strategy for involving the community in an expansion program. It was at this point again in his life, that he reminded himself of his mother's early reading of his astrological forecast, and his parent's counselling to prepare and conduct himself honorably, for someday he could become a leader of men. He assumed that this was in keeping with his parent's wishes and concluded that he should forge ahead and that his strategy would have to be patterned along the following lines.

1. The expansion project had to be big. "Small plans do not stir men's minds." He had heard that statement uttered somewhere.
2. The plan had to be credible and possible to attain. It couldn't be a pipe dream.
3. He had to have a voluntary enlistment of other people to assist him in the project.
4. He had to plan the work, and then work the plan.

One of his first undertakings was to do a certain amount of leg work on the quiet. On the corner of Central Avenue and 14th Street in the city, a piece of vacant property existed suitable for a moderate sized supermarket building with added space for vehicle parking. Through a real estate agent, he discovered it's asking price was listed at $40,000 and that an adjoing lot could be purchased for an additional $10,000.

He contacted the Store Construction Division of Federated Cooperatives (FCL) and ascertained that construction costs would amount to $40 per square foot, and that a building 80 x 150 feet (12,000 sq. ft.) would cost in the neighborhood of $50.000. Other costs involving display fixtures, check-out counters, paving the parking lot and a large marquee sign would take an additonal $10,000.

The 12,000 square feet of space had to be distributed between a small warehouse at the back for receiving the goods, a pharmacy, a hardware department, a coffee bar, the administration office, the grocery, meat and produce sections, and public restrooms. All together the project would require a capital outlay of $100,000 not counting the inventory required to stock the store.

Joseph was not concerned at this time about capital for the inventory. Some of the capital for this purpose could be obtained by retaining the patronage refunds paid annually to the members on their purchases. This amounted to about $15,000 and would purchase some inventory. Most suppliers including FCL would furnish inventory and bill the Co-op on a monthly basis.

Joseph felt that with an aggressive and smart sales effort, he could turn his inventory over, particularly the food inventory at least twice per month. Thus a $30,000 food inventory, would produce about $72,000 worth of sales, considering a 20% mark-up in a given month, and would enable him to operate the food division on the wholesaler's capital. Other arrangements would have to be made for inventory purchased from other wholesale suppliers as and when the time came.

To enable the mobilization of capital for expansion purposes, Joseph consulted with the Department of Cooperative Development of the Provincial Government, to ascertain if the P.A. Co-op would be qualified and permitted to offer for sale to it's shareholders only, a series of Savings Bonds that would enable the mobilization of capital for expansion purposes. He was advised that it was both permissable and feasible based on the security and value of the existing properties, without factoring in the value of any additional property to be purchased.

Without seeking any legal opinion Joseph drafted a preliminary investment prospectus and worked on other premises and calculations. His basic guidelines were:
- *- The Savings Bonds were to mature in five years, but could be renewed for an additional period of time, at the bondholder's discretion.
- *- Bonds would be redeemed on the basis of "first in, first out," (FIFO).
- *- Bonds would carry an interest rate of 6% paid out annually on the anniversary date of the bond.

LIFE'S DETOURS

*- Bonds would be sold in denominations of $100, $500 and $1,000 and were transferable.
*- The bonds were secured by the total assets of the P.A.Co-op, which were valued at $150,000.

As previously pointed out, the expansion program would require a capital outlay of $100,000. Joseph estimated that a sale of the following bond denominations would furnish the required expansion capital.

30 bondholders with purchases of $1,000 each....$30,000
100 bondholders with purchases of $500 each.....$50,000
200 bondholders with purchases of $100 each.....$20,000

Armed with this information and data, and after his first full year as manager, Joseph introduced his plan to a regular meeting of the Board of Directors. During that year he had chalked up an increase in sales volume for the Co-op from $226,000 to $249,000. This was a 10% increase in sales for the year, which added strength to his argument for expansion and weight to his management capability. He was now in a position to impress the Directors, specially Mr. Darnell the president, that this was the opportune time to think and talk growth and expansion.

"Mr. Acker, I think your plan is a bold one. I have reservations about our ability to raise $100,000 in capital to fund such an expansion as you have laid before us," Barney Arnold, the vice president commented.

"Excuse me," Bob Pitchell, another director said. "I happen to agree with Barney. This is a very ambitious program, and I'm not sure the shareholders would respond positively with investment capital to support it."

Jack Powell, chimed in the discussion. "Lady and gentlemen, we are at crossroads with our Co-op. We must consider clearly our position. We cannot stand still. The city is growing, the community is more affluent now than at any time in its history. We may lose out on a golden opportunity. We should take Mr. Acker's proposal very seriously."

Mr. Darnell, the president felt there wasn't unanimous consent between the Directors to enable him to call for a vote on the issue. He turned to the manager and asked: "Mr. Acker, supposing the Directors do not approve the expansion plan you submitted to us today, what action if any do you propose to take?"

"Sir, I haven't given that any thought, but speaking spontaneously from the top of my head, I would have to say that in the first instance, I would be very disappointed. As most of you know, I'm 31 years of age, I'm a cooperator, anxious to develop a career in managing cooperatives. I'm currently earning $300 per month. I know of co-op managers earning two and one-half times this salary. I'm aware that this Co-op cannot afford to pay more unless it has a volume of business to sustain a commensurate salary increase. I believe our shareholders are secretly making a comparison between this Co-op and those Co-ops operating more successfully in other communities or cities of similar size. I believe they are questioning the difference, on the basis of my ability as a manager and yours as directors to lead this cooperative. In other words, they are questioning our credentials as leaders. As Directors the final decision rests with you, as to whether we proceed with an expansion program or remain with the status quo. Depending on the decision you take, I shall have to make my own decision. I do not wish this to be taken as a threat, but in all sincerity and in fairness to my family, I would be forced to go in search of a situation more challenging than I'm managing at present," Joseph replied.

The president suggested that the approval of the plan be tabled for this meeting. He requested the Directors to weigh heavily the manager's proposal, and selected a date in the following week for a special directors' meeting at which the proposal would be the only subject of discussion.

Prince Albert is one of the oldest cities in the province of Saskatchewan. It is situated on the banks of the North Saskatchewan river, about twenty miles west of the fork where the North and South Saskatchewan rivers meet. Together the two rivers unite to form the Saskatchewan river that flows into the Hudson Bay. The area contains rich farm lands, a forest industry, and the city itself is a commercial distribution center and the gateway to the top half of the province. Rich deposits of uranium were being exploited and mined, and the numerous lakes provide a tremendous base for tourism.

A federal penitentiary and a provincial prison were located near the city's limits, and both the provincial and federal governments had regional administrative offices located there. There was no other direction for the community to go, but forward and progressing. The P.A. Co-op was nestled in this kind of a milieu. It had been in existence for 25 years but due to lack of dynamic management and leadership it did not keep pace with the overall growth of the business sector in the community.

"I have a gut feeling that I'm right in my calculations that there is favorable ground here for developing this co-op. If only 10% of the population deals with us, we can safely count on having over 2,000 clients, and with average purchases of $1,000 per family, an annual sales volume of over two million dollars can be achieved. Furthermore if I can manage the enterprise to earn a net profit of only 5% on each

LIFE'S DETOURS

sales dollar, the bottom line would net a global figure of $100,000 annually. Financially the co-op would be in a strong cash position and capable of retiring it's bond obligations to the bondholders as and when they become due," Joseph was saying to himself and he felt good about it.

The following week the directors met as scheduled. The verdict was a unanimous approval of the manager's proposal, and a clear go-ahead signal for Joseph to lead the drive for capital formation and the expansion of the facilities.

It was too late in the year to embark on anything other than the sale of the Co-op Savings Bonds. In consultation with the Co-op's attorney, Joseph prepared the necessary brochures and bond certificates. He held a special session with the directors to have them fully informed about the project, and regular monthly meetings with his staff to make sure they were able to talk intelligently when queried about the project. He launched a monthly bulletin that went directly to the shareholder's home address in an effort to keep them posted on events. He issued periodic press releases and took out some paid advertising announcing publicly the progress being achieved.

He arranged a schedule of meetings covering every rural school house and community neighborhood center within a radius of 35 miles of the city. He dedicated himself to attending these meetings which were the cozy neighborly type, and would patiently and enthusiastically explain the merits of the project.

"Fellow cooperators, supporting this project is like giving your family one of the best breaks it ever had. Please stop to consider that an investment in your co-op is merely an extension of an investment you would be making in your own farm or home, because the co-operative acts to protect your farm and family from market exploitation in both your production efforts, as well as in your consumer needs. Remember, the farmer is the only industrial person in our society that pays the freight both ways. First he pays the freight on the products he ships to market, and then again on the products and merchandise he needs to buy in order to live and carry on with his farming operations. He needs protection. Furthermore, the rate of interest at 6% per annum on your Co-op Savings Bonds, is 1% better than is presently paid by the banks and 2% better than Canada Savings Bonds.

Another criteria to consider is the patronage refund or dividends you earn on your purchases. A family that purchases annually an average of $1,000 worth of merchandise from the Co-op can expect to earn from $50 to $80 in patronage refunds. This means that over a period of ten cumulative years, such a family could receive one year of free spending for merchandise.

You have your choice of purchasing the bonds in three denominations of $100, $500 and $1,000. You may purchase them in one instalment or in monthly or quarterly instalments. The Co-op is permitted to sell only $100,000 worth of these bonds, and when this figure is reached, further offers to sell will be curtailed," Joseph would advise his audience.

"You're an interesting person, very enthusiastic and your enthusiasm is contagious. The members of our women's guild are very supportive of your ideas, and I hear many of our neighbors talking about their intentions to buy bonds and support the Co-op effort," Mrs. Edna Arnold, the president of the Women's Co-operative Guild remarked, as she was talking to Joseph on one occasion.

To everyone's amazement including Joseph's, during the first month of the bond selling campaign over $40,000 had been subscribed. The bond selling fever was high and it seemed like everyone wanted to be associated with the project.

Joseph consulted with his directors, and immediately purchased the vacant corner space he had laid his eye on earlier for $40,000. Once acquired a huge sign was raised, which conspicuously indicated the Co-op's ownership of the property. This together with the monthly newsletter and press releases announcing the acquisition of this choice piece of property on Central Avenue, simply added more fuel to the fire and spurred onward the sale of the bonds. Within six months of the offering the entire bond issue had been subscribed. An application to the Department of Cooperatives requesting permission to sell an additional $25,000, was submitted and approved. All of this tickled Joseph, because he was now certain of adequate capital to finance the inventory as well.

Early in the spring of 1954, the construction division of FCL was contracted for $60,000 to build the store and equip it with a complete line of fixtures. Construction began as soon as the winter frost left the ground and the time alloted for completion of construction was ninety days.

Early on in his capacity as manager of the Co-op, Joseph gradually became recognized as a community leader. In addition to being the manager of the Co-op, he was elected to the Board of Directors of the Prince Albert Credit Union (PACU) and became its vice-president. He was elected president of the local Home and School Association, elected as member of the board of community United Church, joined the Rotary Club, and when these activities were summed up and added to his co-op management responsibility, he found himself with barely any time left on his hands for his family.

While the new premises were under construction, Joseph focused on hiring the additional staff. He was in need of a grocery manager, a hardware manager, a pharmacist, a coffee bar manager, and a number of store clerks. He was able to locate the right people with proper credentials, and when the expanded operations went into full swing his total staff consisted of thirty seven people.

In addition to management of the Co-op, Joseph played a leading role in promoting the development of the P.A. Credit Union. His experience with credit union development at Kayville served him in good stead here. He was elected as a Director of the Credit Union League of Saskatchewan, and became known province-wide as a leading advocate and promoter of credit union development. He was sought after as a guest speaker at credit union annual meetings and district rallies. At the Provincial League level, he was elected as a delegate to represent the provincial league at the annual convention of the Credit Union National Association (CUNA), whose headquarters were in Madison, Wisconsin. A function he discharged for four years.

The store construction was completed on schedule, The official opening of the new facilities was well publicized, and attended by a huge crowd. The event received province- wide publicity, especially in view of the fact that all the capital required to launch this expansion was borrowed from the local members and shareholders, without a red cent being borrowed from any outside source.

The sales volume took an enormous leap, and continued growing at an accelerated pace. From the sales volume of $226,000 annually, at the beginning of Joseph's tenure of management, by the end of the fourth year the sales had topped $1,250.000. Joseph Acker's fundamental belief was in people, their welfare and community development. He trusted people and felt there was more good than bad in every person. This was not always the case, and on occassion he carried this trust to a point of naivety,

On one occasion, he was approached by the president of the local John Howard Society and asked if he would be willing to employ a person, who would shortly be released from the P.A. Penitentiary. The convict, whose name was Gil Oliver, had apparently served a large portion of his time with distinction and was being granted a parole for his good behaviour. Joseph talked the matter over with the grocery manager and they decided to offer him employment as a produce clerk. Other than Joseph and the grocery manager, no one else was informed of Gil Oliver's prison record.

His conduct at the beginning and for several months was outstanding. He was punctual in his work attendance and became skilled at purchasing, displaying and marketing the produce offered for sale. Many clients remarked on the good appearance of the produce section, on the quality displayed and on the competitive prices that prevailed. In reality his produce display attracted customers from other stores. From the standpoint of marketing efficiency, the margin of profit that the produce section produced compared favorably with provincial chain store averages, all of which pleased the grocery manager and Joseph.

Each day, the produce section would discard a certain amount of wet garbage, such as wilted and damaged produce, spoiled fruit and vegetable trimmings. In the first instance, Gil requested permission to use the Co-op light delivery truck to dispose of this garbage at a nearby city wet garbage depot. Permission was granted. Thereafter, at or near the end of the day's business he would clean up the produce section and haul away the refuse, quite often throwing in other wet store garbage. No one questioned this activity. It became routine.

Gil however, detected that he was not being watched and as a result would load a box or two of groceries, which he would secretly pack from warehouse stock and place them in the truck along with the garbage. On the way to the dump he would unload the grocery boxes by a certain roadside tree, which afforded sufficient cover to conceal the boxes.

Following, the termination of his daily shift, he would drive his own car to the tree, pick up the grocery boxes and take them to his apartment. No one was quite sure, for how long he had been doing this.

One day, a lady member of the Co-op phoned Joseph and reported this re-occuring incident, saying she had observed this truck doing this at least once per week for some time. Later in the day a car would come along and pick up the boxes and cart them away. The lady thought this was strange and felt she had to report it.

Joseph phoned the Royal Canadian Mounted Police and informed them of the circumstances. They took the matter in hand, ambushed and caught him in the act. Three days later, Gil Oliver was back in custody charged with theft, lost his parole privelege and went back to prison.

This however, did not deter Joseph from giving employment to underpriveleged people when the opportunity presented itself. The vacancy created by Gil Oliver's absence was filled in by Ben Banik, a deaf-mute, who had worked in the produce section of his father's corner store.

His father went out of business. Joseph in consultation with the grocery manager hired Ben Banik to replace Gil Oliver. Ben turned out to be an outstanding employee.

Joseph took pride and satisfaction in his ability to develop management understudies. Allen Lindell was a young farm lad hired to manage and operate the service station. He turned out to be a fantastic

LIFE'S DETOURS

manager. Joseph felt he would occupy that position for a considerable length of time, since he was such a young man.

The twist came, when his performance was noticed by FCL, who hired him away to be their service station consultant. This promotion for Allen pleased Joseph, but left him without a trained and competent person for replacement. He phoned his brother-in-law Edwin Parker, who had worked with Joseph at Kayville to come and assume this position.

Within a two year period Edwin Parker was offered a position as a Manager of another Co-operative Association in the north-west corner of the province. A position with more responsibility and correspondingly better wages. The Parker vacancy was filled in by promoting Dave Wharton who acquired his experience as a service station employee and had been Parker's assistant.

The P.A. Co-op was on the move. Business was brisk. The hardware department was realizing increased sales in appliances and other big ticket items. The problem facing the Co-op was floor display and storage area for these items. Many loyal and dedicated co-op members understood the situation, and would order the item from the catalog. They waited two or three days for it to come in from the central warehouse in Saskatoon, but others not so loyal, took a different attitude and purchased their needs elsewhere. The result was that the Co-op was losing out on some sales.

A parcel of land was leased from the Canadian National Railways, on their right-of-way spur track. A large warehouse was constructed on that site, which provided ample space for storage. This enabled the Co-op to engage in discounted volume purchases of large ticket items, fertilizers, animal feeds, flour and other commodities.

Many of the Acker friends from the Kayville area would drop in to say "hello," while on their way to the many lakes and abundant fishing grounds in the adjacent areas. Parents and relatives came to visit them and to observe first hand the highly publicized development that Joseph had spearheaded. They were anxious to see first hand how the upward mobility they had attained was rewarding them in terms of an improved and higher standard of living. They were proud of Joseph's achievements and the finer living amenities he was able to provide for his family.

One visitor to their home was "Curly", Joseph's former truck driver from the Kayville area. Along with three of his buddies they drove up to Prince Albert for a weekend. The Ackers owned a cottage, a boat and motor at Christopher Lake. Joseph gave Curly the cottage keys and told the all male group, that the family cottage was theirs for the weekend. He also told them, he would join them on Sunday for a fishing expedition.

On Sunday morning Joseph drove the 40 miles to the cabin carrying with him two bottles of whiskey. He arrived in time to cook breakfast for them, consisting of coffee, toast, bacon, eggs, and home fried potatoes smothered in catsup according to each one's liking. After one or more pre-breakfast drinks of whiskey, the breakfast was gulped down amidst joking and laughter. Then the fishing gear was loaded in the boat and the five men sat in the 14 foot boat powered by a 25 HP motor and drifted away from shore to fish.

Joseph was in charge of manouvering the boat. He knew where the best fishing holes existed. There was a great deal of joke telling, merriment and frolicking going on. Curly reminded everyone that it was now time for another drink. Joseph had insisted that alcoholic liquor, while not prohibited, should not be taken on board the boat.

Curly had concealed a bottle in his fishing kit, and merely smiled and looked at Joseph.

"One drink won't hurt us," Curly remarked as he took out the bottle and unscrewed its cap.

The other men were in agreement. Joseph refused to have a drink at this moment.

As Curly rose from his seat and stood to pour whiskey from the bottle into a one and a half ounce glass, he lost his balance and fell overboard into the water. On his downward fall he apparently grabbed the edge of the boat with his hand in order to save himself and flipped the boat with the remaining people in it, including Joseph.

There were a few moments of despair, as each person struggled to reach shore, or merely to hang on to the boat. The final result was that Curly drowned in this incident, and oddly enough he was the only person that was a good swimmer out of the group.

The weekend had produced sorrow and a funeral instead of happy memories, all due to alcohol. Curly, who had been married for less than a year and was regarded as one of Joseph's dear friends lost his life. For a long time this incident weighed heavily on Joseph's mind and gave him a feeling of guilt and regret.

One morning a gentleman by the name of Ben Woodley requested an interview to talk to the manager. He was shown into Joseph's office.

"Good morning Mr. Acker," my name is Ben Woodley. "I am the district representative from the Retail, Wholesale and Department Store Union (RWDSU).

"Good morning sir," Joseph replied "Have a chair, what can I do for you?"

"I'm here to inform you," he began, "that after talking to a

LIFE'S DETOURS

majority of your employees, they have decided to organize themselves into a collective bargaining unit, affiliated to RWDSU. I'm in the process of submitting the application for certification of the bargaining unit to the Department of Labor. If management does not oppose the certification, your employees can proceed with organizing the unit and after certification, we can arrange a suitable date and time to discuss and sign a collective bargaining agreement. If on the other hand management opposes the idea, then you will be given an opportunity to state your case before the employees. The Department of Labor will call for the employees to vote on the matter, and the outcome of such a vote will determine whether the P.A. Co-op will be a unionized or non-unionized shop. How do you feel about this proposal?

"Mr. Woodley," Joseph began. "I come from the ranks of hard working people, who haven't always received fair treatment. I'm not opposed to unions. In my attempt at managing, I have conscientiously made an effort to share with the employees the benefits of the productivity of the institution, and I will continue to do so - union or no union. However, I must inform you that this is an issue that I must clarify with the Board of Directors, before giving you the answer you are seeking. Give me a week or ten days and I shall give you a response," he concluded.

On that note they parted. Joseph consulted with his Directors, some of which were opposed to the idea of having a unionized shop in a co-operative. They reasoned that the employees were also shareholders and owners of the Co-op, and in addition to their wages they participated in the profits earned by the institution. On the other hand the majority of the Directors including Joseph, felt that a union in the shop would provide an avenue to institute fairness, to air grievances and would probably have a positive effect on the operations.

The directors voted in favor and Joseph notified Woodley accordingly. Within a six week period a collective bargaining agreement of two years duration had been reached and signed. There were some trying times in the aftermath of the signing of the agreement, most of which was due to interpretation of the contract, and the feeling the shop steward had that he was now to be considered some kind of an officer in control of the operations. Grievances of a minor nature, that were previously settled between the department manager and his employees, now became court cases, and consumed the time that could have been otherwise put to more productive use. The Union Representative in order to safeguard his own position, did it by provoking the wrath and agitating the passions of the majority of the unionized employees.

Management was considered with suspicion. The Co-op manager

was portrayed in the same light as the manager of a private business or company at the turn of the century, who was out to accumulate greedy profits, on the backs and sweat of his employees. Joseph did not seek to cultivate, plant or use any employee as an informer. Some of the more mature employees, who saw the folly of the situation would voluntarily talk to Joseph about the tactics the Union Representative would use to disseminate misinformation, degrade shop morale and instigate stinging relations. The relationship eventually became smoother as time went on, but the "management/employee" relations that previously existed disappeared. Joseph became somewhat skeptical of the union leadership and their narrow approach to overall development and people welfare.

The Union Representatives enjoyed high salaries, drove nice new cars, stayed in the best hotel rooms, ate at the best dining places and in general were out to defend and protect their own interests and jobs. Joseph was changing his opinion about the unions. Union leaders were not interested in working with management to improve productivity and to have the employees become partners in the enterprise. They appeared to him like parasites feeding on the backs of their members, sowing dissension and lowering the potentially fertile and fair earnings of other people's savings, investment and effort in the Co-op. Somehow this was diametrically opposite to what Joseph's previously held concept of the union was.

Life for the Acker family although hectic at times, was enjoyable. Joseph had reduced both his intake and the frequency for indulging in alcohol, and this improved greatly the quality of family life. Their two weeks of summer vacation were spent motoring through various parts of Canada and the U.S.A. The family carried a full gear of camping equipment, parked in national, provincial or state parks. They cooked their meals on a gas stove, pitched a tent for the night, and bundled up in their sleeping bags.

They were moments that remained indelibly imprinted in Joseph's mind as being amongst the finest moments he spent with his family.

Joseph enjoyed his management position, his status in the community, and his involvement in the extra curricular activities in which he was engaged. He was approached to enter politics, and to allow his name to stand as a candidate for the Prince Albert federal constituency representing the New Democratic Party. An offer he declined.

Then a long distance phone call came from Regina.

Joseph picked up the receiver - "Hello, this is Acker speaking, how may I help you?"

LIFE'S DETOURS

"Joe, this is Rod Boswell, president of the Credit Union League of Saskatchewan. How are you?"

"Oh, I'm fine," Joseph replied. "What's the scoop, what's so important that you feel you must call me, or is this just a telephone visit?"

"No, I'm calling because the managing director of the League submitted his resignation to me in writing today, and I'm calling to ask you to consider seriously your appointment to this position. The League needs some dynamic leadership at this stage of development, and I believe you are the right person to fill this position at this time. I will be calling a special board meeting for next week, at which of course you will also be present. I really wanted you to have a few days to think this proposition over, and to be aware of my intention and support. I will be talking by phone to the other directors and share my thoughts with them, and as you know the majority have been harboring the feeling that the League needs an overhaul. What do you think? Can I count on you to come prepared to accept the appointment?"

"Listen Rod," Joseph responded. "This is so sudden and quite difficult for me to give a quick and positive reaction to your offer and suggestion. First I must talk it over with my wife. Off hand I would say I'm interested, but there are a few areas that require detailed discussion, the first of which is salary. My present salary is $500 per month and I'm aware that the managing director that resigned was being paid $450 per month. From that standpoint alone the offer is not appealing."

"Joe," Boswell interrupted. "In my opinion, I don't believe salary is an impediment. The League has room for growth and expansion. With an aggressive marketing program of it's services, an accelerated publicity and promotional agenda and careful guidance of it's affairs, the expenditure made for an increase in your salary, could well be an investment in the growth of the League. Give it serious thought, the credit unions in this province need a guy like you to provide quality leadership. I hope you come prepared to accept."

"I'll give it serious and deliberate thought. In the meantime, hold your proposal as close to your chest as possible until I give you my final answer. I would not want my directors here, to learn from outside sources about any move I may or may not undertake. I would like to break such news to them personally, if and when that time comes," Joseph responded.

"I promise to comply with your request. I'll be looking forward to seeing you next week. Talk to you again. Good Bye for now," Boswell said as he hung up.

Chapter 12

A CHALLENGE TO INNOVATION

Up to this point Joseph's career had been a success. His experience in both Kayville and Prince Albert, had made him notoriously famous in the co-operative circles for his ability to increase sales, to promote and to manage. Would he be able to continue on this path, if he made a move into the financial and banking arm of the co-operative movement remained a mystery to him.

He talked it over with Suzanne. She knew that Joseph was full of both energy and ambition and if he once made up his mind, he would be very determined in his way and would proceed to follow his own best instincts.

"I'm very happy with our status here. Our three chidren are in good schools. They attend church Sunday school regularly and have their circle of friends. A move would mean a disruption in their lives and a need to re-adjust themselves to a social environment in a new community. You may do whatever you feel you'd like to do, and to which you think you are best suited. The children and I will understand and give you as much support as we can. We must think in terms of both what's best for you and what's best for the family as a whole. I'm sure you're keeping the same priorities in mind," Suzanne said.

Joseph was aware from his attendance at League Board meetings, that the credit union system that was emerging in the province required innovative leadership. Innovation in the proper areas would establish a sounder base upon which the economic aspects of the system would become more meaningful to the membership. The promotion and injection of a higher degree of technology would spur the system's growth and development. A goal that would have to be attained without sacrificing the philosophy or the social mores - the very foundation upon which credit unions were founded.

At the time, there were about 270 credit unions in existence province wide, some of which were quite inactive. A few were operating under the guise of being credit unions, but were primarily serving the treasurer and a small group of his/her relatives or close friends. For organization purposes, the League divided the province into 12 districts, and each district elected a director to represent the credit unions in that district on the League Board of Directors.

The directors that Joseph knew, were generally managers or officers of the larger more successful credit unions, and were people of integrity, good judgement and progressively minded. They represented the credit unions that were the largest dues paying members of the League, and were interested in making their dues contributions to be as productive as possible. This meant stimulating growth in the smaller credit unions and if their potential for growth was non-existent, mergers with larger neighboring credit unions would be recommended. In any event caution had to be exercised in order to avoid a credit union failure. Particularly, a failure due to fraud or defalcation, from which the publicity produced would tarnish the image of credit unions in general, and especially the more successful and well-run ones.

"Some ideas, I have about developing the Credit Union League (CUL) and the credit unions are not new. Other ideas had been proposed by members of the League Board at their regular quarterly meetings. Some ideas came from other segments of the co-operative and credit union movements continent wide. Good ideas and suggestions that seem to have been misfiled and forgotten. My job will be to PLAN, to PROMOTE, and to PRODUCE. I know these words are worn out and sound like parts of an advertising program, but I don't care. They've worked for me so far and I'm going to make these words work for me all over again. I can let my imagination run free and contain it only to the degree that the ideas would be acceptable to the credit union membership and the financial circumstances of the League will permit," Joseph thought to himself.

With that conviction planted firmly in his mind, he went to the League Board meeting the following week. After a series of questions asked by the League Directors, followed by discussion, he was asked to absent himself from the board room, while they voted on the matter. In a matter of minutes he was called back in to hear the verdict.

"Mr. Acker, the League Board, by unanimous consent has agreed to employ you as Managing-Director. You may take over the position as soon as possible. We have agreed to pay you a salary of $600 per month. In addition, there is a medical and pension plan in effect with no changes. You will have the use of the League owned car and the current budget provides for an expense account to cover meals and lodging when travelling throughout the province. Is this acceptable, and if so, how soon can you assume your duties?" Rod Boswell, the League President asked.

"Gentlemen, I accept your offer," Joseph began. "As you know, I'm not unemployed, and did not run away from the job I currently hold. I'm accepting your offer, because I feel there is a huge potential for credit union growth and development in this province. It will take me a couple of months before I can assume the responsibilities of the position. I'm obligated to allow a reasonable period of time for the P.A. Co-op to find a replacement for me. I must make the physical move to Regina, which includes purchasing a home and relocating my family. But, rest assured I shall pursue the matter with concern and haste. Again, I want to thank you for the trust you've placed in me, and I look forward to discharging the duties of the position to the satisfaction of all concerned."

After the sale of his home, and a farewell party hosted by the Board of Directors of the Prince Albert Co-op, Joseph relocated his family to a home he purchased in an older but central city district and close to schools, shopping and his place of work. All of this was accomplished just in time for the new school year. The two oldest daughters were registered as students in a private girl's school, while the youngest was registered in a nearby public school. He was on schedule in the assumption of the duties of his new position.

He spent the first few weeks in getting acquainted with the characteristics of the League and its intricate relationship with its own affiliated credit unions, and other associated co-operative institutions. He was conscious of the fact that a transformation was taking place, and that he would have to identify precisely the business nature of the Credit Union League, blueprint the path to be followed and seek policy approval from the Board of Directors for its implementation. Simultaneously, it was necessary to acquire and hold the goodwill and endorsement of the other associated Cooperative and Government Institutions with which the League had to interact.

The province's co-operative development was unique, in that at the community level, it was not uncommon to find that a farmer, who was a shareholder of his grain marketing co-operative was also an elected member of that local committee. Simultaneously, he could also be a shareholder in the local consumer co-operative, a board member of his local credit union and president of the community recreational center. All community centered co-operative activities, from which he and his family received benefits and in which he held a vested interest.

That same individual would be elected to represent his credit union to the Credit Union League Annual Convention as a delegate. At the convention, in his mind he would prioritize the credit union's role in

LIFE'S DETOURS

the development of his community, and sustain the adoption of League policies and programs, - but, only to the degree and in terms of how it affected the other co-operative institutions in his community in which he participated. In other words, he had a stake in all of these community institutions and he expected them all to work and serve his interests as well as that of his neighbors.

This type of a grass roots mind-set contributed to a blend that brought the provincial central organizations, representing the various specialized sectors of the co-operative movement to interact with each other in a harmonius fashion. This was the milieu within which the Credit Union League had to function and in Joseph's mind, it was a wholesome one.

The Saskatchewan Co-operative Credit Society (SCCS) was located in the Co-op Block, a building they owned. It was a cousin organization to the Credit Union League, since it was serving the same member credit unions. The difference was that the SCCS acted as a central credit union for the individual community credit unions. It accepted their surplus funds and reserves as deposits, and loaned them funds during peak lending periods. "It was a credit union for credit unions." Individual credit union members could not directly borrow from or invest in SCCS. The local credit union looked after their financial needs.

Joseph knew from the history of co-operative development in the province, from the stories related by his parents and the earlier pioneers about the "great depression", and from his own personal experience that credit unions were born out of a special need. It was during the 1930's the era of the Great Depression, that the commercial banks pulled out of the smaller communities and left them hanging without any financial service. It was also during this period, that the credit union idea had taken hold in parts of the United States and Canada.

Edward A. Filene, the founder, and Roy F. Bergengren, an early pioneer in credit union development, whose names were household words in both Canada and the U.S. are credited with saying:-

"The credit union, a national and normal supplement to the present banking system, is one of many effective ways to promote thrift. It is about the only effective method devised as yet for the elimination of usury as practised on the wage earner and small farmer. It is a means of so educating the people that they will understand our economic system, help in its development and perfection, and protect it with their suffrage. The credit union once developed on anything like a national scale, will exercise a profoundly sane and sobering influence on the masses of the people. It will bring to them an increased opportunity for self-development which will contribute and make for a broadened prosperity."

During the decade of the thirties, the credit union and cooperative seeds took roots in Saskatchewan. Leaders such as Dr. M.M. Coady from Antigonish, Nova Scotia, Roy Bergengren from the Credit Union National Association (CUNA) in Madison, Wisconsin - later followed by Tom Doig and others who came to the province, shared their ideas and motivated the creation and development of local leaders. The local leaders grasped the vision and the philosophy and adapted it to the economic conditions and needs of the people and the times. It was truly an idea whose time had come, and as Joseph discovered in his earlier experiences both at Kayville and Prince Albert, credit unions were needed and were here to stay.

The majority of the communities that had organized credit unions, did so, because there were no banks to serve them. The province's economy was based primarily on agriculture. This meant that there were times throughout the year when the credit unions would be faced with huge fund surpluses. At other times, funds were scarce and needed to meet the credit needs of their individual members. A kind of feast or famine situation. There was a need to stabilize this situation.

In the spring, when the farmers would begin planting their crops and throughout the summer for tilling and other farming requirementss, they would borrow heavily from their credit unions to finance their farming operations. This was the season of the year when the local credit unions, would be borrowing from their central SCCS to supplement their own funds and enable them to meet the loan demands of their members. SCCS had arranged a substantial short term line of credit with a commercial bank to take care of this seasonal loan demand. When the crops would be harvested and marketed in the fall of the year, the loan repayments from the borrowing members would pour in, and the credit unions would find themselves with surpluses and idle funds, which if not invested would have no productive value. These surplus funds would be deposited in an interest bearing account with SCCS, and during the winter months when farming was at a standstill, the funds would bring in earnings to the credit unions, enabling them to pay dividends and interest to their shareholder members commensurate with what the commercial banks were offering.

SCCS on the other hand, would loan these surplus seasonal credit union funds to the Consumers Co-op Refinery to finance the refining and filling to capacity of the fuel storage tanks in readiness again for the following season's farming operations. Two other creditable co-operative accounts that had access to commercial bank lines of credit made themselves available to SCCS as users of short term loans on a "call basis." These were the Saskatchewan Wheat Pool (SWP), the grain marketing cooperative, and Federated Co-operatives Limited (FCL), the central wholesale supply and distribution mechanism for the consumer co-operatives.

In Joseph's mind, the creation and operation of the autonomous local community cooperative institutions, and the manner of integration of their diversified services at the provincial level, without infringing on each others technical specialization, spoke well for the leadership of these organizations.

"I'm delighted to be a part of this system," he was thinking to himself. "I grew up in a farming community made up of East European immigrants and at times my parents and grandparents were referred to as 'greenhorns' and at worse they were 'bohunks'. Yet in this philosophy of cooperation, I find myself in a position of leadership, and I'm being treated with respect and as an equal to any other citizen. This is terrific. What I must try to do is avoid labelling others and treat them as I am being treated. I heard it said, that society doesn't make people positive or negative. Each individual makes himself a complainer or an opportunity seeker, I want to become an opportunity seeker, not in the selfish sense of 'feather-nesting' my personal situation, but of seeking to provide the best service possible for the development of the credit unions and the members that I have been hired to serve."

The Department of Co-operative Development of the Provincial Government under whose aegis the credit unions fell, encouraged their formation and supported their development. Through a field staff of eight qualified people, the department was providing financial and legal counselling, auditing of the accounting records of those credit unions with assets of less than one million dollars, and enacting legislation to conform with their needs. In Joseph's opinion the Department was discharging its responsibilities with distinction, a great deal of understanding and in accordance with the provincial statutes under which it was established.

One specific development the Department undertook was the establishment of a Mutual Aid Fund (MUF), whose objective was to come to the assistance of credit unions faced with financial difficulties. The MUF was funded through annual contributions from each credit union, based on a dues or percentage figure of it's year-end net income.

The MUF was called upon to salvage a couple of credit unions, that had encountered defalcation problems caused through the dishonesty of their managers and the lack of adequate supervision by the Board of Directors and the Supervisory Committee. The two credit unions that were rehabilitated served as prototypes of awareness, to the directors and committee officials in general to adopt measures and guard against such a re-occurence.

The two incidents spoke loud and clear, that in dealing with money - human nature can become frail and lead to greed. It also highlighted the fact that, the persons responsible for the supervision of the credit union, were equally as much to blame for the fraud that took place as the manager who committed the crime; because through neglect of their duties to supervise, they created the opportunity under which the manager was able to perpetrate the act.

After reviewing the services provided by SCCS and the Department of Co-operatives, Joseph resolved in his own mind, that the main function of the CUL would be to embark on improving the current League services. He undertook a survey and made a minute analysis of the entire spectrum of the League operations including it's financial status. He pin-pointed the main areas of concern and prepared, what in his opinion, were suitable solutions in readiness to present to the League directors for their consideration and approval.

His analysis revealed the following issues as areas in need of attention:

* Formulating long range economic development plans.

To encourage and assist each indiviual credit union to survey its local potential and to forecast its growth over a future period of five years. This would enable the CUL to combine the local forecasts into a master provincial plan that would reflect the overall potential, and assist in programming for the future needs of the system. It would also reveal to the local credit union, what its long term operational potential in the community it serves would be.

* Standardization of Forms and Equipment.

The Department of Co-operatives had designed, produced and furnished each credit union with the basic and initial record keeping and legal forms. As the credit unions were growing their needs were changing, calling for an improved system of accounting and record keeping. The larger credit unions had designed their own forms and had them printed at local print shops. Due to their size and volume they were being offered volume discounts that the smaller credit unions were unable to obtain. The piecemeal purchasing of equipment such as, typewriters, adding machines, safes, vaults, and other office supplies was costly, and did not contribute towards standardization or the League's ability to maintain suitable and reduced inventories in such lines in order to meet their overall needs. Computers were coming into use, and there were benefits to be derived if the choice of this equipment was standardized, enabling the development of substantial uniformity throughout the entire system.

It was obvious from the beginning, that the larger credit unions

LIFE'S DETOURS

would always have specialized needs that the smaller credit unions could not use. However, he was pleased to discover that the larger credit unions would bend over backwards in terms of adopting certain measures that were also helpful to the smaller credit unions. They set aside certain selfish concerns in the interest of seeing the credit unions advance as a province wide system. In his opinion, the standardization of equipment and systems was an area in which credit unions were able to support and utilize the CUL to their own much greater advantage and creation of savings in their operations.

* Increased Educational And Training Programs.

What credit unions classify as Educational, the commercial sector would refer to as Advertising and Promotion. There is a distinct difference in the genre of the educational and promotional programs of the credit unions in the sense that their members are treated as owners and consumers of their services, with a right to share in the year-end profits or savings. The commercial banks and other financial institutions treat the users of their services as clients with no further participatory economic rights or claims.

Training on the other hand, is an educational process that embodies a "hands-on" or a "learning-by-doing" approach to new techniques required in a system's operations, or for improving the quality of existing methods and techniques.

In the educational field, the CUL produced and mailed a monthly publication primarily designed to serve the Managers, Members of the Board of Directors, Credit Committees, Supervisory Committees, and the credit union employees. This was to be continued, but expanded to include a wider variety of topics.

The credit unions were scattered throughout the province, but grouped together in the 12 districts. There was a need to get each member of the CUL Board of Directors more involved in the affairs of the district he represented. The Directors generally came from the larger credit unions in their district, and thus were capable of imparting more advanced ideas for the benefit of the smaller credit unions. For this purpose, a League Director's Information Kit together with appropiate visual aids was to be prepared.

The educational and promotional programs had to be beamed at various levels of membership. There were the Directors and Committee persons, the managers and the front-line staff, and the 225,000 members at large . Each level required specific training and knowledge. The programs designed especially for the youth (students), and for teacher training were essential for the long-term advancement of credit unions. Much material to serve these educational and training needs existed. Some of it required updating, while on some topics or areas of operation new materials had to be produced. Schedules for district meetings, special training sessions had to be drafted, personnel allocated, dates publicized and the programs executed.

*<u>Marketing The Credit Union Services.</u>

The activity of marketing the credit union idea and services would accelerate itself if more people were knowledgeable, and could forcefully and intelligently present the issues to the members and the general public. Training members of the Credit Committees in proper ways of assessing and approving loan applications, the Supervisory Committee members in discharging their supervisory duties, and the staff in loan collection procedures, was an area of paramount importance.. The various services would have to be expanded and new services added. The credit unions were already engaged in offering their members over the counter savings and deposit services, loan services, checking services, insurance and financial counselling. Banks were adding other new services such as term deposits, automated teller machines and credit cards. What would the impact of these new banking services be on credit unions, how soon should they enter the field, and what size should they be before embarking on them?

*<u>Orderly Development and Ethical Discipline.</u>

With changing rural conditions in which the small family farm was disappearing, and the formation of larger farm units becoming widespread, the smaller towns were also being affected in the same manner. Insufficient sales volume caused many a small town merchant to fold up and go out of business and the small town to disappear. The credit unions became victims of those same conditions, with the result that many of them would be forced to merge with a nearby viable credit union located in a larger town. In some instances the small credit union would merge its assets completely with a larger one, encourage its members to seek services from the larger one and then it would simply be dissolved. In other situations, the small credit union would merge and convert itself into a branch office of the larger one, offering service only one or two days per week.

This entire process had to be studied and analyzed to ensure an orderly and integrated transformation, with the least possible disruption in the business affairs of the members that were being served. Mail order credit for members moving out of their communities, for military personnel, transfer of accounts, referrals and letters of introduction prepared for the members who were moving and joining a credit union in another district or province, were problems and activities the CUL would be called upon to assist in spearheading, counselling and coordinating.

*<u>Bank Act Changes</u>

LIFE'S DETOURS

The Federal Bank Act would come up for legislative review every ten years. Just as Joseph took over the reigns of managing the League, Canada's parliament was in the beginning stage of opening up enquiries and receiving briefs recommending changes that would be required in the Bank Act. Changes that would place the banking services of the nation in tune with the times. The commercial banks had observed the astounding growth the credit unions had made in the post-war era, and were lobbying the legislators in Ottawa hard and fast to deny the credit unions full banking privileges and access to the "bank clearing centers".

The commercial banks referred to the credit unions as "near-banks", and the credit unions, because they weren't recognized as banks had to refer to their checks as "negotiable-orders." In essence the credit unions through their SCCS central, were now engaged in full fledged banking services, except for re-discounting priveleges with the Central Bank and international linkages to correspondent banks. The Credit Union Leagues from Canada's Western provinces, the Maritime provinces, and the French speaking province of Quebec were lobbying hard for full recognition as a co-operatively owned banking system alongside the commercial banking system.

The banks were powerful in terms of the good banking service they provided and their capital-vested interests. The commercial banks suffered from the stigma that during the depression, they closed their branch offices and abdicated the rural communities and their people. A feat the rural folks never forgot and one which caused organization of credit unions.

The credit unions on the other hand, were powerful in terms of the thousands of members who were their share-holders, and whose votes held enormous political clout. This clout sensitized the political-will of the legislators to deal favorably with the changes that would be requested by the credit unions.

This was the beginning of lobbying by the credit union system on a national level and it had to reflect a sober and truthful exposition of the facts. The CUL in cooperation with SCCS would be responsible for preparing the brief for submission to the specially appointed hearing commission of the legislature, and Joseph felt he would be heavily involved in contributing to its preparation and presentation.
*Intra-Institutional Communications.

Saskatchewan being the banner cooperative province in Canada at the time, had a network of various kinds of service cooperatives, all of which were represented at the provincial level by their respective central organizations. It behooved the CUL to maintain close liaison and good relations with the several central organizations, since as he discovered earlier on, many a single member was a shareholder in more than one kind of a co-operative.

The agenda and schedules of the CUL educational and promotional programs would be designed in such a manner to allow time for the other sister co-operative institutions to attend these seminars and week-end training sessions and to publicize their services. This kind of gesture was practiced throughout the cooperative sector.

Reciprocally the CUL would be invited to publicize its services and activities at their annual shareholder as well as distict held meetings, a responsibility that would fall heavily on Joseph's shoulders.

*Developing Grass-roots Democracy And Leadership.

The credit union system would have to look forward if it was to act as a financial source for the thousands of members who were now its supporters. Many a rural young person who grew up in the province, completed his public and high school education and entered into the labor and productive force of the economy, without having walked into the premises of a commercial bank. This spoke well for the kind of service the credit unions had provided.

In spite of this remarkable record, after interviewing several young people in their early twenties it was concluded, that their concept of the credit union cradled the idea that this was just another banking system. They were not familiar with the philosophy and history of their development, much less with the fact that as a member he was also an owner. He had a right to participate in the election of its directors, a right to voice his opinion on the policies, to question operational procedures and to share in the profits. An awareness campaign would have to be launched that would stimulate grass-roots democracy and develop local leadership.

Joseph prepared and presented a report incorporating all of the above areas, with ample detail and corresponding budgets for the consideration of the CUL Directors. At the same time requesting Board approval to enable him to employ another person as Director of Education.

The idea was to divide the task to be accomplished into two significant parts. The first part would give Joseph a free hand to plan the overall League programs and to carry out the liaison required for the maintenance of good relations system wide, as well as the International, Intra-institutional, and Governmental contacts and relations. The Director of Education, would confine his activities in programming the educational and training programs and see to their execution.

At their subsequent board meeting, the Directors endorsed his report and program for the coordinated development of the CUL and the credit union system. The ball was now in his court to spell out the details in each area and to begin their execution.

He employed Len Channel as his Director of Education. Len was a young man, strong in accounting, having worked as an accountant in one of the larger and more successful credit unions. He had command of the English and French languages, was well versed in overall credit union operations; was aggressive in work habit, had a pleasant personality and a flair for public speaking. Joseph had a gut feeling that he had made a good choice.Together they worked out the details of their program and set about its implementation.

Once Joseph felt solidly in the saddle and in control, the work he performed became routine. He could rise and spontaneously give a talk on the League, its organization, its scope, its services and its accomplishments, quoting a jungle of figures and data from memory. There were times when he would have to research the issue or subject matter and present himself well prepared and documented to contribute to discussions of high level importance. He made himself available to assist Len Channel, the the education director, both in terms of program planning and in the execution.

During the tenure of his management of the CUL, the credit unions were involved in making all kinds of loans. He recalls with delight a specific incident where a newly developing urban community was desirous of building a church. The banks would not advance funds for church loans. The parishioners by and large were members of the credit union, so they decided to seek a mortgage loan from the credit union. Credit Unions were also not legally empowered to lend funds to corporations or companies. The credit union phoned CUL seeking counselling on the matter.

In consultation with the manager of SCCS and others they gave birth to the idea, that if the church were able to get 50 parishioners to sign personal notes in the amount of $1,000 each, and guarantee the repayment of this loan to the credit union, that a loan of that size could be advanced to the church without making it illegal. This idea was transmitted to the credit union, who immediately picked up on it, executed the required documentation and obtained the signatures. The loan was granted and the church building was completed.

While economists were talking about tight money in Canada, the credit unions were continuously on the growth path. Joseph was aware that the system did not have enough funds to meet the full demands of its members, nevertheless the growth was palpable and on an up-hill trajectory. Loans were made for new homes, for small business ventures, for farming, for personal loans to housewives to purchase household furniture, clothing and school supplies. Laborers and professional people obtained loans to purchase automobiles or tools for their specific occupation, for family vacations, and last but not least funds were being made available in limited qauntity for student loans.

A phenomenal period of growth and development during a period of slightly less than 25 years, All in the hands of the people, guided by elected leaders, the majority of whom were farmers who were not experts in finance. What did exist was a high degree of honesty, an abundance of the scarce commodity of common sense, backed by moral integrity and a strong desire to improve living conditions for themselves and their children.

The CUL was affiliated to the Credit Unional National Association (CUNA), whose headquarters were in Madison, Wisconsin. CUNA began as a national association of credit unions, whose initial members were the state credit union leagues in the U.S. Later, the provincial leagues from Canada were permitted to affiliate themselves with CUNA, thus making it international in scope. The CUL of Saskatchewan was affiliated to CUNA, and had a slate of delegates appointed by and from its directors, who would attend the CUNA annual cConventions generally held in the United States.

Joseph had been attending the CUNA annual conventions in prior years when he was in Prince Albert as a provincial delegate. Now as managing-director of the CUL, he was again priveleged to attend and it was at these conventions that he became acquainted with the CUNA staff. The CUNA staff had put an "eagle-eye" on Saskatchewan's credit union growth and diversified development, and were inspired by the progress attained. In addition to being a CUNA delegate, Joseph had been elected to serve on the Credit Committee of the Sask Co-op Credit Society, he was elected to the Board of Directors of the Co-operative Union of Saskatchewan. and further appointed to a couple of CUNA's Committees. All of this, when coupled with the duties of Managing-Director gave him a full agenda. He found himself attending country meetings in the evenings and often his weekends were fully occupied

He was sought after as a guest speaker at credit union annual meetings and at other cooperative functions. He was a believer in the fact that inspiration and the ability to fire up another person's intellect involves speaking the truth, which is more forceful and productive than fiction.

"I have a high respect for and love ordinary people. I consider credit unions and other kinds of cooperatives as instruments by which they can help themselves individually and each other in a collective sense. No, I'm not a communist and have no respect or regard for Communism. I simply subscribe to the philosophy that when people work together under an umbrella of good-will, nobody is left out and everybody can participate and share in the benefits. Such sharing to be commensurate with the individual input of effort and economic contribution. I've been made more and more aware of this fact over the period of time I've been involved in the cooperative movement. I was brought up in a christian home and as a result harbored a feeling that there was a natural instinct in human beings, to seek `self-preservation' through group interaction. No man is an island unto himself is a statement I've often heard," Joseph would say to himself or others when addressing a crowd.

Management of resources was his one area of great concern. He was constantly under the belief that what was really wrong in the world was not due so much to a shortage of resources, but rather due to a shortage of people who knew how to manage resources. The credit union was an institution that amassed the financial resources of many people and was responsible for ensuring the most productive use of those resources. In addition, credit unions had the added reponsibility of sharing with their members, the philosophy of wise management of their individual resources, therefore management of resources was a very crucial component to both the credit union and the individual member's development.

As credit unions grew, the need for skilled management came into focus, and the art and science of good management became a very precise and demanding discipline and career. The ordinary housewife, laborer, or farmer, who was a credit union treasurer in a small community or at a church sponsored credit union in the beginning stages, could no longer fulfill that function satisfactorily and would handicap its growth. Fortunately many part-time treasurers kept abreast of the growth by attending CUL sponsored training seminars and evening classes at local colleges, and were able to upgrade their skills and professionalize themselves. They grew through the ranks from part-time treasurers to full fledged and competent managers.

Leadership for the maximum utilization of resources in the community credit union had to come from the manager. The manager had to be fully cognizant of the resources under his command and make recommendations to the directors for their most productive use. The key resources available to the manager are:

"PEOPLE" - the shareholder members, the directors, committeemen, and all staff play a key role in the credit union. Often this basic resource is not fully utilized or developed. This resource is the key to future growth and expansion. Growth takes place in two dimensions in a credit union. Horizontal growth transpires until all of the eligible people in the area become shareholders and use the credit union services. The dimension of horizontal growth can reach a cap

The dimension of vertical growth applies to financial growth, and financial growth or savings mobilization if properly promoted should be continuous and practically limitless..

"DOLLARS" - this is a very key area, because it involves the trusteeship responsibility of the member's individual business, as well as offering quality financial services and counselling. The financial aspects and results of operation must be shared openly with the members. Dollars are a way of measuring the spirit of good judgement and physical effort.

"PHYSICAL" - the facilities, programs, and services also play a very key role, and must be well planned and managed. Facilities that are conveniently located, exhibiting a suitable sign and well maintained, instills pride of ownership in the members. Trained, courteous and well informed staff add to the image of efficiency, and will move the institution in the direction of its objectives more hurriedly.

Joseph was aware that this three-legged ensemble of criteria for management was extremely important, and he bent his efforts in the design of the CUL training programs and policies to sustain this criteria and move it in the direction of strengthening its base. He urged local credit unions to institute pension programs and other valuable employee benefits in order to retain the trained and experienced staff.

Another aspect for credit union development was the creation of an awareness of the value of "time". Effective use of time applies to everyone regardless of occupation, Unquestionably every person has access to an equal amount of time, because we all have 24 hours in a day to live our lives and to perform our responsibilities. The bottom line in life's accomplishments will reflect whether a person has made full and good use of his time, or whether he has squandered it. There are exceptions to this rule, because problem situations could arise that would impede upon established plans and better use of time. But, these impediments need to be understood and provision made to take care of such situations and not permit them to become a handicap to a person's productivity and contribution to his welfare, as well as that of the society he lives in.

Much as Joseph enjoyed his duties, and responsibilities as managing-director of CUL, he secretly harbored some doubtful thoughts about the future and its direction.

The CUL's income came from dues that were collected from each credit union, based on the number of members each one had. A credit union with 500 members and paying dues of $1.00 per member per year, would pay annual dues of $500.00 Others with a lesser number of members would pay less, and those with more members would pay

LIFE'S DETOURS

correspondingly more. The larger credit unions, with 1,000 or more members felt they should pay dues on a declining scale basis. The argument they advanced, was that they were receiving proportionately less service per member from the CUL, than the medium or small-sized credit unions. They suggested a scale of declining dues based on membership numbers. As an example, a credit union with 3,000 members, would pay $1. per member on its first 1,000 members, 50 cents per member on the next thousand and perhaps 25 cents per member on the remainder. It was a cost-benefit to the large credit unions. The adoption of such a dues paying policy would have minimized the budget and restricted the volume and quality of services the CUL could provide for the smaller credit unions.

The Canadian credit union leagues by and large, with the possible exception of the Desjardin movement in Quebec, had been patterned after the State Leagues in the U.S. Initially the U.S. Leagues did not have central credit unions to serve them, primarily because they were organized in industry, labor unions, government employees or professional bodies. In contrast, the Canadian credit unions were in the larger part organized along community and parish lines. They focused on providing a more complete financial service to their members, beyond the mere accumulation of savings and short-term lending. In view of this broader concept of financial service, the Canadian credit unions led the field in organizing centrals and became more bank-like in their operations.

On the other hand, with the substantial growth of the SCCS, a concept evolved that there might be some duplicity in the services provided by the CUL and SCCS, and that a merger of the two would create efficiency and more homogenity within the system. The CUL services could be absorbed by SCCS and furnished to the credit unions from an Education and Training Department. Such a merger would eliminate the need for the credit unions to pay dues and was an idea favorably looked upon by many of the credit unions. The Canadian leagues were CUNA dues paying members. The dues amounted to .25 cents per member per year. CUNA and the Leagues were instrumental in organizing the Cuna Mutual Insurance Society (CUMIS). CUMIS was an insurance society wholly owned by the credit union system, that insured the share and loan balances of the members in their credit unions. This was an excellent feature that the credit unions were offering their members. The insurance service was only available to credit unions who were dues paying members of their League, and furthermore the League had to be afilliated with CUNA. The Canadian leagues, with rare exceptions supported CUMIS and offered this insurance protection to its members.

The credit unions affiliated with the CUL had another insurance option. The co-op members in the province had organized a Co-operative Insurance Company (CIC), which offered similar protection as CUMIS with competitive premium rates, thus giving the credit unions another choice. Joseph would often find himself at odds when it came to explaining the insurance benefits. Both insurance companies were good and gave the same level of support to CUL, but CUMIS was domcilied in the U.S. while the Co-operative Insurance Company (CIC) was a locally incorporated institution whose headquarters were located in the same city as the CUL. He would elect to support the CIC because it was home based and its investments were being made locally, although he would make it clear that each credit union could select the insurance carrier they wanted.

While the credit union system in general was growing, a few more fieldmen and office personnel were added to the CUL staff, enabling it to step up its service. Joseph was engrossed in his work, attending to the day-to-day needs of a growing system. He would absorb himself in statistical and financial analysis of the system, study the programs and services offered by other leagues, ascertain the probability of potential problems, and plotting the future direction of the system for presentation to and discussion by the elected officials of the system.

Although the one area of uncertainty about CUL's future would creep into Joseph's mind, he was very positive about his work and willing to seek comfort in any changes that were seen looming with regards to the CUL and his position. He was going on his third year as managing-director, and felt satisfied with the progress achieved during this period. He always felt that it was necessary to evaluate the past, in order to make the proper and less costly advances for the future. If the future for the CUL as an institution would disappear, he would certainly find a spot within the cooperative system that would offer him satisfying employment. He was proud of both his record and achievement, and was confident in facing the future.

LIFE'S DETOURS

Chapter 13

TOO PROUD TO BE HUMBLE

The word "good" would be the one word that would best describe Joseph's feeling about his position as managing-director of the Credit Union League. He was imbued with its philosophy and loved his work. The growth of the credit unions was palpable and they were fast becoming financial pillars in the communities they served.

Joseph was in his office. His secretary Pearl Young, rapped on his door and walked in.

"There's a gentleman here by the name of Virgil Derry, wants to have an interview with you. Here is his card. He is the President of Sherwood Co-op Association here in Regina. Shall I show him in?" Pearl asked.

"Certainly, show him right in," Joseph replied.

Mr. Derry, was a respectable and well thought of farmer in the Regina district. He had been serving on the Board of Directors of the Sherwood Co-op for a number of years, and more recently was elected as its president. Joseph had met him on a number of occassions at conventions and other meetings, and somewhat was acquainted with him.

Sherwood Co-operative Association was one of the largest consumer owned co-operatives west of the Great Lakes in Canada. Its annual sales volume had reached $5 million, it had 160 employees and assets valued at over $2 million.

Pearl Young showed Mr. Derry in, introduced him to Joseph, who came out from behind his desk to shake Mr. Derry's hand.

"Good morning, Mr. Acker. We seem to know each other from previous meetings and gatherings. How are you doing? From every source I know, I understand the credit union system is growing and flourishing, and I want to extend my congratulations. You're doing a splendid job. How do you find the workload?" Derry commented.

"Well, thank you for those kind remarks. It takes a lot of people working together to make a system like this a success, but of course I don't mind it, I'm enjoying the work and as a result it is not a load," Joseph replied.

"To make a long story short, I'll tell you why I'm here this morning. Please give me a bit of your time. Mr.Harold Whitney, the present general manager of Sherwood Co-op has reached retirement age and has asked to be relieved of his responsibilities as general-manager. He has suggested that we approach you and ask you to replace him. You have quite an enviable record of both good management, and sales and ideas promotion. I've had an opportunity to discuss it with other members of the Board of Directors. They were all in agreement, that based on your record, you would be a suitable candidate. I'm here to offer you this position with Sherwood. What do you think?" Derry concluded.

"Golly, I've never given this one iota of thought. It never crossed my mind, that I would be approached to become the general-manager of your Co-op. I really don't know what to say. I need some time to think about it. I'm not certain that I want the position. It is a big job. It has different kinds of presssures impinging upon a person, and I'm not too sure I want those kinds of pressures. The job I have now is one that I like and I'm quite happy with it," Joseph replied.

"Yes, I'm aware that the position of general manager of Sherwood is more strenuous than the job you presently have. But you're a young man. We have observed your performance in your other positions, and we feel you possess the qualities that we are in search of. Besides we are in a position to pay you more money than you're presently earning," Derry countered.

"Well Virgil, the last time I had a beer with Howard, your general manager, and we were comparing some notes, he said he was earning $800 per month. Frankly, I wouldn't take the job at that price," Joseph stated.

"You're correct, and we wouldn't expect you to, we can sweeten that part of it. I have no authority at this moment to make you a salary offer, but it is an item open for negotiation, if you decide to accept the job offer," Derry said.

"Mr. Derry, I appreciate the offer and the courtesy of your call. I must think about the matter. Give me a couple of weeks and try me again," Joseph said.

With that they both rose from their chairs, shook hands and parted.

Joseph sat relaxed in his chair and began mulling the whole thing over in his mind. He decided to place a phone call to one of his manager friends at the Pioneer Co-op in Swift Current, Saskatchewan.

"Hello Herb, how are you?" Joseph uttered.

"Hey, I'm great," was the reply from the other end. "What makes you phone, what can I do for you?"

"Herb, this is confidential. This morning I was approached by Virgil Derry, president of Sherwood Co-op. You know him, and he made me a job offer to become their general manager. I am not committed, but am mulling it over in my mind. You are holding an equally responsible position in your co-op. What's a position of the kind Sherwood offers worth?" Joseph asked.

"Hm, so that's the scoop. I guess old Howard decided to retire not because of his age, but because of the business pressure. His sales volume is on the decline and I'm assuming he is under pressure from his Board to do something about it. I understand he will become the president of the SCCS at a salary. That was an unpaid position formerly filled by a volunteer. It's a position of prestige and without any stress. It's a retirement post for him. But to come back to your question, I would not touch that position for less than $12,000 per year," Herb commented.

After a few more exchanges of ideas and information, Joseph hung up the telephone and sat thinking. The year is 1959. His present salary is $600 per month, plus a few other benefits. Doubling his salary would be an accomplishment. There weren't too many executives or professional people earning that kind of a salary at that time. But, then the question arose in his mind.

"Do I want it and could I do the job, if I got it? Its an offer, a once in a lifetime offer. Should I turn it down? Their sales volume is on a water-shed and has been over the last two years. On the other hand its a challenge and if I could turn their sales curve in an upward trend I would be a real hero," he thought to himself.

Then another thought entered his mind. Why did Howard Whitney establish for himself a paid position in SCCS? The CUL of which Joseph was managing-director worked very closely with SCCS. They did not require a public relations person. There was a strategy in play behind a curtain of which he was unaware.

That evening he talked it over with Suzanne, his wife. Since she held no outside job and Joseph was the sole breadwinner in the family, she did not have it in her nature to make brash recommendations. She was fearful that if a situation did not turn out positive, she might be held partially responsible for having made a bad recommendation. She merely urged him to consider carefully his move.

The next day Joseph went in to see Keith Unger, who was the Managing-Director of SCCS, and whom Joseph considered to be a trusted and genuine friend. He was seeking Unger's point of view and advice.

"Keith, I've known you for a long number of years. The co-ops I managed borrowed heavily from SCCS, and I've had a record of good management and repayment. I'd like you to square with me on what appears to me to be a situation, which I don't fully comprehend. I understand that Howard Whitney is resigning as manager of the Sherwood Co-op and coming here into SCCS to take a paid position as president. At the same time, I've been offered the position of replacing Howard as the GM in Sherwood. What does this mean? Does SCCS need a president with a salary when up to this moment, it has always been discharged by a volunteer? Is there a move on foot to step up the public relations activity of SCCS, and cut into the work of the CUL? What is the picture as you see it?" Joseph asked.

"Joseph," Unger began. "I'm glad you came in to talk this matter over with me. I am eager to talk to you about it. Howard Whitney is coming in as a paid president of SCCS, with a low salary. He is retiring from Sherwood and can do public relations work for us. This will assist me, since I'm getting up in age and close to retirement. In the meantime, my workload has been getting heavier and I need some help. The fact that you have been asked to take over the position of general manager and to replace Howard in Sherwood, speaks well for you and your capability. You happen to be one of those exceptional guys that has no need to look for a job, the job comes looking for you. With regards to the future of the CUL, I'm in no position to say which direction it will go - but, it would be my hunch, that over the long pull the CUL and SCCS would be integrating their services and eliminating duplicity and the extra cost," Unger replied.

They exchanged a few more ideas and niceties, then separated. Joseph continued in thought about this matter.

"Should I turn it down and hang on to what I have for as long as it lasts - or should I take the plunge and accept the offer. I'm not sure I can handle it, but rather than admit that the job might be too big for me and turn the job offer down, I think, I know what I'll do! I'm going to price myself beyond their willingness to pay. I'm going to demand a salary of $1,000 per month. They won't pay that much. This enables them to search for someone else, and for me to save face and remain with my pride intact and in my present position," Joseph said to himself.

Ten days later, Virgil Derry phoned Joseph and requested an appointment for a further chat. Joseph advised him to come right over. Within minutes he was in Joseph's office.

"I've talked your situation over with my directors, and they've

LIFE'S DETOURS

agreed to sweeten the salary pot for you, if you decide to come. We will offer you $10.800 as a starting salary. This is substantially more than what your present position pays, or will pay for the immediate future. We hope you'll decide to accept our offer," Derry said.

"Mr. Derry, my decision to fill the position you're offering rests primarily on salary. As you know, the position is a tough one. The union contract will expire this coming October and will require negotiation, and my love for the union has kind of dissipated. Then your sales are on a down swing and naturally you would expect me to remedy that situation. I cannot consider your offer, without a salary of $1,000 per month," Joseph replied.

At this point Derry cut into the conversation. "What you are demanding in salary is equivalent to the salary of the Premier of this province!"

"Then get the Premier of the province to manage the business, I'm happy where I am," Joseph said with a smile.

The upshot of this conversation was that Derry would go back to his Board of Directors and seek their opinion on the salary demand Joseph had advanced. It was mid-June and Joseph was preparing to depart on a much-earned two week motoring vacation with his family. The phone rang, just as they were preparing to lock the front door of their house and depart. Joseph answered.

"Joe, this is Virgil. I knew you were leaving on your vacation and I wanted to catch you before departing. The Board of Directors has agreed to meet your salary demand. When can we expect you to assume the responsibilities?"

"Mr. Derry, thank you for your call. You're lucky, you caught me just as we were going out the door, preparing to lock it. I'll think it over and get back to you after I return from our vacation. See you then," Joseph hung up.

On hearing the news, his feeling was divided. Happy in the sense that his demand had been met, but still indefinite about really wanting the job. The salary was nearly double the amount he was currently earning. The future uncertainty of the CUL was something to think about. Where else could he obtain a position offering this kind of a salary.

The vacation consisted of a motor trip with his family. They took their camping equipment along. The plan called for a trip to Vancouver Island and interior British Columbia.

Joseph's father had suffered a heart attack a few days before and was in hospital recuperating. He had just purchased a new car and offered it to Joseph and his family to drive on the trip.

"This new car, will take you where you want to go and back

without any problems. Have a good vacation," he said as he handed Joseph the keys.

Two weeks later, he was back in his CUL office. By this time word had gotten around about the salary offer made to him, and everyone was quite certain he would resign from the CUL and accept the new position, which in fact he did. He submitted a 30 day notice of resignation to the CUL Directors, and on the first of August moved into the general manager's office in Sherwood Co-op.

He wanted to commence his responsibilities at the very beginning, but wasn't quite sure of where the beginning point would be. There were so many areas to examine and analyze. After being introduced to key members of the staff, he requested Bernard Martin, the personnel manager to arrange a time schedule in which he would have an opportunity to have a half-hour interview with every member of the staff. One hundred and sixty two employees, would take up about 82 hours of his time. He requested that the schedule be contained to no more than six hours per day, allowing him time to attend to other matters of pressing importance that would arise.

He picked up the annual reports and auditors recommendations for the preceding five years and studied them minutely. He spent an untold amount of time in discussing the position of Sherwood with Ronald Layton, the treasurer/accountant. He had a chart prepared outlining the Sherwood's position and sales trend for the preceding three years. During the last two years of that period the overall sales reflected a declining trend and a slight upward trend in operating expenses.

To remind himself, and to show it to staff members as they came into his office for the half-hour interview, he had the chart mounted on the wall to the right of his chair and desk.

Ten days after he took hold of the reigns, he began the half-hour interviews with the employees. The first three or four employees walked timidly into his office and sort of stared at him, wondering what the content and outcome of such an interview would be. Word soon got around through the staff-vine that the interviews were pleasant and nothing to fear.

In the interview, he would talk to his associates about their personal situation. Questions on such matters as:
1. Their families. Were they married or single. Did they have children, etc.,
2. Their job at Sherwood. How long had they been working at Sherwood. Were they happy with their job situation. What could be done to improve their working conditions at the station they were in.

LIFE'S DETOURS

3. What could be done for Sherwood to increase its sales volume, and at the same time control expenses.(At this juncture Joseph would turn to the chart with graphs on the wall, and spend a few moments explaining the situation facing Sherwood to the associated employee.

Finally he would wind up the interview by appealing to the his associate for assistance.

"As you know, I'm your new general manager. I've been hired to be your leader in correcting the problems Sherwood is facing at the moment. I can't do it alone. I have to ask for your assistance. Please go back to your work station and take a pencil and a pad, then start looking around you and find out what you think should be done to improve your work area. First, to help you do your job more efficiently, and secondly to be of greater service to our member/customers and to increase our sales."

Pointing to the graph chart he would say, "For if we cannot make this sales curve go up and hold our expenses within a reasonable percentage of the sales, both you and I will be looking for a job elsewhere. We are in this game together - and we either swim or sink together."

Joseph did not do another thing to alter the operational structure of Sherwood for the balance of that year. The sales volume began growing, the pace was so accelerated that by year-end, the sales had superceded the previous year's volume. The change in employee attitudes as a result of having taken them into his confidence and sharing his problem with them, made them fully aware of the situation and they pitched in to help.

The members of Sherwood, who were also the customers would come up to Joseph and remark,- "What have you done to your staff to fire them up like you did? Some of them phone us at home in the evening telling us about the bargains being offered. Everyone is just plain nice and helpful. It's much nicer to shop here now." Joseph had scored a hit.

From his interviews with the Board of Directors, with his staff, with other members of Sherwood, who were old time shareholders and believers in the cooperative philosophy, he concluded that there were three important problem areas facing Sherwood that had to be addressed if it was to continue growing and making it's impact in the city.

First, a large portion of its sales volume came from the sale of heating oil. In a city of 60,000 residents, Sherwood enjoyed the largest share of the market for this commodity. Natural gas had been piped into the city and home-heating conversion from oil to natural gas was taking place at an accelerated pace. The market for heating oil would be totally eliminated in the city area, and only the rural farm homes would be consumers of heating oil. The loss of this sales volume, would have to be replaced with the selling of commodities of a different genre.

Secondly, the development of shopping centers or plazas were in vogue and several were under construction in the city. Sherwood had a unique location at the corner where two main highways converged. This was considered one of the highest traffic count locations in the city. It was an ideal location for developing a co-operative shopping plaza, but more land was needed.

Thirdly, with the growth of the city and with suburban development, it would be necessary for Sherwood to reach out with branch locations in order to bring its services closer to its members and users.

The Directors requested Joseph to make specific recommendations as to the action he visualized taking in order to be of greater service, to maintain competetive prices based on sales volume, and a profit or savings balance that would be satisfactory to the shareholder members.

He began by negotiating a three year collective bargaining agreement with the union. This matter was out of his hair, and he could now devote more of his time towards the planning of solutions to Sherwood's problems.

It seemed that the ideal situation was to make the existing location at the corner of the two main streets an enlarged family shopping center. There was a four year old, well constructed building facility that did not appear to be properly utilized. The first floor was used for food merchandising. The second floor was completely dedicated to administration offices. The basement housed a cold storage and locker department, which was very popular with the rural folks prior to the electrification of the rural areas. But with the advent of rural electrification, this service was on becoming obsolete. An older building housing the hardware department and a service station were at the same location.. The parking space was inadequate, but additonal land could be purchased from private homeowners adjacent to the location.

Joseph's recommendations consisted of purchasing the required additional land, constructing a new and larger food store, converting the newer building into a department store that would house the hardware, cafeteria, beauty salon, barber shop and a post office in the basement. A pharmacy in one area of the main floor. Men's wear in the remainder of the main floor, with ladies' wear taking up the entire top floor. All three floors to be connected by elevator. The administration

LIFE'S DETOURS

offices were to be moved into leased quarters on the top floor of the Sherwood Credit Union building which was constructed at the same location and annexed by an abutment to the newer Sherwood building.

The Co-op had an established lumber department for some years, and a heating and plumbing department was also in place. The sales and services of these two departments could be integrated, an electrical department added, and a complete "home construction" department developed. This could facilitate the sale of a completely packaged home, that could be delivered and erected on the customer's premises. This idea was most suitable for farm homes, or for city dwellers who owned their own land. This strategy for expanding the use of the existing services would help to offset the loss of fuel oil sales.

There was room for the construction of three more service stations, one on each of the three principal highways leading into the city. These service stations were important because Sherwood Co-op, was the only outlet for the petroleum products coming from the co-operatively owned refinery. As a result, the refinery was not enjoying a fair share of the petroleum market in the city. This was considered a disservice to the refinery as well as to its shareholders, in terms of the sales output and the member's investment in the refinery. To round out the picture a number of smaller neighborhood type shopping centers that would provide basic pick-up food items and a pharmacy to serve outlying suburban areas was suggested.

The estimated cost of this entire package reached one and a half million dollars. After a thorough review and approval by the Board of Directors, Joseph was authorized to purchase the additional land, to hire a consulting firm, to engage an architectural firm, and a construction firm. The construction and renovation period at the main center lasted approximately six months.

Joseph was in the limelight. He had been elected as Chairman of the Co-op Manager's Advisory Committee. A group of co-op managers who acted in an advisory capacity to the merchandising departments of FCL, the central wholesale. The main purpose of this committee was to standardize overall brands to be carried in inventory, to ensure quality and to promote the co-op brands, which were the best money earners for the local co-operatives.

He was elected as chairman of the Finance Committee to raise funds for the construction of a new Orthodox church in the east end of the city. Under his chairmanship pledges of more than $175,000 had been obtained, a new church was constructed and the mortgage burned at the end of a three year period. Joseph's father had moved from the Kayville area and was now the officiating pastor at this church.

In the interval, several other developments took place affecting

Joseph both directly and indirectly. Dolores Chase, who had been secretary to Howard Whitney, the former general manager, and who was also the corporate secretary remained on staff. She was a capable and knowledgeable person, and also had a good relationship with Virgil Derry, the president of the Co-op. Joseph was determined to manage the business in the strictest sense of good ethics, open discussions, and did not harbor secrets or play his cards close to his chest. He would share his thoughts and much of his research information in bits and pieces with members of his staff. It became evident, that the Board of Directors were receiving certain inside information, which Joseph considered privy while being researched and in the planning stage.

Simultaneously, he noticed that certain ideas and suggestions were coming to him from subordinates, most of which alluded to the manager's need for caution. He knew he had to be cautious, but felt that, unless he pushed aggressively forward with his ideas and programs, the activity he had embarked on was going to be delayed, or even scuttled. When he would query the subordinates for the source of his information, they would give Dolores Chase's name. He became suspicious that a clique formed by the previous general manager, together with the president and Dolores, were endeavouring to micro manage the business affairs from the outside. That kind of activity had tp be curtailed very quickly.

He called Dolores into his office, and bluntly told her what his feelings were.

"I must admit that I did share some details with Mr. Derry the President about your activity, none of which was to your detriment, but information can get misconstrued as I see it. I'm the corporate secretary and Mr.Derry has been coming into my office to sign letters or documents which are properly within his domain as president. I appreciate you sharing this feeling with me. I shall try to do better," she said.

"I too, appreciate your cooperation in this respect. It is not my intention to hide anything from the Board of Directors. The aggravation comes in when the president finds out about an idea or an activity, before I make it known to him and before it becomes properly jelled for official presentation to the board. This causes me grief and places me in a defensive position before I have all the facts gathered," Joseph admonished her.

After this brief skirmish, the relations between him and the secretary became cooler. Two weeks later Dolores submitted her resignation and went to work for SCCS as the private secretary to Howard Whitney, the former general manager of Sherwood. This confirmed Joseph's fears about the existence of a clique.

LIFE'S DETOURS

All of the members of the Board of Directors served as volunteers, with only out-of-pocket expenses being reimbursed. These expenses consisted of a per diem of $10 per day plus 10 cents per mile for travel costs. Joseph found that he had a majority of the Board of Directors supporting him, and even more strange was the fact that they occassionally looked askance at Virgil Derry the president. Derry was the pushy type, and would often walk around the co-op facilities like a peacock demonstrating his authority. He was a frequent and chronic complainer about the services the members were receiving. He would say that members complain to him and when asked to divulge their names, he would refuse, stating that it would be a breach of confidence. Nine times out of ten his complaints were unfounded when they were investigated. Most of them were focused toward Joseph, with the accusation that the staff was not receiving proper direction which was the reason for the complaint.

Joseph detected that personal politics were at work in an effort to undermine him early in his administration. He attended a fowl supper at one of the rural community churches one evening and sat at a table next to a gentleman, who happened to be Virgil Derry's neighbor. During the course of the dinner, the conversation drifted around to his position as manager at Sherwood Co-op.

"You know Virgil has a son in university studying for a degree in business administration. One time he suggested to me that he thought his son would make a good manager for Sherwood," the neighbor said.

"Yes, I guess he would," Joseph chimed in. "I don't have a degree in business administration. My knowledge comes from the school of hardknocks. I am now completing 15 years of serving co-operatives in a managerial capacity, and have worked my way to the top from the very bottom. But Mr.Derry is an influential person and could very well place his son in that position after graduation," Joseph said.

He thought about that neighbor's comment for a long time. It was possible for such a situation to develop. It was not common at the time for a university graduate with a degree to step out into the business world and obtain for himself an annual salary of $12,000. Furthermore, why was Mr. Derry a chronic complainer on aspects of the operation which were only brought to Joseph's attention by him.

Joseph generally made an inspection of the various facilities that Sherwood owned every Saturday morning. Some of these facilities were some distance apart. During his tour of inspection he would take time, to converse with the manager in charge of the department, to learn about their problems, and to talk to other employees as well. It happened on one of these mornings, that as Joseph walked into the hardware department, Virgil Derry came in pushing a gas-powered lawn mower. He told the manager it wasn't working and that he wanted it fixed. The assistant manager of the department to whom Joseph happened to be talking, looked at him and remarked.

"You know Mr. Acker, Virgil Derry picked up that mower here last summer, never paid for it, and now he brings it back for us to repair for him. He's the president, but I don't think his action is fair to the other members. In my books, he's abusing us through the privelege of his position," he softly said to Joseph.

Joseph neither agreed or disagreed with him. He shrugged his shoulders and gave the assistant manager a pat on the back and walked away. It was another puzzle for him to solve involving Derry the president. In talking to some of the other department managers. he would quietly inquire if Mr. Derry, as president would seek or ask for special favors. All of the managers stated that at one time or another they had been imposed upon to offer him special discounts on merchandise he was buying. Some of the time under the guise that he could obtain it cheaper elsewhere, in which case he would complain that our pricing policy was out of line, and at other times he would demand a discount simply on the merit of his position as president.

Two or three of the old time department managers were quite used to treating the president in this manner, being under the impression that such a favor would secure their employment position in the co-op. The most glaring example of this kind of paternalism was practiced by the manager of the hardware department. When a new policy was instituted that called for the hardware department to broaden the inventory of Co-op labelled goods, he refused to do so and Joseph quickly fired him.

His firing became a court hearing at the next meeting of the Board of Directors, and Mr.Derry the president was determined to have him re-instated.

Joseph simply stated,- "I'm the manager and I'm responsible to manage this business. As directors you can hold me wholly accountable for either its progress or its failure. If you are not happy with my style of management, you may choose to release me from this position. We do not see eye to eye on merchandising policies in his department, and on a few other unethical performances. However, be assured that I will not reinstate the hardware manager."

The directors voted to support his decision. But it aggravated further the relationship between Mr.Derry, the president and Joseph.

The renovation and expansion at the main center was completed on schedule. Official opening and ribbon cutting ceremonies were held. The day's program was executed on a specially constructed platform on the parking space of the new premises. The agenda consisted of a

LIFE'S DETOURS

program beginning at 10:00 a.m. with band music, followed by a number of speakers and well wishers. The ribbons were cut by the Premier of the Province to both the Department store and the new Food store and the crowd of about two thousand people consisting mostly of Sherwood members and shareholders were exposed to the new facilities and enlarged inventories. The day's events wound up with a parking lot dance in the evening at which famous Canadian radio and television stars entertained the crowd. It was probably one of the most spectacular official openings in the City of Regina and certainly in the cooperative system.

After the official opening, business continued to be brisk and sales were steadily on the rise, registering an increase of more than a half million dollars for the remaining three months of the year, and winding up the year at slightly over five million dollars. The sales lost due to the loss of the fuel oil market were being recaptured.

Joseph was continually analyzing ways and means to keep the staff motivated, and not to permit enthusiasm and the sales momentum to cease. Monthly staff meetings were held in an effort to keep the staff informed, and an in-house bulletin was prepared by the personnel department, which was directed exclusively to members of the staff and their families.

A monthly prize would be awarded to the best employee of the month. Such an employee would be chosen by shopping members who would cast ballots in favor of the employee of their choice, and deposit their ballots in conveniently located collection boxes. The award would be based on the number of ballots earned, as well as his work proficiency as judged by his immediate superior. The employee would be awarded a gift of cash and treated to a dinner in the company of his superior and the general manager.

On the basis of their merit, each year a few employees would be selected to attend short courses at the Western Co-operative College for skill improvement. Others from the administrative staff would attend management seminars.

Specialized training programs for updating staff on new technologies being introduced and incorporated in household appliances, home, yard and farm equipment, and for new products were regularly held within the respective departments. It was Joseph's belief that the more informed his staff was, the better would be their performance.

Another program known as the "HUMAN TOUCH" program was also instituted. It was a program designed to make the Co-op employees more conscious of their relations with the member-customers. Each employee was issued with personalized business cards, which carried his name, address, telephone number, and the department with which he was associated. On the back of the business card, the Human Touch points of importance were listed to constantly remind the employee of the program's objectives. It was also a message to the recipient of the card, a message to indicate the character of the task the employees were endeavouring to accomplish, and the corporate image to be developed. The Human Touch points listed were:

H	- Hearing	T	- Train
U	- Understanding	O	- Open Minds
M	- Motivate	U	- Use All Resources
A	- Acknowledge	C	- Communicate
N	- Notice	H	- Honor.

A pocket size pamphlet was prepared enlarging on each of the points listed above and handed to each employee. The theme was made a subject of discussion at the regular staff meetings. The whole idea was to develop the Co-op and its employees into an institution whose people were concerned with supplying the needs of its members in an ethical, humane and dignified manner. And it worked.

Sales continued to increase and the productivity per man hour of labor input was above average in many departments when compared to national industry averages. In the grocery or food department alone, an annual sales volume of $2.7 million had been attained with an average inventory of $49 thousand. This meant an inventory turnover of 55 times per year, or better than once per week. This produced two valuable interpretations. First, that the food items at the Co-op were fresh due to their rapid turnover, and secondly the wholesalers sold their goods on 15 day payment terms, which in effect enabled the Co-op to finance the inventory with the wholesaler's credit terms.

Many other efficiencies of this nature were implemented and an "eagle's eye" was constantly held on the expense side of the operations. Joseph held a general concern and respect for people. As soon as a co-worker or a member customer would come into his office, he would immediately ask that coffee be served; he would find the time to chat, to listen and to make him or her comfortable.

"Everybody has their flaws including me. I'm trying to rebuild my personality, and am on the alert to improve and maintain good relations with everyone associated with the enterprise," Joseph would say to himself.

More than one million dollars in profit was realized over a three year period under his management. He was pleased with the operations and more pleased with his accomplishments. However, in silence he was disappointed with the attitude of the board of directors. Out of the nine directors that constituted the board, five were farmers, one was a

LIFE'S DETOURS

housewife, and the remaining three were professionals in the provincial civil service. None of the civil servants were earning a higher salary than Joseph at the time, and the farm members of the board were good farmers and may have had a higher income, but were as conservative as most good farmers are. The result was that over a three year period Joseph had not been granted a salary increase, and remained at his starting salary of $12,000 per year. To his knowledge a salary adjustment for him had not even been considered by the board, and he was preparing himself to present his case for discussion to the next meeting of the directors.

It was a mid-week afternoon, he was at his desk preparing and discussing a plan for a new service station to be built at the entrance of the main east-west highway into the city. With him was the manager of the Petroleum Division and the manager of the principal down town service station. They had just completed their analysis and the two assistants were on their way out of his office, when the phone rang.

"Hello, this is Joseph Acker speaking. How may I help you?"

"Hello Joseph, how are you?" the voice from the other end of the phone line replied. "This is Bill Sorenson calling you from Madison, Wisconsin. You'll remember me I'm sure from the convention we attended together about three years ago last spring. I'm the director of the World Extension Division of CUNA."

"Oh I'm fine, yea, of course I remember you and the time we had a drink together in your hotel room, how are you?" Joseph said.

"Oh, I'm fine too and extremely busy. What are you up to these days. Had to phone the Credit Union League in order to find your whereabouts," Sorenson replied.

"Well, I'm pretty busy too, as you may have learned. Just got over a sizeable expansion program at this co-op I'm managing, and there are still a few facilities to add before the program is fully rounded. But we're moving ahead," Joseph said.

"The reason I'm calling," Sorenson chimed in, "is because I want to make you an offer. Our division has been awarded a contract by the United States Agency For International Development (USAID), to organize and develop credit unions in the South American republics. I can't think of a better person to head up our training program for this effort than you. I'd like to have you come on board on this venture with us. What do you think?"

"Bill, this is sudden but at the same time it's good news for me. I've dreamt and cherished a position that would give me international exposure. Naturally, I'll have to discuss it with my wife, but I'm sure she'll consent. My question is, what will my salary be, and how much time will you allow me for closing down operations here? he answered.

"Well, what is your present salary?" Bill asked.

"I'm getting $12,000 per year plus benefits," Joseph answered

"Well Joe, if you're willing to come on board, I'll offer you $16,000 to start with, and corresponding increases thereafter based on the policy of the CUNA/USAID agreement. How does that sound to you?" Sorenson advanced.

"At that figure Bill, I'm your man. Give me 60 days to clear up my business here. I will be applying to the U.S. Consulate in Winnipeg for permission to immigrate to the U.S. I don't know what all the requirements will be, but certainly a letter of certification of employment from you would be very useful. Don't you think?" Joseph said.

"Sure deal, I'll tell you what I'll do. I'll send you an application for employment form by mail. Fill it in and return it to me as soon as possible. Then on that basis I will follow up with a letter certifying your employment, and we will proceed from there. If there is other data required we can supply it and vice versa. We can keep in contact by phone. Is that okay?" Sorenson replied.

After the phone conversation Joseph's spirit shot up sky high. He left his office and went home to break the news to Suzanne. She also felt good about it. The job at Sherwood had been nerve wrecking, and often he would come home very moody and exhausted. A change from a boiler pressurized job to one that was not so highly competitive would be a welcome change. The children too, were exposed to the news after they came home from school and were excited about the fact that we were going international. They were cautioned to keep the news in the family, until Joseph would break it officially to the Sherwood directors, to the staff, and to the news media.

At the board meeting which was held on the second Friday of the following month. Joseph did not submit his request for an increase in salary, rather he submitted a letter of resignation. They were taken by surprise at the good offer he had received.

"We were on the verge of increasing your salary at this meeting," Karl Walker, the vice president said. "I don't suppose you would consider cancelling your plans and remaining here with us?"

"No, my mind is now made up. Had you offered me an increase a year ago, I would have possibly considered your proposal, but in all sincerity, I was beginning to feel that my effort and input in Sherwood was not highly valued. The subject of appraisal of the manager's salary should be an annual exercise. I was ready to bring it up at this meeting, but ten days ago I received this offer and I've presented it instead," Joseph said.

His resignation was received with regret. It was approved with thanks by the directors and on that note the meeting adjourned.

Chapter 14

GOING INTERNATIONAL

Joseph had submitted his resignation, and had sixty days in which to wind up both his personal affairs, as well as squaring the affairs of Sherwood Co-op and leaving the working files current and in the best of condition. He subscribed to the Eskimo-land theory, that if you'd like to find the wood box full, then fill the wood box for the next person before departing.

He sat behind his desk making a list of the activities that had to be attended to. He was in thought.

"There is an old saying, that roses have thorns. I felt that I would bump into a few thorns at Sherwood, but overall the job would be rosy. From my previous experience I should have known that a dichotomy to the situation existed somewhere, and the solution rested on having to look at the situation from both sides. Perhaps I should have reversed the old saying to read - thorns have roses - and since there are more thorns than roses, I should have engaged myself in a strategy to deal with more thorns. At Sherwood I had to put up with one big thorn, but then, that may have been the stepping stone for being available to accept the call to an international position. The road of life will be decked with some thorns and we've got to accept that notion and be prepared to make detours. I'm sure there will be some thorns to contend with on the international scene as well, but I'll cross that chasm when I come to it."

Somehow the pressure was off, but there was still a great deal to be done in readiness for their move to the United States. The CUNA offices were located in Madison, Wisconsin and he was expected to relocate there. United States immigration requirements had to be attended to and met. The first step consisted of obtaining physical and medical reports. Passports had to be secured for all members of the family, except for Grace, their youngest daughter who was included on

LIFE'S DETOURS

Suzanne's passport. This called for a trip to a passport photographer, followed by trips to the city police station in order to obtain the personal conduct and fingerprint reports for each family member.

Armed with this data, Joseph took a couple of days off and together with Suzanne they motored to Winnipeg. He filed the required documentation seeking entry into the U.S. at the Consular Office there and the following day was given a personal interview. At the interview, he presented his employment contract and another letter from CUNA which stated that his services were required as soon as possible. Both of the documents helped to accelerate the processing of the documents for early entry into the U.S. In any event the Consular Officer said it would take from six weeks to two months before approval would be received.

The listing of their home with a real estate broker brought quick results, and a sale was consumated within a two week period. Joseph had withdrawn his contribution of fiften years to his co-op pension fund, which amounted to roughly $27,000. He immediately invested the amount of $25,000 as a down payment on a commercial building valued at $125,000. It was an older two storey brick structure, situated on a lot with 160 feet of frontage on the main street and 250 feet in depth parallel to the other street, and very centrally located. The mortgage payments amounted to $800.00 per month with interest at 8% per annum.

The redeeming feature about this purchase was that the main floor had three tenants, consisting of a bank, a drug store and an appliance store. The second storey contained ten one-bedroom and two two-bedroom apartments. There was a monthly income from all sources adequate to meet the mortgage payments, the taxes and other maintenance expenses.

It was programmed to pay for itself in 15 years, and Joseph felt that this would be the place he would retire, when that time came.

There followed a series of going-away luncheons and dinners. Friends came from near and far to say farewell and to pay tribute to the contribution he had made to community life in the province. He had been named in the book of "Who's Who in Saskatchewan".

The local pastor of the United Church of Canada who was a close friend of Joseph's said to him;- "Joseph, I believe you can be a real missionary in the international field. It could be that in the future economic development might have to go hand in hand with the teaching of the christian doctrine. It would be difficult to convince a hungry peasant and his family, that Christ exists and is concerned about the poor, or that the missionary himself is concerned about their plight. The old Chinese proverb - that it is better to teach a man to fish, rather than give him a fish - is the key to development and to the spreading of the gospel as well. I wish you well in your undertaking, and I hope you don't forget to send us a message from time to time, telling us about your work and your adventures. God Be with you and your family."

The authorization to immigrate was being delayed for whatever reason, and CUNA wanted him to launch plans for program development in Latin America. It so happened, that under the Credit Union National Association and the Agency for International Development (CUNA/AID) contract, Joseph happened to be the first employee hired. He was a third country national and not an American citizen. His knowledge of cooperatives and his expertise in making them work was the ingredient that was being sought irrespective of citizenship. He left his family behind and flew to Madison to become acquainted with the terms of reference of his employment, and to purchase a home for locating his family when they would come. All of which he accomplished.

Two weeks later word came by phone from Suzanne that their immigration documents had arrived and they were ready to move. He flew back to Sakatchewan, hired a mover, packed a few personal belongings in their car, hooked the boat and trailer behind and departed for Madison, It was a distance of 1500 miles, and it would take the better part of three days to make the journey.

The post war speed limit of 55 miles per hour was still in effect in both Canada and the U.S. The Ackers were cruising along with Joseph not paying any attention to his car's speed. He came upon another driver and simply passed by him and continued driving. The car he passed followed for perhaps a half mile at Joseph's speed, and then turn on the blue and yellow flashing lights. It was a highway patrol ghost car. Joseph pulled by the roadside, stopped and rolled down his window. The officer got out of his car and came to Joseph's car.

"Good morning," the officer said. "Do you realize you've been driving over the speed limit. I've clocked you at 62 miles per hour."

"Officer, the truth of the matter is that I did not pay any attention to my speedometer. We are on our way out of the country and in the excitement and conversation, it merely slipped my mind and my foot may have gotten a bit heavy," Joseph said.

"May I see your driver's license," he requested.

Joseph obliged by handing it to him.

"What do you mean when you say you're on your way out of the country," the officer said, while examining the operators license.

"Officer we are moving as a family to the United States and we are on our way to Madison, Wisconsin, where we will be establishing our new home," Joseph replied.

LIFE'S DETOURS

"What will you be doing there and how am I to believe you?" the officer queried.

Joseph showed the officer the immigration documents, and the letter of employment. He took a quick glance at them, and handed them back.

"Okay, I will not cite you for speeding on this occassion. I will give you a warning citation instead. It would not be worth our while nor yours to bring you back to court in Canada for a minor speeding ticket. Seven miles over the speed limit calls for a fine of $7.00. I urge you to drive carefully. Take your family to their new home in safety. Good Luck," the officer said with a smile.

"Thank you, Sir," Joseph said, as he rolled his window back up and proceeded to drive.

The remainder of their three day journey went without any further incident. They arrived in Madison early in the afternoon of the third day and drove directly to their new home. It was bare inside and their household furnishings were not due in until the following day. The family expected this to happen. They came prepared. Each one brought in their sleeping bag from the boat they trailed and rolled them out on the living room floor. These would be their sleeping quarters for that night.

The children made a quick survey of the new home. It was different. It was located on a hillside with the garage entrance at street level. From the garage a five step stairway raised one to the basement level and another flight of stairs elevated one to the main floor. The view from the living room window overlooked the street and the houses on the opposite side. The street was well treed. From the kitchen one walked outside on the back patio. There was a flower bed bricked in and three oak trees further back in the yard, on which a couple of squirrels were surveying us.

Everyone seemed please with the choice of the new home Joseph had made. They walked together a block and a half down hill to a McDonald's fast food service, ate their evening meal there and retired for the night.

The next day was a Friday. Joseph was off duty until the following Monday. The moving van arrived. The furnishings were unloaded and placed in their proper places and the unpacking took place over the week end.

This had been the third move for the Ackers. It was ten days before Christmas, and there was time to get Tabetha and Eleanor registered for school classes before the Christmas vacation period. Grace was only three years old and too young for kindergarten. Carolyn the eldest of the girls, was nineteen years of age and she quickly

LIFE'S DETOURS

obtained employment with Madison Newspapers Inc. The entire move went very smoothly considering what moves are like.

Back at the office, the World Extension Division of CUNA was located in an area on the second floor of Filene House. The building bore the name of Edward A. Filene, the founder of Credit Unions in the U.S. and it housed the entire operations of CUNA. Joseph was assigned an office next to Bill Sorenson, his superior. His work commenced with interviewing and interviews and by reading existing files on the various countries.

One of his first interviews was with the CUNA managing director. His name was Sydney Allen. Joseph knew him on a personal basis. He had been invited as a guest speaker to one of the Saskatchewan Credit Union League conventions. The interview with Sid Allen was a courtesy visit and very informal.

"Joseph, I'm delighted to have you on board with us on this exciting venture upon which we are embarked. As you know the U.S. Congress has initiated and signed an accord known as the Alliance for Progress with all of the Latin American countries. The agency created by the government to carry out the terms of the alliance, is known as the Agency for International Development (AID). CUNA as an institution has been fortunate to be called upon to assist in the creation of this progress and in the formation of better ties with these countries," Allen began.

"They need credit unions and cooperatives in their countries as tools for development, just like we needed them in ours. Communism is making rapid inroads into these neighboring countries. President Kennedy and his administration feel that grass roots institutional development on the economic level, and leadership creation under voluntary and democratic circumstances is one sure way to preserve freedom and combat the establishment of communism," he continued.

"The statistics in our country prove that community institutions of all kinds help to develop leadership and a higher quality of citizenship. You are the first employee to be hired by CUNA/World Extension Department under the CUNA/AID contract. As Director of Training for all of Latin America, you have a big job on your hands. But, I am convinced that you are the right person to fill this at this time." Allen concluded,

To Joseph this long winded introduction by Allen did not appear like a speech, but rather like an emotional outpouring of sentiment expressed from his innermost convictions. Almost to say, that he was prepared to go a long way in helping President Kennedy fight the goals of the cold war not with the building of armaments, but rather with the building of understanding, neighborliness and goodwill.

LIFE'S DETOURS

"I also feel good about coming on board," Joseph exclaimed. "I agree wholeheartedly with the sentiments you have just expressed and I sincerely hope I can fill the size of the order to the satisfaction of all concerned. You know that the majority of the Canadians hold a very high regard for President Kennedy and that includes myself. I shall make an effort to deliver the very best."

At this point Allen looked penetratingly into Joseph's eyes, inched his chair up a bit and comfortably laid his hands on the table that separated the two of them. He began to speak softly.

"Joseph since we are both colleagues and friends, I feel compelled to share a personal problem with you. A problem I'm confronted with, which disturbs me. Please treat it confidential as I know you will. I supported your nomination for training director in our World Extension Division (WED), because I was fully aware of the good work you did up in Canada. I believe you are the right person for the job. But, what is happening here at the moment is that there is a move on foot to have me ousted from the position I now hold. I've been managing director of CUNA for four years. The assistant managing director, Ronald Rhodes, whom you know, has been campaigning underhandedly to have me deposed. My intuition tells me that he might be successful at the forthcoming annual meetings of CUNA in May. His ambition is to personally replace me as CUNA's managing director. My purpose for sharing this with you is to inform you about the situation. Ronald is an extremely jealous and vicious individual and should he detect too much fraternization on your part with me, he may after my ouster or resignation make your own position more difficult. This bit of information and advice is offered strictly to enable you to govern yourself accordingly," Allen said.

"Gee, thanks Sid, I appreciate your information and the confidence you have placed in me. I'm sorry to hear about your circumstance and would hate to see you leave. What brought all this about?" Joseph queried.

"It's too long a story for me to relate at this moment, but I've talked to my wife Peggy, and we've decided to invite you over for dinner next Friday night. Come about 7:00 p.m. and bring the whole family," Allen said.

"Thanks, we'll do that," Joseph replied.

After exchanging a few more pleasantries and program ideas they parted company. His next interview appointment was with Ronald Rhodes, the Assistant Managing Director. The timing was on schedule. Joseph knocked on his door.

"Walk in," came the voice from within.

Joseph walked in carrying a smile on his face. Ronald was on the telephone but signalled to Joseph to take a chair facing his desk.

Joseph also knew Rhodes from previous occassions when he was a delegate representing Saskatchewan at CUNA's annual conventions.

"There is a difference in the attitudes of these two top people. Minutes before Joseph had been in the managing director's office, who had the courtesy to come away from his desk, suspend telephone calls, and hold the interview with Joseph in an adjacent den or small meeting area next to his office," he thought to himself, while listening to Ronald's phone conversation. Ronald soon hung up and extended his hand for a handshake across his desk.

"Hi Joe, glad to have you on board. How've you been? They told me your were in, but that you were also busy settling down your family. I hope everything is okay." he saido

"Yep, we're all in and settled okay and ready to make things move. I too am glad to be on the CUNA team, and I hope I can deliver to everyone's satisfaction. From the little I've been able to learn about my responsibilities, it looks like I'm going to have my hands full," Joseph replied.

"You sure are," Ronald chimed in. "You know from an operational standpoint, the world extension department hasn't been doing too well. We haven't been getting a big enough bang for our buck. I hope you can give it close scrutiny and inject some new blood and ideas into it. Frankly, I don't believe the present executive leadership in the department has what it takes to give it the dynamic leadership required and particularly now, when we are embarking on a more aggressive international development program under our contract with the U.S. State Department," Rhodes said.

This puzzled Joseph. He didn't like what he heard Rhodes say about his superior. Here was this man talking as if he were the king pin in the establishment and no one else mattered. He smiled as he replied.

"I'll certainly make an effort to do my best, and work together with the other players in the team, so that we can develop the kind of a program that both CUNA and USAID will be proud of," Joseph uttered.

"Take a couple of weeks and scrutinize the background and current status of the department's activities. After you have a good grasp of the situation, I'd like to have another chat with you," Ronald said.

The conversation between the two continued for a few more minutes, following which Joseph departed.

As he went walking back to his office, he couldn't help thinking about why he should report directly to Rhodes, when according to the best rules in any organization, one reports first to his superior who in turn reports to his superiors. He soon found out that office politics

LIFE'S DETOURS

were rampant. Yet he also knew, that "nice and charming" guys could also finish last. Where was that happy medium.

"I think, I'm between a rock and hard place in this outfit, and I'll have to figure out the best way to do my job. I don't want to by-pass my immediate superior, and I certainly don't want to get involved or caught up in the office politics. I'll have to be extremely careful and play it by ear. I'm not going to give up this job easily, nor without first giving it the good old college try," Joseph thought to himself.

The next day Joseph had an opportunity to have a long talk with Bill Sorenson, Director of the WED, and his immediate superior.

"Bill," Joseph began. "Yesterday, I had interviews with both Mr. Allen and Mr. Rhodes. From the casual conversation I had with both of them. I detected that there was a measure of conflict between the two personalities. Personally, I would not want to get caught in the middle of any conflict. Tell me, am I correct in this assumption?"

"You are correct, CUNA has always been known for it's internal conflicts. There is a power struggle going on between Rhodes and Allen. Rhodes is attempting to replace Allen as managing director and he may succeed. I've had very good relations with Allen and not so hot with Rhodes. The World Extension Division of CUNA is fortunate. We have good support from the National Directors, and now that we have a contract with USAID we are even more secure. That does not mean that we should not deliver the very best performance we can. What it does mean is that to a very high degree we are shielded from the office politics and we want to keep it that way," Sorenson said.

"I'm glad of the early awareness of the situation. It gives me an opportunity to be cautious and to put a better handle on my work. It's good to know from what direction the wind is apt to blow. I take it then, that our situation in WED allows us to a great degree to circumvent the power struggle that is evidently going on." Joseph uttered.

"That's correct. We don't want to get involved in the personal politics of the power struggle. From time to time I'm drawn into it. There should be no reason for you to become embroiled in it, unless you allow yourself to be drawn in," Sorenson said.

"Supposing one of them, either one, calls me in and requests that I report to him on a certain matter. I can't refuse. What do I do?" Joseph asked.

"You must follow their instructions. However for your own sake and mine. Don't report on any matter to either of them before you have reported it to me, and we've had an opportunity to discuss it. This will demonstrate that we are working together as a team and it will make for good relations between ourselves," Sorenson concluded.

"Good," Joseph said. It was exactly what he wanted to hear. He returned back to his office to continue in his research and investigative work.

Early in the New Year Joseph was programmed to accompany Larry Gonzales for a four week tour of six South American countries. The countries to be visited were Brazil, Uruguay, Bolivia, Peru, Ecuador, and Colombia. Larry was an employee of the CUNA/WED but not under the USAID contract. He was an American citizen of Mexican ancestry and was fluent in Spanish. He had visited some of these countries before and had an idea of their developments. He was extremely helpful because Joseph could not articulate in Spanish, so Larry would act as his guide and interpreter.

The purpose of the trip for Joseph was strictly exploratory. He wanted to find out first hand what was going on in terms of credit union development, what institutions if any were involved in their promotion, organization and supervision. He wanted to determine what their training needs were and the best way to go about developing training materials to suit their needs.

The first stop on the tour was in Rio de Janeiro in Brazil. It was a two day lay over in which we visited The Confederation of Brazilian Credit Cooperatives (CONFEBRAS). Here we found in existance a cooperative credit system being developed, patterend almost in whole after the Caisse Populaire movement found in Quebec, Canada. A few urban credit cooperatives had been organized using the Catholic church and the parish it served as the bond of association for its members. They were in need of technical assistance and seed capital.

We proceeded to Montevideo, Uruguay. where a three day conference sponsored by the Organization of the Cooperatives of the Americas (OCA) was being held. The conference brought together the cooperative leaders from all the countries in the hemisphere. It was three days of speeches, suggestions and debate concerning the principles, the methods and procedures of co-operative development in all fields of endeavor including credit. The conference was carried out in both Spanish and English utilizing simultaneous translation. It did not produce earth shaking conclusions. The steering committee of the conference, in making their final summation of the activities, indicated that since it was the first conference of its kind, it contributed towards the building of goodwill; that many of the ideas shared by some delegates were new to others, and that they could be adopted and utilized in the development of cooperatives in their respective countries. In the evaluation process, delegates were asked if conferences of this nature should be repeated again and with what frequency. The results were not released at that time.

LIFE'S DETOURS

For Joseph, the conference was beneficial in the sense that it gave him an appreciation of the kind of development that was in progress, and an opportunity to meet a host of country leaders.

Following the Punta del Este Conference in Uruguay, Larry and Joseph proceeded to visit the remaining countries on their list. They found a localized but evolving movement in Bolivia promoted by an American Catholic priest of the Maryknoll order. Peru was experiencing a similar situation with another American Catholic priest, backstopped by the Catholic church, who had initially launched a credit union high up in the Andes amongst descendants of the Incas at Puno, Peru and later developed a Federation of credit co-operatives.

Ecuador had a little different situation, in that the credit unions were being sponsored under a government to government agreement between USAID and the Department of Co-operatives of the Ecuadorian government. It was making some headway, but principally around parishes located in urban centers.

The two man team spent about three days in each country, and made a major stop of one week in Colombia. Here the development of the Co-operativas de Ahorro y Credito (Credit Co-operatives) under the leadership and guidance of their national federation known as UCONAL had made significant headway. The progress registered was again in the formation and organization of these credit co-operatives in the urban areas, using the industrial, parochial or professional bonds of association to link the members into groups. There were no credit co-operatives in existence in the strict sense of serving a rural populace of small farmers. UCONAL/Colombia was the only Latin American Federation that was uniquely marketing the CUNA Mutual Insurance protection policies to its affiliated credit co-operatives, and appeared to be more developed. It was here that two seminars which had been planned in advance took place, and Gonzalez was requested to be a guest lecturer. Joseph was also asked to deliver a talk, which he did, and which was translated by Gonzalez to those in attendance.

They completed their tour and returned back to Madison, and Joseph was asked to submit a report on his findings. The report was given at a debriefing session in which both Allen, the managing director, as well as Rhodes the assistant were present. Sorenson and Gonzalez were also present. Joseph's report was brief for two reasons,

In the first instance, due to his inability to communicate in the Spanish language, he highlighted only the main observations and findings in connection with the purpose of the trip. He stated that in his opinion, the credit unions organized in the urban areas were functioning in a fashion, because they were able to obtain better quality of managers and employees. There didn't appear to be any kind of widespread uniformity in their accounting systems.

The USAID Missions contacted in those countries without exception, were eager to assist the local governments in the promotion and organization of rural community type credit unions. The commercial banks showed no interest in serving those areas, therefore the credit unions would serve as a source of credit for the peasant farmer and rural dwellers. Their only present source of credit was from the money lender who charged usurious interest rates of up to 20% per week.

Secondly, he made a recommendation to the effect that if we are to develop training materials for the use of their credit unions, particularly in the rural areas, we should start off by selecting a country and launching a pilot project. The training materials for directors, managers, employees and members would then be produced to suit their needs. It was obvious that the U.S. and Canadian training materials which were for the most part oriented to industrial type credit unions, were inappropiate and too advanced for their use. Something more basic and focused on the laws of their land, and the need of their small farmers, teachers, laborers and small entrepeneurs was required.

Bill Sorenson, Joseph's superior spoke first.

"Joseph your recommendation is a good one. We will take it under consideration, discuss it with AID/Washington and hopefully gain acceptance. Naturally, they will ask me if we have a suitable technician in mind to execute the proposal. I have no one else in mind but you. Would you be willing to live in a South American country for a period long enough to launch a pilot project and develop the prerequisite materials?" Sorenson said.

"Sure, I'm game, how soon will this come about?" Joseph asked.

"Knowing with what speed the government bureaucracy moves, I imagine that if our proposal receives favorable consideration it will take from two to three months," Rhodes said.

"That's correct," Sorenson added. "First it must be approved by AID/Washington, then the proposal has to go to the appropiate USAID Mission in the country where the project is to be launched. The USAID Mission and the Government of the country in question must put their stamp of approval on the project. Where do you suppose the best country would be for launching this project," he asked.

"Larry and I discussed this matter on the plane during our return flight, and we concluded that Ecuador would be the best country for a number of reasons. First, the USAID Mission in Ecuador is already offering support to the credit unions organized in the country and showed the greatest interest in developing rural credit unions. Secondly, they have a large number of small farmers (mini-fundios) in

LIFE'S DETOURS

the sierra region of the country, therefore the potential for organizing and launching a pilot project would appear very favorable," Joseph stated.

"I'm totally in agreement with Joseph," Larry Gonzalez added, "and I'm in agreement with Bill that he would be the most suited candidate to go down their and launch the project. He has a rural and agricultural background and the experience and know-how to put credit unions together and make them function. His only drawback is that he can't speak Spanish."

This kind of a statement made by Gonzalez was truthful in a sense. At the same time it sounded to Joseph as if he were only half-qualified for the project. Joseph wanted to get away from Madison and the power struggle that was going on and which he felt would get worse before it got better.

"If it's going to take three months before the project becomes a reality, I can learn Spanish in that period of time," Joseph said.

"I can read, write and speak Romanian. It is a cousin language to Spanish and is a member of the Latin rooted Romance languages. I can read and understand French having studied it in Canada during high school. I can enroll for night classes in Spanish at the University, and submerge myself to study and in three months I'll be able to articulate in Spanish."

Gonzalez looked a little surprised at Joseph's spur of the moment commitment. Earlier he had mentioned to Joseph, that he should probably have a full time interpreter with him and suggested the name of a likely candidate for the job.

"After all the government will pay his salary and it won't cost CUNA any money," Gonzalez had hinted to Joseph during their flight back home.

"I believe Joseph can do it," Allen the managing director chimed in. "Henry Ford, once said that anyone who stops learning is old whether at 20 or at 80. Anyone who keeps learning stays young. The greatest thing in life is to keep your mind young. I believe CUNA should pay the cost of the course. It is an opportunity for us to send a seasoned technician in credit unions, who can can articulate in their language and thus make his work and ours more effective. I'm all for the proposal, and Bill, I suggest you follow through on this matter as rapidly as you can."

This debriefing session broke up on a friendly note, and Joseph felt good that his recommendation had been accepted and that action was being seized upon to follow through. He lost no time in enrolling for night classes. CUNA paid the bill. He took two hours of classes each evening in conversational Spanish, five days per week. Joseph could read Spanish without any difficulty, since it read the same as Romanian and the grammatical structure of the language was basically the same. His aim was to learn to speak it. He quickly put to memory fifty of the most frequently used verbs together with their conjugations. He memorized the numbers, the days of the week, months of the year and many travel, restaurant and hotel expressions. From there he kept on studying and learning the language in general, and the technical terminology as it related to his work.

Joseph kept himself occupied by holding training seminars for international students that came to the U.S. to study credit unions, and to see them in operation. He would program and accompany the students in visits to credit unions which were generally located in the State of Wisconsin or nearby Illinois. This enabled Joseph to transport the students by car, and keep the expenses within the framework of the budget. He was also invited to several of the larger credit unions in both the U.S. and Canada to be their guest lecturer, and he would accept such invitations when the time schedule and his work permitted.

It was at one of the training seminars at which a half dozen international students were in attendance that Joseph received a shock. It was perhaps the greatest shock event in his life up to that moment. He was in the midst of a lecture to his students in one of the CUNA meeting rooms, when suddenly the entrance door to the meeting flew open and in walked Anette Tomaino, one of the secretaries in the WED department. She had a puzzled look on her face and looking directly at Joseph said in a loud voice.

"President Kennedy has been shot. It just came over the radio now," she said.

At first Joseph couldn't believe what he had heard.

"Are you certain? How could that be?" Joseph asked.

He knew from the news media that President Kennedy was supposed to be in Dallas, Texas on that day. Surely, the shooting wasn't fatal he thought to himself.

He asked Rachel Thomsen, the class interpreter for that day to share the news item with the class and asked her to tell them, that they were dismissed for the balance of the day. Joseph went back to his office and turned on the little radio he carried in his brief case. He listened to the events as they were coming over the airwaves from Dallas. Yes, he was fatally shot, wounded and died.

Joseph felt that the Americans had suffered a huge loss in the death of President Kennedy. His family also felt the trauma and being new in the country, they were wondering what was going to happen next. How secure would they be? What would the State Department strategy and policies be with respect to credit unions? Did the

LIFE'S DETOURS

communists arrange to have Kennedy killed? Did they make the right move, when they left Canada and came to the U.S.? There was a lot of anxiety.

In Joseph's family certain changes had also occurred. Their oldest daughter Carolyn who was 20 years of age, had requested her parents permission to return to Canada. This took place eight months after her immigration to the United States. She had been corresponding with her boyfriend whom she had left behind in Canada. At that time he was a cadet in the Royal Canadian Mounted Police, but had since graduated and was assigned to a detachment in the city of Port Alberni on Canada's West Coast. It was a difficult decision for Joseph and Suzanne to make, but one which they knew was inevitable. "There is nothing static in life. Life is a perpetual moving phenomenon. Sooner or later she would have to leave home and seek her own fortunes in the world," Joseph said to himself.

They also knew that her departure signalled the break-up of their nuclear family. Carolyn had been a fine daughter and Joseph was very proud of her because, while she tried to please her parents, she also showed a high degree of self-confidence, good judgement and independence. It was in the basement of their home, that Joseph constructed a plywood box, placed most of Carolyn's earthly belongings in it, including an old fashioned "Royal" typewriter which he though she might use, being a secretary.

They took her to Verona to catch the Soo Line train coming from Chicago and going into Regina, Canada. The parting at the train station was emotional.

"Carolyn, take good care of yourself. Make sure you stop over in Regina and vist the grandparents for a day or two before you proceed to the West Coast. Be sure to write us often and to give us your phone number, and say "Hi" to Larry," Suzanne cautioned.

"Yes I will," Carolyn said hugging and kissing, as the steam engine pulling the pullman passenger cars rolled into the station. Moments later the whistle blew again and its departure was announced.

"God bless you and good luck," were her dad's parting words. The remaining Ackers stood on the station platform and watched the train disappear slowly into the horizon until they could no longer hear its dying noise and rumble.

They returned to their home with Eleanor, Grace and Irma Barazza, the exchange student from Ecuador staying with the Ackers.

Tabetha the second oldest daughter had left home a few months before and travelled to Ecuador. She was just sixteen years old, but very mature for her age. She went to Ecuador to live with the Barazza family, whose daughter was with the Ackers in Madison. Jose "Pepe"

Barazza, Irma's father, was a Supreme Court Judge in Ecuador. The objective here was to have Tabetha attend school in Quito to learn Spanish, while Irma was enrolled at a public school in Madison to learn English.

The arrangement was worked out the year before by a near relative of the Barazzas, who happened to visit Madison and the Ackers as a credit union observer from Ecuador. The arrangement worked out to the benefit of all concerned. The Barazzas sent their daughter very little pin money for out-of-pocket expenses, and Joseph added a little to her allowance, as if she were his own daughter. He also forwarded a monthly allowance to Tabetha in Ecuador. Irma was treated as a member of the family and would accompany the Ackers on their weekend jaunts or picnics to the lakes and parks. She returned to Ecuador after the school term ended in June.

Their daughter Tabetha did not come home, because she was told that there was a pending move for the entire family to be posted to Ecuador for a two-year assignment.

During this time, and because the approval of the pilot project recommendation had been delayed beyond the expectations of CUNA, Joseph had made another trip to three countries in South America. This time he required no interpreter since through his study of the language, he was proficient enough to travel and articulate on his own.

Everyone was amazed at how quickly he had grasped the language and at how well he spoke it. He visited Ecuador again and while there, learned that the project had been approved together with a corresponding budget.

He visited with Tabetha and shared with her the news about the whole family coming to Ecuador. He gave her fifty dollars, and advised her to continue her studies and to stay put pending the family's arrival.

Joseph returned from his second trip only to discover that Carolyn had written from Canada and announced her marriage to Larry Weaver, her long time boy friend. The wedding was set for the latter part of May and she requested that if it were at all possible, she would like to have the family attend the wedding and for her dad to give her away. Joseph had accumulated sufficient vacation time to enable him to do this, and at any rate he wanted to use up this amassed time before departing for overseas. The entire family, including Irma Barazza motored to Canada's West Coast. Joseph did walk his daughter down the aisle, and jokingly said to her that if she was about to change her mind, she would have to do it very quickly.

She smiled and whispered, "No dad, it's for keeps."

The wedding was a small affair held in late April and Larry's parents were also present. They returned to Madison only to discover

LIFE'S DETOURS 233

some revolting developments.

As was suspected, Ronald Rhodes had decided that before Joseph could proceed on his overseas assignment, he had to have an industrial phsycological test, to determine if he was fit and the right candidate for the task. Sorenson told Joseph that this was not necessary, but Rhodes as acting managing director had to show his authority. Furthermore, it was a scheme subtly drafted by Gonzalez, hoping in one way or another to get his recommended interpreter, who was his friend cut in on the deal.

Joseph had a friend in AID/Washington whose name was Allen Pitchell, and who was the backstopping officer for the CUNA/AID program in the State Department. He phoned him and related his story.

"Go ahead and take your phsycological test," Pitchell counselled. "I'm sure you'll pass the test with flying colors. But, whether you pass the test or not, you can be sure that you are the candidate for the pilot project assignment in Ecuador. We have a number of people, who have gone on overseas duty, who have not had the test and they are doing fine."

Joseph said his prayers that day with all the fervor at his command. He didn't know why he harbored a fear of having to undergo psychological tests, but he did. He motored to Chicago on the appointed day and wrote a two hour test, followed by an oral interview.

"You are certainly qualified to undertake the task assigned to you. You have made good marks on your test, and I'll mail the results to your superiors tomorrow. I wish you good luck," the psychologist said

On his way back to Madison, Joseph felt really good about the outcome of the test and the fact that now it was only a matter of another week or two and he would be on his way to Ecuador.

Two days later as was expected, the report from the psychological test came in. Sorenson called Joseph into his office.

"In relation to your job description, which we had to furnish the psychological laboratory, you're test came out above average. You are well qualified to furnish the technical skills required to meet the demands of the work for which you have been nominated. I congratulate you. I couldn't have done better myself. On the Q.T. I don't believe Rhodes could have done equally as well. You are now ready to go on your assignment, and I would urge you to leave at the earliest possible date. When do you think you could depart?" Sorenson asked.

"We have a buyer for our house, in fact, we have a deposit and as soon as the sale is consumated, we'll be ready to leave. At the outside, I would say we could be ready to leave within a week," Joseph said.

It was only two years ago, that they moved from Canada to the U.S. He was pulling up stakes again and another move was necessary.

He had been advised that the USAID Mission in Quito would supply them with furnished housing. As a family, they were to pack clothing, bedding, bathroom supplies, other personal effects and an automobile. There was no need to ship furniture.

The Ackers sold their Madison home and realized a capital gain. They held a yard auction sale and sold their furniture. Other personal and household items were placed in storage. The movers came and packed the belongings that were going to Ecuador, including their automobile.

The Ackers were not permitted to depart from the U.S. without a clearance from the Internal Revenue Service. A partial year income tax report had to be filed. All other documents were in order. Since they weren't U.S. citizens they were travelling with Canadian passports. It was the first week in October. Irma Barazza the exchange student had left a couple of months earlier. Joseph, Suzanne, Eleanor and Grace had flown from Madison to New York's La Guardia Airport. They had a four hour layover at La Guardia and at one o'clock after midnight they boarded the Panagra Air Line bound for Miami, Panama City, and Quito.

LIFE'S DETOURS 235

Chapter 15

IMPLEMENTING A PILOT PROJECT

"Welcome to Quito, Ecuador. We have just landed at the Mariscal Sucre Airport. The time is now 8:30 a.m. We are in the same time zone as New York, there is no need to change your watches. Please remain seated with your seat belts fastened until we've come to a complete stop, and the captain has turned off the seat belt lights," the stewardess cautioned.

It was an overnight flight, and everyone was tired and at the same time excited. As the family deplaned this sunny Friday morning, they first caught sight of Mount Cotopaxi with its snow capped summit and a few clouds forming a halo arount its near peak situated to the south of the city. To the east stood stately Mount Antezana, over whose rim the sun had just risen minutes before. The near Mount Pichincha to the west appeared to be ready to slide unto the city of Quito. A city whose center consisted for the most part of cobblestoned streets and buildings bearing the stamp of seventeenth and eighteenth century architecture and ancient cathedrals. The city appeared to be cradled on a plateau surrounded by these mountain giants. A handful of modern buildings could be seen on the northern periphery of the city, of which the Quito Hotel was the most recently constructed.

"Where is the equator, I can't see it?" the four year old Grace asked after they had entered the customs and immigration section of the airport. No one had any idea what she expected to see, but she had heard talk, that Quito was on the equator and was wondering where it was.

"We will get to see it all after we settle in and we find our way around," her father replied.

Alejandro Ramirez from the USAID Mission transport division and Enrique Salazar from the CUNA/AID program were on hand to assist the Ackers in expediting the procedures for entry into the country.

Initially they entered the country as tourists. Their resident visas and diplomatic priveleges were to be accorded at a later date.

"We've been looking forward to your coming for some time. Sure glad you were able to make it," Salazar said as he introduced himself and shook hands with Joseph.

"I guess, I can say I'm glad to be here also," Joseph replied. "For awhile it looked like the project we have been contemplating to establish here, might not come off."

By this time Alejandro Ramirez had checked the Acker's baggage and had loaded it on to a Jeep station wagon. They were driven to the Embajador Hotel, where prior reservations had been made and where the Ackers would be housed until they were furnished with more permanent housing facilities.

"This is Friday, and you're all tired from the trip. Take the balance of the day and get over the jet-lag. My wife Lois and I will come over and join you for dinner this evening. I'll also bring you some material you can look at over the weekend, and your assigned duties will commence on Monday morning. We'll pick you up and take you to the office," Salazar said as he left.

All of a sudden the Ackers felt strange and lonely.

The road and street they drove on from the airport was made of cobblestone in places. There were Indian women walking along the edge of the road in brightly colored skirts with babies bundled on their backs. They were leading their donkeys, that also carried cargos of green vegetables, firewood, bags of charcoal and other goods on their backs. The houses were located behind high walls. The wall tops were adorned with protruding cut glass. The language spoken was strange and Joseph was the only person that understood and spoke it. On a street corner, an Indian woman was frying pork meat (fritada) in a large steel `wok' shaped pan, on a charcoal fire out in the open. She would sell pieces of meat together with a big boiled potato, and a spoonfull of hot pepper sauce to hungry by passers. This was a different culture. Joseph assured his family that although it would be difficult at first, they would eventually all get accustomed to it.

During the day their daughter Tabetha, who had been living in Ecuador came over to visit with them. She related in detail experiences she encountered during her year in Ecuador. She could converse in Spanish and assured her sisters that they too, would have command of the language in a short period of time. Suzanne, her mother looked at Tabetha with satisfaction, and wondered if she would personally learn to speak the language. They told Tabetha that as soon as they were assigned permanent housing she would be expected to come home and join the rest of the family.

LIFE'S DETOURS 237

That evening was spent in the company of the Salazars. They dined together and later withdrew to the quarters in the hotel where the Ackers were housed, and spent another couple of hours talking about life in Ecuador. The Salazars had children in the American School in Quito, which had an American curriculum and classes were taught in English. That helped to unravel some of the doubts that their daughter Eleanor had. Grace was old enough to be enrolled in kindergarten and this would be attended to at the appropiate time.

Monday at the office was a day spent in orientation and visits to the Mission Director, the various heads of departments, and in getting identification cards, driver's licenses and other permits. At the time, Ecuador was being governed by a Military Junta, and Joseph was cautioned about the need to be prudent in both what was being said and done. At the request of the Ministry of Agriculture and Cooperatives a meeting was arranged with Dr. Luis Robles, the Minister in charge. Joseph was accompanied by Enrique Salazar, the CUNA Program Director in the country.

Dr. Robles was a tall, slender man who had received some of his education in economics from Texas State University and was fluent in English. He had a good grasp of U.S. culture and prior to becoming a government minister, he taught economics at the University in Quito. Like a teacher, he began his conversation with Joseph.

"I have said that we live in an hour of decision for humanity. Our generation will decide whether mankind shall live or die, whether atomic energy and the other marvels of modern science are to be used to create a better and fuller life for all mankind or for the destruction of civilization and most of the life on earth. If we do nothing, then surely we are on the path of self-destruction. However, I'm confident that through cooperation at all levels of human endeavor, we can turn the tide in favor of mankind and a better life," he stated looking directly into Joseph's eyes.

"Dr. Robles, I agree with you wholeheartedly, and the truth of the matter is that, quite apart from the fact that developing and working with co-operatives is my profession, I also subscribe and believe in the philosophy," Joseph replied.

Dr. Robles interrupted and took up the conversation again.

"I've had an opportunity to review your bio-data and I'm impressed with the volume of experience you bring to this task. I commend CUNA and AID for hiring technicians of your caliber from outside the U.S. boundaries. You are from Canada, aren't you?" he asked inquisitively.

Joseph nodded in agreement and was prepared to talk, but Dr. Robles had not terminated.

"Our aim in Ecuador, is to carry out a program of creating institutions and developing leadership, and I can think of no better way of doing so than by the organization of co-operatives. In the early stages of development in your countries, at the community level both the church and the school were the primary institutions that gave impetus to leadership development, the rural cooperatives followed. In our situation, both the church and the school came from the top down, with the result that our rural villages lack the leadership with vision and know-how to initiate development.

It is my feeling that the development of a rural credit program for our small farmers, businessmen, and housewives at parish levels throughout the country, will enhance the economic conditions of the rural families, as well as teach them that they can be masters of their own destiny. Mr. Acker you can rest assured that you have the wholehearted support of this Ministry in your undertaking. If there is anything we can do to help in your effort, please do not hesitate to call on me or my associates," he concluded.

Both Enrigue Salazar and Joseph thanked Dr. Robles as they shook hands and exited from his office.

Joseph felt good about the interview. Firstly, he was happy with himself because of the kind remarks Dr. Robles had made about his person, and secondly because the remarks were made in the presence of Salazar, who was in fact CUNA's overall program director and Joseph's superior, and whose experience in co-operatives was much narrower.

"Since we will be organizing the rural credit unions on a parish basis, it is my feeling that we should approach the Catholic church hierarchy, and explain our program to them as well and to seek their good-will and support," Joseph said to Salazar.

"We have already done that," Salazar replied. "You see the credit unions organized in Quito and Guayaquil, as well as some of the smaller urban centers were organized on a parish basis. There are only a handful of credit unions organized on an industrial or professional basis, like the teachers, the railroad, and some transport workers. We have brought the credit union idea to the attention of the church authorities, and we have their concurrence. I will be accompanying you to the parish in which the pilot project will be launched, and we will make a point of discussing the project with both the parish priest and the bishop of the parish," Salazar concluded.

Salazar the CUNA program director, and William Simmons the USAID/Ecuador backstopping officer had scoured the country prior to Joseph's arrival in search of a suitable parish area in which a pilot project in rural and small farm credit could be launched. They pinpointed three areas, which Joseph visited in the following week. Out of

LIFE'S DETOURS

the three Joseph selected the village and parish of Julio Andrade in the province of Carchi in Northern Ecuador. A province bordering with Colombia.

Two weeks after arrival in the country, Joseph had settled his family in permanent housing. It was a home with three bedrooms upstairs and an open air verandah from which the surrounding snow-capped mountains, as well as a good portion of the city could be viewed. The main floor consisted of a living and dining room combined, the kitchen, a suitable pantry, a laundry room and the maid's live-in quarters. The drive-in garage was attached to the main house, and a high-walled cement block fence encircled the property. It was a new structure and it was adequate for the moment. The children had been registered in schools, the school fees paid, and the school bus would pick them up each school day.

Upon the recommendation of Lois Salazar, with whom Suzanne struck a close acquaintance, a full time live-in maid was employed, and a part time gardener. The Ackers were told that although the Americans were "do-it-yourselfers", it was improper for them, considering the wages they were receiving, not to give employment to local people. The maid was hired at U.S. $30.00 per month, with Saturday afternoons and Sundays as "days off." The gardener was receiving $15.00 per month for two days of work per week. In both instances the wages paid were above those they could obtain from working for their own people, and was one of the reasons why many Ecuadoreans were striving to get hired by the American "gringo" households.

On the third week after arrival in the country, Joseph and Salazar scheduled another trip to the selected project site at Julio Andrade. The person they met with again was Padre Jacinto Aguilar. It was Joseph's second visit to the parish.

"I did not expect you to come back," Padre Aguilar said to Salazar. "I remember your visit here about two months ago and again last week, but I felt your visits were routine, and that you have forgotten all about us."

"We are here this time to let you know that we have decided to choose this parish as the site of the first pilot project in agricultural credit for small farmers. We want to discuss the project and its function in depth with you," Salazar said.

"I'm glad, I'm glad," the Padre said. "What were the principal characteristics that made you choose this parish for the project?"

"Padre Aguilar," Joseph began. "Your parish has been chosen because it resembles in large part the agricultural area and the crops produced from where I was born and brought up in Canada. Your major production comes from potatoes, but the area also produces corn, and some cereal crops and livestock. The difference is that our farms are mechanized and larger in size. But at one time our farms were also smaller in size. In your case, all your farmers are small farmers, two to three hectares (4 to 6 acres). You have rich soil. I noticed your Sunday afternoon livestock market is quite active and lastly the nearest bank is located in Tulcan, which is 25 kilometers (15 miles) away. Very few if any of your small farmers go to Tulcan to obtain bank loans for their production credit needs. Fertilizers, insecticides, fungicides are not used and better quality seed is not available. These inputs cannot be obtained without adequate cash or credit. In addition from our last visit here, I observed your personal enthusiasm and I feel that if we harness your enthusiasm, together with our technology, and surround ourselves with a group of your better farmers, we can make the project a success," Joseph explained.

"You are correct," Padre Aguilar said. "Our farmers have not been introduced to the more modern methods of raising crops or livestock, and as far as credit or bank loans are concerned, they simply have no access to such a source. There are two or three money lenders who prowl around the Sunday market and lend money to our campesinos (small farmers) at usurios interest rates. Sometimes, they lend the money as an advance on their crops, under the condition that the crop is to be sold to them when harvested. Two of the money lenders I understand come up from Quito. The situation is not good, and I'm sure we can organize a good credit union to serve a useful purpose in this parish," he said.

"Padre Aguilar," Joseph spoke up. "There are a few preliminary things we must do, before we can launch the project. Here are some things I can do and some things for you to do in order to help us get started.

Firstly, announce from your pulpit next Sunday that a general meeting of all the parish residents will be held after the worship service on the following Sunday. Explain the purpose of the meeting and also extend an invitation to the housewives to attend. This will provide time for word to get around in the parish, and for us to have as many folks as possible in attendance.

Secondly, based on your knowledge of the farmers and the people in your parish, invite a group of ten to fifteen of your best parishioners to come to the meeting and to be prepared to accept positions on the Board of Directors, on the Credit Committee, and on the Supervisory Committee.

Finally, we must find a person in your parish that is considered a leading citizen, that can do some basic record keeping and whom we can appoint as the manager of the credit union. Is this order too tall? Do

LIFE'S DETOURS

you think you can fulfill this obligation in the time frame I have mentioned?" Joseph concluded.

"As you know this credit union has been in existence about a year and a half, but we were not aware of its development potential or the kind of service it could provide. I believe we can do it. I will call on the present directors and a few other people I know immediately, and we'll lay the groundwork ready for you. Now what are you going to do?" the Padre asked.

"I'll get back to Quito, and employ an Ecuadorean to be my national counterpart. Then together we will prepare all the necessary materials for us to get started. We already have some materials, such as membership applications, bank books, savings and deposit slips, and so on. What I must do is draft and produce a loan application form for farm loans, and other educational and training material especially adapted for the use of farmers and rural residents. Both the counterpart technician and myself will return with these documents prepared at least one day before the meeting. After the meeting, I propose to remain here in the parish, and work together with and train the newly appointed manager. I will be conducting training courses for the Board of Directors and the Committees. It will also give us an opportunity to hold futher mass meetings and training sessions with the farmers themselves. How does that sound to you?" Joseph concluded.

"Muy bien," the Padre said. "I'll hurry this thing along as much as possible. You understand, that we're not like your people in the U.S. We do not have telephones. Our rural roads are simple trails used for walking, riding, or for hauling freight and supplies on the backs of horses. The activity will be much slower, but we'll do the best we can."

Salazar and Joseph returned to Quito over the narrow cobblestoned road with their Jeep station wagon. It was an eight hour drive each way through steep ravines and numerous antiquated villages. One village that struck Joseph as being unique was a village of black people, located in the Chota Valley about half way between Ibarra and Julio Andrade. The houses constructed in this village were patterened along the African style, made out of woven reeds, plastered with mud and a grass thatched roof.

The story was, that the people living there were descendants from a group of slaves that were shipwrecked off the coast of Colombia, and had found their way to this tropical valley high up in the Andes by following the down flow of the Mira river whose mouth dumped the waters into the Pacific ocean just off the coast of Colombia. Joseph stopped many times in this valley on his way to and from Julio Andrade during his stay in the country. He noted that there were one or two albinos amongst the population, and he saw two individuals chained to a tree. The locals explained that those chained were mentally deficient and would inflict injury to others. One explanation offered for some of these abnormalities, was that they came from the inbreeding of the inhabitants due to their isolation and numbers.

Joseph had been allocated a Jeep vehicle without a driver by USAID. This was for the use of Joseph and Pablo Espinosa his counterpart technician in the project. Together they returned on schedule to Julio Andrade. They found that Padre Aguilar had dutifully performed the assignment left with him. Everything was ready for the meeting to take place on Sunday, the next day after church mass.

Annexed to the church a sort of an amphitheater had been constructed, and it was inside this structure that the meeting was held. Joseph had prepared a flip chart with Spanish titles covering the complete outline of his talk, and stationed himself at the bottom of the amphitheater. The crowd of about 300 men, women and children sat on the stairs looking down at the speaker. Enrique Salazar, William Simmons, Victor Escalante and others drove in from Quito to witness the activity. They were interested in observing Joseph make his presentation in Spanish, and at the same time wanted to gauge the attendance in terms of the number of people, and the kind of interest that had been generated.

Victor Escalante, who was the national counterpart to Enrique Salazar, and was the Managing Director of the Federation of Credit Unions in Ecuador (FECOAC) acted as the chairman for the meeting. It was a bright sunny day in October. The meeting was opened with the singing of the Ecuadorian National Anthem followed by a short prayer recited by Padre Aguilar. The chairman then requested Padre Aguilar to say a few words and to introduce Joseph, who was scheduled as the main speaker.

This was the first time that Joseph would be making a complete presentation in the Spanish language. He could feel his discomfort, but plunged into it.

"Senoras y Senores, thank you for coming to this meeting. First of all, I will ask your pardon for errors I will be committing as I try to use the Spanish language in making this presentation to you. I am delighted to have this opportunity to share with you the techniques that were used in our countries, that improved the incomes and standard of living of our farmers and rural people. I am convinced we can duplicate this development here in your community if we get organized and work together."

"The credit union is a local people's bank. You will be the owners and shareholders of this institution. Through the democratic process, you will elect from amongst yourselves people to serve on the Board of

LIFE'S DETOURS

Directors and Committees. Padre Aguilar tells me that there are more than 1000 families in this parish. If each family were to save 5 sucres per week (U.S. $1 = 20 sucres), a family would save 260 sucres in one year, and 1000 families would mobilize savings together of 260,000 sucres. Five sucres is the cost of one package of cigarettes in your country. If each family saved 10 sucres per week (50 cents), the amount generated in one year would double to 520,000 sucres or more than one half million sucres. In ten years the sum would add up to more than 5 million sucres. In other words you would have your own bank, and you would be shareholders in it."

"This money would be used for loans to the farm families in this community to assist you in increasing your production and therefore the family income. From what Padre Aguilar tells me, and some of you have told me, that the farmers in this community are unable to purchase high quality seed, fertilizers, fungicides, and insecticides, because they do not have the money with which to purchase these commodities, all of which are necessary production aids,"

At this point Joseph could see many campesinos looking at each other and nodding their heads in approval of his statement.

"Then what about diversifying your production," Joseph continued. "When I was growing up on my father's farm we would raise cattle, hogs, sheep, and poultry, in addition to the field crops. If the crop happened to fail due to drought or hail or early frost, we could always pull ourselves through for another year by selling livestock or poultry. Can that be done on your farms on a smaller scale? For example, how many housewives here could raise 100 chickens for the market, if they could obtain a loan to purchase the baby chicks from the hatchery in Quito?" About one dozen hands went up.

"Each family could raise a few chickens. A couple of milk cows would supply the family with milk, cream, butter and cheese. This would give employment to other family members. It would contribute to the family's food supply and good health, and leave more of the proceeds from the sale of your crops to be used for farm and home improvements, for sending your children to school, and for elevating your standard of living," Joseph argued.

The crowd listened intently to his raggedly spoken Spanish, and did not appear to become restless. Joseph knew from experience that he would lose their interest if the talk lasted more than a half hour. He hurried to get his main points in.

"With good seed, fertilizer, and insecticides used at the right time, a campesino could triple his potato production. Why don't you do it? Because you do not have a source of credit. Those of you that take fertilizer on credit and offer to pay for it after the potato harvest, are paying as much as 5% interest per month to the "chulquiero" or money lender. That amounts to 60 percent per year. You would pay 1% per month at your credit union or 12% per year.Thats an enormous saving. Don't you think?" Joseph asked. Again heads were nodding in agreement.

"Right after we adjourn this meeting, we will call another meeting to order, for the purpose of reorganizing the Board of Directors and Committees. As you know, this credit union has been in existence for the past year and a half, but is dormant in its activities. Sr. Alberto Cardenas, whom you all know has agreed to become full-time manager if his appointment is approved by the directors. With your help and cooperation we want to breathe new life into your credit union. I urge you to remain and participate in this discussion as well.

Later as your credit union develops, and with the approval of your Board of Directors we will be drafting lending policies and procedures. These will be made known to you through printed brochures and pamphlets. I will remain in your community for the next two to three weeks to assist and train your Manager. We will conduct a series of training sessions with your directors and committees. Finally, together with Sr.Cardenas we will be travelling on horseback to attend "kitchen" meetings in your own homes and to answer questions you may have about this pilot project. I wish to thank you very much for your patience and your attention. I shall now turn the meeting back over to Senor Escalante to continue with the agenda. Muchas Gracias!" and with that Joseph terminated his presentation.

The meeting continued in orderly fashion. Those that remained to attend the reorganization meeting were highly enthused. That evening Joseph together with Espinosa his counterpart, and a few of the directors gathered at the only eating place in the village to have their dinner. The lady of the house said she could prepare pork stew, with boiled potatoes and bread, but we would have to wait awhile since she did not have it ready. We agreed to wait and in the meantime ordered and imbibed in a few quart bottles of beer.

Rural Ecuadoreans in that area generally drink a more inexpensive sweet whiskey imported from Colombia. A kind of liqueur. It is made from sugar cane and is called "aguardiente," which means "toothwater" in English. Drinking beer with an American was a luxury for sure, and especially when the American displayed his generosity by paying for it. Joseph felt dry from the talk he presented as well as from just plain chatting with people. He thoroughly enjoyed his beer. The continued chatting and appraisal of the day's activity between Joseph and the Ecuadoreans made the time pass by. He noticed a sincere desire on their part to want to be friends, to be helpful in the project and offered their service in any way that it could be used.

This was a character trait that made Joseph feel good about associating with them. After all, they were simple peasants who had been exposed to an elementary education at the parish school. They were able to read and write and do some simple arithmetic, and were sound in their logic and in their arguments. Time flew by and soon the dinner was served. A white cotton tablecloth was spread across the table, a bowl of cabbage soup was first served, followed by the pork stew and boiled potatoes. Not having had a noon day meal, the food served was adequate, tasteful and filling.

Joseph and Espinosa his counterpart housed themselves at a hotel in the nearby city of Tulcan, and would commute back and forth with their jeep. They spent the entire next week in training the manager, and the one girl "Lolita" who would be the full time attendant and bookkeeper in the credit union. It became evident that while Alberto Cardenas the manager, was capable of counselling the farmers in their loan and supply requirements, he was somewhat deficient in his mathematics. Lolita on the other hand was quite good at her arithmetic, and with the use of a hand operated adding machine did quite well in calculating time and interest rates on both savings and loans.

During the day, Joseph, Pablo and Alberto, the manager would rent horses and make visits to the homes of selected campesinos in the parish. A day's rental for a horse was 20 sucres ($1.US). These visits were made for the purpose of telling the story, and killing negative rumors that would spring up. The money lenders were especially proficient in originating negative rumors.

At one home they were invited to remain for the noon day meal.

"We can't stop here for a noon day meal. This man is a poor campesino, with five children running about in his yard. How can he afford to feed us three men?" Joseph said to Espinosa, his counterpart.

The campesino insisted, saying that his wife was all prepared to feed all of them.

"Senor Jose," Espinosa whispered quietly to Joseph. "We must accept his invitation, otherwise we would hurt his dignity."

They agreed to remain and after tying their horses to a fence post and feeding them a bit of freshly pulled grass, they joined the campesino for the noon day meal. It was served at a fairly large table in the kitchen of their home. A wash basin was passed around for each person to wash his hands, and this was followed by a towel for drying them. They were asked to sit down at a table of rather crude lumber construction. It resembled the likes of a picnic table found in the parks in the U.S. It had an oilcloth covering. The meal consisted of potato soup, roasted guinea pig and boiled potatoes, served with a side dish of very hot sauce made from hot chili peppers known as "aji."

"Senor Jose," the campesino began. "Some of my neighbors have said to me, and I agree with them, that if we mobilize together a quantity of capital and the manager runs away with it, we are the losers. Or supposing people borrow from their credit union and fail to repay their loans, then those with savings in the credit union will lose their savings. Aren't we correct in this thinking?"

"Yes you are correct. But, we have taken certain precautions to see that this does not happen. In the first place, the manager and his bookkeeper are bonded employees of the credit union. A bond is an insurance certificate issued by an insurance company, which guarantees the replacement of capital, which might be stolen or defalcated by the employees or officers of the credit union. Your credit union carries such an insurance policy through the Federation in Quito. If Senor Cardenas runs away with your money, the insurance company will replace it, and they will chase Senor Cardenas for the rest of his life to collect it from him. They will prosecute and make him answer for his deeds before the law. In any event, the money is replaced. With regard to the non-repayment of loans, this is a different matter. In the first instance every campesino borrower will be expected, in fact required to attend at least eight hours of classes, at which his responsibilities will be clearly explained. We will also demonstrate to the campesino how to use credit both wisely and productively, so that he can afford to repay his loan. In addition to this training, he may be asked to obtain a guarantor or a co-signer to vouch for his integrity and honesty. Finally, if the loan is a large amount he will be requested to hypothecate personal property which he owns. Our experience in Canada and the U.S. over the years, clearly demonstrated that farmers are generally very honest people and repay their obligations, unless God-created circumstances prohibit them from doing so," Joseph replied.

"That's good," the campesino replied. "I shall tell my neighbors about this. People are talking about your project. Some like it very much and others are not so sure."

By this time, the meal hour and discussion had terminated. Joseph offered to pay the farmer something for the meal, but he refused to take any money, so he gently slipped a 20 sucre bill under his plate so as not to be noticed. They thanked the farmer and his wife for their hospitality and departed.

For the next three weeks, Joseph and his crew covered the entire parish. Each Sunday after mass, they would conduct classes on how to raise chickens, angora rabbits or hogs; on how to build an inexpensive hog shed, rabbit hutches, or a chicken house. This would include simple plans and cost estimates.

LIFE'S DETOURS

In the training seminars Joseph would use a blackboard and develop projects using figures the campesinos would give him.

"Look" he would say. "How much would it cost you to buy a one-year-old brood sow?"

After a wide range of discussion amongst themselves, they would offer Joseph a figure.

"One thousand sucres," ($50 US), they would say.

"All right. You can go to the credit union obtain a one thousand sucre loan for one year and buy a brood sow. The sow can produce two litters of piglets during the year. At the end of the year, you can sell the sow for what it cost in the first place or maybe even more, and repay the credit union loan. You find you will have no debt and two litters of pigs free and clear - minus the shelter and feed for the sow during the year. Is that good farming and good business? Joseph would ask.

At one campesino's farm located near the village an experiment was conducted, wherein two plots of land were used for demonstration purposes. Plot A consisted of four hundred square meters (1 sq. meter = 1.196 sq. yd.) of land, planted with potatoes in the traditional manner using small local whole potatoes for seed. The seed was dropped into the rows by hand with spacing of approximately 10 inches, and the space between the rows being about two feet. The potatoes were planted during the full stage of the moon, which they said was the best time for planting.

Alongside, plot B of similar size was planted without considering the moon's stage. The seed used were sections of a large selected potato that contained one or two eyes. These seed eyes were spaced in the rows about 12 to 15 inches apart and a 24 inch space between the rows. Parcel B was treated with an application of fertilizer at the time of planting, and once more at about half time during the growing season. Parcel A was not fertilized. At the appropiate time during the growing season, both parcels received similar kind of insecticide treatment.

Throughout the growing season, there was an exceptional difference in the quality of the crop. The fertilized parcel had sturdier, full bodied leaves, and each plant carried more blossoms than the unfertilized plot. On Sundays after church the campesinos and their wives would walk to this demonstration spot, and examine the difference in the plant growth that was unfolding with great curiosity.

An accurate record was maintained of the crop inputs, and of the end result. The harvest was the real test. Plot B produced two and one-half times more potatoes, larger in size and of better quality than Plot A. Due to the size and better quality the crop brought 49.65 sucres ($2.50 US) more per hundred weight than the regular crop from plot A. Both plots required the same amount of labor in terms of cultivation, insect treatment and harvesting. The additional cost consisted of two bags of fertilizer valued at 95 sucres ($4.45 US), and the increased income amounted to $26.25 over the Plot A income. The word spread like wildfire, and this was all it took to convince the parish campesinos about the value of using fertilizer.

" I believe I should be compensated for the time I took to explain to my neighbors the benefits that are being derived from the planting method you used," Hernan Torres the farmer on whose land the experiment was conducted said to Joseph with a smile on his face.

"Don Hernan you're a good man. You've been repaid for your effort by the increased production on that small parcel, and the technical know how you gained from the experiment. Had it not been for the experiment, you'd be planting your potatoes the traditional way for many more seasons, don't you think?" Joseph replied grinning.

"I'm happy with the results of this simple experiment. I suppose that if Plot B handn't produced as well or even failed, I would've been blamed for not having planted the crop during the moon's full stage, and perhaps asked to make up for any crop deficiency or monetary loss. Thank God for that," Joseph said to himself.

The credit union at Julio Andrade virtually took off. The parish was convinced that credit, use of chemicals and the new technology would bring higher returns for the land and labor investment. Joseph would watch closely and with satisfaction the month by month statistics and reports that reflected the growth that was taking place.

Six months had gone by. Bill Sorenson, Director of the World Extension Department in Madison had resigned. He was replaced by Ben Hartman, a seasoned technician in overseas development of credit unions. He too, lacked the know-how to adapt the credit union from consumer to production credit. Ronald Rhodes who was now the Managing Director was raising issues about Acker's program in Ecuador. A telegram came in from from Madison addressed to Enrique Salazar.

"CUNA concerned about progress being made by Acker in developing pilot project on agricultural credit. Request Acker prepare and submit immediate report detailing development to date. AID/Washington concerned." Sent by Ronald Rhodes.

This surprised Joseph who had been working his butt off, producing office and training materials, conducting seminars and getting the project launched. He reported monthly on his activities. He wasn't sure what was at the root of this out-of-the-blue demand.

"Enrique, I'd like to have a meeting with William Simmons, the USAID backstopping officer to this project," Joseph said to his superior.

LIFE'S DETOURS

Enrique arranged the meeting that very day. By this time Joseph had become better acquainted with Simmons. They walked into his office.

"What's your problem Joe? We've been watching the good work you're doing, yet I understand the big boss in Madison wants a minute by minute accounting. What gives? What kind of a guy is he anyway? Don't you send him any reports?" Simmons asked.

"Joe has been submitting reports to me, and I've been incorporating his activities along with ours. This may have not come across sufficiently clear to Head Office. I'll be phoning them tomorrow. Hopefully, we can get the matter straightened away," Salazar said.

"Bill as you know, I've made copies of my reports to you as well as to Enrique. I can surely prepare a summary report tomorrow and shoot it in to Madison. The telegram however, states that AID/Washington is concerned about the status of the program and this is where I believe you come in. In my opinion, I feel the pilot project is off and running, and I'm now prepared to expand the program to other rural credit unions interested in the production credit program. All of this will be done within the terms of my contract and its time frame," Joseph stated.

"You're absolutely correct Joe. I believe we've all failed a bit in reporting separately on your project. We've done the same thing as Enrique. That is, we've included excerpts from your reports in the Missions general report to AID /Washington and I believe your activity and project has not been sufficiently identified with the result that it gets lost in the mix. Tell you what. Write a summary report for CUNA, and give me a copy and I'll pass it to our backstopping officer in AID/Washington. I'll follow this up with a phone call to him and we'll get the matter rectified. How's that?" Simmons said, as he gave Joseph a wink.

The pilot project was heading in the direction of a complete success. It became a showcase in its operations, and was used as an example for other parishes to emmulate.

"Pablo," Joseph said to his counterpart. "From now on Julio Andrade is your baby. I would suggest that you visit them twice per month for the next two to three months. Once at month-end until we are satisfied that Lolita and Alberto Cardenas know how to close the books and prepare the monthly financial statements. Then during the month at the meeting of the Board of Directors, to ensure that they are served with properly prepared and complete reports, also to assist them in solving problems that may arise."

"Don Jose, I'm very happy to follow your instructions, and I'm delighted to be associated with you in this work. I've learned so much from you, and I would like to accompany you on the other projects as you go about launching them." Espinosa the counterpart said in an almost pleading voice.

"We will certainly work together. My contract is good for three years, during which time I'm obligated to develop at least 36 more credit unions with production credit programs. As you know, last week we took 15 credit union managers to Julio Andrade to see that operation, and we had a solid week of training for them. These credit unions are ready to go, just as soon as we can get around to train their directors, committeemen and the campesinos," Joseph said.

"Yes, I know," Espinosa said. "I understand that you and your family will be leaving next week for your vacation and home-leave back to the U.S. Since you will be gone for about six weeks, I'm anxious to proceed with the training and the initiation of a few of these credit unions during your absence. Would you mind if I did that?" Espinosa asked.

"Not at all, I welcome your suggestion very much and urge you to move ahead with implementation of the projects in accordance with our planned schedule. As you know last year our daughter Tabetha terminated her high school here in Ecuador, and returned to the U.S. to attend college. She took a course in business management, and about a month ago we received a letter from her saying she was engaged and that she had planned her wedding to coincide with our home leave. I don't want to miss that event," Joseph replied.

"I would agree, as the bride's father you'll have to be there to give her away. I congratulate you," Pablo said.

"There are also the Peace Corps Volunteers, who have been assigned to the credit union project in Ecuador, and we should strive to make full use of their capabilities. They are academically well prepared, and are motivated to render assistance to the people in the villages in which they live.

They displayed great interest in this program during the special in-country training session we held for them, and I believe they can be real helpful in teaching the credit union accounting system, lending policies, procedures, and using credit as a tool for production. The volunteers can teach the rules of order for running a meeting in a democratic fashion. They're good. Look at the good work that Volunteer Ernest Kramer is doing in Julio Andrade. He's been very helpful," Joseph explained to his counterpart.

"You know Senor Jose, there is such a thing as mental telepathy (telepatia cerebral), because I've been thinking the same thing you just mentioned. Would you request the P.C. Volunteers to cooperate with me during your absence, and we can do a lot of work together," Pablo

LIFE'S DETOURS

stated.

"Sure, I'll chat with them at next Monday's staff meeting. I know they'll be delighted to assist," Joseph replied.

Joseph was pleased with the initiative displayed by Pablo Espinosa his counterpart. After all, Joseph's job was to work his way out of a job, by training others. He felt that the sooner he could be relieved from his job by the national understudy and counterpart technician, the better a technician he became himself.

"I have a simple theory," Joseph would say. "My job in this business is - training people, to train people, to train people, ad infinitum."

The following week, Joseph, his wife Suzanne, and daughters Eleanor and Grace found themselves in Phoenix, Arizona on a much earned vacation and home leave. Allen Acker, Joseph's youngest brother, who had been a resident in Phoenix for some prior years had leased a furnished apartment for them, and had also assisted their daughter Tabetha with the wedding plans and arrangement. The Ackers met Thomas Pratt, who would soon become their son-in-law and were impressed with Tabetha's choice. About the only thing left for Joseph and his family to do was to enjoy their vacation and pay the bills, including the wedding costs.

Chapter 16

A SHIFT IN THE TIDE OF EVENTS

The furnished apartment the Ackers occupied was situated near the downtown area of Phoenix. They had moved in and after having a short visit with their daughter Tabetha and brother Allan, they went about the business of unpacking suitcases and generally settling in. They had descended overnight from a cool spring like temperature in Quito at an altitude of 7,500 feet above sea-level, to an altitude of about 1,000 feet above sea level, to face the hot June temperature in Phoenix. This called for an adjustment of their physical bodies to both altitude and temperature conditions.

That same day Joseph wasted no time in renting an automobile. They drove to a nearby supermarket to make a few food purchases, and to enjoy the comfort of shopping in the "big U.S.type" supermarket. The city market where the Ackers shopped in Quito had no push carts, instead they would pay a native Indian to carry a large woven wicker basket on his back. Suzanne would go to the different sections in the market, such as the dairy section, meat section, and vegetable section, At each section the goods purchased would be paid for right there and then, and placed in the wicker basket on this man's back. When the shopping was completed, the Indian would carry the basket to the car, unload it, receive his tip and disappear in search of another customer. "Shopping here at home is a leisurely and enjoyable event as compared to Ecuador," their daughter Eleanor said. "In Ecuador, you'd hurry because you would be constantly thinking about the man carrying the basket on his back and feeling sorry for him."

The Ackers retired to their beds earlier than usual that day. They were tired and Suzanne complained of a crippling headache. About an hour before midnight, Joseph was aroused from his sleep by the falling of the table lamp, that sat on a night table which separated the two twin beds in the bedroom. One bed was occupied by Suzanne and one by

LIFE'S DETOURS

himself. Joseph raised himself in bed, replaced the lamp in its place and switched on the light.

He was amazed to see Suzanne on the floor beside her bed, and in a kind of a physical struggle with herself. He jumped out of bed immediately and went to raise her back into bed.

"What's wrong Mom?" he said. "What happened?" "Are you hurt?"

Suzanne would not talk. She had gone into a state of limpness. Joseph picked her up and laid her back on her bed.

He ran into the daughter's bedroom.

"Eleanor," he said to the eldest of his two daughters, "wake up quickly and help me. Mom is very sick. We need a doctor. Would you stay watch over Mom, while I run downstairs and knock on the landlady's door and ask her to phone for a doctor."

The Ackers were not familiar with any doctor in the city, so the landlady placed a phone call to her personal doctor, who arrived within the hour at the apartment. By this time Suzanne had regained her composure, and was resting quietly on the bed. The doctor gave her a quick check for temperature, blood pressure and heart beat and asked her a few questions.

"I'm going to write her a prescription to do her over the weekend, but I'd like to see her at my clinic on Monday morning," he said as he looked at Joseph and signalled to him to follow him into the kitchen.

"Mr. Acker, your wife has all the symptoms common to patients who suffer with a brain tumor. Bring her in on Monday, and we will give her a battery of tests, and determine the nature and exact cause of her illness," the doctor said and with that he departed.

"This situation is certainly going to dampen our vacation and holiday spirit. In addition, Mom may find herself in the hospital, instead of at her daughter's wedding, which is to take place within a week's time," Joseph thought to himself.

The following week, Suzanne had undergone all her tests, and the X-rays and diagnosis proved conclusively that she had a brain tumor the size of an English Walnut on the left side of her brain. The date for surgery was fixed to follow their daughter's wedding,

The wedding was held as scheduled, and immediately after the wedding Tabetha and Tom her busband departed on their planned honeymoon.

"This vacation and home leave turned out to be a nightmare for us, I'm not concerned about the medical costs, since CUNA is providing excellent medical coverage for the me and my family, but the plans we had mapped out for our vacation must now be cast aside. It turns out that this is a time of stress for me. This surgery is on the brain,

LIFE'S DETOURS

it is critical, and heaven forbid - it could even mean death or some sort of long term disability," Joseph said to himself.

Carolyn, their oldest daughter and her husband Larry attended the wedding and were still present, but would have to return to their jobs in Canada within a two week period.

The predicament seemed a bit puzzling for Joseph, and in his pensive moments he felt he was carrying a burden, a degree of stress. He was secretly sharing Suzanne's pain and her own uncertainty about the outcome of the surgery. He thought about events that transpired during their twenty-five years of marriage.

"I should have showered more love and attention on Suzanne as well as the children. I didn't do it. I was a good provider, and I dedicated much effort and time to the economic aspects of family welfare. The nature of my work took me away from home for long periods at a time, but when I was at home I failed to grasp the opportunity to spend qaulity time with them. Instead I sought pleasure and enjoyment in boozing with my buddies. At this point, he recalled some of his father's early drinking bouts and felt remorseful. He recalled his mother's admonishment - `to always remember, one reaps what he sows,' and as the - `twig is bent, so shall the tree grow.' Could this really be me? Have I followed my father's footsteps?" Then, as if to compensate for this guilt, he turned his thoughts to a more positive judgement.

"Suzanne is a good woman and through this trying time for her, she will need to feel our love and moral support more than usual. I'm going to do all I can to make things better for her. We will all have to rally behind her and show our appreciation and care," Joseph thought.

Suzanne underwent surgery on schedule. She was led into the operating room at 9:00 a.m. and brought into the intensive care ward at 4:00 p.m. Joseph was there waiting for her when she was brought down. She was still under heavy sedation and unconscious. Dr.Brown, a renowned neuro-surgeon, by whose hands the surgery was conducted, looked tired, exhausted, came up to Joseph when he saw him.

"We had a very successful surgical operation, and the good news is that the tumor was benign. She will regain some consciousness within the next hour, and should be feeling better by tomorrow." he said. "Its been a hard day's work."

"Thanks Doc," Joseph replied. "I'm sure you did your level best and we're very grateful. You look tired."

Joseph came close to Suzanne's bed.

"Mom, can you hear me. Dr. Brown says your tumor was benign, and that you'll be okay. Honey, I'm pulling for you.

LIFE'S DETOURS

He said you'll feel better by to-morrow," Suzanne gave a low grunt with a trying smile.

He gazed at her in her helpless state and was emotionally moved. He prayed that she would recover and get back to her normal self. As a married couple, they were a "balanced" pair. It seemed that each one's weak points were offset by the other's strong points.

"Maybe we were an odd couple, but I wouldn't have it any other way," Joseph thought.

According to Dr. Brown, her recuperation would take up to six months or better, since the right side of her body was suffering from paralysis and her speech was somewhat impaired. This was to be expected, and there was still a month left before their vacation would terminate. Joseph knew that Suzanne would be unable to travel back to Quito soon, so he made arrangements for further rental of the apartment. He knew that Eleanor, their daughter who was now 16 years of age, could look after her mother until she would be fit to travel.

During the course of these family events, other dynamics were at work within the CUNA organization. Joseph received a phone call from Madison, Wisconsin.

"Joe this is Ronald Rhodes calling. How are you. We're sorry to learn that your wife underwent major surgery. How is she?" he asked.

"Oh, hello, good to hear from you. Thanks for asking, Suzanne is just fine. Making steady progress, but it will take a few weeks before she can travel," Joseph replied.

"I'm calling to let you in on some good news. CUNA and AID/Washington have agreed to open a regional office in Panama City, from where we can serve the whole of Latin America. Everything south of the Rio Grande. We have appointed Robert Long as the Director of the Regional Office. The reality is that Long is now in Panama arranging for office space, and he will be hiring his staff, most of which must be Spanish speaking. However, there is one appointment to the staff that was made in agreement with AID/Washington. You have been appointed as Director of Training for all of Latin America, and I congratulate you." Rhodes said.

"Gee thanks, how did all this come about so sudden? Joseph inquired.

"The truth of the matter is that your production credit program looks very promising. AID/Washington would like to see every country in Latin America adopt it as a part of their total rural development programs. You've done an outstanding job in Ecuador. Even beyond my personal expectations and the reports coming in from every direction both to our office and in Washington speak very highly of the program. The USAID/Mission in Quito stated that they were amazed with the speed with which you implemented the program. They were also quite taken up with the impact the program made on every segment of activity it touched. The methods you used in simplifying the technology to a level where rural people could understand it, and then transfering the technology effectively to your understudies and the others involved in the program speaks well for your effort," Rhodes continued.

"I'm delighted to hear your comments. I'm not quite finished with my task in Ecuador. I'll need another year to fulfill the contract obligations. Then I also have this problem on my hands with my wife's health," Joseph stated.

"We're prepared to make your transition from Ecuador as smooth, but as quickly as possible. In the first place, if you need an extra couple of weeks to be added on to your vacation in order to take care of Suzanne, that can be arranged. What I'm saying here now is that we need you in Panama, and we need you to initiate and direct the production credit program in all of the Latin American countries, with the exception of Cuba. I'm personally counting on you to do it," Rhodes said.

"Just thinking it over quickly, I think it can be done. The fact that I would be stationed in Panama, removes me from living in Ecuador, but does not prohibit me from visiting the country and continuing to provide consultations to the national counterpart, the program and to observe and measure the progress of that country program. Then of course, we could commence to unfold an agenda and offer technical assistance to the credit union systems being developed in the other Latin American countries," Joseph replied.

"We are sending another technician to Ecuador to replace you as the Country Program Director for CUNA. I suggest you go back to Ecuador, spend four to six weeks in orienting your replacement and write your exit report. This is the end of June, perhaps you could assume your duties in Panama by the first of October," Rhodes said in a tone of voice that sounded almost demanding.

Joseph found it hard to understand the sudden change of attitude in Rhodes's position. Some three months before, he sent the telegram complaining that the program was not moving fast enough in Ecuador, and that the reports were weak. Then all hell breaks loose. He wants to move with the speed of fury to get the program initiated in every country in Latin America. Perhaps later, Joseph would discover what the circumstances were that caused this hasty and unforeseen turnabout.

Suzanne's recovery made remarkable progress. In their discussions they agreed, that Joseph would return back to Quito alone and terminate his duties there. He would pack and ship their personal

LIFE'S DETOURS

belongings to Panama City. Suzanne and their two daughters would remain behind in Phoenix and join him in Panana after he had obtained suitable housing.

On his return to Quito, Joseph found the program moving ahead without any hitches.

"How's Suzanne, and we understand you're going to leave us," was a chorus heard from every hand shaken, as program officials, associates and friends greeted Joseph back.

Simmons the USAID Rural Development Officer phoned Joseph and asked him to come over to his office for a chat. Joseph complied.

"Joe, the day after you departed on your home leave, a team of two people came in from Washington. One was a sociologist and the other an economist. They came in specifically to study and analyze the much touted production credit program and its component parts. They spent one week here, and gave the program very high marks. They said it was the type of a program, that should be part of a rural development package in every country," Simmons said.

"This is sure good to hear. Now I'm beginning to put together the pieces, that urged Rhodes back in Madison to phone and tell me about the changes that took place. I guess you've heard about my being moved," Joseph replied.

"We're sorry to see you go," Simmons added. "But, being stationed in Panama and having the role of a roving type technician, will enable you to stop in Ecuador on occassion, or as requested and give us the benefit of your knowledge. I congratulate you on the work you've accomplished here, and on your move. That should mean a promotion for you," Simmons said.

"Hopefully a promotion is being considered. I haven't asked for the promotion. It was offered. One assumes that with the promotion, there comes a corresponding salary increase!" Joseph replied smiling.

"I'm sure you'll do well. Good Luck. It was a pleasure to work with you and to watch a professional at work," Simmons added as they shook hands and parted.

The next few weeks for Joseph consisted of devoting sufficient time in orienting Jack Sobley, his replacement as Country Program Director. He conducted a total review of the program with Pablo Espinosa his Ecuadorian counterpart, whose job remained now to expand the program countrywide.

He wrote and submitted his exit report, and had the family's personal effects shipped to Panama. While all of this was going on, he was honored with the presentation of a Merit Award by the Ecuadorian Federation of Credit Unions, and also attended several farewell parties which had been organized in some rural credit unions, at which he was awarded Certificates of Merit.

Joseph met the October deadline he had set for himself to arrive in Panama City. The Latin American Regional Office (LARO) was established and functioning. He reported to the office, and met Robert Long, the Director of the Regional Program.

"Hello Joseph, sure glad to meet you," he said as he rose from his desk chair and extended his hand for a shake with Joseph. "Have a seat. I was really anxious to meet you and to chat about the work we're responsible to perform together."

"I'm also pleased to meet you. It looks as if we have a huge challenge ahead of us," Joseph replied.

"You bet we do! Both Washington and Madison have great expectations about the possibilities of the production credit idea you've so creatively instituted into the credit union programs. I'm not a cooperative technician myself. I come from the administrative field in government, and I suppose I've been chosen for this task, in order to have a blend between a government point of view and professionals like yourself, who know how to put the nuts and bolts to-gether to make a system work," Long added.

"I've been putting together a staff. Enrigue Salazar with whom you've worked in Ecuador, will be my assistant for administrative purposes. and I'll be hiring a few more technicians especially a writer and publicity expert. You are however the pillar in this program, and if it wasn't for the production credit program, I doubt very much if this regional office would have been established. You will be glad to know that along with your transfer here, you are back again as Director of Training for all of Latin America, but this time with an increase in your salary. Your salary is now equivalent to that of a GS-15 in government. That's a good salary. You're one of the highest paid employees in this office," Long added.

"You know, I've been receiving more accolades lately, than I can carry. I'm not sure that I'm totally responsible for the program's success. Many other folks were involved in making it a winner. But,I'm very grateful for the increase in salary. It is certainly recognition for my effort. It also means more hard work on a continuing basis," Joseph said in a humble way.

"The territory we have to work in is huge. There are 16 countries in Central and South America, excluding the three Guayana., Then there are a number of island countries scattered throughout the Carribean. Our main and immediate thrust will be in South America. Some countries have programs, and have gone so far as to organize their own federations. But, they have no financial backbone and don't know how to go about mobilizing capital. In addition, their training

LIFE'S DETOURS

programs have to be upgraded, their operational systems reviewed and their managerial skills sharpened. You have a big job on your hands."

"Mr. Long," Joseph began to say, when he was interrupted.

"Call me Bob, and I shall call you Joseph. We'll cut out the formality, roll up our sleeves, and push forward to meet our goals," Long said.

"No problem, calling you Bob is easier than Mr. Long." Joseph replied with a smile. "I need a few days to seek housing and to bring my family in from Phoenix. As you know, my wife is recovering from brain tumor surgery. Then before I draft any specific work program, I'd like to make a tour of the countries in question, with a view to determining what programs exist, and what resources we have to work with."

"I would be the last person to attempt to tell you how to go about organizing your work. You are here because we are certain you know your business. Take whatever time is required to seek living accommodation, then bring your family in as you've suggested and make preparations to travel as you see fit. We will have a secretary, who among other things will be responsible for making flight reservations and purchasing tickets, and we have an adequate travel budget for you," Long said.

They parted. It was a good meeting Joseph thought to himself. His mind drifted to his childhood days, and his mother's hope that someday he would be a leader of some sort. "I've probably reached the pinnacle of my career. I wonder if this is the maximum leadership position I could attain? I'm now 50 years of age. Maybe this'll be it, but I'm content. I hope I can make this phase of the work confronting me successful."

Joseph could read and understand French, having studied it in his high school days in Canada. He could read, write and speak Spanish fluently, and he had studied Portuguese.

He felt equipped and confident that he could travel in all the Western Hemisphere countries from the North to the South Pole and not feel estranged.

The Acker's personal effects had arrived from Quito. After a hectic air trip with much turbulance, Suzanne and their two daughters arrived from Phoenix, and Joseph had them settled in a three bedroom home situated on a hillside location in Golf Heights overlooking the golf course in Panama City. Eleanor registered for classes in the Canal Zone Junior College, while Grace attended elementary school in the Canal Zone. A housemaid was flown in from Ecuador to live in and do the housework, while Suzanne was still in the process of recuperating.

Since his air travel would be costly, Joseph planned to be in the field about three weeks out of each month. That would give him one full week to ten days at home. He arranged by telephone or telegraph with program contacts in each country dates for meetings. He took his first trip to Venezuela, Brazil, Argentine, Uruguay, Paraguay and Chile. It gave him on the average about two days in each country, with a day in between for travel.

Venezuela was the first stop. Joseph found a development of consumer cooperatives organized by the civil servants. They operated credit departments restricted to the financing of merchandise, such as television sets and other major appliances. There was a parish credit union operating in the city of Barquisimeto and another in Merida, both in the western part of Venezuela. There was a need here for trechnical input and training.

Brazil was the second stop. In Rio de Janeiro a small development was taking place embracing several parishes in which credit unions had been organized along French-Canada's Caisse Populaire's lines. They were strictly the urban type extending small amounts of credit for consumer and personal loan purposes. Not much could be done by way of production credit, except for maybe some small loans to urban artesans. A need for a heavy input of technical know-how and training materials was clearly evident in this situation.

"Brazil is a big country, it must have zillions of small farmers. I must find out more about this country," Joseph said to himself.

He phoned the President of the Agricultural Development Bank of Brazil in Rio.

"Si Signor," Ricardo Madrugal, the president said."We have plenty of small farmers in northeast Brazil. I want to meet and talk with you. How long will you be in our country?" he asked.

"Not too long on this occassion. I'm on a research and study tour. I still have a couple of days to spare here," Joseph replied.

"I invite you to join me tomorrow, as early as possible. I will pick you up at your hotel, and together we will fly over our country in our bank's aeroplane. This will give you an opportunity to view some aspects of our agricultural setting, and we can discuss your ideas about production credit and see how we could incorporate your methods in our current operations. Would you be available?" Madrugal asked.

"I would be delighted to join you sir," Joseph replied. "Call for me as early as you like. I'll be ready."

The two-hour air tour of Brazil's countryside, covered only a small segment of this huge country. They flew over a portion of the States of Minas Gerais and Sao Paulo, both situated in the south central part of Brazil. Joseph saw well developed pastures clustered with large numbers of livestock. There were painted buildings, vineyards, fruit

LIFE'S DETOURS

farms and corn fields. Farms that were fenced and as well developed as anything we had in the U.S. These areas were settled at the turn of the century by German, Italian and other European immigrants.

"We have branch offices in these areas, and the farmers here make good use of the bank's lending services. They call on the government agronomists, veterinarians and other specialists to provide them with counselling. The farms may not be as large as your American farms, but they are large enough to be economic units in terms of our Brazilean economy," Madrugal advised.

Joseph agreed and felt there was no need for his type of program for those areas.

Conditions changed drastically, as they turned and flew northward over the provinces of Bahia and Pernambuco. Flying at low altitude, Joseph could see poor roads, small patches of poorly cultivated farm land, lesser numbers of cattle, and fewer vehicles on their roads. From the lush green fields and pastures of Southern Brazil, they were flying over an area imbued with a greyish brown tinge and with less green in its composition.

"This is the area in which a large number of our small land owners are located. They need our help. In the first instance, they have no understanding of good farm management practises, and secondly the farmers do not have adequate credit facilities available to them. We can provide the facilities. The problem lies in teaching these small farmers how to use the credit that can be offered to them in a productive way. This is where I think the kind of program you've been talking about can be helpful for us," Madrugal said, and without giving Joseph a chance to voice an opinion he continued.

"I would like to have you come back. Do a survey in a given area and launch a pilot project for us. I can give you a good technician to work with you, and we can incorporate your ideas and techniques in the operations of the Bank's branch offices located here in Northeast Brazil. Do you think that's possible?" Madrugal asked.

"Sure thing, we can work with you on such a program if you request our help in writing," Joseph replied.

They parted company, on the understanding that as soon as an official request would be received from the Agricultural Development Bank of Brazil, Joseph would program a date and time frame in which he could make himself available for further consultation and advice.

"The Development Bank of Brazil is not a credit union or a credit co-operative. But it is essentially doing the same thing in terms of extending credit. It does lack other important elements for community development, such as local ownership, leadership development, savings promotion, and educational and training programs on a continuing basis. There might be a remote possibility for these rural bank branches to be converted into locally owned credit unions at some appropiate future date, but this was an idea whose time was premature. At any rate, our assistance should not be withheld to a non-credit union entity such as the National Bank, even if the purpose differs from the CUNA objective of developing credit unions and credit union federations, along with the production credit program. The focus of increasing food production in the third world countries still falls within the parameters of what the U.S. Government policy advocates. and after all, our taxpayers are funding this program," Joseph was justifying in his mind the reason why he had made a commitment to offer technical services to a government owned bank.

"We have 26 credit unions here in Argentine, with 131,000 shareholder members, and about $80 million in deposits. We have a National Federation capable of extending technical assistance and leadership. Of course, we still have much to learn with regards to the types of credit we could extend, and about the most up-to-date methods and techniques in banking and especially rural banking. Our credit unions are located in the larger centers of the country, and we deal with the larger estancia owners and ranchers. We do not have the kind of a production credit program such as you have described," Arturo Escandon the managing director stated.

"You have a fairly well developed system, and I'm not here to tell you what to do. You folks have come a long way in your development, without the CUNA technical assistance.

I would however add that you have possibilities of extending your credit services to the smaller farmers in the peripheral areas of your larger centers, by establishing branch offices in selected smaller rural communities, and promoting savings, as well as extending loans for increasing their production," Joseph countered.

"Your observation is good, and that is a field, a potential and a method that we haven't explored. Send us a package of your program materials, and drop in to see us on your next visit. We may need some help from you. I will propose these thoughts to the Board of the Federation and we'll see what action we might take." Escandon said.

Uruguay was next on Joseph's itenirary. Here he found a struggling Federation with 20 credit unions, mostly in urban centers. They had about 60,000 members and $4.5 million in deposits. They were very receptive to Joseph's ideas and felt that the coastal credit unions could be of great financial help to their small fishermen and landowners, who simply did not have a source of credit outside of the moneylender. Joseph agreed to return and assist in planning a long-range development program, and to introduce the production credit idea

LIFE'S DETOURS

to the Federation technicians, who would them impart it to their affiliates.

The visit to Paraguay was productive in a sense. Joseph met with the Director of Cooperatives, who at first, did not appear enthusiastic about credit unions.

"General Stroesner, our president authorized the establishment of an Agricultural Development Bank and credit to the small farmers is handled by this bank," the Director stated.

"I agree that the Development Bank can be of great service to a small segment of your farm population. However, it does not offer rural communities an opportunity to organize their own locally owned financial institutions. The Development Bank has only two other branches to serve the whole country. Credit unions teach people how to save, how to use credit wisely and provide for local leadership development," Joseph invoked.

"Well, we don't want too many leaders in our country. Under General Stroesner we have a benevolent dictatorship, and our people are content. There is a danger that through organizations of the credit union type, communism could creep into our society, and we don't want that. We do have some cooperatives organized, but we don't believe we're ready for a widespread development of the kind you speak," the Director stated emphatically.

"Sir, I'm not here to force anything into being. I'm merely stating that these are the kinds of technical and material services we can offer. It's your choice to accept our offer or to deny it. As you know, the program was one launched by our late President Kennedy, and is intended to assist our Latin American neighbors in improving incomes and elevating their living standards," Joseph replied.

They parted with the understanding that the Director would investigate the possibility of launching a credit union program from the ground up. Joseph handed him his call card. He would communicate his decision to Joseph at a later date. The final upshot of this meeting resulted in Paraguay going for the program, hook line and sinker, and CUNA recruited and furnished an on-site technician to assist in their development.

The agricultural development officer of the USAID Mission in Santiago, Chile, felt that this was an inopportune time for widespread credit union development in that country. The Chilean dictatorship did not look favorably on the existing cooperatives and in reality restricted the formation of any new ones. They advised Joseph to act with caution. A visit to the office of the Chilean Federation of Credit Unions convinced Joseph that a desire for expansion was there, but the feasability to do so was arrested by the political climate and economic instability in the country. It would have to go on the back burner for awhile.

Joseph returned to his office in Panama and submitted a report on his findings.

"How do you see the situation?" Long asked Joseph.

"A couple of areas of immediate promise. Another couple of areas are in the making, and a couple must rest on the back burner until more interest is aroused," Joseph reported.

"It is my feeling, now that my initial visits are concluded, that we should sponsor a one week seminar in Ecuador. We would invite the current leaders from the Federations of all the countries to attend. We could invite certain individuals from the government agencies that work closely with the cooperatives or have supervisory authority over them. I believe that once they see the pilot project in operation and feel the swell of pride and enthusiasm that exists, they will entertain the idea of introducing the program within their own countries," Joseph stated.

"Your report and your ideas are okay. I suggest you pursue your objectives with as much urgency as possible," Director Long said as he puffed on his big cigar.

Joseph set about immediately and drew plans for the Ecuador seminar. Then he mailed seminar notices to all the Federations and Government agencies in all of the South American countries. In the meantime he prepared for himself an itenirary to cover the remaining countries, he had not yet visited. Colombia, Peru and Bolivia were on that list. He would visit Ecuador to arrange the logistics for the seminar, and to request the Ecuadorian Federation to assist in the seminar in its role as the host country agency.

Bolivia was his first call. He found a struggling but vibrant Federation organized under the direction of Padre Glen Powell, a Maryknoll missionary from the U.S. Joseph had met him some three years earlier at the Cooperative conference which had been held in Punta del Este, Uruguay.

"We have a few credit unions organized here in Cochabamba. We have none so far in La Paz. We have a handful of leaders that require more technical knowledge and training with regards to credit union operations. Since I received your letter of invitation to the Quito seminar, and the announcement that you were coming to Bolivia on this visit, I've arranged for you to deliver a talk tonight in one of our church halls. We have summoned credit union leaders to attend this meeting. I hope this meets with your approval," Padre Powell said

"No problem, it is always easy to talk about money management. So many people know so little about the fundamentals of managing

LIFE'S DETOURS

resources," Joseph replied.

"We also have one very good credit union in Santa Cruz. It is not affiliated with our effort here in any way, but has been making great strides and is instrumental in granting loans for the construction of homes," Padre Powell added.

That evening Joseph had an opportunity to expound on the merits of practising thrift, of borrowing wisely. and repaying the loan promptly. Above all he illustrated how production credit can enhance the growth of a credit union by increasing the productivity and income of the borrowers enabling them to garner more savings. He talked about leadership development and responsibilities and about the huge potential that was awaiting to be tapped for development.

His visit to Peru was productive as well. Another Maryknoll missionary had started a credit union, some years back at a place called Puno, high up in the Andes mountains. It was organized amongst the descendants of the Incas, and was a successful venture. Padre David Stern the priest, later moved to Lima the capital city and gave leadership for organizing many more credit unions, both in Lima the city, as well as countrywide.

"The development in Peru is making progress," Padre Stern said in describing their set-up. "We have credit unions here in Lima that are organized in employee and professional groups. Every parish in the city has a credit union to serve its parishioners. Outside of Lima, the credit unions are organized primarily on a parish basis."

Padre Stern was a proud man. He had gained prestige and was well known in international circles for the work he had accomplished amongst the Inca people at Puno. One could immediately sense that with Padre Stern you did not give advice, but rather sought it.

"What do you see as valuable technical assistance coming from us at LARO to the system you pioneered here in Peru?" Joseph asked.

"We're growing constantly. There are about 150 credit unions in operation now, and we have room to double this number. There are more than a quarter million members and over $2 million in savings and deposits. When I need help, I go directly to CUNA in Madison or the State Department in Washington. I've had a private interview with the deceased President Kennedy, you know," he said.

Inevitably one could not help but feel the piercing and absolute vibrancy of Padre Stern's ego.

"Yes, I'm fully aware of your good work here in Peru. Our Latin American Regional Office (LARO) in Panama needs your skills and prestige in extending the system continent-wide in Latin America. We've organized a one week training seminar in Quito, and invitations have been mailed to credit union federations and other allied agencies to send participants. I'm in charge of this seminar. I'd like to have you favor us with your presence and to deliver a couple of lectures. Will you accept this invitation?" Joseph asked.   Padre Stern replied by asking,-"Who pays my expenses?".

"LARO will pay your travel and out-of-pocket expenses, and we can arrange to pay you an honorarium as well, for lecturing," Joseph replied.

"No, I'm not seeking an honrarium. I'm a credit union man. I was merely asking that my expenses be paid. What role would you have me play at the seminar?" he asked.

"In my opinion and with your permission, I'd like to bill you as our keynote speaker on the morning of the first day. You may select any theme you feel comfortable with. Perhaps a philosophical theme peppered with some ideas that would set the tone for the week's seminar," Joseph said.

"What about the second lecture?" he asked.

"In this case, I suggest you deliver a message posing aspects of the technical operations and problems of credit unions based on your experience," Joseph proposed

"Sounds like something I could do. Would you mail us a copy of the week's program as early as you can. I believe we will sponsor a couple of our people to this seminar. There ought to be some new ideas we could bring back to serve us here," Padre Stern said.

They parted company. Joseph felt he had won the day and Padre Stern's goodwill. This was important for the overall success of the seminar and for developing a good foundation for the production credit program. He was tired and returned back to Hotel Bolivar, where he changed into clothes more casual and comfortable.

He came down into the bar. It was near empty. He ordered and drank two double scotches on the rocks quite hastily, and then stepped out unto the street.

It was about 5:30 in the evening. Near the entrance, shielding herself from the sun, stood a well-dressed and attractive lady. She appeared to be in her early forties.

Joseph had seen her in the hotel the day before. She looked toward him and smiled.

"Buenos dias, senora," Joseph said. "It's a beautiful day isn't it?".

"Good evening," she replied. "I saw you speaking English to a gentleman last night. Are you an American?"

"Yes, I am," Joseph replied.

"I have a sister in Miami. I'll be going to join her as soon as my divorce proceedings are over here." she said.

"Oh, I'm sorry to hear about your divorce," he replied. "Are there

LIFE'S DETOURS

any children involved?"

"Yes, I have two children. A girl ten years of age, and a boy eight. They are now at my mother's place in Callao on the coast. My divorce will come through next week. I'm here to get my passports and visas. The children are coming with me. I should be able to leave in about ten days."

As she spoke she came nearer to Joseph who was leaning against one of the pillars to the main entrance of the hotel. He felt just a bit light headed from the drinks he had consumed, and thought the lady would make a good companion to spend an evening with.

"Are you in Peru on business or as a tourist?" she asked.

"On business," he replied.

"What do you do? Are your offices in Miami?"

"No, my office is in Panama. I'm a consultant in the field of credit unions. Have you got a moment? How'd you like to join me for a drink in the bar?" Joseph asked.

"I wouldn't mind that." she said. "I have a little time to spare."

They entered the bar. Joseph ordered another scotch for himself and a pisco-sour for her.

"What is your name," she asked.

"My name is Joseph, and yours?"

"My name is Amanda Zazueta, but after next week it will be Camargo. I revert to my maiden name." she said.

Their conversation delved into and explored both their lives. She was aware that Joseph was married. He ordered another two drinks, and the conversation continued.

"I'd like to invite you up to my room. Would you care to come? Joseph asked.

"No, I'm afraid I must refuse your invitation," she said, as she touched his hand with hers. "It's the wrong time of the month for me. Besides, I'm not quite over my divorce. Infidelity has been the cause of it. My husband chased other women. When I go to America, I hope I find another man with whom I can share my love and feelings, and spend the rest of my life with him. Infidelity is dangerous for it bewilders the stable order and introduces notes of deception and betrayal into a marriage intended to be harmonius."

Inspite of his intoxicated disposition Joseph understood and felt humiliated by her sermon. He dropped the subject and ordered dinner instead. They ate their dinner and parted.

The next morning Joseph awoke with a huge hangover. He tried to recount what took place the night before. He could remember the woman he had met. He recalled some of their conversation, and her sermon on infidelity. He could not recall their parting. He grabbed a taxi, went to the airport and checked in.

There was a wait of one and one half hours before his plane would depart. He strolled over to a book stand. There were two shelves with new and used pocket books in English. By coincidence he picked up a book on infidelity, and began leafing through it's pages, stopping occassionally to read a line or two.

"If love makes the world go 'round, what does infidelity do? Stop it in its tracks? Does it give life spice or make it unbearable? For as long as people have been falling in love, they've been falling out of love and trying to find comfort in the arms of another." There was more to read but Joseph looked up from the book in thought.

"I did the wrong thing last night." It was his first attempt to engage in an extra marital affair. He felt a measure of guilt.

"Thank God, it didn't work out. Good thing this happened a thousand miles away from home. Suzanne will never find out about it. I'm really ashamed of myself. But then, what's bad for marriage is often good for literature and for book writers," he thought to himself.

He placed the book back on the shelf, just as the flight was being called and proceeded toward the embarkation gate.

On his return to Panama, he stopped in Colombia where a good credit union system was unfolding. The Managing Director, Vicente Gutierrez met Joseph at the airport.

"We are on the verge of tremendous growth and expansion in our country," Gutierrez said. "Our Federation known as the Union Cooperativa Nacional de Ahorro y Credito (UCONAL) has about 150 affiliated credit unions with 150,000 member- shareholders and $20 million in member deposits. For the most part, our credit unions are organized amongst labor groups in Bogota, Cali, and other larger cities in the country. We have a small number of rural parish credit unions, but they are undercapitalized and furthermore we don't have all the right training materials for them. In addition, we believe that if a source of seed capital were available, the dynamics of growth in our system would really unfold," Gutierrez reiterated.

"I've garnered much useful data from this trip. Our experience in the U.S. and Canada bears out your suggestion, for the need to establish a central source for lending funds to be used as seed capital by the smaller and under-capitalized credit unions. In addition a central source will assist them to stabilize their fund management capability after they reach a certain size," Joseph said agreeably.

"Then of course, we are very much interested in the aspect of lending for productive purposes. We have a need for training materials at all levels of our operations, with special emphasis on management training. We have bookkeepers and accountants, but they lack

LIFE'S DETOURS

managerial skills. The idea of your seminar in Quito is a good one. You can be sure that a group from Colombia will be there," Gutierrez said.

Joseph returned to Panama. He reported back to Long, the LARO Director.

"My report will be brief," Joseph said. "I feel that there are three areas that require our immediate attention.

First, preparation of training materials. Some of these materials like the management training substance, can be general in nature. The production credit materials need to be tailored to meet each country's specific needs. Technical assistance and training should form part of the materials package.

Secondly, there is a need to study and find ways and means to assist the national federations in each country to set-up, organize and capitalize a central credit union.

Thirdly, the Quito seminar should highlight amongst others, two important topics, namely:

1. Credit as a tool for production purpose,and
2. Management Skills.

Furthermore, I believe we here at LARO should develop a model Credit Union Law and furnish it to the federations. As I covered these countries and spoke to the credit union leaders, I found a wide divergence in the laws under which they operate. A model law would act as a guide line to enable them to petition their governments for an improved law under which they could operate.

This is substantially my report. Priority will be given in terms of technical assistance to those federations that are willing and ready to initiate the production credit program immediately. Those federations in countries like Brazil, Chile and Paraguay, which for whatever reason are not yet ready, will be assisted later. However, through the media of the publication going out from here, they should be kept informed on the progress being made by participating federations," Joseph stated.

"Your comments are well taken," Long replied as he drew a puff from his long cigar. "Where do we go from here?"

"I will immediately draft the training schedule for the seminar and mail it to all the federations, including those in the Carribean. In addition to Padre Stern, I will line up the other lecturers, amongst which you are included. The logistics have been spoken for and final arrangements are looked after by the Ecuadorian Federation," Joseph replied.

"Prepare the budget for this seminar and carry on," Long said as they parted.

Chapter 17

NEW HORIZONS

The seminar was well attended. All of the continental countries were represented as well as Mexico and the Dominican Republic. A total of 42 trainees in attendance.

At the seminar Padre Stern chose as his topic for the keynote address an excerpt from the philosophical writings of Thomas Paine.

"The world is my country, all mankind are my brethren, and to do good is my religion."

Padre Stern did a marvelous job in his keynote address, by blending in human philosophy with grass roots economics to conditions in Latin America, and world wide in general.

"We have a responsibility" he said, "to help those less fortunate than ourselves. Credit unions are not a giveaway program. It is not giving away fish to people. It is teaching them how to fish, so they can help themselves. No man is an island unto himself. We must live together and learn to live together. He reminded the trainees, that Christ himself did not teach us to pray selfishly and only to `My Father'. Through the Lord's Prayer he has taught us to pray to OUR FATHER - and when we ask him for OUR DAILY BREAD - we do not ask Him only for - `My Daily Bread'. Credit unions are a practical way for us to put our Christian faith into everyday practical use," Padre Stern concluded.

He was loudly applauded for his presentation. It was a good kickoff for the seminar.

One of the seminar's highlights for the trainees was the bus trip from Quito, high up in the Andes, to the pilot project on production credit at Julio Andrade. This took up two of the days on the training timetable.

The trainees were amazed at the progress that had been made in this community in such a short period of time. They were exposed to

LIFE'S DETOURS

projects of improved potato crops. They saw projects involving one or two dairy cows, and hog and poultry raising. Local peasants offered testimonials as to how credit assisted them in their small farm ventures to become more productive. Everyone talked enthusiastically about the project and its achievements.

They were particularly taken up with the presentation made by Alberto Cardenas, the manager of the Julio Andrade Credit Union.

"Gentlemen, slightly more than two years ago, we had here a dormant credit union. Now, we have more than half a million sucres ($25,000) in loans to about 280 members. We had no capital of our own. Now we are operating with 20% of our own capital and the remaining 80% borrowed from the Co-operative Bank in Quito."

"Upon the recommendation of Mr. Acker, the CUNA expert, we adopted a policy of retaining 5% of every loan made, and adding this amount to the member's share capital as a saving. When the borrower repays the loan, he pays the entire amount plus interest. In this way the member accumulates savings by increasing the amount of his share capital in the credit union," Cardenas said.

One of the trainees requested clarification.

"You mean you lend a member 105% of what he actually needs for his project, you retain the extra 5% and apply it to his share capital in the credit union, and give him the 100% balance for his project. When he repays the loan, he repays the entire amount he borrowed (105%) plus the interest, and he has then increased his share account by that additional five percent. Is that correct?"

"Yes it is," Cardenas replied. "We call this compulsory capitalization or forced savings. The combined capital that is retained from all the borrowing members forms the basis of the capital structure. That is how we choose to mobilize local funds for the credit union. In addition to the voluntary deposits our members make into their share account, they are compelled to save as they borrow. For example, if we lend 500,000 sucres during the year, we can make the share capital grow by 25,000 sucres. Eventually we will replace the capital we borrowed from the Co-operative Bank, with our own funds."

All of the trainees felt that the principle of using compulsory savings to capitalize a credit union was a good idea. It is also democratic. The member who borrows more, contributes more to capital formation, because he needs more. Percentage wise each member shareholder contributes equally. Yet each one contributes in accordance with the volume of capital he uses for loans.

Robert Long, the Director of LARO was introduced and asked to speak to the trainees. He was a tall man, and could not articulate well in Spanish. He conveyed his message through the interpreter. Apart from extending his personal greetings and that of his colleagues, he expounded on a simple theme.

"The credit union is an economic institution with a moral/social conscience," he began.

"I'm going to speak to you briefly, to simply remind you about a few principles I read somewhere, some time ago, written by someone whose name I do not recall."

"Economics is human nature in action. The credit union is an institution reflecting human nature in action."

"People will always buy more of the good product whose price is fair."

"There will always be employers who will hire people that can produce the most."

"Too much debt will eventually destroy a man or a government."

"Borrow wisely for productive purposes, and repay your debts promptly."

"Remember nothing is ever - FREE - someone has to produce to pay for it."

"Capital should be rewarded with a fair return."

"The person who steadily learns more, will by the same token earn more."

"The safe and happy individual, family, or nation is the one which spends less than it earns."

"These are some standards that we must learn to live by, and no amount of government regulations or other rules can change them. Credit unions can teach and help people to live within these bounds and to be prosperous and happy," Long concluded.

The lecturers spoke on themes that were so down to earth; that made so much common sense and yet were so necessary.

Throughout the seminar's workshops, Joseph Acker was a leading lecturer in both the topic of production credit, as well as the subject of management.

"How many of you in this audience are managers?" Joseph asked.

Out of the forty-two trainees in class only five hands went up.

"What's the matter with the rest of you? Why aren't you a manager? he asked, pointing to a trainee in the front row.

"I'm an agronomist," he replied.

"What about you sir, what do you do?"

"I'm the Director of our Federation," he answered.

"And you sir, you're not a manager, what occupation do you have?" Joseph asked.

"I'm an accountant in the school district," he said

"This is a gross error people make," Joseph remarked. "People

LIFE'S DETOURS

think that because they do not carry a title of - manager - that they are not managers. Management is a science and an art that every human being with a sound mind possesses. Every adult person has at his disposal resources, energy and time. How that person uses these three elements depends on their ability to combine and manage them with beneficial results for themselves and others."

"Management plays a vital role in every phase of human endeavor. It is especially essential in this program of using credit for production purposes. Everyone associated and involved in this program should be aware of the management concepts and their application."

"If people are to be linked to progress, growth, and development, there must be understanding. How can under-standing be developed and who is responsible?"

"The people! All of the people, regardless of their occupation or status in a community."

"What are the first requirements? To understand! - to pinpoint the need, and to discover a solution to fill that need."

Joseph delivered his talk on management using a graphic illustration which he himself drew on the blackboard. He went about describing the components of his illustration. Using the credit union as the institutional base, he depicted a mechanism, that could assist people in reaching pre-determined objectives.

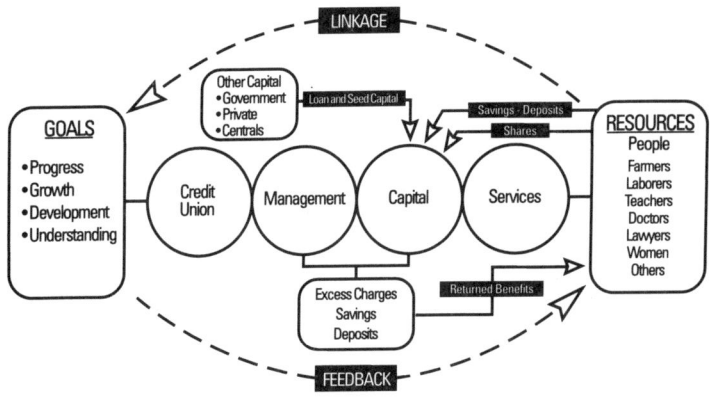

"Check on the resources in your own community. The basic resource consists of our people. People in every walk of life who can come together and link themselves to the attainment of both individual and common goals. The credit union provides the linkage insitution.

With proper management, a credit union could mobilize capital, and the feedback will be a full range of financial services at cost to those it serves. Over a reasonable period of time, people should be able to see results, both in terms of the development of the institution as well as in their own personal lives," Joseph expounded.

He knew the seminar had motivated and impacted the trainees, by the comments made on their evaluation sheets.

The Paraguay, Bolivia, Peru and Colombian delegates had requested Joseph's presence in their country immediately, and he promised he would attend to their needs as soon as he could.

He felt fulfilled and grateful. Grateful for the fact that through credit unions and cooperatives, he had found a way to be of great help to others, while at the same time he was realizing a satisfying career in leadership for himself.

"Thank God for the genius of Raiffeisen and Desjardin and Filene for having given birth to the idea of credit unions, for without such a system, how else would it be possible for honest, hard-working people, of limited means to break away from the stranglehold of the `unscrupulous money-lenders', to uplift themselves and to provide a better future for their families," he thought.

He returned to Panama, and discussed the seminar and the direction to take for program implementaion.

"I believe, you should hire yourself an assistant as an understudy as soon as you can. This task is far greater than we had imagined and the demand on you will leave you no time for your family," Long said to him.

"Good idea," Joseph remarked.

"We have Romero Beltran who has been with CUNA as an interpreter for some time. He has no practical experience in operating credit unions. but understands their structure and philosophy. What do you think?" Long said.

"Yes, I know Romero. I believe we can work together. Let's give it a try," Joseph responded.

Romero was taken on strength, and working as a team they visited the countries requesting the inclusion of production credit into the development of their overall credit union system.

Joseph and his understudy were in Ecuador doing a critical analysis of the initial pilot project at Julio Andrade. A telegram arrived from Panama.

"God took your mother into his care. She passed away last night. Funeral will be on Monday. Signed Dad."

LIFE'S DETOURS

Joseph was expecting this news. His mother was a victim of cancer. On his last visit to Regina a few months earlier, he had visited with her in the hospital. She had undergone surgery for the removal of a cancerous kidney. Following that she enjoyed life for about three months. Then her condition worsened, she wound up in the hospital for a second time and now she was dead. That last visit he had with his mother remained indelibly imprinted in his memory.

"The cancer is now in my bones. It is terminal. I feel and I know I'm going to die," she said. "I'm too young to die at 68, but that is the way life has been ordained for me. I miss my family and I would have enjoyed being a few more years in the company of my children and grandchildren.

But, I'm grateful that my children are all married, settled and in their proper places. I've asked every person to forgive me for any hurts I may have caused them. I tried to be a perfect mother, but being human I've failed in some areas."

Joseph had to leave. He kissed his mother on her forehead as she was lying on her pillow in the hospital bed. He squeezed her hand as he looked again into her tearing eyes and departed.

Now she was dead.

He telephoned Panama and sought permission to attend the funeral. Permission was granted.

The next day Saturday found Joseph flying from Quito to be present at his mother's funeral. He would miss her. She had been his favorite.

It was a big funeral. For the memorial service the seating capacity in the church for 300 people was packed. The pews and balcony were full, and people were standing in the narthex. As a minister's wife she was well known and well respected. The pall bearers were her son-in-law, a nephew, and her four living sons.

"She held meaning in life for a lot more people than just for me," Joseph thought as he viewed her coffin being slowly and reverently placed into the hearse for the mile long drive to the cemetery. He watched with tears and sorrow as the coffin was lowered into the grave. He sobbed with a feeling of deep emotion, for he knew that her coffin, and her body would decompose and finally join the elements from whence it came.

"May God rest her soul eternally in peace - I loved my mother," he said to himself.

Back in Panama, he continued with his work. Travelling from country to country, and at home long enough to write a trip report, spend a weekend or two with his family and pack a clean change of clothes. Then off again.

He thought about his father, who was now a widower and living alone. Joseph's sister and a brother were nearby, but he often wondered about his dad and how he was faring.

The novelty had worn out of the travel routine. Joseph was secretly yearning to get back to a less boisterous and quiet life.

At times he was unhappy with his work. He was considered a third country national, working on a program contracted with the U.S. Government. He could not have access to confidential government documents on the countries he would be required to visit and work in. He was also burdened with and deplored the thought of having to pay taxes to two countries.

He could return to Canada, pick up a job and manage the property of which he was now an owner. The property he had purchased in Regina before leaving, had paid for itself in nine years instead of fifteen as originally planned.

"I think I'll quit and go back to Canada," he told Long one day.

"You're not serious, are you?" Long asked surprisingly

"Yes, I am. Although I love my work, I'm not a U.S. citizen. I cannot have access to confidential information. This to a degree hurts my pride because here I am a leading technician, forced to be accompanied by someone who is American, but knows nothing about my business. It makes me feel untrustworthy, and yet I understand that this is the way it should be. I carry the extra burden of having to pay taxes to both countries. Then there is my dad, who has been widowed and I'm a bit concerned about his welfare," Joseph added.

"Joe the reports coming in from every country you've worked in rave about your knowledge and your uncanny ability to transfer it to others. I would personally hate to see you leave us. Why don't you become an American citizen, or don't you want to? We still need you. You could bring your dad to live with you here in Panama," Long said.

"If I wanted to become an American citizen, I wouldn't qualify, because I do not meet the citizenship requirements. You see, I haven't lived a full year in the United States yet," Joseph replied.

"The question is - do you want to become an American citizen?" Long asked again.

"Sure, but as I said, I don't qualify," he repeated.

"Tell you what, I'm going to discuss your situation with our Ambassador here in Panama. He too is familiar with your good work. Work that you've performed here in Panama. We'll see what he says," Long said.

A couple of weeks went by. This was Joseph's third year in Panama, and he and his family would soon qualify for another home leave and vacation. Together with Beltran his associate, they were now

LIFE'S DETOURS 277

preparing for a full-fledged introduction of the program into Mexico and the Carribean.

Long called Joseph into his office.

"I have good news for you," Long said. "The Ambassador informs me that if you're willing to become a citizen, there is a way to circumvent the residency requirement."

"How's that going to be done?" he asked.

"Apparently, it's been done before for others. A bill will be prepared and submitted to Congress, which will merely state, that all this time, that you have been working on this program under contract with USAID, shall be considered the same as time spent in the United States. This then qualifies you to be sworn in as a citizen. I've got a package of forms here for you to fill in and sign. The Bill would have to be sponsored by a Congressman or Senator from the State in which you were last a resident," Long said.

"Good. I don't know any Congressman or Senator personally, so that leaves me holding the bag again."

"No, I suggest you fill the forms in, and we'll send them to the CUNA office in Madison, and we'll ask Rhodes to petition a Wisconsin Congressman to sponsor your bill. okay?" Long added. "Okay - let's give it the old college try," Joseph said.

The necessary forms were filled in and submitted to Ronald Rhodes in CUNA. Rhodes in turn made the other required contacts. In the meantime Joseph continued going about his work. Programs were either introduced or instituted in every country south of the Rio Grande with the exception of Cuba. The production credit aspect of the CUNA/AID program was now moving ahead in full swing. Joseph reduced the length of his trips. He would spend more time in planning, developing training materials and with his family. He counted on Beltran, his understudy to perform a good deal of the preparatory legwork on any given assignment.

An air-gram message arrived through the Embassy from the U.S. Embassy in Laos.

"USAID/Laos requests permission from USAID/Panama and CUNA to release Acker for a six-week assignment in Laos. Purpose to review the small farmer credit program here. Background information and terms of reference air-mailed via Embassy pouch." It was signed by William Simmons.

Acker was requested to be interviewed by his superior, Robert Long.

"Are you willing to go?" Long asked. "The cable is signed by Bill Simmons, and you know him from Ecuador."

"Bill Simmons - Hm! - He was the USAID backstopping officer

in Ecuador, during the stage of development for the pilot project. Sure I know him. Nice guy, but he expected you to work most every weekend," Joseph said with a grin.

"That'll be a real change of scenery for you Joe. The Vietnam situation is still percolating. But Asia is Asia and you'll have a chance to do some good and see that part of the world too," Long added.

"Well, if it wasn't for Bill Simmons, I don't think I'd really care to go. But our program here is doing pretty well. Beltran is on top of the thing. If you feel you can do without me for a couple of months. I think I'd like to go," Joseph said.

Both Long and USAID/Panama agreed that he could be spared from duty for a couple of months. Joseph was pleased.

It was time for home leave and for the family's vacation. Their daughter Eleanor had preceeded them to the U.S. and was now enrolled as a graduate student at the Arizona State University. The Ackers were left with only their youngest daughter Grace at home.

He talked over his Laotian assignment with Suzanne. They agreed that Suzanne and Grace their youngest daughter would accompany him back as far as the U.S. where they would remain until his return from Laos.

After their arrival in Phoenix, Arizona and prior to his departure for Laos, he received a phone call from CUNA advising him that Congress had approved his status which enabled him to become a U.S. citizen. He contacted one of the county judges, who conducted an examination of his knowledge about the U.S. Constitution, history and how it was governed.

The answers he gave must have been to the Judge's satisfaction.

The Judge ordered Joseph to raise his right hand and take his "Oath of Allegiance," then shook his hand and congratulated him on becoming an American citizen. The next day Suzanne was also sworn in, while Grace their youngest daughter, because of her age automatically became a citizen, but with the right to declare her status when she attains the age of twenty-one.

Joseph departed on his exploratory mission to Laos, while Suzanne and Grace remained behind in Phoenix.

The Laotian expedition was strictly an invitation for Joseph to look over the USAID/Laotian program for small farmer credit and rural development. Joseph saw a great need and good possibilities.

"Would you be prepared to come to Laos, and give leadership to the formation of a small farmer credit program, utilizing the credit union mechanism for its implementation? Something similar to what you did in Ecuador," Bill Simmons said to Joseph.

They discussed the housing and educational facilities. Because of

LIFE'S DETOURS

the war going on in neighboring Vietnam, in which the Laotians were also involved, the security situation for him and his family was also discussed. Laos was considered a "hardship post" and for that reason a package of additonal amenities was available.

"Speaking off-hand I'm prepared to accept your offer. Let me first discuss it with CUNA and then talk it over with Suzanne. After my return to the U.S. within a day or two, I'll cable you my intention." Joseph assured Simmons.

One week later, a cablegram from Phoenix was dispatched to Simmons in care of the USAID/Mission in Vientiane, Laos.
"YOUR OFFER ACCEPTED".

THE END

LIFE'S DETOURS

ABBREVIATIONS

ADB	-	Agricultural Development Bank
AID	-	Agency For International Development
AID/W	-	AID/Washington
CUNA	-	Credit Union National Association
C.O.	-	Commanding Officer
COL.	-	Colonel
CUL	-	Credit Union League
DEPHR	-	Dept. of Education, Publicity and Human Relations
FECOAC	-	Federacion de Co-operativas de Ahorro y Credito del Ecuador
FCL	-	Federated Co-operatives Limited
GEN-MGR.	-	General Manager
LARO	-	Latin American Regional Office
MD	-	Managing Director
OCA	-	Organization of Cooperatives of America
P.A.	-	Prince Albert
SASK	-	Saskatchewan
SCCS	-	Sask. Co-op Credit Society
SWP	-	Saskatchewan Wheat Pool
USAID	-	U.S. Agency for International Development
V.P.	-	Vice President
WED	-	World Extension Department

LIFE'S DETOURS

ORDERING INFORMATION

Please send_____copies of "LIFE'S DETOURS" at $8.95 plus $2.50 shipping and handling. (Arizona residents add 7% sales tax)

to me____ as a gift____

Be sure to include your name in either case.

My Name   (Please print)

Street   Apt.No.

City   (State or province)   Zip Code

Gift for   (Please print)

Street   Apt.No.

City   (State or province)   Zip Code

My gift card should read:

From_____

I enclose $_____ (Please remit in U.S. Funds)

Make check payable to: Marva Enterprises

Mail To: Marva Enterprises
                  P.O. Box 7615
                  Mesa, AZ. 85216-7615
                  U.S.A.

(This page may be photocopied)

LIFE'S DETOURS

From:

_____

_____

_____

TO: Marva Enterprises,
      P.O. Box 7615,
      Mesa, Arizona. 85216-7615
      U.S.A.